LOVE IN THE WATER .

Clay felt an uncharacteristic attack of shyness.
Perhaps it was because she wanted Josh Lewis to
be important in her life and that magnified every
action.

Half turned away, fumbling with her shoulder
straps, she stole a glance at Josh. He was looking
at her, smiling. Clay laughed and they both tore
off their clothes, grabbed the fruit basket and
champagne and ran down into the sea.

Josh and Clay lazed for a while in the warm, clear
water, eating chunks of pineapple from the basket
that floated on the surface and passing the Dom
Perignon back and forth . . .

Also by Meredith Rich in Sphere Books:

BARE ESSENCE

Virginia Clay

MEREDITH RICH

SPHERE BOOKS LIMITED
30–32 Gray's Inn Road, London WC1X 8JL

First published in Great Britain by
Sphere Books Ltd 1983

For Barbara Lowenstein,
with love and gratitude

TRADE
MARK

Printed and bound in Great Britain by
William Collins Sons & Co. Ltd, Glasgow

PART ONE
The Present

Chapter 1

THE air conditioning in Bangkok's Don Muang airport was not noticeable. Josh Lewis took off his wilting linen jacket, lit his first cigarette of the day, and walked through the revolving glass door to the arrivals platform. It was not yet noon, and already the temperature was ninety-four. The heat shimmered above the concrete roadway.

A stray lock of dark-brown hair stuck to his high forehead. He ran his fingers through his hair to push it back into place and strolled to the end of the platform. There was nothing to look at, only hangars and runways. He tossed the cigarette on the cement walk and stomped on it. It was too hot to smoke, and he was trying to cut down. He wiped the sweat from his brow and headed back to the terminal.

A white Datsun taxi screeched to a stop several feet away from him. The door opened, and a leggy good-looking woman stepped out. Her tall, slim figure looked terrific in the white cotton-twill trousers and oversized shirt she wore belted with a wide black-chamois sash. Her shiny shoulder-length chestnut hair swung as she moved her head. She appeared immune to the humidity.

The young woman hailed a porter and pointed to the trunk of the cab, then to another cab that had just pulled up behind. The passenger space of the second cab was filled with large silver cases. She handed each cab driver two hundred *baht*. From the back seat of the first taxi, she dragged out three navy Sportsac shoulder bags of varying sizes and two other dark-brown cowhide cases.

Out of habit, Josh lit another cigarette and watched the porter unloading six, seven, finally ten metal cases, roughly the size of orange crates. Photographic equipment, he guessed. Whatever it was, there was certainly a hell of a lot of it. Last came two large leather Botega de Veneta suitcases. The porter enlisted another's aid, and they shouted noisily at one another in singsong Thai as they tried to balance the tenth metal case on top of the brimming second cart.

"Oh! No . . . no!" The young woman rushed over. Her accent was American. "These four here must be carried separately. On another cart, please."

The small Thai porters smiled at her. It was obvious they did not understand. "Yes . . . yes," one of them finally said, nodding.

"You see . . ." the slim beauty pointed to the cases in question. "These go . . . there!" She indicated another porter walking by with an empty cart. "And please hurry. Bring them to the Philippine Airline counter . . . Philippine Airlines," she repeated. "You understand?"

The porters bobbed their heads up and down in unison.

Josh Lewis dragged on his Gitanes, amused by the perplexed porters, who busily began rearranging everything between the three carts. The young woman, carrying a handbag in addition to the five shoulder bags, strode into the terminal, walking effortlessly in spite of the apparent weight she was balancing. He wondered if she was traveling alone. At any rate, she had made him forget about the heat.

Lewis followed her inside, intrigued. The only scheduled Philippine Airlines flight that noon was to Manila, his destination.

At the check-in counter, a uniformed Philippine Airlines agent began ticketing the baggage as the porters unloaded it. He tried to maintain his professional aplomb in the face of this mountain of cases. "Have you any carry-on luggage?" he asked.

"Yes, these."

The Filipino rose on to the balls of his feet to look over the counter. "One . . . two . . . Oh, no, miss, you cannot take five. It is not allowed. You must check three of them."

"Oh, dear," the woman said, widening her large smoky-gray eyes. "But they have to go with me. They contain film, and cameras and lenses that are breakable. Some of them are irreplaceable . . ."

The Filipino smiled, shaking his head. "You are asking me to break a rule," he said. "I cannot do that."

The woman smiled appealingly. "No, no. I'm not asking that." Josh Lewis admired her performance. The problem was obviously one she had encountered often, and she handled it with a well-practiced, naive charm. "It's just that many of the other passengers, I'm sure, are *not* using their allowed quota. So you see, in terms of weight, my three extra bags could just as well belong to someone else. You see what I mean?"

"No," the Filipino said. "I mean, yes, I know what you are saying, but we must be strict about our rules. Besides"—he pointed to her twelve check-through bags—"you are already overweight."

She sighed. "Well, yes, but of course I'll be paying for that. But these *must* go on board with me. Air India allowed it yesterday . . . and Pan Am last week . . ."

"Maybe so, but your total overweight is far over the limit. Let me see . . ." He checked the scale. "That will be an additional ten thousand *baht* please."

Lewis made the quick mental calculation as the woman opened her credit card case and handed the agent her green air travel card. Five hundred dollars. It looked like a good time to step in.

"Excuse me," he said. "I couldn't help overhearing your conversation. If I can help by taking some of your carry-on bags, I'd be happy to."

"Oh, *thank* you. I'd really appreciate it."

Lewis glanced at her travel card on the counter. The name on it was Clay Fitzgerald. He turned to the ticket agent. "Ms. Fitzgerald and I are traveling together. I'll take the extra hand luggage. Oh, and while we're at it, why don't you check a few of those cases through on my ticket? I checked in with only two lightweight bags . . ."

"But, sir—" The Filipino shrugged. "Oh, all right, all right. The flight today is not too crowded."

"And make sure to put the lady in the seat next to me."
He turned to Clay Fitzgerald. "If that's agreeable."

She nodded. "After all," she said, "we're traveling together."

He grinned and put out his hand. "My name's Josh Lewis."

"Clay Fitzgerald."

The public address system announced the last boarding call for the Philippine Airlines flight to Manila.

"Aha," Josh said. "They're playing our flight. Shall we?"

He picked up his share of her hand luggage, and they headed for the gate.

The tiny brunette Filipino flight attendant brought their Bloody Marys as soon as the plane reached its cruising altitude. Clay Fitzgerald smiled at her lean, handsome seat companion. He had just put out his cigarette because he noticed the smoke was bothering her.

"I'm trying to give it up, anyway," Josh Lewis said. His long legs were stretched out into the aisle, and Clay guessed he was several inches over six feet. "It doesn't help my jogging at all."

Clay laughed. "I guess I'm lucky. I smoked in college, but I never really got hooked." Clay poured half the miniature bottle of vodka into her spicy tomato juice. "Well, cheers."

"To you, too." He smiled and tore open his complimentary bag of peanuts and rice crackers. "What takes you to the Philippines?"

"I'm going to photograph the Moro pearl divers in the Sulu Archipelago."

"Real pearls? I didn't think there were many of those left."

Clay shook her head. "Not a whole lot. Most of the oyster beds have been pearled out. Since the Japanese invented the perfect way to culture pearls, that's virtually the market now. Anyway, I'm doing a two-part piece for *International Geography* magazine on natural and cultured pearls."

"You photograph underwater?" Josh leaned forward with interest.

Clay nodded, munching on a rice cracker.

"Wild." Josh grinned. "No wonder you travel with so much gear."

Clay's gray eyes shined with amusement. "It's not easy. Sometimes I have to buy an extra plane ticket in order to take my stuff." She raised her glass. "Thanks again, for coming to my rescue."

"My pleasure," Josh said. He had a way of focusing his dark-brown eyes on her that made her feel she was the most fascinating woman he had ever met.

"Some underwater photographers travel lighter than I do. But when I'm working, I like to take a lot of cameras down with me. That way I don't have to keep coming up to change film and lenses or filters. The underwater camera mountings and strobes are what take up most of my luggage."

"I must say, I was intrigued when I saw you . . . arriving in two taxis."

"Yes . . . in New York, I can make it to the airport in one Checker cab."

"Is that where you live?"

Clay nodded. "I think so. The past few months I've been there for a total of four days. Anyway . . . what about you? Are you on holiday, or are you getting ready to do a film in these parts?" Clay had recognized Josh Lewis's name immediately. He was one of Hollywood's hot young directors, of that generation that seemed to burst full-blown from the UCLA film school a few years back. Clay had seen in the papers that he had just won the *Grand Prix* at the Cannes Film Festival for writing and directing *Victorian Pastoral*.

Josh grinned wryly. "I'm doing a picture that starts shooting in two and a half months. On location. Except we still don't have the location. That's what I'm scouting now."

"So you've just checked out Thailand, and now you're considering Manila?"

Josh nodded. "It really boils down to the amount of co-operation we get from the local governments. Shooting in Asia is full of red tape." Josh Lewis's black lashes, Clay noted, were long enough to trip over.

"What's the film about . . . or is it a top-secret project?"

Josh laughed. "It's not going to be a film. It's a movie. An adventure-thriller. Sex, violence, the works. I contracted to do it last year when I was desperate for financing to finish editing *Victorian Pastoral*." He shrugged. "It'll be easy enough. The challenge is keeping it from melding into the genre. Making it better than it has to be. It's called *Golden Triangle*."

"Oh, I read the book. It was on the best-seller list last year."

"That's the one. But it's taken something like ten rewrites to get a decent screenplay." Lewis elaborated on the ethics of making pictures for love versus money, and Clay watched his face as he spoke. He was what she and her college friends used to describe as "ugly-handsome." The best kind, as far as she was concerned. The overall appearance was attractive, although certain features, with the exception of his eyes, stopped short of total perfection. His forehead was a shade too high. The nose had obviously been broken and improperly reset or possibly broken more than once. Although his hair had been shaped expertly, there were hints of childhood cowlicks separating curls on the crown of his head. Such imperfections kept a potentially perfect face from being boring.

"Anyway, enough of the shop talk," Josh said. "How long are you going to be in Manila?"

"I have a flight south tomorrow at the crack of dawn."

"Will you have dinner with me tonight?"

"I'd love it. But please let *International Geography* foot the bill. You saved them a lot of money today."

"Ah," Josh said. "I always did love a woman with an expense account."

Clay tried to remember an article she had read recently about Josh after his success at Cannes. She did not recall any mention of a wife, and he certainly did not appear to be gay. Still, she told herself, anyone as attractive as Josh Lewis was not likely to be unattached.

"I'm staying at the Manila Hotel," she said.

"Great. Me, too. We can share a couple of taxis in from the airport."

Like many other famous old Asian hotels, the Manila had been restored and enlarged to meet the demands of a burgeoning tourist industry. An eighteen-story concrete-and-glass tower that would have been at home in Miami Beach now loomed behind the original formal gardens and landmark building that had been constructed in 1912. It was a constant challenge to the knowledgeable traveler in Asia to procure rooms in the old sections of those hostelries where the genteel elegance of eras gone by still emanated from the rooms and lobbies.

Clay's room, with a view of Manila Bay, was ornately decorated with a dark mahogany bed of the Spanish colonial period and rattan chairs and end tables. The lamp bases were large inlaid bronzeware figurines from the Mindanao region, and the walls displayed carved wooden frames with religious prints by Filipino artists.

Clay showered, unpacked her favorite white-silk crepe de chine pants, and picked out a lacy strapless white-linen top to accentuate her tan and her smooth, broad shoulders. She hung them in the bathroom and turned on the hot water to steam out the wrinkles while she put on evening makeup and sprayed her body lavishly with Diorissimo *eau de toilette*. She had just finished dressing when the phone rang.

"Hi, it's me," Josh Lewis said. "If you're ready, I'll stop by and pick you up. Did you make reservations at the restaurant?"

"Yes, sir . . . nine o'clock. That'll give us time to walk there and see the sights along the way."

"Hmmm, free dinner with guided tour thrown in. This *is* my lucky day. See you in a minute."

This is my lucky day, too, Clay thought as she gave herself a quick last-minute once-over in the bathroom mirror.

The Zamboanga restaurant on Makati Avenue in the Makati district of Manila City was filled with the lively multilingual conversation of patrons who ranged from local Filipino and wealthy American and European travelers to a collage of exotic faces from various Oriental countries. The medium-sized room had been transformed into a jungle of potted palms and bamboo trees. Large baskets hung from the ceiling, brimming with brown and purple *waling-waling* orchids. Each table was laid out with native woven abacá placemats and a small hurricane candle.

After the waiter brought their San Miguel beers and took their food order, Josh smiled at Clay, his brown eyes gleaming with good humor.

"Two miles of guided tour was a bit more than I'd bargained for. I'm starving."

"Me, too." Clay laughed. "Really, on my map, this looked much closer to the hotel. But don't you think it's nice to get the feel of a new city on the first evening?"

"Sure. I only wish I'd worn sneakers." He reached in his pocket for his cigarettes, then thought better of it.

"Listen, I don't want to thwart your vices. I can stand the smoke."

"No . . . you're good for me. My, er, most recent lady was a chain smoker. I escalated to over two packs a day with her around."

"Well, I suppose when you get home you'll escalate again . . ."

"She said tactfully . . ." Josh gave Clay a wide grin and took a sip of beer. "No . . . that lady is *finis*. No permanent relationships at the moment. What about you?"

Clay paused. "I'm more or less in the same situation."

"More or less. What do you mean exactly?"

"Well . . . I've been seeing someone, but . . . I've been away a lot this year."

"Yeah . . . distance is hell on relationships," Josh agreed. He signaled the waiter for another beer. Clay noticed for the first time a tiny mole on his right earlobe that resembled a pierced earring.

The waiter appeared with the beer and their first course. Clay had ordered *lumpia*, a salad of heart of palm and small pieces of shrimp and pork wrapped in a tissue-thin crepe. Josh had chosen the *sinuam* soup, a spicy shellfish concoction.

"My thanks to *International Geography*," Josh said. "This food is terrific."

Clay and Josh sampled each other's entrees—*lechon,* roast suckling pig stuffed with tamarind leaves; clams steamed and served in bamboo baskets with a sauce of spices and *kalamansi,* a small green Filipino citrus similar to a lemon. For dessert, they ordered *bibingka,* a pudding made of rice and coconut milk, baked in a clay oven and topped with fresh cheese and salted duck eggs.

After dinner they strolled a leisurely, circuitous route back to the hotel through Chinatown, in the district of Binondo. At midnight, the section was still bustling with activity, crowded with small restaurants and shops offering Chinese pastries, herbs, incense, and curios and tiny hole-in-the-wall factories turning out toys and novelties and bamboo kitchen supplies. Families with small children were eating dinner in the backs of the shops or on the sidewalks in front. Horse-drawn carts with tourists wove in and out of the traffic jam on Ongpin Street.

"Okay . . . what next?" Josh asked as they arrived back at the hotel. "There's the floating casino. Or one of the night clubs."

Clay shook her head. "It's been a long day, and I have to be up early. Let's just have a drink."

They sat at the hotel's Jungle Bar and ordered Philippine rum on the rocks. They had talked almost nonstop since that morning in the Bangkok airport, and the comfortable silence of new-old friends set in. Clay stirred the ice in her drink with her index finger.

On the road, strangers met, passed time, and traded stories, then went their separate ways. It had happened to Clay many times, and she accepted it as a part of the life she had chosen for herself. But Josh Lewis was special; that much she knew from spending the day with him. He was witty, sensitive, interesting. And wildly attractive. She did not want him to be a one-night stand.

"Okay," Josh said finally. "We have to see what we can work out."

"What?"

"I want to see you again. What's your schedule? How long are you going to be photographing those virile young divers?"

"Hmmm." Clay smiled provocatively. "Depends on how virile and young they really are. And the weather. If all goes well, about a week."

"My director of photography's flying in tomorrow. We'll be here at least that long. So . . . how about next week, same place? Give me a ring when you get in and I'll greet you with champagne."

"Oh, San Miguel will do." Clay smiled. "I'm a woman with simple tastes."

Josh signed the bar check and saw Clay to her door. He caressed her bare shoulder lightly with his hand. "Are you going to invite me in?"

Clay shook her head. "I have to be up at four-thirty in order to catch my plane."

"Hardly seems worth the trouble to sleep."

"No, Josh. Not tonight."

He leaned over and kissed her. "Okay. Next week, then. Get good and rested down there." He kissed her again.

"Hmmm." Clay pulled her body away. "You make it hard to say good night."

"No . . . you're the one who makes it hard."

Clay giggled. "I'll see you next week." She kissed his cheek quickly.

"Be careful," Josh said as she closed the door. "Watch out for sharks."

Clay took out her contact lenses and put them into the electric cleaner with distilled water. Squinting nearsightedly out the window, she slipped into her nightgown. It was the first time she had met someone on a plane worth getting to know. And she had not been so turned on by a kiss in a long time. Things were looking up.

Chapter 2

"EXCUSE, miss . . . would you like some *tuba*?" the young Filipino waiter asked as he cleared the remains of Clay Fitzgerald's lunch—a salad of papaya and *curacha*, a native shellfish that tasted like something between crab and lobster.

"Oh, no, thank you." Clay looked up, smiling. "Just the check, please." She pushed her chair back and stretched out her long, tanned legs. A gecko lizard scurried past and into the shadow of a wicker planter filled with fragrant, white-petaled *sampaguita* flowers.

From her table on the veranda restaurant of the Lantaka Hotel, Clay gazed out at the shell vendors and the fishing craft anchored in the shimmering Sulu Sea. She had been in Zamboanga for two days and had nearly succeeded in clearing her head of the various annoyances that had pestered her since leaving Manila.

First, there had been a bomb hoax at Manila International airport that had grounded all flights for six hours. And, of course, there were the usual hassles about her carry-on luggage. Because of the delay, the flight was fully booked, and the agent could not sell her an extra ticket. Fortunately, the kindness of strangers prevailed once more, and a cheerful middle-aged Filipino couple had carried on her excess camera cases.

Once in Zamboanga, Clay discovered that the air compressor she had arranged to rent was in faulty condition, so Hadji Ali Kiram, her guide, was forced to drive all the way to Davao City for another one. In the meantime, the Taluksagay pearl farm she had planned to photograph turned out to be a run-down operation producing inferior,

12

irregularly shaped pearls. To top it off, there were reports of Muslim unrest, and that morning's newspaper had recounted a guerrilla uprising near Davao. Clay was worried that her guide would be delayed getting back.

Zamboanga, sprawled along the southwest tip of the southern Philippine island of Mindanao, was Clay's stepping-off point to the Sulu Archipelago. It was known as the "City of Flowers." In the distant outskirts of town, vivid patches of orchids and lush green coconut plantations sloped toward the cloudless blue sky. In the foreground, Zamboanga's low skyline was accented with church steeples and the glistening minarets and domes of mosques.

The night before, Clay had slept in one of the free tree houses in Pansonanca Park, which had a fully equipped kitchenette and magenta Bougainvillea blooming outside the screened windows. Although it was possible for anyone to obtain permission to stay there, it was easy to understand why the town's mayor gave preference to honeymooners; it was a perfect place to make love all day.

Making love was still something she had to look forward to with Josh Lewis. Clay smiled as she indulged in the fantasy of him arriving in Zamboanga unexpectedly, too impatient to wait a week before seeing her. She conjured up Josh's unevenly handsome face and the sound of his deep voice.

"Meez Clay?"

Clay looked up, disoriented. The voice belonged not to Josh but to her guide, Hadji Ali Kiram. "Hadji! You're back! I was afraid that you'd run into trouble . . ."

"No trouble, Meez Clay. But traffic. Road very crowded." The short, muscular man smiled. His teeth, what was left of them, were crooked and stained brown from chewing betel nuts. Hadji, a Moro Muslim who had once been a pearl diver, was serving as Clay's guide for the week and had provided the boat they would use. He was also her interpreter for the local native dialect of *chabacano,* an adaptation of the Filipino Tagalog language with trilled r's and multiple syllables.

"I got the air compressor. Now I go fix motor of my boat."

"Oh, no. What's wrong?" The sun was in Clay's face, and she squinted up at Hadji. She could not bear the thought of any more delays.

"Minor problem, Meez Clay. Not serious. Will take only an hour to fix."

"We can still leave at dawn?"

"Oh, yes. You bet." The lines around his mouth deepened when he smiled.

"Terrific, Hadji. I'll buy food at the market this afternoon, then come and load my equipment on. So we can leave as soon as the sun comes up."

"You bet," Hadji said again. "See you later."

Clay paid for lunch and walked the few blocks to the midtown Barter Trade Market, where she purchased a large straw basket and enough fruits and vegetables for the trip to the archipelago. On the way to Hadji's boat, she stopped by another market for bread, soda crackers, bottled water, and beer. When she arrived to load the provisions on the thirty-five-foot wooden boat, Hadji was nowhere to be found. Instead, a collection of tools was spread out on deck next to a pile of cloths black with grease.

Clay dropped the basket of food into the cooler and wandered back on the dock. None of the other fishermen had seen Hadji. Sure he would show up eventually, she loaded the rest of her equipment into the galley. Then she opened a San Miguel and watched the sunset, wondering what Josh was doing at that moment.

"Meez Clay?" Hadji Ali Kiram called out from the dock. "I go get part for motor." He was bare-chested, wearing faded jeans with holes in the knees and a red kerchief headband.

"What about the motor?" Clay asked with dread. "Is it almost fixed?"

"You bet . . . in a few minutes."

"We'll still be able to get away tomorrow . . . early?"

"You bet. You be ready at five-thirty?"

"You bet." Clay smiled.

The next morning, as the sky turned from rosy gray to deep blue, Hadji's boat chugged slowly along the balmy coastline, past fishing craft, thatched houses perched above the sea on stilts, and natives heading to market in *bancas,* small motorized dugout canoes.

Hadji pointed to a nest of wood rafts, each with a vividly colored, patterned sail. "You see those *vintas?* That is a Badjao community. Sea gypsies. They live offshore and come on land only to bury their dead." Hadji waved to a group of young Badjao boys flying kites, and they returned the greeting enthusiastically. "The sea is calm. We will reach Jolo by midmorning," Hadji said.

"Good. I'll be down in the hold recharging my strobes and filling my aqualung."

"You bet. I sure hope we don't have problems with divers."

"Problems?" Clay stopped and turned to face him suspiciously. "What sort of problems, Hadji?"

"Oh . . ." He shrugged. "You know, not all pearl divers are like me. Some of them superstitious. Don't want people to see where they dive. Specially not take photographs."

"Hadji—why am I hearing this now? You assured me that everything would be fine."

"Well, maybe so. My cousin, Hakim, don't object to you diving with them. But he say that Abdul, the owner of the diving boat, he not happy about woman coming there."

Clay sighed. Now that Hadji had raised the problem, she was sure he would have a solution to offer. And she was sure it would cost her. "What do you think I should do?"

"You have something you could give Abdul . . . as a present?"

"Well, I'm paying him and the divers a hundred *pesos* each to photograph them."

"I know, Meez Clay. But Abdul very proud man. If you have something special to give him, it might . . ."

"Okay, Hadji. What is it you actually told Abdul I'd give him besides the hundred *pesos*?"

Hadji looked innocent. "I no promise . . ." He broke into a nervous grin under Clay's stare. "Well, maybe a transistor radio."

"Hadji! I don't have a transistor radio with me."

"Maybe then a camera?"

Clay shook her head. "My cameras are expensive . . . and I need them all."

"A tape recorder?"

Clay sighed again. "Okay . . . I suppose I can part with my cassette recorder. But not until I've interviewed the divers."

Hadji smiled. "You bet, Meez Clay. Abdul will be happy, I think."

"He better be," Clay said under her breath as she went into the cabin.

Hadji anchored in a clear blue-watered cove on the northwest coast of Jolo, alongside the divers' boat. A seven-foot manta ray circled the boats curiously, and out in the deeper water porpoises flipped merrily above the surface.

"You wait here," Hadji told Clay as he climbed over to Abdul Hasim's boat. The heavy-bearded Muslim was older than Hadji, Clay guessed, probably in his mid-fifties. He greeted Hadji with a smile and an embrace but glanced over at Clay with impenetrable coolness. Clay smiled and nodded, but Abdul Hasim scowled at her. The other divers remained quiet, merely observing the situation. They were perfectly happy to be paid extra for doing their jobs.

Hadji and Abdul walked to the bow, keeping their backs to the others. They spoke in a heated mumble, looking at Clay from time to time. She felt as if she were exhibit "A." *Everything will be all right,* she told herself. She had come this far; she was not about to let Abdul ruin her story.

Abdul raised his voice. Hadji smiled pliantly. After several minutes, Hadji walked to the side of the boat and called over to Clay.

"Meez Clay? I don't know. Abdul say men are superstitious. These are pearl grounds for black-lipped oyster. Very rare. They afraid other people will come here when they see the story. Take away all the oysters."

"No one will know *where* the pictures are taken. Underwater shots and shots of the men on the boat—that won't give away the location."

Hadji nodded and went back to explain that to Abdul. There were more raised voices, with Hadji gesticulating wildly. Finally, the burly man motioned for Clay to come on board his boat.

"So . . . you take good pictures of us?" Clay was surprised that he spoke English. Although she knew that English was taught in Filipino schools, she had assumed that out on the archipelago the natives would not have much use for it.

"I'll do my best."

"You send me copies of magazine story?"

"Oh, yes. For you and all your family and friends."

Abdul nodded, silent.

Clay sensed that it was time to play her trump. She could interview the divers in longhand. They wouldn't have all that much to say, anyway. She fetched her Sony tape recorder and presented it, along with ten blank tapes, to Abdul.

While Abdul examined the cassette recorder, Clay told him how grateful she was to have found him and assured him she would not disrupt the divers' routine. Abdul nodded again, turning the little Sony over in his large brown hands. Finally, he stared deep into her eyes.

"I decide, Meez Clay, that you okay. You no tell anybody where we dive?"

"I'll say only that it was off the coast of Jolo. And Jolo is a big island."

Abdul gazed at her again, then smiled for the first time, displaying large white teeth, all intact. "You may dive when you want."

Later, Clay appeared on deck of Hadji's boat in her shiny red lycra Blue Water wet suit, neophrene foam boots under her fins, and a buoyancy compensator vest strapped around her chest and back. On her wrists, over the wet suit, were her underwater watch, depth gauge, and a compass.

Clay set her cameras on deck: two Nikonos marine cameras, one with a 15 mm. wide-angle lens and one in a housing with a 16 mm. semi-fisheye lens; two Nikon-F cameras in aluminum and lucite Ocean Eye housings with 55 mm. micro-Nikkor lenses; another Nikon-F with a 105 mm. micro-Nikkor lens with a special extension port to shoot tiny fish; six Subsea Mark 150 strobes, two attached to each housing; and, finally, her Luna-Pro light meter in a plexiglass housing she had made herself.

Clay attached the backpack that would hold her twin diving tanks, positioning two straps over her shoulders and one around her waist. Hadji helped her on with the tanks and put in place the regulator and submersible pressure gauge. Just as she was moving to put on her mask, she happened to glance over at Abdul's boat. Abdul Hakim and all twenty divers and haulers were watching her with such rapt attention, Clay felt as if she were performing a reverse striptease. She smiled and waved, and twenty-one Muslims smiled back shyly.

The pearl divers, Clay knew, used no equipment at all. Since they went down for a minute and a half to four minutes at a time, they did not have to decompress in order to avoid the bends. These Moro Muslims had trained themselves to hold their breaths for long periods of time underwater. Hadji had told her of a diver who could stay under for fifteen minutes, but he was crippled now because he came up too fast once and an air bubble had burst in his brain. Pearl diving was a dangerous occupation. The bends could cause death, paralysis, blindness, and convulsions. In addition, the divers worked in waters that were infested by sharks.

Abdul explained to Clay where the divers would be working. She put on her mask, mouthpiece, and a twelve-pound weight belt and lowered herself into the water with two cameras. Hadji dove down eighty feet with Clay to deposit the three other cameras on the sea floor, then returned to the surface to act as Clay's topside buddy in case she needed any sort of assistance.

Clay spent an hour shooting closeups of the divers as they rapidly gathered white-lipped and black-lipped mollusks into their sacks before drawing back to record the scene with a wide-angle lens. After two hours and ten minutes, Clay began her ascent to thirty feet, then twenty, finally spending a half hour at ten feet on the edge of the reef, photographing an inquisitive black-tipped reef shark, a large sea turtle, and myriad multicolored smaller reef fish.

The pearl divers made as many as forty rapid dives a day. Clay limited herself to two dives, three hours each. The rest of the time was spent on Abdul's boat photographing the divers and haulers as they opened the oysters in their search for pearls.

"The divers lucky if they find three black pearls in a thousand shells," Hadji said. "White pearls are a little easier to find, but not much." He handed Clay a plate of raw *lapu-lapu* fish marinated in *kalamansi* juice.

"Ah! Meez Clay, come here!" Abdul called out from the other side of the boat. "See what Mahakuttah here has found." He held up a black pearl which was a dark metallic-gray color, about the size of a large kernel of corn. "This is about five years old ... not bad."

"Not bad at all," Clay exclaimed. "It's beautiful." She picked it up carefully and held it in the light of the late-afternoon sun. "How much do you think it will bring?"

Abdul shrugged. "Maybe two thousand, three thousand *pesos*." Clay calculated it to be three to five hundred dollars. "At the end of the season, we sell them all, then split the profits among the divers, the haulers, and me, of course."

Clay jotted notes in her pad. "Is there any way an experienced diver can tell, before it's opened, if an oyster will have a pearl?"

Hadji and Abdul laughed together. "If only we knew that, we would be rich men," Hadji said.

Clay spent five days with the Moro divers and shot over

seventy rolls of film. Under other circumstances, she might have stayed longer, stretched it out for a week or so. The divers had accepted her completely and went out of their way to point out special underwater sights to her. She was enjoying herself, and she knew her work had been good, even spectacular.

But back in Manila there was Josh Lewis, and Josh Lewises did not come along every day. She was a little afraid he might be gone by the time she got back there. In this part of the world, people's plans changed. She knew she could always track him down again if she missed him in the East. But running him to ground in Los Angeles would lose some of the fine spontaneity of this far-corners-of-the-earth meeting. If something were going to come of the relationship, it would have to happen now.

So Clay packed up her gear and said her good-bys. Hadji returned her to Zamboanga, and a few hours later she was on a plane back to Manila.

Chapter 3

JOSH Lewis squeezed lime juice on to his fresh mango slices and looked out the window across the morning brightness of Manila Bay. There were only two things he could be sure of about today. It would be hot. And precious little would get done.

So far, Lewis and his cinematographer, Lars Knudsen, had spent seven days of frustration, exasperation, and siestas and seven nights of San Miguel beer and Johnnie Walker whiskey.

Knudsen looked at the clock on the wall of the hotel's coffee shop. "I must go. I'm touring the facilities at Metro Manila Productions at ten." He stood without enthusiasm, fit and athletic looking with a blond beard. Only the crease across his forehead and the slight sagging of his eyelids gave notice that he had stepped over the line into his forties. "I have a hunch we are still going to wind up getting most of our equipment from Sydney."

"What a life." Josh Lewis sighed. "Harvey should roast in hell for putting us through all this bullshit."

"Even better, he could roast right here," Knudsen quipped in his Anglicized Swedish accent. He glanced glumly out at the heat that was beginning to fry the flagstones on the terrace, beyond the air-conditioned sanctuary of the dining room. "Well, see you later."

"Okay, Lars."

Lewis summoned the waitress for another cup of the rich Philippine coffee, which he liked black, and lit a cigarette.

Harvey Schaffner, he thought. This exercise in futility was Harvey's fault. The studio had made Harvey the pro-

ducer on *Golden Triangle* when the original producer
suffered a stroke. And the bastard had started right in with
cost cutting, by sending Josh and his cinematographer
hopscotching around Asia in search of economy facilities.
It was a power move on Harvey's part; big-budget tighten-
ing would look good to the studio. And he knew it would
burn Josh's ass.

They had been friends once, Harvey and Josh. They
had been a team at UCLA film school. After graduation,
they had made a low-budget student comedy called *Way
to Go*. By a fluke, the picture was accepted for the annual
film festival at Lincoln Center in New York. Although it
did not make much money when it was distributed after
the festival, the good reviews launched Josh and Harvey.

They did a couple of throwaway comedy-horror movies
for American International that grossed big. By 1973, the
major studios were opening their doors to the young pro-
ducer-director team. Over the next six years, they turned
out four highly successful films, including *Shadows of One
Another*, which won Josh an Oscar nomination. But the
next film, *The Maze*, was a fiasco from start to finish.
During the filming, the female star was busted for possession of cocaine, and the male second lead broke his
shoulder in a motorcycle accident. The film went over
schedule and over budget. The studio came down hard on
Harvey, and Harvey took the picture away from Josh
and recut it. Josh went into arbitration and won. But by
then the whole thing was a shambles. The studio dumped
it furtively into regional release, and it was a financial
disaster.

Harvey, however, had a knack for Hollywood survival.
He produced another picture immediately, and it was a
surprise hit. After that, everything he touched turned to
box-office platinum. Around the same time, Harvey went
after Josh's girl friend, a young actress named Marcy
Sims, and married her.

For Josh, the recovery from *The Maze* had been tough-
er. He made a modest-budget picture that won critical
praise but only a small (though enthusiastic) audience.
Josh felt that the studio had not given it the distribution it

deserved, and he suspected Harvey Schaffner's hand at work pulling strings behind the scenes.

It had taken Josh nearly a year to get financing for *Victorian Pastoral*. Now, however, with the *Grand Prix* at Cannes in his pocket, he was solidly back on his feet. There was his contractual obligation to the studio for *Golden Triangle* to get out of the way, but even that had promised to be an interesting challenge. Simon Regnery, the producer, had guaranteed him carte blanche. But then Simon had had his stroke, and Harvey was assigned to the picture.

Josh had fought it, but contractually he was locked in. Finally, he had to grit his teeth and make the best of it. Harvey, on the other hand, seemed to take a perverse pleasure in the assignment. They squabbled over every pre-production detail. Things that Simon had approved were ruthlessly disputed by Harvey until Josh was raw with exasperation. Why the hell couldn't Harvey just leave him alone and let him make the picture right? Actually, Josh knew the answer. Meridan Studios had suffered two multi-million-dollar flops over the past year, and budget fever was running high in the board room. Harvey had been assigned to the picture in no small part because of his reputation for cutting costs and coming in under budget.

So, although relations remained strained between Josh and Harvey, they were stuck with one another for the duration of *Golden Triangle*.

Josh finished his coffee and signed the check. As he stood up, he took one last look around the coffee shop, which was still full of late-rising tourists. He had half expected to see Clay Fitzgerald there this morning. In fact, he had been looking for her for the past couple of days. Now he was beginning to think that her plans might have changed. You could never tell with women like that. She had seemed to like him, but beautiful women, Josh knew from a lot of experience with them, could put on charm and the impression of interest in a man as easily as they put on perfume. What the hell, it had only been a plane ride and a dinner date.

On the way back to the lobby, he stopped at the Associated Press news ticker. There was another item about Muslim unrest in Mindanao—a factory had been bombed by the guerrillas. He had been hearing talk about problems down there all week, although there had been nothing about it in the English-language Manila *Journal*. Still, it had him worried. He hoped Clay hadn't been caught up in any violence.

Josh ordered a car for ten-thirty to take him around the island. He stopped at the cashier to change a couple of traveler's checks, and as he turned to head across the lobby, the first thing he saw was a mountain of metal cases being hauled through the door by three sweating bellhops.

"Clay!" he said.

Clay appeared in the doorway behind the cases, wearing a fatigue-green jumpsuit and loaded down with three shoulder bags. Her face lit up when she saw him.

"Josh! You're still here!"

"Riveted to the spot," he said. "I haven't left the lobby since I saw you last for fear I'd miss you."

She grinned. "And I thought chivalry was dead."

"I'm glad to see you back. I had visions of you being blown up in a guerrilla attack on an oyster bed or carried off by some dashing Muslim freedom fighter who would fall in love with you and refuse the ransom."

"The guerrillas were off on another part of the island. I did see a lot of sharks, though. But they weren't carrying guns."

Josh looked alarmed. "Sharks . . . I forgot to worry about them. Oh, my God . . ." He gave her the once-over. "You appear to still have all your parts."

"Sharks don't bother divers much. But of course you Hollywood people can only relate to *Jaws*." She smiled at him. "Thanks for worrying about me, though."

"Well, I had a lot to lose. We were just getting to the interesting part last time I saw you, if you'll remember. I had a reservation to pick up where we left off when you got back."

"You were going to bring champagne."

"So I was." He looked at his watch. "It's ten thirty. I have a car and driver waiting for me to take me location scouting. Want to come?"

"I'd love it. Let me just check in and change clothes. I'll be as fast as possible."

"Ah, the very quality I admire in a woman."

"See you in fifteen minutes," Clay called back as she headed for the reservations desk.

"Terrific. I'll order the champagne."

The car was a Toyota Celica. The driver, a young crew-cut Filipino, wound along the roads at a relaxed pace. Clay and Josh sat in the back seat.

A bottle of Dom Perignon rested in a silver bucket of melting ice on the floor. It was nearly empty. A hotel basket of fruit was on the seat beside them. They drank from bathroom glasses bearing the monogram of the Manila Hotel.

"If this were L.A.," Josh said, "we'd have a block-long Continental. Stereo and TV in the back, a bar stocked with every kind of liquor and drug, a fold-out bed with magic fingers, and the Los Angeles Philharmonic in the rumble seat."

Clay laughed. "This way is kind of nicer, don't you think?"

"Well, I've never had a very good time in a Hollywood limo, but I think if Toyota wants these things to catch on with the executive set in tinsel town, they're going to have to work out some sort of a deal with you."

"Without Clay Fitzgerald," Clay purred in a sexy spokeswoman voice, "a Toyota is only a car."

"That's it," Josh said. He leaned over and kissed her.

They drove north, past the peninsula of Bataan and the island of Corregidor. Josh had been taking notes, and both he and Clay had been shooting pictures along the way. By early afternoon—the hottest part of the day—they wound up on a deserted stretch of the island of Luzon.

"Look at the sea." Clay sighed. "Doesn't it make you want to rip your clothes off and jump in?"

Josh leaned forward and spoke to the driver. "How do

we get down there?" he asked. They were on an elevated road running along a ridge a couple of hundred feet above the beach.

"No roads," the driver said. "Have to walk."

Josh looked at Clay. "You game?"

"Them's fightin' words where I come from."

"Pull over here," he told the driver.

They got out with the champagne and fruit and their camera bags. Clay stood at the edge of the road, looking down at the glistening water. Josh went over and spoke to the driver. As he walked back to Clay, the car roared off.

"Where's he going?"

"For more champagne."

"Where on earth is he going to get it?"

"Beats me. But it should take him a while."

Josh found a sort of a path that took them down the steep, overgrown hillside. It levelled off gradually until it came out on to a short scallop of clean sandy beach. Palm and bamboo trees and dense underbrush grew out to the water's edge on both sides, leaving them a half moon of sand about thirty yards long and twenty yards deep. Their beach was along the edge of a bay, protected from the ocean, so that the water lapped gently up on the sand with a graded drop off into a deeper blue.

"Shall we eat first?" Clay asked, setting down the basket of fruit. "Or swim first?"

"Let's do both."

Clay was wearing a magenta-gauze sundress. Josh had been amazed when she had come down to the lobby. "My God," he had said, "this is the first time I've seen your legs. They're fabulous!"

Suddenly, on the verge of exposing all the rest of herself to him, Clay felt an uncharacteristic attack of shyness. She had skinnydipped before, sometimes with people she did not know much better than she knew Josh. And she wanted Josh, wanted to see his body, wanted to show him hers. Still, there was this sudden modesty, and she did not know why. Perhaps it was because she wanted Josh Lewis to be important in her life, and that magnified every action.

Half turned away, fumbling with her shoulder straps, she stole a glance back at Josh. He was looking at her, smiling.

"I feel as if we're getting ready to do *From Here to Eternity*," he said.

Clay laughed, and they both tore off their clothes, grabbed the fruit basket and champagne, and ran down into the sea.

Josh and Clay lazed for a while in the warm, clear water, eating chunks of pineapple from the basket that floated on the surface and passing the Dom Perignon back and forth. At first, they just talked and smiled and looked at each other, but soon Josh's foot drifted over and began to trace a line up Clay's thigh, gradually moving up until it reached the hollow of her hip, and then across to curl his toes in the softness of her pubic hair.

"Mmm." She sighed. She came toward him, and he pulled her body against him and kissed her. "Lie back," she whispered. "Float."

Josh let his legs come up and spread themselves on the surface, and she moved in between them.

"Very reminiscent of a shark's fin," Clay murmured as she slid her lips down around him. Her hair shielded Josh's belly from the sun.

"Hmmm. I hope you don't do this to all the sharks you know."

"Hardly any . . ." she tried to say, but it came out sounding more like a mumble.

"Don't talk with your mouth full," Josh whispered. "Don't talk at all."

Before long, they raced ashore and stretched out in the warm white sand in the shade of a coconut palm. Josh kissed Clay's breasts, bringing the brown nipples to stiff attention.

"You have a wonderful body," he said. "And this is a nice place to see it for the first time."

"I know. I feel as if we've been shipwrecked on a deserted island . . ." Clay's full lips met his for a long, probing kiss. A gentle breeze glanced over them, cutting the midday heat.

Clay moaned as he pushed deep into her and wrapped her calves around his shoulders as he thrust again and again with growing urgency. She dug her fingers into his buttocks and shuddered with a little cry as she came, then clung to him as he came.

Out in the lagoon, the basket of fruit and the nearly empty bottle of Dom Perignon mixed with the salt water and drifted away, like a sumptuous message from a cast-away land.

By six o'clock, Clay and Josh were back in Manila having a drink at the Manila Hotel's Jungle Bar with Lars Knudsen, whom they had run into in the lobby. The three of them chose a small table toward the back, as far as they could sit from the happy-hour musical trio, a Filipino *rondallas*, or string band, robustly belting out Musak favorites.

Clay smiled at Lars after they were seated. "It's really a thrill to meet you. In college, I used to read copies of *American Cinematographer* the way some people read Tolkien. With total awe."

Knudsen stroked his beard. "Oh, so you were a cinematographer groupie? A rare breed . . . nearly extinct. And you used to spend all your time off campus at the nearest art cinema?"

"Of course. Five or six films a week. Now I barely have time to catch up with the big ones." She smiled at Josh. "Don't worry . . . *Victorian Pastoral*'s at the top of my list."

Lars leaned forward. "Ever since Josh told me about you, I've been haunted by your name. Now it comes to me. You did the underwater sequences for that PBS documentary . . . the one on the North Sea oil drilling . . ."

"Yes . . . *Fortune Under the Sea*."

"That's it." Lars nodded. "The film itself was so-so, but your footage was excellent."

Josh looked at his watch. "Oh, shit. I was supposed to call California. What time is it there now?"

"Late," Clay said.

"Around two A.M." Lars said.

Josh shrugged. "That's not so bad. I don't mind waking up Harvey Schaffner. He probably hasn't gone to bed yet, anyway. Order me a San Miguel. I'll be back soon."

After Josh left, Clay and Lars launched into a discussion of marine photographic equipment and techniques. From there, they slid into a comparison analyses of films with underwater sequences, everything from *The Deep* and *Raise the Titanic* to Cecil B. DeMille's *Reap the Wild Wind*.

Lars sat back, relaxed. "Don't get me wrong—I am a happily married man. But why is it I never get to meet anyone so attractive on a plane? My luck is always to wind up next to German businessmen."

Clay laughed. "It's usually young mothers with screaming infants for me. They always ask me to watch the baby for them while they go to the john. Which, of course, makes the baby scream even more."

Lars picked up the bottle of beer he had ordered for Josh and split the contents between his glass and Clay's. "Josh could be hours. He's talking to our producer, which probably means they're arguing."

"Yes, I gathered that Josh and the producer don't get along." She paused. "How do you like working with Josh?"

"This will be our third film together. That says something." Lars lit an aromatic Manila cigar and watched the smoke spiral over the table. "I like working with Josh. He's a professional . . . absolutely meticulous. He knows what he wants and how to get it without stifling the people who work with him. Josh is flexible enough to listen to ideas and to use them if he thinks they're good."

"That's very impressive." Clay moved her chair a little to avoid the trail of cigar smoke.

"Oh, yes," Lars continued. "I also like the fact that he's still learning. Most directors at his age have found their niche and are comfortable working within its boundaries. Josh is *never* contented. He's not afraid to extend himself."

"Josh told me he's a tyrant on the set. Is that true?"

Lars was thoughtful. "Well, Josh expects people to work

as hard as he does. If they do, everything is fine. If
not"—he made the sign of a razor cutting his throat—"he
has no tolerance. He will replace crew members who are
not holding their own. So in some quarters he has a rep
for being difficult." The Swede laughed. "Hell, so do I.
That's probably why Josh and I get along so well. We're
alike in many respects."

"Alike?" Josh returned and sat. "I'm not Swedish, and
I don't smoke cigars. What's this man been telling you anyway, Clay?"

"He's been assuring me that you are much misunder-
stood by the Hollywood unions."

Josh chuckled. "That's one way of putting it. Listen, I
don't think I can take this music much longer. What do
you feel like doing?"

"I'm ordering room service and tucking in early. To
read," Lars said.

"How boring!" Clay said. "Why don't you go out with
us?"

Lars shook his head. "Josh told me to get lost after one
drink. I've had two and a half . . ."

"You liar!" Josh laughed. "You know we'd love to have
you join us."

"My Nordic blood can't stand all this heat and humidity. It exhausts me."

"Well, then I have good news for you. It looks as
though, after all this, Bangkok is back on. Harvey's been
talking to some Thai businessmen in L.A. who say they
can provide everything we need. On the cheap. So now we
have to zip to London to work it all out with Fred Justin."
He looked at Clay. "Fred's our production supervisor."

Lars smiled. "I never thought I'd look forward to England for the climate, but after this . . . Do you want me
to stop off at the travel desk and check on flights?"

"Sure. I'll see you at breakfast."

"Okay. Around eight, then." Lars paused and turned
back to Clay. "And you, too, I hope."

Clay nodded. "Probably. Anyway, I enjoyed meeting
you."

"So . . ." Josh said when they were alone. "What shall we do this evening?"

"I have my handy guidebook right here. Let's see . . ." Clay turned to the section on Manila and its environs. "There're the Bat Caves of Montalban, best seen at dusk."

"We'd never make it in time."

"Hmmm, this sounds good. The Bamboo Organ of Las Piñas . . . twelve feet wide, several hundred bamboo pipes?"

"No. I have a better organ for you to see."

Clay laughed. "Well, it doesn't measure twelve feet. Anyway . . . on to Tagaytay Ridge, with about as fine a view as we're likely to see anywhere. Or cockfighting in the suburbs, jai alai—or there's always the magnificent Manila Bay sunset."

"Okay. I vote for that. Should be pretty soon now."

Clay and Josh moved out to the terrace to watch the huge sun drop behind feathery orange and purple clouds. They stood by the railing with their arms held lightly around each other's waists.

"Mmm . . . it *is* magnificent," Clay said.

"Yeah . . . but when was the last time you saw a rotten sunset?"

Clay laughed. "When I'm in New York, I seldom see one at all."

"You look wonderful tonight. I don't think I told you."

"But I haven't had time to change . . ."

Josh kissed her cheek. "Some women don't need clothes. You'd look great in anything." He paused. "I'm trying to figure out what we're going to do."

"I read about a restaurant that specializes in aphrodisiac seafoods. Sounds like a must."

"Hmmm." Josh was pensive. "I mean after tomorrow. When am I going to see you again?"

Clay sighed. "I have to go to Bombay for a day or so. Then back to New York to write my story."

"What about London?"

"What about it?"

"Why don't you stop by there on the way to New York?"

"The trouble is," Clay said, "I'm behind schedule now. My editor wants the story as soon as possible." She paused, and they watched the sun sink over the horizon. "I suppose I could air express my stuff to Kodak and write the story in London . . ."

Josh smiled. "There. You see? Where there's a will . . . Anyway, Brown's Hotel, whenever you can make it."

"Let's say Thursday. I'll wire you if there's a change."

"There better not be. Now that that's set, what'll we do for our last evening together in this part of the world?"

"I hate to waste time by going out to dinner. Of course, there is the aphrodisiac seafood . . ."

"Hell." Josh grinned. "We can always order oysters from room service."

Chapter 4

THE Taj Mahal Hotel's splendid old section, built in 1903, spread out like an exotic stately mansion overlooking Bombay's famous stone arch, the Gateway to India landmark on the Arabian Sea. Behind it stood the towering white edifice known as the "new wing."

Clay's room in the "old Taj," comfortably done up in British Colonial style, overlooked the cosmopolitan city, which was cleaner, more efficient, and obviously wealthier than other Indian cities. The long sweep of waterfront, backed by crescent-shaped Marine Drive winding through hills covered by mansions and expensive high-rises, reminded Clay of Rio de Janeiro's Copacabana Beach. Elsewhere, the modern industrial buildings gave a hint of Los Angeles, and the double-decker buses called to mind Hong Kong. Living amid all of this were Hindus, Christians, Parsees, Jews, and Muslims, speaking dozens of different languages and dialects, ten of which were taught in Bombay's elementary schools.

After a room service breakfast of Darjeeling tea and toast with lime marmalade, Clay got ready to go out. She began by fitting two cameras and five lenses into one of her shoulder bags and tucking ten extra rolls of EPY film into a side pocket. The phone rang.

The hotel's overseas operator announced: "Miss Fitzgerald? I am ready with your call to New York."

"Thank you," Clay said, and waited through an assortment of clicks and sputters. "Hello . . . hello. Owen?"

"Clay! Where the hell are you?" The Alabama drawl of Owen Thomas came through suddenly, as clearly as if he were in the next room. He was Clay's editor at *Interna-*

tional Geography. For the last two years, they had also
been seeing each other, more or less seriously—more for
Owen, less for Clay.

"In Bombay. Listen, I've had a bit of a change of plan.
I'll air express the film to Kodak and have them deliver it
directly to you when they've processed it. I'm going to stop
off in London and write the story there. I'll be back sometime next week."

"Clay, we need the story as soon as possible." His voice
sounded hurt as he took on his professional tone.

"I know, sweetie. But I can write it just as fast in London . . . fewer interruptions."

"But, honey, I miss you. I haven't heard word one from
you for the past two weeks. I was worried."

"Oh, Owen, I'm just fine. Everything with the Moro
divers went smoothly. The shots are going to be fabulous."

"Well, I'm glad. But you could've called or cabled me
just so I'd know you were okay." Owen sounded miffed.

"This is the first chance I've had . . . I've been out in
the middle of nowhere, you know. On a boat."

"Why're you goin' to London, anyway?"

"I thought I'd stop off and see some friends. After
all this time in Asia, I'm longing for a change."

"Well, it'd be a change if you came to New York. I
miss you . . . and I'd like to think you missed me, at least
a little."

"Of course I do, Owen. You're one of my best friends
and—"

"Hell, Clay, that's not what I meant!" Owen snapped.

"Please, Owen, let's not go into that over long distance.
I *do* miss you. And I'll call you as soon as I get back next
week."

Owen sighed. "All right, Clay."

"Need anything from London?"

He sighed again. "No, Clay, nothing at all. Good-by."

Clay sat on the bed for a few moments after she hung
up. She liked Owen. But she had always known that she
didn't want to spend her life with him. Still, she felt a
little rotten lying to him about London. Clay kept hoping

that they could settle into being friends, but that was not what Owen had in mind. And now there was Josh.

It would be easy to fall in love with Josh, but she had to be careful not to rush things. Travel romances tended not to spill over into the realities of everyday living. Clay knew that she would have to keep reminding herself of that fact when she was in London with Josh. In the meantime, she was anxious to rip through her photographic assignment in Bombay so she could get to London as soon as possible.

Clay gathered her camera bag and other paraphernalia and headed for the lobby to mail off some postcards. Handing her key to the desk clerk, she ventured out into the humid ninety-degree heat.

A teenaged Indian boy in jeans approached Clay as soon as she reached the sidewalk. "Hey, miss?" He spoke in accented English. "Nice day. You want to take a boat to the Elephanta Caves? I will get you special price."

"No, thanks," Clay said, walking on.

The tall, gangly boy followed her down the street. "Where you going?" he called out.

"The pearl brokerage center." Clay clutched her handbag and camera case close to her body as she wove along the crowded walkway.

"I take you there. Only one rupee."

Clay held up her map of Bombay. "No, thanks. I know how to get there."

"But I know short cut. Through alley."

"*No* thank you!"

The boy laughed. "Oh . . . you think I am going to rip you off?"—he pronounced it "reep yawf." "No, miss. I go with you to make sure you get there safe. Please, miss. One rupee." He smiled. There was a scar over his left brow.

Clay knew that in India someone was going to hustle her every step of the way. She might as well have an escort to keep the others at bay. "Okay, deal. What's your name?"

"Ajay. I have a cousin who works at the pearl center. I will introduce you."

"All right, Ajay. My name's Clay. Let's go."

Bombay is the only Indian city where cattle do not have the undisputed right of way, but the streets were jammed, anyway, with pedestrians, cars, taxis, scooters, horse-drawn tongas, and rickety bicycles darting everywhere.

For the next twenty minutes, Ajay led Clay through a maze of narrow streets, full of the cacophonic bustle of the city's six or so million inhabitants. Barbers sat out on the street while customers knelt to be shaved. Merchants with open-fronted shops and street vendors hawked an incredible variety of foodstuffs and wares, from hunks of meat completely covered with flies to brilliantly colored bolts of silks and cottons. Beggars squatted before thatched huts nestled in the shadows of antiseptic white high-rises. All along the route, people slept on the sidewalk and were stepped over by everyone, including the street sweepers who pushed litter up and down with brushes made of twigs. Clay stopped to photograph a bored snake charmer with two cobras, blowing indifferently into a flute of gourd and bamboo. Perched a foot away from the snakes, an ear cleaner industriously swabbed his clients' ears with slivers of bamboo dipped in sweet oil.

Finally, as Clay was beginning to wish she had taken an air-conditioned taxi, they arrived at the bustling pearl brokerage center.

"You see, miss?" Ajay smiled. "I take you by short cut."

Pearls from the Persian Gulf between Saudi Arabia and Iran, the largest area of natural pearl production, are shipped to Bombay. There they are cleaned by immersion in hydrogen peroxide and sun-dried. In the pearl brokerage center, they are sorted and drilled, and the finer grades are sold to Western dealers. Many of these pearls wind up in Paris, a major distribution point, and eventually, the United States.

The Bombay pearl brokerage center was a hot, packed, noisy nucleus of the pearl industry.

"One mollusk in a hundred yields a natural pearl. The odds of finding high quality rise from there," Shahid Khalaf explained. Khalaf was a highly respected pearl dealer whose family had been in the pearl business for generations. Clay had a letter of introduction to him from the Indian Embassy in New York.

"It's hard to believe. Look at *all* those pearls!" Clay said as she attached a 55 mm. macro lens with a bellows unit onto her Nikon F-2.

Khalaf nodded. "Only a handful are really extraordinary." He held up a cream-colored slightly oval-shaped pearl over half an inch in diameter. "This is a baroque, one that is imperfect in shape."

"It's lovely." Clay leaned in for a closeup.

"Yes. But not terribly expensive. A pearl's value is based on its color, luster"—he turned the pearl around and around in his fingers— "translucency, texture, size. And shape, of course. The scarcest pearls are round. Next come pear shaped, egg shaped, teardrop . . . then button, baroques, half pearls, seed pearls . . ."

Clay reloaded the camera with Ektachrome Professional film while Mr. Khalaf talked. The stout older man took obvious pleasure in handling each pearl with his short, chubby fingers. Before putting a pearl back on its tray, he wiped it with a soft cloth.

"You know, a string of pearls should be wiped clean after every wearing. Cosmetics and perfumes can work their way into pearls and pit them. By the way, they should be strung with silk—it's much stronger—and restrung every six months or so. The string should be knotted in between each pearl . . ."

"So if the necklace breaks, the pearls won't all spill off?" Clay suggested.

Khalaf nodded. "Also, it keeps them from rubbing together. Pearls will last if treated with great care. There is a story about the treasure from the estate of a very rich maharajah. Mr. Arpels of Van Cleef and Arpels was offered the chest of pearls. But when the box was opened and he picked one up, the pearl disintegrated into a white powder, like chalk. You see, those beautiful pearls had been locked away in a vault for many years. Pearls *need* light and air . . . or they will become dehydrated." Khalaf shook his head with sadness. "What a loss."

Clay changed to her other Nikon F-2, equipped with a 24 mm. wide-angle lens. "But nowadays most of the pearls that come on the market are cultured and harvested," she said.

"On pearl farms . . . oh, yes. I deal mostly cultured pearls now . . . but the *crème de la crème*, you understand. Such as the black pearls from French Polynesia that have been cultured recently by Jean-Claude Brouillet . . . they are very hard to come by." Khalaf smiled, his dark eyes gleaming. "But one has connections . . . one has to in this business.

"Here . . . you see this one?" Khalaf continued, holding up a round, creamy, rose-hued pearl about two centimeters in circumference. "Pure, even color. A strong Orient—overtone—with a high luster. Good semitranslucency. The body, the background color, you see, is the pinkish cast." He held the pearl up to a magnifying glass. "You see this scratch! This minuscule blemish slashes many thousands of dollars from the market price. A perfect pearl must have no dent or scar of any kind."

"But the scratch is barely visible through a magnifying glass," Clay said, switching back to her 55 mm. macro lens in order to get a shot of the blemish. "The pearl still looks perfect to the naked eye."

Shahid Khalaf grinned so wide that the gold fillings in his back teeth were visible. "Yes, indeed. It is possible for a rich man to pay a great deal of money for an inferior pearl obtained from an unscrupulous dealer. If you buy pearls, Miss Fitzgerald, you must go to someone highly reputable."

"Or know exactly what to look for." Clay smiled.

"Ah"—Khalaf waved his finger at her—"it takes *years* for the eye to distinguish flawless quality . . . and perfect color." The plump man pulled a key out of the breast pocket of his Western-cut suit and unlocked an antique teak cabinet. Inside was a steel safe the size of a large television set. "It is time to air my beauties." The Indian chuckled as he clicked through the combination and lifted out a wooden tray covered with black velvet. "I will show you some pearls, Miss Fitzgerald, the likes of which you will never see again, I daresay. Excepting perhaps in a museum."

Clay exclaimed over the beauty of the two dozen or so pearls set before her. They differed in size, shape, and color, and Clay clicked pictures rapidly. "I feel as if I'm gazing into the queen's jewel box! I've never seen anything so beautiful. No wonder people are buying pearls as a hedge against inflation. To own one of these would make you feel like royalty."

"This one"—Khalaf held up a pear-shaped black pearl, roughly the size of a quail egg—"was given to an Indian princess by her lover. She was bidden to throw it back into the sea, so the legend goes, to save the young man who was dying of a mysterious disease." Shahid Khalaf set the pearl on a white-sain cloth so Clay could photograph it. "As she was about to toss it into the water, she received word that her lover had died. She cursed the pearl and sold it instead. Supposedly, every owner since then has met with ill luck. Many people are superstitious about black pearls."

"Obviously *you* aren't," Clay said, changing film.

"No. Not about black pearls in general. This one, however, I purchased for a specific buyer. I am merely keeping it until he returns to India to claim it." He indicated several other dark pearls. "You may be interested to know, the category of black pearl includes also gray, bronze, dark blue, bluish-green, and metallic green." Khalaf held up pearls of each luster to illustrate his point.

"Well, if I'm ever in a position to afford one, I'll come back to you, Mr. Khalaf," Clay said as she shot, rapidly switching cameras and lenses. "What makes pearls different colors? Is it something in the oyster or the ocean? I mean, I know black-lipped mollusks produce the black pearls of the Philippines, but what about all the hues?"

"The color depends on the part of the world the oyster comes from. Of course, the best pearls are produced in salt water." Khalaf showed Clay a teardrop pearl with a violet overtone. "This is called a Madras pearl, from the Indian Ocean between India and Sri Lanka—because of the color. You see . . . reflected light comes from its surface. This *reflection* is what makes pearls appear pink or yellow, green, purple, orange, blue . . ."

"I want them all, Mr. Khalaf." Clay grinned. She pointed to a round white pearl. "How much would that one cost?"

"Ah, Miss Fitzgerald, you have good taste. This is one of my finest—an Oriental pearl from the Persian Gulf. The value of a pearl is estimated by multiplying a base rate by the square of the pearl's weight. The base rate fluctuates often, as you can imagine. Of course, now they're at an all-time high. And even a tiny increase in a pearl's size can have a large effect on its value."

Khalaf wiped the perspiration from his face with a white-linen handkerchief and continued. "This is why appraising pearls is more complex than other gems. A necklace of pearls as fine as this would sell today for around five and a half million rupees . . . about five hundred thousand American dollars."

Clay's gray eyes widened with amazement. She broke into a smile. "Just charge it to my account, Mr. Khalaf. Or would you prefer a check?"

The Indian laughed and looked at his Swiss watch. "I am afraid I have a luncheon engagement. Perhaps you can return around three o'clock, and I will show you something very special."

"Thank you, Mr. Khalaf. I'd like that. In the meantime, I'll wander around and photograph some of the other activity going on around here."

As Clay gathered her equipment, Ajay, her young Indian escort, reappeared. "I take you to my cousin now."

"Okay, Ajay. Lead the way." They pressed through the crowd. There were a number of Westerners milling about, but Clay was one of the few women. At five feet nine, with two cameras strapped around her neck, she drew a number of open-mouthed stares.

A hand reached out from the welter of bodies and touched her shoulder. She smelled sweet talcum and heard a peculiar clipped drawl that she recognized instantly, although the last time she had heard it had been ten years and ten thousand miles removed.

"Well, Clay! Clay Fitzgerald!"

"Hello, Beau," Clay managed to say, hoping her voice somehow stayed neutral.

Beau Yates held her familiarly by the shoulders, grinning at her at arm's length. "Well, if it's not my little sister."

"No, it's not, Beau."

He laughed. "Just in a manner of speakin', honey. Well, damn! I don't know how I even recognized you. You've turned into quite some piece of woman, Clay."

Clay stepped back a pace, shrugging off his hands. Beau Yates, at thirty-one, exuded a good deal more worldly confidence than he had when she had last seen him. He was expensively dressed in a white silk suit of Italian cut. His blond hair was neatly trimmed below a straw Panama. His face, still handsome, was fuller now, and there was a muscular thickness to his body that she did not remember. Overall, he gave the impression of sleek and prosperous good health; but there were shadows around his pale-blue eyes that belied that impression, and the eyes themselves still made her shiver.

"So what are you doin' in this part of the world?"

"A story for *International Geography*. And you?"

"Business. Got my own import company."

"That's nice. Well, so long, Beau. I've got an appointment."

"What, with your little woggie friend there?" His eyes darted, leering.

"Oh, for Christ's sake, Beau . . ."

"Come on now, Clay," Beau drawled. "Your voice is so cold I'm almost freezin'. Why not let bygones be bygones, or however the sayin' goes? Who'd of thought we'd run into each other way out here in India? Hey, how about havin' a drink with me? Melt the ice. We got a lot of catchin' up to do."

Clay shook her head. "No, Beau. I don't really think we have anything to say to each other."

Beau Yates grinned, and she saw that bright glint in his eyes that had always scared her. "Still the same old Clay. You're no better than anybody else, honey. But you've still

got that stick up your ass. Too bad . . . because otherwise
you're a hell of an attractive woman."

"Good-bye, Beau," Clay snapped. She turned to leave,
but Yates grabbed her arm.

"Hey, relax, why don't you?" He turned her toward
him, pushing his face too close to hers. "Here we are, halfway across the world. It's got to be fate, so don't let's fight
it. I've got plenty of money. Let me show you a good
time."

"Let go of my arm."

"Oh, *sorry* . . ." He released his grip. "Didn't mean to
touch the vestal virgin. Guess you still have some growin'
up to do, Clay. That body of yours doesn't make you a
woman."

Ajay scurried after her as she squeezed down a narrow
aisle of the crowded pearl market. "*Now* you ready to
meet my cousin?"

He had to call twice and tug on Clay's arm. She spun
on him, and she saw him cringe away in alarm at what
must have been a ferocious look on her face before she realized it was Ajay, not Beau. She composed her face
quickly.

"No . . . I'm sorry, Ajay. I've changed my mind." She
dug in her pocket and handed him two rupees. "That's all,
Ajay. Thank you." He did not argue. He took the money,
bowed hurriedly, and disappeared into the throng of the
market.

For a quarter of an hour, she tried to throw herself into
work, shooting the frenetic activity of the market through
her 20 mm. lens. But even the familiar mental and
mechanical processes of photographing could not absorb
her. The work was no good. Her eye was off, and her
hands were still shaking with anger. As she was unscrew-
ing a lens filter to change it, the glass dropped to the
floor and broke.

"Shit!" she muttered. "Shit!"

Surprised faces turned to her.

"Oh, God *damn* you, Beau Yates!" she muttered under
her breath, and pushed her way through the crowd and
out of the Bombay pearl brokerage center. Her nerves

were still vibrating when she reached her hotel. She could not wait to get out of India. The poverty and filth disgusted her; there were too many faces.

She knew she was overreacting. She told herself that she had nothing to fear from Beau Yates. But it made Asia seem unpleasantly smaller if he could turn up there.

Chapter 5

CONVERSATION was interrupted by a knock on the door of Josh Lewis's suite at Brown's, an understatedly elegant, old-fashioned hotel in the Mayfair section of London. Josh, dressed in counterpoint to the traditional surroundings, answered the door in an old T-shirt, chinos, and bare feet. He broke into a grin at the sight of Clay Fitzgerald.

"It's the lady with the luggage . . . welcome!" Josh kissed her quickly on the lips and peered out into the hallway. "What happened to your entourage?"

"Still trying to fit everything into the elevator. So I hopped on another one."

"Well, come in. How was your trip?"

Clay shrugged. "It was . . . okay."

In the living room, Lars Knudsen rose and greeted her continental style, with a kiss on both cheeks. Another man stood and gazed at her quizzically.

"Clay, this is Fred Justin, our production supervisor. We're just finishing up. Can I order you a drink?"

Clay shook hands with Justin and declined the drink. "I'd love to take advantage of your tub, though. The plane was crowded, and the air conditioning was barely working."

"Here . . . this way." Josh led her through the oak-paneled bedroom. "I'll be through in about fifteen minutes. Take your time and I'll join you."

Clay smiled. "I'm glad to see you again."

"Me, too." Josh kissed her forehead.

The bathroom door burst open, and Josh walked in, naked.

"Too late," Clay said. "My Vitabath bubbles are almost gone."

"With your hair slicked back like that, you look like a boy."

"Gee, thanks." Clay smiled. "Does that turn you on?"

Josh wedged himself in the tub, facing her while water splashed over the sides. "Not the way you think. So . . . how was Bombay and the pearl center?"

"Fine. But it gets depressing after a while, looking at all those pearls and knowing you can't have them."

Josh puffed at an imaginary cigar. "Stick with me, kid, and I'll buy you a necklace of pearls."

"Only the real thing . . . nothing cultured for me."

"I always suspected that you were a woman who scorned culture."

Clay laughed. "Just your type, right?"

"Right." He kissed her wet knees. "Hmmm, very tasty. I really have a thing for knees, you know."

"A knee fetishist?"

"Yes. And shoulders." He scooped up a pile of bubbles and mounded them on her shoulders, sculpting the foamy soap down over her tanned breasts with his fingers. "And breasts. I didn't mention them, did I?" Josh skimmed the last of the bubbles off the water's surface and recovered Clay's breasts and rib cage. "This is more fun than icing a cake."

"Hmmm, I'll say. Although I do feel a bit like the latest model of bathtub toy."

"You're not a toy to me, Clay." Josh grinned but then paused and looked seriously into her deep-gray eyes. "I missed you."

That look again, Clay thought. Josh Lewis was irresistible. She leaned forward and kissed him. She hadn't realized until that moment exactly how much she had missed him. "Me, too," she said.

Josh scooped up handfuls of water and washed away the remains of the soap bubbles on Clay. Trying to move closer, he bumped his elbow. "English tubs really aren't made for long-legged Americans, are they?"

"No. But then neither are most American tubs." Clay giggled.

"I feel as if I'm wedged in a sardine can."

"Packed in water, our label should read. Anyway, my toes are wrinkled." Clay stepped out, reaching for a towel. "It's all yours."

"Hell, that wasn't very romantic."

"As you said, you have to be *small* to do it in a tub."

Josh sponged the soap off his body and got out. "Someday we'll have a tub for two. Custom made for us. How tall are you, anyway?"

"Five nine." Clay smiled. "But I've finished growing."

Josh opened Clay's towel, pressing his wet body against hers, and closed the towel around them. "Were you a gawky teenager?"

"I suppose. But I didn't really like boys, so it didn't matter."

Josh kissed the top of her wet head. "Did you like girls?"

"No, horses." Clay laughed and pressed her fingertips to Josh's mouth. "*Don't* comment on that one."

"I wouldn't touch it. Your secret's safe with me." Josh disengaged himself from the towel. At the basin, he lathered up with shaving cream. "As you might have noticed, I didn't shave this morning. I keep thinking I'll grow a beard, like Lars and Fred Justin, but I never last out the day."

"Good thing. I hate razor burn." Clay hugged Josh's waist from behind. He kissed her hand and left it white with shaving cream.

Clay yawned. "Sorry. I didn't sleep much on the plane. I feel like a zombie."

"I figured you would. I didn't plan anything for tonight."

"If I have a nap, I'll be ready to go out later."

"Get in bed. I'll give you Mr. Josh's super back rub."

"Hmmm, thank you. My lower back is screaming for help."

"Oh, yeah . . . I think I hear it."

Clay stretched out on the bed, and Josh sat on her buttocks, his knees straddling her hips. "God, you have a well-developed back. It's really nice." His fingers dug into her shoulders and slowly pressed their way down her spine.

"Hmmm, that feels fabulous. I promise I'll do you later."

"Just relax," Josh whispered. "Concentrate on relaxing, loosening up all those muscles." He kneaded, rubbed, and caressed every inch of her back and hips while Clay murmured her delight.

When he finished, Josh stretched his long body out next to her. "Are you sleepy? Would you like the special after-back-rub massage now or later?"

Clay kissed him lazily. "Now . . . I think it'd make me sleep better."

He was already hard. She took hold of him. "You seem to be keeping it in shape," she said. "Seen any action while I was away?"

Josh grinned. "Sure. I haven't seen you for nearly three days."

"Oh?"

"There were so many I can't keep track."

Clay laughed. "Really?"

"I'm not telling you a damned thing." He nibbled on her neck and made her giggle.

"Okay. Have it your way," Clay said.

"All right, you asked for it."

Josh shifted into a sitting position and pulled Clay on to his lap, pushing himself deep within her. Clay stretched her arms up toward the ceiling and threw her head back in pleasure as she slid up and down.

"Oh, Josh. You . . . are . . . wonderful." She leaned over and kissed her way around his face. Her fingers twisted around the curls and cowlicks of his dark-brown hair.

Josh pulled her close to him, and their torsos moved and sweated together. Clay's body was flushed with excitement. She moaned and gasped for breath as they rolled and turned and changed positions. The athleticism of Josh's lovemaking was exhilarating, and Clay felt revitalized from the adrenalin surging through her body.

Later, when they were lying on the thick dark-green carpet, tangled in sheets, Clay felt so totally disoriented that she was not sure whether they had spent minutes or hours making love.

"Whew!" Clay laughed as they disengaged themselves from the covers. "I feel as if I just ran the four-minute mile."

Josh held her in his arms. "Four minutes? Madam, you do me an injustice."

They lay together on the floor in contented silence. After a few minutes, Josh realized that Clay had drifted off to sleep, and gently he moved her back on to the bed, pulling a blanket over her.

"Josh?" Clay called out from the telephone in the bedroom. "I finally reached Lord Asquith. He's invited us out for the weekend. I said yes. Is that okay with you?"

Josh stood in the doorway. "Sure. I'd love it. I have theater tickets for Saturday night, but I can switch them."

"Great. You'll really like Jamie. He was a good friend of my father's. I haven't seen him since before my father died, eight years ago."

"Oh? You know, you've never told me anything about yourself . . ."

"I consider myself a boring subject," Clay smiled. "Anyway, are you ready to hit Portobello Road? We can have tea at a little place I remember near Hampstead Heath, and—"

"Stop . . . stop! One thing at a time. You're wearing me out. I'm going to need a vacation from my vacation."

"What do you mean? You've spent most of the past week in bed." Clay grabbed a jacket out of the closet. "Come on, let's get a little exercise. The *outdoor* variety."

By Saturday noon, Clay and Josh felt very much at home at Lord Asquith's country manor, Winston Knoll. The sprawling brick Tudor house in the Cotswolds had been in Lord Asquith's family for seven hundred years.

Lord Asquith took a sip of wine. "To dine well in England, Somerset Maugham said, one must eat breakfast three times a day." The gray, dignified man chuckled gently. "But I rather think my cook, Mrs. Granger, disproves Mr. Maugham's aphorism."

"She certainly does," Clay said, tasting the portion of fresh blackberry posset the butler had set before her.

"I'd love to watch her concoct the pâté she made with herbs from your garden," Josh said. "It was superb."

"Oh, you cook, Mr. Lewis?"

Josh grinned. "I worked in a restaurant kitchen when I was at UCLA film school. I've liked to cook ever since. In fact, it relaxes me."

"Oh, you Americans are so amusing," Lord Asquith said. "And Clay, I suppose you, too, are a gourmet cook."

"Not at all." Clay laughed."But I'm quite good at ordering in Chinese. That's what you do in New York when you're too lazy to cook."

"Ordering in Chinese?" Lord Asquith was impressed. "I didn't know you were a linguist, my dear."

"No, no. Chinese food. Ordering it on the phone."

"Oh, that's frightfully amusing!" Lord Asquith laughed robustly. "Next time I'm at the Carlyle, I'll have to do it. Don't you think room service would be appropriately horrified if a Chinese waiter delivered me dinner in a large brown bag?"

Asquith rose and led them out to the west garden. "Come now, I'll show you the stable, Mr. Lewis." Lord Asquith, in his conservative three-piece banker's suit, strode across the manicured lawn where peacocks roamed at large.

"I'm very anxious to see it," Josh said, keeping pace.

"Clay mentioned when she rang up that you own some racehorses in California," Lord Asquith said.

"Only three. But I plan to buy more. I bought a ranch last year . . . Unfortunately, I haven't been able to spend much time there."

"There have been a few changes since you were here

last, Clay. My goodness, it's been over ten years." Lord
Asquith shook his head. "I still miss your father."

Clay took Lord Asquith's hand as they made their brisk
way to the stables. "I do, too." She turned to Josh. "My
father and Jamie were partners, in a way. Jamie scouted
thoroughbreds in England for Daddy, and vice-versa."

"Yes, we co-owned quite a few as well. We had extremely good luck together. One of my biggest stakes
winners, Loblolly, I purchased from your father. Now
Loblolly supports the farm with his stud fees." Lord
Asquith strolled on ahead.

"You never told me your father bred horses," Josh
whispered.

"Well, it was a long time ago. I don't like to talk about
it."

They entered a large courtyard surrounded by horse
stalls, a maroon barn, and a large stone cottage that housed
the farm office.

"Ah," Lord Asquith reminisced, "under Mac Fitzgerald,
The Willows was one of the finest breeding farms in the
States."

"Was?" Josh asked. "I thought The Willows was still
thriving."

"I suppose it is, actually," Lord Asquith said. "But it's
not the same now . . ." He trailed off.

"Oh, look! Darcy's Landing—my old favorite." Clay
patted the bay mare in stall sixteen. "Hello, lady. Remember me?" She kissed the white star on the horse's forehead.
"It's good to see you again. May I ride her later, Jamie?"

"Of course, my dear. She's as frisky as ever. You ride,
don't you, Mr. Lewis?"

Josh nodded. "When I was a boy, my folks lived near
the Santa Anita race track. My nickname was Peewee
back then, and I wanted to be a jockey."

Lord Asquith laughed. "Oh, my."

"Yes . . . the summer I was fourteen I grew nearly a
foot. I think that's when I decided to switch to film making." Josh grinned and put his arm around Clay as they
walked around with Lord Asquith, admiring his race

horses, young foals, and the yearlings that he would sell at Tattersall's in Newmarket later in the season.

"Oh, I nearly forgot. I have something quite amusing for us to do tomorrow. I think you'll be interested in this, Mr. Lewis," Lord Asquith instructed a groom to saddle up horses for Clay and Josh, then continued. "A wealthy industrialist, or rather ex-wealthy, is holding a private horse sale tomorrow. At his soon-to-be-former estate, near here. I'm interested in one of his French-bred yearlings. I think I can strike a deal with him before the auction. At any rate, would you care to join me?"

"Oh, yes," Clay said.

"I would, too," Josh added. "But what about exporting horses from Great Britain?"

"Well, it's still true that no horse bred on an English breeding farm will be accepted into the States for fear of disease. The horses being auctioned tomorrow, incidentally, were bred and foaled in France. Of course—oh, here you are!"

The young, ruddy-cheeked Welsh groom came up quietly, leading Darcy's Landing and a chestnut horse for Josh.

"Splendid," Lord Asquith said. "I'm afraid I won't be able to join you. I must go over the billing with my comptroller. See you at drink time. Seven-thirty. A nice young couple, Felicity and Michael Henderson, will be joining us for dinner. They've restored a rather sweet cottage down the road, but they work in London. Oh, I'm running on, am I not?" He pointed westward. "If you head in that direction, you'll get to Sudeley Castle. It's open to the public now, and I think you might enjoy it. Quite interesting, as castles go. All right—off with you. Have a pleasant ride."

Clay and Josh cantered off toward an ocean of tall grass and red poppies swaying in the breeze.

"I think I could get used to this life," Josh called to Clay.

"Me, too. It's a far cry from the bridle path in Central Park."

Sunday noon, after a "full-cooked English breakfast" consisting of trout armored in bacon, rumbled eggs with Scottish salmon, kedgeree, breakfast kippers and haddock, sausages, kidneys, ham in whiskey sauce, glazed guinea fowl with juniper berries, and fresh fruits in orange shells with Cumberland sauce, Clay and Josh climbed into Lord Asquith's Silver Cloud and drove with him to the nearby estate of the bankrupt industrialist, Perrin Archer.

"I'm going to have a chat with Archer," Lord Asquith said. "You two have a look 'round. I'll find you later."

Clay was glad that she had thought to bring her pink-linen Bill Blass up from London. It was the only suit she owned, and it was just right. The men and women who were bunched around the stalls for a pre-auction look at the race horses were all outfitted as if they were going from there to have tea with the royal family.

"Let's start at those stalls over there," Clay said. "They're not as crowded."

Josh handed her an auction program. "Yes, let's see what we'll buy."

For the next twenty minutes, they went from stall to stall discussing seriously the various merits of the thoroughbreds going up for sale.

"I'm beginning to get in the mood to bid at this auction," Josh said to Lord Asquith as he joined them. "You said these horses have not been on an English breeding farm?"

"Technically, they haven't," Lord Asquith said. "You see, Archer's place here isn't a stud farm. Most of his horses were bred in France."

"Oh, look!" Clay pointed to a beautiful gray filly, the color of a silver fox.

"Nice," Josh said. "I've always been a sucker for a gray horse."

Clay looked up the horse, number twenty-three in the catalogue. "She's a two-year-old . . ."

"Yes, her sire was a stakes winner and a grandson of Nearco," Asquith added.

"Secretariat's great-grandfather was Nearco!" Clay said enthusiastically.

"Yes," Lord Asquith continued, "and the dam was a winner of the French 1000 Guineas, at Longchamp. As I remember, the filly was bred in France and raced a few times there this past winter. Won or placed every time, Archer told me. Then bucked her shins, and he brought her over here to mend. He had hopes of racing her at Epsom this summer."

Lord Asquith spotted several friends in the distance, "Excuse me, Clay, Josh . . ." He headed off into the flock of aristocracy, horse breeders, and blood-stock agents.

"I can't get over this filly," Clay said. "Look at her conformation. She's absolutely perfect. I haven't seen a horse this beautiful since . . . for a long time."

"She is a beauty. But bucked shins . . . she could recover and buck them again."

"True. But with the right trainer she could have a wonderful career. And when she retires, you can breed her. She'll make money both ways."

"What do you mean, *I* can breed her? I'm not buying her . . . What's her name, anyway?" Josh looked in his program. "Oriental Pearl."

"See?" Clay said excitedly. "Even her name's symbolic."

"For you, maybe. But . . ."

"Oh, Josh, you'd be a fool not to bid on her. Look at that bloodline. She'd be a fabulous blood mare later on. You've got to do it, Josh! *Look* at that horse and tell me she couldn't win the Kentucky Oaks. Or the Derby, for that matter."

"Stop . . . stop." Josh laughed. "I admit she looks good. And you're probably right—she would be a good broodmare to own."

"Exactly! And if you race her for a couple of years first . . ."

Josh shook his head. "No point in risking that. It's expensive, and if she hurt herself, I might wind up with nothing."

"You'd buy a horse like that and not race her? All she needs is to be retrained. Come on, Josh. Buy her!"

"Well . . . if I did, it would be to get her in foal next year."

Lord Asquith reappeared. "Ah, you're still looking at that filly? Come along, I have reserved seats at the sales pavilion. Archer refused to talk privately . . . he's really up against it. I'll have to bid on that yearling after all. Turns out Mr. Combs is interested, too."

For the next couple of hours, race horses, brood mares, and yearlings were brought on to the open-air sales paddock while the bidding progressed down the auction program. Lord Asquith was outbid by Leslie Combs's Spendthrift Farms for the yearling, but he wound up purchasing a two-year-old colt that had won its first three starts at Longchamp in Paris.

"Oriental Pearl is coming up next," Clay whispered to Josh.

"Okay, okay. You've convinced me." Josh grinned. "Besides, I'm getting auction fever."

"Then you *will* race her?"

"No. I told you. I need a brood mare."

"You're making a big mistake, Josh."

"If you think she'll make such a great stakes winner, then why don't *you* bid on her?"

"Oh, Josh. You're—"

Auctioneer Lawrence Schuster fingered his gavel. Oriental Pearl was led into the sales ring. The filly gazed at the American and foreign breeders gathered before her and lifted her head. She looked quite pleased with herself. Her handler led her in slow circles around the ring. She pricked her ears as Schuster went into his spiel.

"Filly, number twenty-three. The bidding will commence with five thousand pounds." The energetic auctioneer glanced at the crowd. "I have five thousand . . . five . . . fifty-five hundred . . ."

Clay nodded.

The auctioneer continued, "I have six thousand . . . six . . ."

"You really *are* bidding," Josh said. "You're not serious?"

"You bet I am," Clay whispered. Several other bidders,

including an American in a flamboyant plaid sports coat, brought the figure up to eight thousand pounds.

Josh signaled a bid of eighty-five hundred. "Where on earth would you keep a horse in New York City?" he asked.

Clay nodded to the auctioneer: nine thousand pounds. "I'll board her with some friends in Virginia. The Randolphs. They have Blue Hill Stud."

Josh nodded. "Have it your way, then." He turned back to the auctioneer. Someone in back, an American woman had just bid ten thousand. Josh upped it another five hundred.

Clay bid eleven thousand. She felt exhilarated. Her cheeks took on a rosy flush as blood pounded through her head. She knew it was irrational, bidding against Josh. But something from the past, an intense passion for thoroughbreds—a feeling she thought she had buried with her father—was pushing its way from deep in her subconscious.

Clay forced herself to think quickly, specifically, about her finances. How would she pay for Oriental Pearl? There was her savings account stash and a few thousand dollars worth of stock dividends that were gathering interest in a daily cash accumulation fund at Merrill, Lynch. She had been saving to buy a boat in the Caribbean. Her plan had been to live on it part of the year and charter it out the rest of the time to pay the maintenance expenses. Well, the boat would have to wait.

The woman in back bid up, followed by Josh, then Clay. One by one, the other bidders dropped out.

Clay felt the gentle hand of Lord Asquith touch her elbow. "Clay, my dear, are you sure this is the right thing to do?"

Clay smiled at his concern and squeezed his hand, "No, but I want to race that horse. I have a feeling . . ." She bid twelve thousand, remembering the handful of rare gold coins her grandfather had left her. They were sitting idle in a safety deposit box. With the current price of gold, surely they were worth a decent chunk of money, perhaps ten thousand or more.

Josh bid twelve five. The woman in back brought it to thirteen five. The auctioneer looked at Clay. She signaled fourteen.

Fourteen thousand pounds, at the current rate of exchange, was around thirty-three thousand dollars, Clay calculated quickly. She knew she had launched into temporary insanity, gambler's fever. She was behaving like an auction junkie. Besides the purchase price, her sensible side reminded her, there would be shipping fees to transport the horse to Virginia. And storage and food and vet bills and insurance. Then there was the cost of retraining, track fees . . .

The auctioneer's eyes were on Clay. "Sixteen thousand . . . do I have sixteen?"

Clay's palms began to tingle, the way they did when she was nervous. She looked at Oriental Pearl and felt again an irresistible need to own the horse. There were wealthy friends in New York she could tap. Perhaps she could convince one or two of them to go into partnership with her. Oriental Pearl was a spectacular horse, a good risk. If she could raise the money, the gray filly would pay her back.

Clay nodded: sixteen thousand pounds. Thirty-eight thousand dollars. Now her entire body began to prickle. She looked at Josh's strong profile. He was the most exciting man she had come across in a long time. The other impracticalities aside, if she bought this horse, what would it to do their relationship?

Josh bid again and smiled at Clay, but she detected no real amusement in his eyes; he wanted the filly as much as she did. And he had a stable ready for her.

The bidding was up to eighteen thousand. The auctioneer glanced at Clay again. She took a slow deep breath and looked at the fabulous gray filly. She wanted Oriental Pearl as much as she had wanted any horse in her life.

But Clay shook her head.

Josh squeezed her arm and bid eighteen. The woman in back offered twenty, then upped Josh's twenty-one by another thousand pounds.

Clay tightened her grip on Josh's arm. "We've got to get her!" she whispered.

Josh bid twenty-three. "I'm not going much higher, Clay."

The gallery was quiet, and the auctioneer started calling in the bid. "Twenty-three . . . I have twenty-three . . . twenty-four . . . do I hear twenty-four? Twenty-three once . . ." He looked at the woman in back, then Josh.

"Sold to the gentleman for twenty-three thousand pounds."

"Josh! She's yours!" Clay threw her arms around him ecstatically. "Congratulations!"

"Good show." Lord Asquith shook Josh's hand. "A fine filly. A good price, too."

Josh beamed. "Thanks to Clay. She's the one who picked her out."

"Please race her, Josh."

"No, honey. Too expensive. I *need* a brood mare."

Clay Fitzgerald sighed with frustration, but she kept her mouth shut. She was determined to change Josh's mind.

Chapter 6

"WHY, Clay, it *is* you! I said to mother, 'That's Clay.' And she said, 'It can't be. What would *she* be doing here?' And I said, 'I'll bet you it is.' Then, when you started to bid, I recognized your voice. From where we all were sittin' in back, I couldn't see too well. We were late arrivin'." Audrey Yates Babcock paused for breath and gazed up at Josh Lewis. She shielded her turquoise eyes from the sun with her hand and smiled.

"Audrey, this is Josh Lewis. Josh . . . my stepsister, Audrey Yates."

"Actually, it's Babcock now . . . but not for long. My divorce'll be comin' through soon. Well, Mr. Lewis. You've got yourself a fine filly. I shouldn't have given in to you so easily."

"What? I was bidding against you?"

Audrey grinned. "Yes. And Clay . . . why on earth were *you* biddin' against Mr. Lewis?"

"I was toying with going into the horse business, Audrey. On a small scale."

"Oh, you always did have a mind of your own." Audrey giggled. "Anyway, come with me. Mother and Kenny are over there somewhere."

"Kenny? He's here?" Clay turned to Josh. "He's my half brother. I haven't seen him in years. He'll be ten next March."

"Mother says you never forget his birthday. And you send him postcards from all over the world. My goodness, you're so busy these days. I'm surprised you've never gotten married. Oh, *there* they are! Mother! Look who's here."

58

An attractive petite woman with short, curly platinum hair extended a gloved hand to Clay. "Well, Clay. It's been a long time. I'm surprised to see you heah, of all places."

"Yes . . . well . . . Josh, this is my stepmother, Sunny Fitzgerald, from Virginia."

A pale, slim young boy with large gray eyes, like Clay's, and sandy hair stepped up hesitantly. "Clay?"

"Kenny!" The boy was the image of their father, Mac Fitzgerald, and Clay's eyes filled with tears as she knelt down to hug him. The boy squeezed her tightly. "Oh, it's so good to see you!"

"We've been to Paris," Kenny said. "I sent you a postcard. Did you get it?"

Clay shook her head, smiling. "I'm sure it's home waiting for me. I just sent *you* cards from India and the Philippines." Out of the corner of her eye, Clay could see Audrey flirting as she chatted animatedly with Josh. She also noted Josh's approving once-over of Audrey's appearance. She had on a ruffly multiprinted Saint Laurent garden dress that rested two inches above her shapely knees.

"When I'm older, will you take me on one of your trips? Maybe next year? I'll be eleven then."

"Of course. Maybe your mother will let me take you to the Caribbean for spring vacation."

"Oh, golly. Mom! Did you hear that? Can I go with Clay next spring to—"

"Perhaps, Kenny. We'll see. Now say good-by to Clay, and run find Nanny."

"Mother," Audrey called out. "I've just convinced Mr. Lewis to have a drink with us at the inn. You'll come, too, won't you, Clay?"

Clay's stomach knotted. She knew she was no longer the ugly duckling to Audrey's swan, but old reflexes die hard. "Well, actually," she said, trying to smile, "Josh and I have to get back to Lord Asquith's to pick up our things. We're heading back to London this evening."

"Oh? Well, then, you all stop by and have a drink on your way to London. The inn is right on your way."

"Good idea," Josh said. "We'll see you later."

Audrey scribbled something on a notepad she took out of her purse and handed the sheet to Josh. "Directions. Ah wouldn't want you to get lost," she said sweetly. She swept a loose strand of her long blonde hair away from her face and kept her eyes locked on Josh. "See you later, Mr. Lewis. You, too, Clay."

Clay embraced Lord Asquith affectionately. "Thank you for everything, Jamie. It's been wonderful seeing you again."

"It's been my pleasure, Clay. I'll ring you next time I'm in New York. We'll order in Chinese." Lord Asquith chuckled. "And Mr. Lewis, I wish you much success with your filly. You're sure you can find your way now? Drive with care."

Clay and Josh waved a final farewell, and took off in their rented BMW.

"After the Silver Cloud, this is a bit of a jolt." Josh grinned. "What a great weekend." He turned off the Winston Knoll drive and on to a winding two-lane back road. "I don't understand, Clay, why you never told me about your family. And that you're Mac Fitzgerald's daughter."

"I didn't think it was interesting," Clay said flatly.

"Why not? I told you about my ranch and my racehorses. Of course, I'd be interested."

Clay shrugged. "It's not a part of my life that I particularly care to talk about."

"From the tone of your voice, I'm beginning to suspect you're mad at me."

"No."

They drove along in silence for several kilometers.

"All right," Josh said finally, "what've I done?"

"If you had any sensitivity at all, you'd have seen that I do *not* want to have a drink with my stepmother and Audrey."

"Well, I thought it would be the polite thing. I figured you'd probably want to see your family."

"They're *not* my family. I haven't had any family since

my father died. Except Kenny . . . and I haven't actually seen him since he was a baby."

"Well, I'm sorry. But look—it's been a long time since you've seen them."

"Not long enough. I'd be perfectly happy if I never saw them again. There's a lot you don't know, Josh, and I'm sorry, but it's really none of your business."

"All right." Josh sighed. "We'll have a quick drink. Then we'll head back to London. Okay?" He smiled.

Clay did not smile. "One drink. That's all."

Audrey Babcock greeted them at the door of the White Stag Inn. She had changed into Oriental white silk damask pants with a brocaded jacket by Ungaro. Her hair was piled on top of her head, with fine wisps spilling down her long neck.

"I hope you all didn't have any trouble findin' it." She led them into a cozy oak-paneled room with an immense stone fireplace. "Seems silly to be havin' a fire in June . . . but these English inns get cold as a tomb at night."

Sunny Fitzgerald had not bothered to change her beige Adolfo suit, but she had added diamond ear clips and a choker of seed pearls to dress it up. Two other couples, the Edgecombe Meades and the Amos Outhwaites, American horse people whom Clay vaguely remembered, stood to greet them, along with a ruddy-complexioned older man, Sir Ian Elliott. After everyone shifted around and the waiter brought two more chairs, Clay noticed that Audrey had switched places with Edge Meade in order to sit next to Josh. Audrey immediately began quizzing him about his ranch in California and the movie business. Amos and Janet Outhwaite, on Clay's left, engaged Clay in polite small talk as the waiter took drink orders. Across the table, Edge and Mary Meade were gossiping with Sunny and Sir Ian.

Clay studied Sunny. Her stepmother's jaw had slackened a bit, and the laugh lines around her eyes were more permanently creased, but Sunny still looked good. She had to be in her late forties, Clay figured.

As if suddenly aware of Clay's scrutiny, Sunny Yates looked at Clay.

"Where's Kenny?" Clay asked. "I thought he'd be here."

"Oh, God, no. He's not allowed to socialize with the grownups when we travel. He's havin' dinner in his room with Nanny."

"Would you mind if I went up to see him for a few minutes?"

"Do as you like," Sunny replied. "Room thirty-one. Tell Miss Gibbons I want him put straight to bed as soon as you leave."

Clay looked at her watch. It was just past seven, an early bedtime for a nine-year-old. "I'll be back soon," she told Josh, and excused herself.

"Oh, Clay! I was hopin' I'd get to see you again." Kenny Fitzgerald hugged her and introduced Clay to his nanny, an exhausted-looking woman of an uncertain age.

Clay opened her handbag. "Here's a little something for you. Some shells from the Sulu Archipelago. Do you know where that is?"

Kenny thought for a second. "Northeast of Borneo. You know that globe you sent me for Christmas last year? I use it all the time. Geography's my best subject, next to math."

Clay laughed. "Math was my worst subject! I couldn't survive today without my calculator."

"Kenny!" Miss Gibbons said sternly. "Time to get ready for bed."

"Oh, can't I stay up a little longer and talk to Clay?"

"Your mother wants you to keep to your schedule." She handed the boy a dime-sized white pill that he swallowed obediently with a glass of mineral water.

"What's that for?" Clay asked.

"Asthma," Kenny said. "I get attacks a lot. Especially at night."

Clay put her arms around him and kissed his soft, curly hair. "Poor baby. I'm sure you'll grow out of it. I have a friend who did when she was in her early teens."

Tears filled the boy's eyes, but he blinked hard to control them. "Why don't you ever come and visit us? I wish I could see you more."

"I wish so, too. But it would make me sad to come to Virginia. I'd miss my father too much."

"He was my father, too," Kenny said. "Except I don't remember him. Just pictures. Mom doesn't talk much about him."

"Kenny," Miss Gibbons returned. "I told you—"

"Yes, ma'am, I'm comin'." He hugged Clay.

"We'll spend more time together," Clay promised. "Now that you're getting older, I'm sure your mother will let you come visit . . ."

"No, she won't! She said you live a wild life in New York."

Clay laughed. "Well, don't go believing everything you hear about me. Okay?" She kissed his cheek. "Sleep tight. We'll see each other soon."

"Promise?"

"Yes, we'll work it out somehow."

Kenny hugged her again and then retreated to the bedroom under the nanny's forbidding glare.

Josh was sipping his second Skol lager when Clay returned to the round table near the crackling fireplace. Audrey was still gazing attentively at Josh. The others were swapping horse stories.

"Hi." Josh smiled. "I ordered you another wine."

"I haven't finished my first. Besides we have to go."

"Well . . . not yet."

Audrey leaned forward. "Oh, Clay . . ." Her round azure eyes sparkled with a sensual innocence. "I've just about convinced Josh for y'all to join us for dinner . . ."

Edge Meade spoke up drunkenly. "Damned fine trout here. Worth it."

"Thank you, Audrey. But no. I'm due back in London. Josh can stay if he likes." She picked up her handbag and extended a polite farewell to the rest of the group.

Josh rose and caught up with Clay as he headed outside. "What's going on? Are you really leaving for London now?"

"Yes."

"Well . . . I'm not ready to go. I'm having a hell of a good time. It's a very congenial group. And I'm learning a lot about the horse-breeding business."

"Well, fine. Great. I'm glad to hear it." Clay strode across the gravel to the rented car.

"Damnit, Clay. They invited us to stay for dinner. It's dinner time. I'm hungry. We can drive back to London right after."

"You can do anything you want. I told you before that I don't want to be around my stepmother. Or Audrey. But I'm sure she'll do her best to keep you entertained . . ."

"Oh, so that's it. You think I'm interested in her?"

"She's certainly interested in you! I didn't know women still got away with being that obvious."

Josh sighed. "She's just fascinated by the movie business. She knows you and I are together."

"Oh, Josh, really. Since when would that stop her?"

"You're just going to leave me here?"

"I'm sure one of the others can give you a ride to London."

"Clay, you're being stubborn. You're making a big deal out of nothing. I'm merely trying to be polite. After all, Audrey bowed out of the bidding and let me buy the filly."

"If she bowed out, she had a reason."

Josh shook his head with exasperation. "You really have it in for her. You're not being reasonable."

"Be that as it may, I don't want to spend another minute here. But I wouldn't dream of asking you to tear yourself away from such a prestigious group of horse breeders."

"You're being ridiculous!"

"And *you're* being totally insensitive to my feelings."

Josh put his hands on her shoulders, resisting the temptation to shake them. "You're overreacting," he tried to say calmly. "I don't see why we can't have a pleasant dinner before we drive back to London."

"I'd love to have a pleasant dinner. But not here."

Clay started up the motor. "Order the trout," she called

out the window. "I hear it's worth it." She pulled on to the main road and careened down the right-hand side before remembering that the British drive on the left.

Josh Lewis stood in the parking lot and looked up at the full moon. The evening air had a chill to it. "Shit!" he said as he strolled back into the inn.

By the time the Outhwaites dropped Josh off at Brown's Hotel later that evening, Clay had checked out, leaving behind a curt note saying that she had been called back to New York. Josh crumpled it up and flushed it down the toilet.

Chapter 7

GARNET Turner turned the three locks of the Central Park West apartment she shared with Clay Fitzgerald and stepped in, rebolting the latches. She glanced through her mail and set it and her briefcase on the marble table in the foyer. Halfway down the hall to her bedroom, she heard a noise. She stopped and listened. There it was again, a rustling sound. It came from the kitchen. Her body tensing with fear, she tiptoed back to the front door and quietly began to unlatch it.

"Hello! I thought I heard someone."

Garnet pivoted around, pressing her hand to her chest. "Oh, my God . . . Clay! You nearly gave me a heart attack. I thought someone had broken in."

Clay laughed and hugged her friend. "I'm sorry. I got back a couple of hours ago. I was rummaging around trying to find something to eat."

"There's not much. I've been out nearly every night. Anyway, what are you doing here? I wasn't expecting you before the end of the week."

They walked into the small living room, and Clay collapsed on to the art deco sofa that was left over from Garnet's marriage.

Clay shrugged. "A classic story. Woman finds man, woman gets man, woman loses man by blowing it."

"What's the matter? He didn't like having it blown?" she teased. Garnet was black. A tall, model-slim beauty whose dark-brown skin glowed with health. Her hair was cut close to her head, and she wore gold African hoop earrings. Her teeth looked very white in her dark face, and they flashed now as she grinned. "All right, tell mama."

"It's not funny. I made an ass out of myself."

"Oh, God. Surely not." Garnet lit a Now. "Who was this dude, anyway? Your card didn't give me much to sink my teeth into."

"Josh Lewis . . ." Clay stared at her friend. "You've cut your hair, and I didn't even notice."

"Oh, yeah. A few weeks ago. You like it?"

"Yes, it's very sleek."

"Actually, I was going for punk." Garnet laughed. "Let's get some wine and go out on the terrace. Are you talking about Josh Lewis the director?"

Clay nodded.

"When he won the big prize at Cannes, there was an article on him in the *Times*. And *People*. And I think the *Enquirer* had him linked up with Farrah Fawcett . . . or was it Brooke Shields? Anyway, he looks like pretty nice stuff." She opened a bottle of Soave Bolla. "So let's have the rundown."

Over the better part of the bottle of wine, Clay related the story of her chance meeting with Josh Lewis at the airport all the way through to their disastrous last evening together. "I really came unglued, seeing Sunny and Audrey. If I'd kept my cool, everything would have been fine. I could have waited in London for Josh and apologized. But I just took off in a huff. I'm sure he's mad as hell now. I can't believe that at the age of twenty-eight I'm still doing such stupid things."

Garnet tossed her hand in the air. "Well . . . well . . ."

"See? Even you can't think of anything comforting to say. There's no way the man will ever get in touch with me again."

"I'm sorry, Clay. It sounds like loads of fun while it lasted. Meanwhile, your friend Owen Thomas has been calling every two seconds to find out if I've heard from you. He was afraid something had happened."

Clay poured some more wine in her glass. "Well, there's always Owen."

"He still seems to be mad about you."

"I know. He's sweet. But it always comes around to the same thing. Getting married, giving up work, settling down, raising kids." She shook her head. "That's not what I want."

"Isn't it, Clay?"

"Well, not with Owen. And I'd *never* give up work." She put her feet up on a wooden planter brimming with candy-striped petunias. "Anyway, enough about me. Who've *you* been seeing every night?"

"An English professor at Columbia. I met him when I started teaching that night course in journalism."

"Is he white or black?"

"White . . . you know me. He's divorced, has two kids living with his ex-wife on West End Avenue. And he's real nifty. Very well built." She laughed. "You know . . . good enough to eat."

"Which reminds me of food. I'm hungry," Clay said. "Want to order in?"

Simon's, a tiny bôite on West Sixty-eighth Street near Owen Thomas's office, was vibrating with lunch commotion. Thomas, decked out in Ralph Lauren's western garb, spoke so softly in his Alabama accent that Clay had to strain to hear him above the din. He was auburn haired and boyish looking. At thirty-three, there was still a smattering of freckles spanning the bridge of his thin, aristocratic nose.

"I was worried about you. I had this premonition that somethin' was happenin'. I've never felt that way when you were off before."

"Just the usual threat of sharks, sudden monsoons, that sort of thing." Clay smiled. "Anyway, I have a great idea. After I've finished the cultured-pearl piece, I want to do something on those incredibly beautiful poisonous fish in the Red Sea."

Owen Thomas grinned, shaking his head. "David and Annie Doubilet did it already. Didn't you see last month's *National Geographic*?"

Clay sighed. "They always beat me to it. Well, what about something cute on sea otters?"

"That's not a bad idea. I'll talk to Ed about it." He reached his hand under the table and rubbed Clay's thigh. Her instinct was to move her leg, but the space was too cramped. "Clay, I've been doin' a lot of thinkin' while you were gone. About us."

"Owen, I told you—"

"Now wait, hear me out." His brow was creased, and his hazel eyes were serious. "I know we've been over this in the past. But the moment I met you, I knew you were the one. I know you don't think you're ready. But darlin', if you'd just give it a try. Heck, you could even keep workin' for a year or so if you really want to . . ."

Clay stared at the sautéed Coho salmon, untouched on her plate. "Owen," she started, "you know I like you—"

"Oh, shit," he said, draining his martini glass. "Skip the platitudes."

"All right," Clay said. "We've been seeing each other for two years . . ."

"And I've been askin' you for about twenty-three months."

Clay nodded. "And my answer's always been the same."

"Not quite. Six months ago you said you'd think about it. You said to give you a little time. Well, I gave you a little time."

"You're right. Six months ago I thought I might—I thought I was about ready to settle down . . ."

"And now you aren't?" Owen pushed away his Chinese vegetable salad and folded his arms neatly on the table.

Clay smiled. "Well, the moment has passed."

"Okay. Who is it? There's someone else. I can tell."

"No . . ."

"Then we're not worse off than we were before." He flagged down the waiter for the check. "Look, let's go up to your place and talk there."

"No. You think if we make love everything will be all right."

"You've never had any complaints before."

"That's not the point. I like seeing you. I like working with you. I like going to the theater and dinner and movies. But I guess I don't love you."

"You mean you never loved me?"

"No. I mean yes, I did. Oh, hell, I don't know." She smiled and caressed the back of his neck with her hand. "I don't want you to be mad at me. I want us to keep on being friends. Please?"

Owen sighed and handed the waiter his American Express card. "As friends, do I still get sleeping privileges?"

Clay laughed. "We'll see."

"Want to go to the movies tonight? *Victorian Pastoral* is playin' around the corner from my apartment. I could cook somethin' afterward."

Clay's mood dove to the pit of her stomach. "Oh, er, I'm still feeling jet lag. I have to unpack tonight and sort through those slides for you."

"You're not bein' very friendly. I thought—"

Clay laughed. "Maybe tomorrow. But I've already seen *Victorian Pastoral*. In London." She lied.

Later that week, Owen called. "Ed wants you to shoot a story on the undersea world off Baja. As an accompaniment to a piece that Meade Lindsay is doing."

"Well, sure. When would you want it?"

"As soon as possible. I made a reservation for you on the nine P.M. flight to L.A. You can make a connection tomorrow."

"My, you are in a hurry. You must've already made another date for tonight."

Owen laughed. "Ed wants it to run in the November issue. So you see the rush."

"Okay, okay. My tan was beginning to fade, anyway."

"Great. I'll send a packet of info over by messenger. Will you be there the next couple of hours?"

"Looks like it. Packing."

"Okay, toots," Owen blew a kiss into the phone. "Have fun. Call me when you get back."

Garnet Turner called out from the kitchen. "Hey, Clay, phone for you."

Clay was lugging her equipment out to the hall elevator. "Take a message. I'm running late."

Garnet appeared in the doorway. "It's long-distance. He has an accent and says it's important."

"Okay. Will you ring for the elevator?" She ran into the living room and picked up the extension.

"Hello, Clay? This is Lars . . . Knudsen."

"Lars! How are you? *Where* are you?"

"Back in L.A. Listen, something has come up. Our second-unit underwater cameraman, Toby Jackson, has to be operated on for a slipped disc. He will be out of commission for several months. I want to know if you will consider taking his place. For *Golden Triangle*. We've decided to shoot in Thailand. August through October, including pre-production."

"Well . . . this is sudden. I'm kind of booked up right now."

"Look, Clay. I like your work. I really want you. It would be an excellent opportunity for you."

"I know. I'd like to do it, but . . . Does Josh know about this?"

"No. Not yet. I handle my end of things. He gives me complete autonomy."

Garnet shouted from the hall. "Hey! I can't hold the elevator forever."

"Listen, Lars, I'm on my way out the door. To Baja, but I'm flying to L.A. first."

"Great! Come by my office at the studio tomorrow at noon. We'll talk about it, and I'll take you to lunch."

"Lars . . ." Clay hesitated. "I don't think I can do it. I want to, but . . ."

"But what?"

"Josh. He and I . . ."

"Look, you'll be working for *me*. I don't know what happened between you two, but this is a good chance for you, Clay. A major film, big budget. I want to try some effects that have never been done underwater."

"Okay, Lars. I'm not promising anything. But I'll see you tomorrow."

"Good! *Bon voyage*. My office number is 843-7800."

Clay thought about it all the way to California. By the time her plane touched ground, she knew that she would work on Josh's picture. It was destiny. There was no point in fighting it.

And besides, she told herself, smiling, Lars was right. It was a great opportunity for her.

Chapter 8

LARS Knudsen leaned across his cluttered desk at Meridan Studio and kissed Clay on both cheeks. "Good to see you! Clay, this is Peter Zaidenberg. If you join us, you'll be working underwater with him."

"I can't think of anybody I'd rather work underwater with." Clay smiled at the medium-height muscular man. "I've been a fan of yours for years."

"Yes." Lars laughed. "The old man here has been pretty busy. And he just celebrated his thirtieth birthday last week."

"Thanks for the compliment, Lars. I'm thirty-four." Zaidenberg grinned.

"Oh, well, then you *are* an old man. You see, Clay, we need young blood around here."

For the next hour, Lars and Zaidenberg filled in Clay on the screenplay, the special effects they were after, and the equipment they would be using.

"Okay, Clay . . . have you made up your mind yet?" Lars rubbed his beard with his right hand.

She threw up both arms. "I surrender. I'm really excited about it."

"Now . . . money."

Clay shook her head. "My agent's Cary Lloyd. Slug it out with her."

Lars laughed. "Okay, I'll call her this afternoon. What about lunch?"

Peter looked at his watch. "I promised Linda I'd meet her at Harold's Place to get a present for her mother's birthday. Glad we'll be working together, Clay. See you in Bangkok."

73

After Peter left, Lars, pulling on a beige tropical-wool jacket, said, "Peter's wife Linda is Josh's script supervisor. She's about your age. I think you'll like her. Now . . . I made a reservation at Ma Maison. Unless you have another preference?"

"No, that's . . ."

The door swung open, and Josh Lewis burst in. "Hey, Lars, a minute? Oh." He paused. "Clay. Hello."

"Hello, Josh."

"Clay's taking over for Toby Jackson," Lars said.

Josh smiled, but Clay could not read the expression in his eyes. "Well, great. Welcome aboard the sinking ship."

Lars looked concerned. "What's happened?"

"Another hassle with Harvey over budget. I told him we had to get a thousand-amp. silent Landrover-based generator from Australia. But he's come up with a two hundred fifty amp. unit in Bangkok. He wants us to make do with that and the local noisy units. That shmuck!"

Lars shrugged. "It's okay. We can improvise. I worked on a film in the jungle a few years ago. We built a thirty-foot-high sandbag enclosure to house a five hundred-amp. generator. It brought the noise level down remarkably well."

"Yeah, we can do something like that. But I'm sick of hassling over petty cash! Oh, hell." He sat on the edge of Lars's desk.

"We're on our way to lunch," Lars said. "Want to join us?"

"No. I'm late for a meeting." He started out, then he turned back to Clay. "You busy after lunch?"

"I have a plane at six."

"Well, I want to show you something. I'll pick you up in two hours. At the restaurant. If you're free," he added as an afterthought.

"Okay. Ma Maison."

"Good enough. Lars, I'll see you in the screening room at five-thirty."

Over seafood salads and Perrier, Lars regaled Clay with industry stories. Although she enjoyed herself, part of her consciousness was occupied with trying to figure out Josh Lewis. Outwardly, he had appeared as if everything were fine between them, but she knew it couldn't be after her fast exit from London.

By the time Josh picked her up in his beige Toyota jeep, she was both excited and apprehensive about seeing him again.

"You keep showing up in my life," he said, turning onto the freeway. "I can't seem to shake you."

"Do you want to?"

"I don't know. I don't think so." Josh kept his eyes on the traffic while he pulled a Muddy Waters cassette out of a box on the floor and shoved it in the tape deck. "I still haven't figured out what happened. You sure left in a huff."

"Well, I'll admit I probably wasn't functioning reasonably. But . . ." She trailed off. She did not want to apologize for behavior in a situation that Josh, in part, had insisted on creating. On the other hand, she did not want to start another fight.

"You're a pretty complicated lady when you want to be."

"Would you prefer me to turn down the job Lars offered?" Clay asked.

"No. I think you're mercurial, but I'm glad to see you again." Josh looked at her and smiled. He patted her thigh. "At least your knees show when you sit down." She had on khaki culottes and a safari jacket designed by a friend of Garnet's.

"I'm happy to see you, Josh." Clay wanted to slide closer to him, but the jeep's bucket seats were separated by a stick shift. "Are we headed for your ranch?"

Josh nodded. "Our mutual filly friend arrived this morning."

"Oriental Pearl! I can't wait to see her."

Josh exited off the freeway, and five miles later drove through the white iron gates of the six hundred-acre ranch he had bought from the estate of a silent movie star. The drive to the main house was flanked by corral fencing and immense eucalyptus, ash, and oak trees. Before they reached the sprawling one-story white frame house and pool pavilion, they turned and drove over a wooden bridge, following a gravel road through the pastures to the stable and barn.

"Eventually, I want to invest in a herd of Santa Gertrudis cattle. But horses are the first priority."

"This is really beautiful."

"Thanks," Josh said. "I love it here. One of these days I want to fix up the main house and live here full time. It needs a hell of a lot of work . . . Here we are."

He pulled the jeep up by the barn, and they went to find Josh's stable manager, Lucky Repetti. He was in the stall with Oriental Pearl. A big sheep dog bounded up and yelped with joy at seeing Josh, putting its huge paws on his waist.

"This is Elsa," Josh said. "The constant love of my life. And Lucky. This is Clay Fitzgerald. How's it going?"

Lucky shook hands with Clay. "Pretty well. She's a little nervous, but she and Elsa hit it off right away. Elsa hasn't wandered off ten feet since the Pearl arrived."

The gray filly snorted and looked at Clay and Josh. Almost as if in recognition, she walked over to Clay, who patted the horse's neck fondly. "Hello, girl. Welcome to the U.S.A. You're going to like it here. Lots of yummy alfalfa and a much better climate than England." The horse brushed her nose against Clay's hair.

"Oh, Josh . . . she's even prettier than I remembered." She stepped back and looked the filly over. "Her leg's looking much better," she said, glancing at Josh out of the corner of her eye. "Practically healed."

"You wouldn't be trying to start up an old argument again, would you?"

She looked at him innocently. "What do you mean?"

Josh laughed. "Well, as a matter of fact, I've been thinking about it."

"About what?"

"Putting Oriental Pearl into training. Racing her."

"Josh, you mean it?"

"I'm thinking about it. That's all. My regular trainer is

too busy to take her on. I've made a few calls, but I haven't come up with anybody good enough who's free."

"I know somebody. Eddie Landry. He's the best."

"Yeah, I know his name. But he's retired now, isn't he?"

"Well, he was a great friend of my father's. I could at least call. He might recommend somebody."

Josh put his arm around Clay. "Sure, that'd be great."

A phone rang in the stable office, and Lucky ran to get it. He returned a moment later out of breath. "For you, Josh. An Audrey Babcock."

"Oh, shit," Josh said. "I'll be back in a minute. *Please* don't take off with my jeep," he called to Clay.

Lucky Repetti showed Clay the other horses, and Josh rejoined them a few minutes later.

"Audrey's changed her mind. She wants to buy Oriental Pearl for a brood mare. She's willing to pay me ten grand more than I paid, over and above the shipping fees from England."

"Oh, no. You *can't* sell her," Clay said with alarm.

Josh shrugged. "Oh, I don't know. Sounds like a pretty good deal."

"Josh, you'll be making the mistake of . . ." But Clay saw from the glint in Josh's eyes that he was teasing her.

"No, I've come this far with the Pearl. I'm willing to risk it all."

Clay hugged him. "Okay! Let me track down Eddie Landry and see what he has to say."

Clay started across the yard to the office, then came back. "One question. How did Audrey happen to find you here?"

"She must've called my office first." He paused. "Listen, we're getting along fine. Let's not talk about Audrey."

"Did you take her out after I left London?"

Josh put his arm around her and walked toward the office with her. "Let's not talk about Audrey," he said again, and kissed her cheek with tenderness. "Remember, I'm following *your* advice about racing the Pearl. So notch that on your belt."

Clay knew that she had better not pursue the question of Audrey. "Okay, I'll call Eddie."

After she had made a dozen phone calls, Clay went back to the stable and found Josh in Oriental Pearl's stall. "Eddie has a farm in northern Utah, and he's sick of retirement, *and* he's started doing some training again. As a favor, he's agreed to take on the Pearl. You're to have her shipped out to him when her leg's completely healed. Here's the info." She handed him a note.

"Terrific! You really know how to deliver, don't you?" He kissed her cheek.

"I've got to go. My plane."

"Can't you take a later one? Tomorrow?"

Clay shook her head. "No. I wish I could."

"When will you be back?"

"I won't. I'm going straight from La Paz to New York, with a connection in Houston."

"Then when am I going to see you again?"

"In three weeks. Bangkok."

Josh laughed. "What a perfect place to be working together."

On the drive back into town, Clay though about Audrey. Audrey wanted Josh, apparently; she was sticking with the chase. But for now, safely tucked away in Virginia, Audrey was not much of a threat.

Besides, Clay would have Josh all to herself in Thailand.

Chapter 9

BANGKOK, Thailand, is also called Krung Thep, the "City of Angels." Once it was known as the Venice of the East. In those days, an intricate network of canals, or *klongs*, wove through cosmopolitan bustle and squalor to rural orchid farms and back again. Now most of Bangkok's canals have been filled in to make way for cars, trucks, buses, and *thuk-thuks*, three-wheeled motorized pickups that are cheaper to hire than the air-conditioned taxis. The resultant blend of carbon monoxide and noxious industry pollutants, combined with the crowding together of over four million souls, gives Thailand's capital a strong claim to the title of World's Most Polluted City. In August, toss in the daily summer torrential monsoon rains, ninety-degree heat, and intense humidity, and Bangkok is a difficult place, at best, to shoot a film.

Fred Justin, the British production supervisor, and his staff had been in Thailand for a month, obtaining various government permits and clearances, renting equipment and props, lining up Thai actors and extras, and scouting indoor locations.

In early August, Justin met Lars Knudsen, Clay, and the rest of the film unit at Don Muang airport, waving duty exemption forms for their photographic and film stock. It took several hours for an endless series of customs officials to put their stamps and signatures on the itemized forms. Finally, the entourage crept through the heat and bumper-to-bumper traffic to the Oriental Hotel, a refuge of relative quiet perched alongside the Chao Phya River and next door to the French Embassy.

After two days' rest from the day-long flight, the group

assembled for fruit, croissants, and coffee at the hotel's Riverside Terrace, overlooking the legendary River of Kings.

Lars Knudsen flicked away a fly and forked into the deep coral meat of his papaya. "Is everyone rested?"

"You must be kidding," Linda Zaidenberg, script supervisor and Peter's wife, said. "This nine-hour time difference has me really crazy."

"Yeah," Peter said. "We got up around four A.M. and drank beers from the mini-bar in our room because we couldn't sleep."

"You Californians have it easy," Clay said. "It's a twelve-hour difference for me." She spread marmalade on to her roll, trying to ignore the bees hovering over it.

"Well, I hit Patpong Road last night," Bill Lacy, Lars's assistant, said.

"The red-light district? *Already?* God, you must have quite a libido," Linda joked.

Lacy's long-jawed face remained dead-pan. "Just checking it out. I want to get an idea of what's there when I need it."

"What is there?" Clay and Linda asked in unison.

"You know, the usual. Bars, strip joints, lots of Thai massage parlors. And skin shows. Every two steps, someone tries to hustle you into going to one. They even hand you a little card, a menu, kind of. Printed in English on one side, French on the other." He paused to pour more coffee into his cup.

"Come on, save the suspense. What're the entrees?" Peter Zaidenberg asked.

"Lesbian sex show, man-woman fuck, pussy write letter ... things like that."

"Pussy write letter?" Linda said. "You mean . . ."

Bill nodded. "Just what you think. And pussy use chopsticks, pussy open Coke bottle, pussy smoke cigarette."

"Did you go to see it?"

Lacy grinned shyly. "Well, actually, I did. I went to a place called the Montmartre. It's kind of a ripoff, but I guess it's part of the Bangkok experience. They usher you upstairs into this sort of seedy living room with a bar in the corner and chairs around the wall and coffee tables. And then these sweet Thai girls, some of them really pretty, whip off a robe—they don't even do a sexy strip—and lie down on the floor a few feet away from where you sit. They go right into action—no music, no buildup. She lights two cigarettes in her mouth, sticks them in her cunt, and smokes them. Each girl seems to have a specialty. When she's finished, she runs out of the room, and the next one goes on."

"Was it a turn-on?" Peter asked.

Bill Lacy shook his head. "Hardly. You're mostly furious at yourself for spending six hundred *baht* on something so ho-hum."

Clay figured rapidly. "Six hundred baht . . . that's . . . divide by twenty . . . help, somebody."

"Thirty bucks," Lars said.

"Thirty bucks for pussy write letter? She must write some letter."

"Wasn't part of *The Deer Hunter* shot on Patpong Road?"

"Yeah, I think so. All the Russian roulette stuff with Chris Walken."

"Don't worry. They refrained from pussy blow brains out." Lacy laughed. "Anyway, now that I know my way around, I'll be glad to take any of you on a guided tour."

Lars laughed. "Dropping thirty dollars in a tourist clip joint doesn't sound to me like you know your way around."

"Experience, Lars, experience." Bill Lacy sat forward and pushed his glasses back up the bridge of his nose. "You know, the thing is, the girls have sort of a shy-sweet quality. Kind of in-between hookers and girls looking for boyfriends. I think I'm going to fall in love with a Thai woman while I'm here. So many of them are really beautiful. Especially the ones from up north. They're taller, and—"

"Jesus. You've been here less than two days, and you're already an expert on Thai women," Linda said. "Well, Clay, shall we tell the guys what *we've* been up to?"

"What?" Fred Justin asked. He had just pulled up a chair to join them. "Patpong Road II?"

"We took a tour of the Wats, the temples, by *thuk-thuk* yesterday. Much more rewarding than Patpong Road," Linda said.

"Except my lungs may never be the same from all the exhaust fumes," Clay said. "But we covered the whole city. Then we came back from the Grand Palace by public river taxi . . ."

They ordered more coffee and exchanged more tourist tales, while they watched a variety of boats putter up and down the Chao Phya River.

"All right," Lars said finally, lighting his pipe. "Are you up for taking a holiday at the seashore? We have to comb the Siamese Gulf for locations."

"The car and driver will be here around eleven," Fred Justin said. The Englishman was an efficient, easygoing man with black hair, a salt-and-pepper beard, and astigmatic blue eyes. He wore glasses only to read and squinted the rest of the time.

"Oh? So this is not an optional choice?" Clay said. "What you mean is—run upstairs and get your gear and meet me in the lobby at eleven."

Lars nodded. "The trip's only optional for Linda."

"You think I'm going to let you go off and leave me? Josh won't be here for another five days. So this really is my holiday."

Lars borrowed Clay's map and spread it open on the rectangular table. "I want to head southwest, down the peninsula to Hua Hin. That's about as far away as we could afford to shoot. Then, after we've looked it over, I want to come back around the coast to Pattaya and check it out there."

"What about Phuket?" Bill Lacy asked. "It's supposed to be beautiful. And they've just enlarged the airport."

"No good," Fred Justin said. "Too many hassles. There's occasional guerrilla fighting in the jungles near there."

"What do you want us to pack?" Clay asked.

"Enough for three or four days. And your scuba gear. I want you and Peter to check out underwater conditions."

"Let's see." Linda giggled. "If it's Tuesday, it must be Hua Hin."

"Ugh," her husband groaned. "Are you sure you don't want to just stay here and sleep?"

Five days later, the film unit was still in Pattaya. Lars had decided that the resort area, nicknamed the Thai Riviera, would be the most efficient location to shoot the underwater sequences of *Golden Triangle*. They had spent the better part of each day in a rented blue fishing boat named *My Friend*, skirting the coral reef around the offshore islands until they had pinpointed several excellent spots where the Siamese Gulf water was clear enough for underwater shooting and deep enough to achieve the effects Lars and Josh were after.

It was Bill Lacy's thirty-fifth birthday and Linda and Clay decided to throw a surprise party for him in Clay's room at the Regent Pattaya. They made a shopping list and divided it. By six, all that remained for Clay to find were some birthday candles. She had tried several places along the narrow main street of Pattaya old town with no luck. Thais in the big hotels and shops spoke English, but away from the tourist traps, few Thais spoke anything but their native dialects. Clay had learned to count in Thai, so she could bargain, and she knew a few basic phrases such as *sawat dee kha*, the general greeting, and *khob khun kha*, thank you, but she could not find any word close to describing birthday candle in her Berlitz guidebook.

"Hey, *dai prod*, miss. You need help?" A teenaged Thai boy, darkly tanned with a wide grin and white teeth, caught up with her.

Clay smiled at him but continued walking. He trailed slightly behind. "Miss, you look for something? I help you find." The boy was wearing a cowboy hat and a T-shirt that said, "Never Give a Sucker an Even Break."

"Do you know what a birthday candle is?"

The boy looked confused, then smiled. "A big light exploding in the sky! Yes?"

"No. That's a Roman candle." Clay explained that she needed tiny candles.

"Yes. Yes," he said excitely. "Come. I show you."

The boy led her to a shop down a side street where a toothless old woman rummaged through musty inventory that looked as if it had not been touched in decades. At last, she produced a box of pink birthday candles, made in Brooklyn, U.S.A. Clay paid ten *baht*, fifty cents, for them, knowing there was no point in quibbling about the color or haggling over price.

Back on the street, the boy stayed with her. "I see you before," he said. "Yesterday. Putting diving stuff in the boat you rent. You a diver?"

Clay nodded. "I take pictures underwater."

The boy's eyes flashed. "I dive, too. I know the water around here, I know the reef and the islands. You need guide?"

"I'm sorry. We're going back to Bangkok tomorrow. I won't be back here for several weeks." Clay enunciated clearly so the boy could understand her. He bobbed his head up and down and smiled constantly. Actually, she wasn't sure whether he comprehended or not.

"My name is Som Pat Dai. You call me Pat. My mother live in Bangkok. Maybe I go visit her and be your guide there. She work for British family. That is how I learn so good English."

"Well, I don't really need a guide."

"Oh, yes. Water around here is . . . difficult. I know it. I take you where you can shoot good pictures. I know where treasure ship is, under the sea. Many ships go down in the Gulf of Siam. Even one of Marco Polo's ships with treasure from Chinese temple. Worth millions of *baht* in gold. I know where to find it. But I need fancy scuba to search. I take you to see it."

By the time Clay reached her hotel, she had begun to like Pat. He was a vivacious talker and full of teenage braggadocio, but he was friendly and seemed well intentioned.

"If I come to Bangkok, how much you pay me to be your guide?"

"I told you, Pat. I don't need a guide. I can find my own way around."

"But you do not speak Thai. I can help you. One hundred *baht* a day?"

Clay shook her head. Five dollars was reasonable, but she did not need her own personal interpreter. "No. Pat ..."

"Eighty *baht*? I take you to places tourists never see."

Clay walked into the lobby. The hotel was a new one, built during the boom of the early seventies, and the modern glass and steel structure loomed high above the green choppy water of the Gulf of Siam. "No, thank you, Pat." She reached into her purse and took out a ten-*baht* coin. "Thank you for helping me find the candles."

"Forty *baht* a day. But you buy me lunch."

Clay laughed. "I give up. I'll look for you when I come back to Pattaya, okay?"

"Where you stay in Bangkok?"

Clay started to lie, then looked at Pat's trusting Thai face and couldn't. "The Oriental. But *don't* come there. I don't need an interpreter."

"What is your name, miss?"

"Clay."

Pat bowed his head. "I will see you again, Khun Clay. I will look after you." He tore out the front door seconds before the doorman could nab him for hustling a guest.

Chapter 10

CLAY stepped out of the shower and wrapped herself in one of the large white bath towels. She walked out of the bathroom and down the steps that divided the hotel room into a split-level suite into the sitting room. The room was a comfortable temperature now, and she closed the balcony door that she had opened to dilute the effects of full-blast air conditioning.

There was a knock at the door. "Clay, it's me, Linda."

She opened the door and let in the small freckle-faced redhead.

"You're not dressed yet?" Linda said. "It's nearly time to head out for dinner."

"You go ahead," Clay said. "I'm going to stay in and check over my equipment."

"Oh, come on. Big eve-of-shooting dinner. Old Bangkok tradition." She looked at Clay. "What's the matter?"

Clay shrugged.

"Is it Lars?" Linda asked. "Is there something between you two?"

"Lars?" Clay smiled. "No."

"It's somebody, though, isn't it?"

Clay nodded. "Josh," she said.

"Josh? Really?" Linda sat down on the wooden-armed chair. "How long has this been going on?"

Clay gave her a quick rundown of the relationship. Linda listened, amazed.

"Boy, you can sure keep a secret."

"*I* can? What about him? He's been here five days, and we haven't been alone together five minutes. He's friendly enough, but there's nothing more. When I was in California, I thought we'd patched things up. Now . . . I don't know what's going on."

"You've never been with Josh on a shoot before."

"No. You know that."

"He's a different guy. A total perfectionist. High tension all the time, a real borderline ulcer case. I think it's fear of failure. Maybe he doesn't know how good he is. Or maybe that's what makes him so good. Anyway, when he's shooting or getting ready to shoot, he's all business."

Clay was drying her hair with a towel. "Business? I don't know. It doesn't look like business to me." She tried to smile. "Unless it's the pasta business."

Linda laughed. "What, Natalia?" Natalia Ferrari, the film's female star, was a temperamental Italian beauty with long raven-black hair, breasts like round loaves rising with plenty of yeast, a wide mouth, and green eyes bordered with thick black ribbons of mascara. Josh had been spending a lot of time with her since they had arrived in Bangkok. "Don't worry about Natalia," Linda advised. "She may be gorgeous, but she's not the type of girl men marry, as we used to say. She's neurotic as hell. Besides"—Linda leaned forward, hand to mouth in a dramatic *sotto voce*—"she's supposed to be gay."

"Natalia Ferrari? A lesbian?" Clay was genuinely surprised.

"Oh, I'm sure she knows how to do it with men. But her heart is with the ladies."

Clay grinned broadly. "Ah, the fickle world of the silver screen. All lies and illusion."

"Ain't it the truth? Come on, Clay," Linda said. "Put some clothes on and join us. We're going for Indian food. A little lamb *vindaloo* will pick you up. You can't turn yourself into a hermit just because Josh is acting like an asshole. Besides, I happen to know that Natalia isn't going to be there tonight."

"That shouldn't really make any difference," Clay said. Then she smiled. "But maybe it does. Okay. I'll be down in ten minutes."

Tables had been pushed together to accommodate the film

crew at Café India, an excellent Indian restaurant down the street from the hotel. The group with Linda and Clay included Josh, Lars, Fred Justin, Bill Lacy, Peter Zaidenberg, and Nick Reynolds, the handsome male star of *Golden Triangle*. Natalia Ferrari, as promised, was absent. Josh was defending her.

"Listen, don't put her down," he said, breaking off a piece of *alu paratha*, an Indian potato bread. "She's nervous, that's all. This is her first English-language movie."

"Oh, Josh, she may have nice tits, but she's a pain in the ass," Linda said. "She's changed rooms three times, threw a tantrum to get her own bodyguard . . ."

"Diplomacy is a big part of being a director," Clay said. "They teach it to you at the Famous Director's School before you're even allowed to direct a short."

Nick Reynolds sat up and assumed a deep TV announcer-type voice. "Here at the Famous Director's School you'll learn how to soothe the feelings of volatile actors. You'll learn phrases like 'Great, darling,' and 'One more time—we had a technical problem.' And that's not all! You'll learn to wield authority, to say, 'Roll 'em' . . . 'Cut!' . . . 'Quiet on the set.' How to fire writers, antagonize your crew. All this and *much* more! For a free brochure, at absolutely no obligation, call this number. Today!"

They were all laughing, including Josh. "All right," he said, "I can take a joke as well as anyone. You're all fired."

Clay looked around for the waiter to order more Singha beer. Her eyes brushed past a man with short blond hair sitting alone at a rear table, oblivious to their laughter and reading the *Bangkok Post*, the city's English newspaper. She couldn't see his face. It was tilted toward the paper. But there was something familiar about him.

"Clay!" Bill Lacy raised his voice. "I asked you a question. Didn't you hear me?"

"Sorry. Just distracted." She smiled.

"We have a quiz going. Can you remember who played the original Saint. Was it Louis . . ."

"Shush!" Linda said. "Don't give her any names. We're looking for a first reaction here."

"Let me think . . . Was it George Sanders? Or . . ." A hand touched her shoulder gently.

"Clay? It *is* you. I wasn't quite sure."

"Will! I . . . can't believe it! This is really amazing." She turned to the others. "I'm sorry. This is Will Stone, an old friend." She went around the table firing off names. "Pull up a chair, Will."

"Well, no, I'd block the aisle. Why don't you join me at the bar for a drink? I'd hate to bore the rest of you with old-times' talk," he said amiably to the others.

"Yes, this group gets bored very easily." Clay threw a hundred-*baht* note on the table. "That should cover my share. If you will excuse me, I'll weave my way to the bar."

Clay sat on the stool next to Will. This time he kissed her cheek in greeting. She was aware of Josh's eyes following her. *Good,* she thought, *let him wonder.*

Will smiled. "What'll you have?"

"Oh, I don't know. A brandy, I guess."

"I can't get over it. Seeing you here, of all places. You look more beautiful than ever, Clay. I like your hair longer. It's more feminine."

"Thank you. You look wonderful, too." Will Stone had aged little in eight years. The tanned weather lines in his face were deeper, but he seemed as fit as she remembered. And his blue eyes were still as electric. "But tell me. What are you doing here? On holiday or—"

"No. I left Key West for good. I work here now. I travel around, but I'm based in Bangkok."

"More treasure ships?"

Will smiled. "Oh, no, babe. I'm done with that. No, I'm in on the ground floor of a new company. They're import-export. Among other things, I manage a pearl farm. You know, cultured pearls?"

"Oh, yes, I know all right." She told him about her pearl assignments for *International Geography.* "In fact, they want me to do a piece on pearl farms in Japan and

Southeast Asia while I'm here. I'd love to photograph yours."

"Fine," Will said. "It's down the peninsula. Off Phuket."

"Great! I have a free day this weekend."

"Well, it'll be a while before I go back there again," he said evasively. "My little Clay . . . a photographer . . . working on a movie. I can't get over it." He paused and gazed into his drink. "You know, over these past years, I've thought of you often . . ."

"Oh, Will . . . you . . ."

"No, let me say this. I've never forgotten you . . . or what you did for me."

"I don't know what you're talking about."

"Yes, you do. I owe you a debt of long standing. But I'm going to be coming into quite a bit of money before long. I have every intention of paying you back."

"Let's not talk about the past," Clay said. "I want to know . . . are you married? Do you have kids?"

Will shook his head. "No twice. You?"

"No twice." Clay laughed.

Will finished his drink. "Listen, instead of ordering another here, why don't you come over to my place? I have a bottle of four-star Hennessey . . . and something I want to show you."

"All right. Just one drink. I have an early call for tomorrow."

Will contemplated her intently. "You don't hold any grudges against me, do you Clay? I mean—"

"No, Will. Only good memories."

Will kissed the tip of her nose. "You've always been quite a gal . . ." He laughed. "Quite a *woman*." Will settled up the tab. "All right, F-stop. Shall we?"

"I hate being called F-stop," Clay chuckled. She waved good night to everyone.

"Don't forget," Lars called out. "Six o'clock."

The others said good night. Josh merely nodded and watched Clay and Will, through the restaurant's window, walk down the shadowy street toward New Road.

Will Stone's apartment was actually a tiny suite, rented by

the month, in the Hotel Ran Khai, a run-down establishment with a bar in the lobby that featured go-go dancers and disco music. The room itself was painted infirmary green, and although the paint was peeling off the ceiling, Will had attempted to do what he could to spiffy up the place. The wall by the couch was covered with a huge map of southern Thailand and the Gulf of Siam. Around the rest of the room he had hung various photographs and some not-bad watercolors, copies of Buddhist Davaravati art by local artists. The unraveling wicker hotel furniture looked as if it had been rescued from the last days of Saigon. The overall effect was pretty seedy. Clay was dismayed to see Will Stone living like that but she tried to conceal it.

"I'm not here very much," Will said as if he had read her mind. He flipped a switch, and the ceiling fan began to whirr squeakily overhead. "Have a seat. That one over there's the most comfortable."

Will went into the bedroom and returned with the Hennessey and two bathroom glasses.

"The glasses lack a certain elegance befitting the occasion," he said. "But the cognac makes up for it." He poured and handed Clay a glass, and they clinked "To . . . ?"

"Let's make it *tchin-tchin*." Clay took a sip. "You said you had something you wanted to show me."

Will appeared distracted for a moment. "Ah, yes. Wait right here." He went into the closet off the foyer, and Clay could hear him shuffling boxes around.

"Be patient," he called out. "It's stuck all the way in back. Okay . . . found it." He returned with something hidden in the palm of his hand.

"This is actually for you. A present."

"A present? But . . ."

"Close your eyes and open your hands . . . Come on."

Clay obeyed. "I feel like a kid." Will placed something flat and cool into her hand. At the same instant, a kiss gently tickled her forehead. Clay opened her eyes, pulling away slightly.

"I couldn't resist," Will said. "But don't worry, I'm not making advances."

Clay looked into her palm. It was a silver coin, Spanish. She held it under the lamp and made out the date: 1612. "Oh, Will . . ."

"It's a cob. Remember? Cut from a bar of silver and hand stamped. Minted in Potosí during the reign of King Phillip III. Anyway, I found it the summer after you left. It's the oldest coin I ever uncovered. I could never bring myself to sell it. I've kept it as good luck. But now that I've found you again, I want you to have it."

"You think I need luck?"

"Ah, babe, we all need it, don't we?" He had pulled up a chair directly facing her. "You know, *you* were my good luck once. If it hadn't been for you—"

"Please, Will. I told you. I don't want to talk about the past. It's over."

Will leaned in closer, his eyes locked on hers. "No, Clay . . . it doesn't have to be. It's a miracle we found each other again. I want you as much now as I ever did."

Will's mouth headed toward Clay's, but she turned her head away just as the telephone rang in the bedroom. "Damn," he said, and went to answer it.

Clay stood up and hung her bag over her right shoulder. Moving to look out the window, she discovered that it faced on to a dark alley, so she went toward the foyer. When Will walked back into the room, she noticed, for the first time, that his shoulders had begun to hunch a bit.

"Thanks for the drink" she said.

"It was good to see you again, Clay."

She was surprised that Will did not attempt to convince her to stay longer. Nor did he kiss her good night. His eyes looked tired suddenly. He picked up a pack of cigarettes from the coffee table and grabbed the rumpled cotton jacket he had taken off when they came in. His eyes picked up something on the table across the room, and he went to get it. It was the Spanish coin.

"Clay, I really want you to have this."

"But it must be worth a fortune. I can't accept it."

Will opened her shoulder bag and dropped it in. "I want

you to. You have no choice. Consider it your good deed for the day. Helping an old man ease his conscience."

Clay smiled. "Will, you're hardly an old man. You haven't changed a bit."

"Thank you. You don't know how good that makes me feel." He opened the door and took her arm. "I'll see you to a taxi."

"No, don't bother. It's only a couple of blocks. I've studied karate. I can protect myself."

"Are you sure?"

"Positive."

"Well, then, if you don't mind, I have to get some papers together. That call . . . I have a meeting with a colleague."

"Good night, Will. Thank you for the coin. And I do want to tour your pearl farm sometime soon."

"What? Oh, the pearl farm. Sure. I'll give you a call about it."

Clay walked down the three flights of stairs rather than wait for the creaky elevator. The initial euphoria of seeing Will again had faded. Eight years ago, he had so much going for him. Now he seemed a bit out of it. He was still attractive and in good shape for mid-forty, and he did not appear to drink as much as he used to, either. But something nagged her about him. If things were going so well, why was he living in a depressing place like this?

She walked through the lobby, past the raucous bar and another door that led to the Honey Massage Parlor. Outside, the street was wet from a flash storm. A crowd of people, both Thais and tourists, were gathered around a young Thai man dressed in a colorful Hill Tribe costume, playing a flute of long reeds stuck through a piece of gourd, a sort of Oriental pipes of Pan. She stopped to listen.

Her mood improved with the haunting atonal music. She pulled her Nikon out of her shoulder bag and spent the next few minutes shooting the musician and onlookers. The night was hot, and there was a strong smell of jasmine in the air. Long ropes of jasmine dangled from the wooden Buddhist spirit house outside the hotel. Every

Thai Buddhist kept a dollhouse-like shrine on a post in their front yard, that held their daily offerings of flowers, incense, and food to keep away evil spirits.

Replacing her camera in her bag, Clay glanced up to see Will emerge from his hotel. He crossed the street, and a moment later a black chauffeured Datsun pulled up to the curb. Will Stone got in next to someone in the back seat. The car backed on to the sidewalk and turned around, slowly heading toward where Clay was standing. She stepped back into the crowd and stared into the car as it passed. The other man had leaned forward to instruct the driver. He sat back again and for a brief moment glanced out of the car window in her direction. His face was illuminated by the purplish street light.

Clay gasped and remained motionless as the car turned left on to Silom Road. Then she walked the three blocks back to the Oriental.

Up in her room, she took a bottle of Kloster beer from the mini bar and noticed that her hands were trembling as she pried off the cap. She took the bottle and walked out on to the little balcony that overlooked the Oriental pool and terrace. Beyond, the dark waters of the Chao Phya flowed quietly, and the running lights of the ferry drifted across from Thonburi on the far side of the river.

The beer was good, and cold, and after a while Clay began to relax. She was in Bangkok, Thailand, the far side of the world. The street had been dark, the car had been moving, and she had only seen the face for the barest flicker of a moment.

But even as she tried to reassure herself, she knew she had seen him well enough.

It was her stepbrother, Beau Yates.

Beau again. First in Bombay, now here. It was a coincidence, certainly, but it gave her a dark, cold feeling. She was a long way from the Virginia horse farm where she had been born and raised and where she had first encountered Beau Yates. But just glimpsing him had brought those days back with intense clarity.

PART TWO
The Past

Chapter 11

THE dark-green Chevy horse van shimmied over the cattle guard and wove down the road. It flashed past a white sign bearing a race horse silhouetted in green and the green letters Willows Stud Farm. A smaller sign beneath advised: Absolutely No Salesmen. A hundred yards farther on, the van turned in at the business entrance and raced up the gravel road that led to the stables and office. The truck lurched to a stop, and two men jumped out. Both wore jeans and sweat-soaked shirts.

"Okay, Buck. You can take care of it from here. I'll see you later. About five? Up at the house."

"Sure thing, Mac. Give Clay my congrats." Buck Smith grinned, displaying the oversized teeth for which he was nicknamed.

"Yeah, if I make it in time." Mac Fitzgerald pulled the gold-scrolled watch from his shirt pocket and checked it. The watch was monogramed with K.M.F., initials of the men in his family as far back as his great-grandfather in Scotland, the original Kenyon McCracken Fitzgerald. "Hell, forty-five minutes to dress and get there." He took off and ran the eight-tenths of a mile to the main house.

"Mr. Mac! Thank goodness. Do you know what time it is? We're gonna be late." Nonah Hughes, the black housekeeper and cook, was dressed in her best church dress, a prim navy blue with lace collar and cuffs, size thirty-two and a snug fit.

"I'm rushing, Nonah. Is Miss Smith ready?"

"She's puttin' on a hat. She laid your clothes out on the bed for you."

"Okay . . . five minutes." Mac Fitzgerald took the ellip-

tical stairway two steps at a time, ignoring the pounding of
his heart. He brushed past Nell Smith with an apologetic
smile. "We had a flat coming over the mountain from
Waynesboro. Don't worry. We'll make it."

"I'm sure we will, the way you drive. But I'd like to get
there alive if you don't mind."

"You and Nonah go ahead and get in the car. Do you
have the present?"

"Right here," she called through the closed bedroom
door. "I wrapped it for you." Lovingly, Nell fingered the
small box, covered with gold foil, from Keller and George,
the Tiffany's of Albemarle County, Virginia.

Mac Fitzgerald was already in the shower and could not
hear her. The cold water running over his muscular body
revived him, and his breathing slowed to normal. It was
eighty-five degrees out, unusually hot and humid for early
June.

Wrapping a towel around his waist, he went to the basin
and checked his face. He had shaved this morning before
he left the house, around four-thirty. Now he detected a
dusting of whiskers but decided it could pass. He splashed
English Leather on his handsome, aristocratic face. His
daughter said that he resembled the actor Charlton Heston. He smiled at his reflection. Not bad for forty-seven.
But he was not getting any younger. And here was Clay,
his only child, his *baby*, for chrissakes, graduating from
high school and going off to the University of Virginia in
the fall. It had all happened too quickly.

Mac let the towel drop on the bathroom floor, dashed
into the bedroom, and grabbed a clean pair of boxer
shorts. His eyes caught sight of the picture in the polished
silver frame on his bedside table. Himself, at thirty-six,
with Clay, round faced and quizzical, not quite six. And
Eleanor, as beautiful as she had ever been, at thirty. A
month after the picture was taken, the Cessna 110 she was
learning to fly had crashed into Afton Mountain in the
fog. He flinched. The thought of it, even after eleven
years, caused an involuntary shiver down his back.

It had been awful; that day, and a month later and a
year later. He and his young daughter had been so lost.

They had managed a semblance of life-goes-on during the days, but after dusk the tiniest memory could trigger tears in both of them. The Willows seemed so empty without Eleanor's laughter and the impromptu parties she loved to throw. The tragedy, the void, was always with them, like an invisible undershirt clinging to their bodies, covering their hearts.

Slowly, Mac had lifted above his grief long enough to realize that their mutual misery might do permanent damage to little Clay. She had always been a serious child, alert and aware of the injustices of life. Now he was afraid that if something did not occur to change the structure of their day-to-day routine, the child might sink into a depression that only years and skilled psychiatrists would be able to unravel.

The answer had come quickly. Buck Smith, Mac's farm manager, had mentioned that his unmarried sister, Nell, was looking for a job. She was a craftsperson; she created dolls that she sold to a shop in town, but she wasn't making much money. She had been trained as a secretary but hated the conformity and inflexibility of nine-to-five life. Mac had met her on many occasions. She was a quiet, plain woman, but Buck told Mac that she loved children; his own kids adored her. So Mac decided to give her a try. He brought in a decorator to fix up one of the guest suites and hired Nell Smith to come and live at The Willows as a companion for Clay.

Wrestling his tan cotton gabardine suit from the polyethylene cleaner's bag, Mac quickly finished dressing. Nell Smith and Nonah were waiting in the car, a forest-green Pontiac station wagon with "The Willows Stud" hand painted in white on the door next to the driver.

"Hold on to your hats, gals. Keep your eyes closed if you have to. We're going to make Commencement before it commences."

"I was afraid of that," Nell said. "We have twenty minutes, and it's a half-hour drive. Plus we have to find a place to park . . ."

"We'll make it." Mac accelerated down the long driveway, hitting fifty-five as he careened on to the main road.

He turned on the radio and punched the buttons until he located a local station with easy-listening music: Mantovani instead of the Beatles, the Rolling Stones, or one of those other groups Clay played incessantly on her bedroom stereo.

Mac wove in and out of the sparse traffic with ease.

"Oh!" Nell's fingers grasped the dashboard. "We just missed that truck."

"Yeah, by a mile. Now just relax."

Mac pressed his foot on the accelerator to take advantage of the open road ahead. He reached for a Chesterfield. Nell pushed in the car lighter for him and held it while he lit his cigarette. Mac gave her a grin of thanks, and she told him to keep his eyes on the road.

Nell Smith had worked out well; she had been with them for over ten years now. Clay had taken to her from the beginning, and before long the little girl was smiling more, doing well in school, making new friends. At home, she and Nell were always involved in projects, making dolls or puppets and a puppet stage. Later, it was miniature furniture and a doll house; still later, pottery and photography. Last year, Nell had urged Mac to buy Clay a Nikon camera for her sixteenth birthday, and since then, Clay had been photographing the horses for the brochures he sent out. She was doing a hell of a job, too.

"Mr. Mac, I can't stand it! Please slow down." This time the terrified voice belonged to Nonah, who was sitting in the back seat.

"Not much farther. I think I've set some sort of a record." Mac exited off of I-64 and glanced at Nell, sitting quietly next to him. She was single-handedly responsible for yanking Clay back into the world. He owed her a big debt of gratitude.

He remembered a time when Clay was about ten. It was a Saturday evening, and he and his daughter were having dinner together. Nell had been away with Buck and his wife that weekend. As the meal had progressed, Clay had grown thoughtful. Finally, she had spoken up.

"Daddy, I have a serious question to ask you."

Mac looked into her huge gray eyes and smiled. "Well, I'll try to give you a serious answer."

"Why don't you marry Nell, daddy? I mean, she lives here most of the time. And if you were married, she could be here all the time. We could go on trips together and stuff like that."

Mac put two teaspoons of sugar in his coffee and stirred. "Honey, you know I have the highest regard for Nell. She's a wonderful person. I know you're crazy about her, but I'm not going to marry her. I don't love her."

"But you *like* her. Why can't you marry her, anyway? We could be a *real* family."

Mac picked up his napkin and wiped a cookie crumb from the corner of Clay's mouth. "We *are* a family, honey. All of us here at The Willows—Buck, Nell, Nonah and Pete, the rest of the boys. Not a conventional one, I'll hand you that, but a family just the same."

"Then you won't ever get married again, daddy?" Clay gazed at him searchingly.

"I don't think so, Clay. I loved your mother very much. No one could ever take her place."

"Don't *I* take her place, daddy—sort of? Don't you love me as much as you loved her?"

"Of course I do, baby." He pushed his chair back and held out his arms. Clay rushed into them and wrapped her own around him tightly.

"I'll never ever leave you, daddy."

"And I'll never leave you, baby . . ."

The station wagon turned right off Route 250 west and through the stone gates of St. Anne's School. Mac Fitzgerald sped up the driveway, ignoring the fifteen mile per hour limit, and skidded into a nonparking space on the grass. He pulled out his pocket watch. A few minutes past eleven. If the proceedings had not started yet, as usually happened with these events, they would not have to tiptoe in quietly and sit in back. Mac rushed around to open the car doors for Nell and Nonah.

"Come on, gals. We don't have all day."

Chapter 12

INSIDE the claustrophobic gymnasium at St. Anne's Episcopal School, Clay Fitzgerald sat perspiring with her graduating class in a semicircle facing the schoolmates and families packed in for the occasion. She squinted hopelessly at the blurred faces. She had decided not to wear her glasses. As a result, she could barely see the features of the person two chairs away, much less make out her father and Nell. She returned her attention to the podium where Headmaster Halquist was delivering his opening address.

Clay was certain her father would not make it back from Harrisonburg in time. He would probably pull up as the crowd was dispersing, full of apologies about flat tires and traffic. But it was all right. Today, she was so happy to be graduating that nothing could spoil it. She looked forward to a quiet summer—taking pictures, riding horseback, attending the Saratoga yearling sales with her father. Maybe she could even convince him to take her someplace for a final spree before college.

Clay felt a nudge to her ribs. Genie Davis, the girl sitting next to her, whispered, "Wake up! They're getting ready to announce the art prize."

". . . great pleasure to announce," the headmaster said, "that this year's prize goes to Clay Fitzgerald. For her achievement in the art of photography."

Clay hurried up, almost tripping on the hem of her long white-organdy dress. The room broke into applause, and she could hear her best friend, Robin Randolph, call out, "See, I told you!" above the clapping.

The rest of the event, even the handing out of the diplomas, was a blur for Clay. Being singled out for the art prize seemed to signal to her that the next four years of college would be a breeze. She had talent!

After the ceremony, Clay quickly found her father, Nell, and Nonah out on the lawn.

"Daddy! I never thought you'd make it! I bet you just got here." Clay hugged him and the two women.

"Hell, no. We were just a couple of minutes late, baby. We didn't miss much. Buck and I ran a little behind schedule, but I made good time getting here." He smiled at Nell Smith and the large black woman. "Didn't I, ladies?" Nonah smiled and rolled her eyes skyward.

"Doesn't matter," Clay said. "Mr. Halquist's speech was deadly boring." She glanced around and was chagrined to see the object of her comment standing within earshot. She flashed him a smile and blushed. The headmaster nodded stiffly; she could not tell if he had overheard her.

Mac Fitzgerald beamed. "I'm so proud of you, Clay."

"I was keepin' my fingers crossed about the art prize! But I had a feelin' you'd win it," Nell said.

Mac turned to Nell. "Buck's sending one of the boys to pick up you and Nonah to help with the shopping. He'll be along anytime now." He put his arm around Clay and kissed her cheek. "I want to take my daughter for a special celebration lunch at the Boar's Head before we go home."

Clay squinched up her face. "Thank you, daddy, but do we have to? I'm just about to die in this dress. It's so hot, and I look terrible." Several strands of her chestnut hair were beginning to escape the chignon Nell had created for her earlier that morning. Her glasses, which she had put back on, kept sliding down her nose.

"Don't be silly, baby. You look beautiful. And I kind of wanted to talk to you, alone. It's a special day."

"Well . . . okay. But I hope we don't see anybody we know. I look so . . . ostentatious!"

"Run say your good-bys, honey. My reservation's for one o'clock. It's almost that now."

"Champagne, honey? It's a day for celebration." Mac

and Clay Fitzgerald were comfortably seated in the Old Mill Room, a plush, tartan-carpeted dining room in Charlottesville's elegantly colonial Boar's Head Inn.

"No, thank you, daddy."

"Okay, then," Mac said to the waitress, "bring me a Bloody Mary and the roast beef."

"I'll have a club sandwich, I guess," Clay said. She felt as if all eyes in the room were focused on her, the giraffe in the frilly dress. "And a Diet Pepsi."

Mac pulled the present from his suit pocket and placed it on the table in front of Clay. "Happy graduation, my love."

"Oh, daddy! What is it?"

"Why do people always say that? Open it, baby, and find out."

The white cardboard box contained another box, a small one covered in royal-blue velvet. Clay opened it slowly. Inside was a gold flower ring with petals of pear-shaped rubies and three marquise emeralds for leaves.

"It's . . . beautiful, daddy." Clay leaned over and kissed her father on the cheek. "Really. Just beautiful." It was, but Clay wondered when she would ever wear it. It was too sophisticated for her taste, which ran to a turquoise and silver ring she had favored for so long that the stone was worn down. But she did not want to hurt her father's feelings. "I'll . . . love it always."

"Your grandfather bought those stones from somebody who was in debt back during the Depression. He tossed them into one of his bank boxes, and I didn't discover them until a couple of years ago. I decided then to have something done for you. Nell designed the ring and had the jewelers make it up." Mac laughed. "She was afraid you wouldn't like it because it was too fancy. But I told her a woman can never resist jewels."

Clay grinned. "Well, some women can, daddy. But I know I'll treasure this more and more as I get older."

Mac downed his Bloody Mary and ordered another. He nodded distractedly to some friends on the far side of the oak-beamed room, then looked back at his daughter. "Enjoying yourself? This isn't so bad, is it? Having lunch with your old man."

"It's fun, daddy. I only wish I could have changed clothes first."

The waitress brought their food, and they ate in silence for a couple of minutes. Clay could tell her father's mood had shifted. She was afraid she had not seemed enthusiastic enough about the ring. She held up her finger.

"I really love my ring, daddy."

"I'm glad, sweetheart. Now, er, there's something I want to talk over with you. Something very important."

Mac seldom spoke so quietly. Clay put down her dill pickle. "Is something . . . wrong?"

Mac smiled. "No. No, just the opposite. I have some great news. I didn't want to tell you 'til you'd gotten through your exams and graduation, but—"

"What, daddy? You're being very dramatic."

Mac patted his daughter's hand. "You're right. It's just that I'm not sure how you're going to take this. I had rehearsed this speech, but the words are eluding me now. The thing is—I've found somebody I want to marry."

Clay was stunned. Her mouth worked ineffectually for a few seconds before she could bring words out. "What? Who? Do I know her?"

"Not yet, baby. Her name is Sunny Yates, and she moved to town last fall. I met her at a party at the Jessups' in April. I know you'll like her, Clay. She's a widow, and she has a daughter who's at Hollins and a son just back from Vietnam. He'll be going to the university this fall . . ."

"When are you getting married?" Clay asked, crushed. This was supposed to have been *her* day. Why did her father have to spoil it? Surely he could have waited until tomorrow.

"Well . . . soon, in a month or so. That is, if you'll grant me your permission."

"But I've never even *met* her! You're marrying someone I've never laid eyes on. How *could* you?" She blinked fiercely, too late to stop the tears that seeped down her cheeks underneath her gold wire-rimmed glasses.

"Sweetheart, you're going to meet her. Tomorrow night. She's coming out to the house for dinner."

"Does Nell know about this?"

"Nobody knows. You're the first person I've told. You know that."

"But . . . you haven't known her very long. I mean, are you sure you want to get married so soon?"

"Sunny's the first person I've met since your mother who has even made me think about marriage. I'm getting older, Clay. And you're almost grown, going off to college . . ."

"Well, not far. I'll still be living at home."

Mac nodded. "But in another year or so you'll want to get a place of your own in town. Then you'll meet someone and get married. I guess I'm trying to hedge my bets. I couldn't bear to be alone after you've gone off to have a life of your own."

"But I'm not going off anytime soon. I'm only seventeen."

Mac leaned forward and took Clay's hands in his. "You're going to like Sunny. She's a warm, wonderful person. Just like her name."

"Are you . . . in love with her?" Clay hated this conversation. She wanted to be someplace else.

Mac Fitzgerald's hazel eyes sparkled. "Yes, Clay, I am. Very much. I know you think your life is going to change drastically, but it won't. After Sunny and I get married, life'll go on the same as it is now. Except you'll have a mother, someone to talk things over with when you don't want to talk to me."

"I don't need a mother. I have Nell. I can talk to her about anything. Look, daddy, you have a right to get married again, I guess. It is your life, and I probably will leave home sooner or later. But this Sunny Yates is *never* going to be my mother!" In her outburst, Clay knocked over the Diet Pepsi with her elbow. The brown liquid oozed along the white-linen tablecloth and into her lap, on to her organdy dress. "Oh, no . . . oh, dear. I'm sorry." Clay escaped from the dining room, crying, and did not stop until she had reached the car.

Mac Fitzgerald sighed and signaled for the waitress to bring the check. *Every silver lining has a cloud,* he thought to himself.

The beige Mercedes 190 SL drove slowly past the Spring Mountain country store and cautiously turned right on to Route 6. The car was a 1962 model, nearly ten years old, but when Sunny Yates bought it, she knew that it would stand her in good style for a long time. The days of its usefulness were coming to an end, however. Now that she was marrying Mac Fitzgerald, the handsomest and nearly the richest catch of Albermarle County, she supposed that Mac would give her a new car. A Jaguar would be nice, or perhaps a more sedate Aston Martin.

As she turned west, the sun glared into her eyes, and she reached into the glove compartment for her dark glasses. She sped past a sign, Loblolly Pines, Planted in 1932, and smiled with satisfaction. It was her first visit to the famous Willows Stud Farm. Mac had not wanted her to visit until he had told his daughter that they were getting married. *Strange,* she thought, *driving to a place for the first time and knowing that you were going to live there forever.*

At least she hoped it would be forever. It had taken her a long time to find a man worth marrying: wealthy, attractive, and unattached. In New Orleans and Atlanta, the rich ones were either married, homely, boring, or closet gay. Most of her friends had contented themselves with that lot. But Sunny had held out. And gotten out.

Moving to Charlottesville was the best thing she had ever done. The small city was intellectual and cosmopolitan because of the university and proximity to Washington, D.C., and the surrounding countryside, with its rolling green hills, retained the beauty of another century. She had met so many compatible people.

And now there was Mac. He did not exactly send her into ecstasy when they made love, but she had decided that he was just out of practice. Mac was virile and more than willing to try new things. There was plenty she could teach him. Besides, everything else was so perfect, she could afford to wait a while longer for sexual satisfaction.

Sunny drove through the gate to The Willows and along the imposing two-lane driveway that cut through the sixteen-hundred-acre estate. It was easy to see how the place got its name. The thick-trunked, tall willows along the length of the drive were probably over a hundred years old. On one side, Holstein cattle were converting the Wavertree grass into milk for the Monticello Dairy in Charlottesville. On the other side, behind the whitewashed country fence, were acres of flat fields for the sleek thoroughbred horses. One, a chestnut stallion, raced the sports car for a quarter of a mile before it lost interest and galloped off toward a hill on the horizon. The road straightened and the white Tuscan-columned brick mansion came into view.

Sunny felt herself growing more excited as she drove nearer; there was a prickly feeling in her palms and between her legs. Here she was, thirty-nine, and practically having an orgasm over a house. No, it was not only the house. It was the history, the life-style, the money. Old money, her favorite kind.

Sunny slowed down and tilted the rear-view mirror to check her makeup. The sun had burned fiery highlights into her shoulder-length blonde hair. She pushed her sunglasses up and looked at her blue eyes, framed by plum eye shadow and black lashes. She wondered how many other women her age looked as young. As she drove the car around the circle to the front of the house, she squirted herself with Chanel No. 19.

Mac Fitzgerald was standing on the large front porch as she drove up. He came down the steps and opened the car door for her. "Did you have any problem finding us, darlin'?"

Sunny gave him a quick kiss and smiled. "Not at all. But I drove slow so I could take in the breathtakin' beauty of this country. And The Willows Stud, in particular."

Mac put his arm around her and led her up to the porch. "I'm glad you like it. I'll give you a tour of the place before dark. But let's have a drink first. I want you to meet Clay."

"I can't wait. I've been lookin' forward to this moment for so long. My, those English boxwood are just huge. The gardens are so immaculate!"

"Well, you'll meet Nonah, our cook. Her husband, Pete, is our head gardener. He used to work for Mrs. Smith when she had Rose Hill. That was about the most beautiful place in the county."

Mac led Sunny through the two-storied hall and into the immense living room. She took one look and made a mental note to call in the decorator as soon as they returned from the honeymoon. The antique furniture was beautiful but obviously had not been reupholstered in years. The American Empire sofa and gold floral Aubusson rug she would keep. Everything else would have to be recovered or reconsidered.

Mac extracted a bottle of Bollinger from the silver ice bucket. "I know you like champagne. Shall we?"

Sunny pinched his cheek affectionately. "Of course, darlin'. Just the thing for our walk through the stables." She winked at him seductively and followed his gaze to the French doors that led to the patio. A tall girl with thick glasses and long straight hair stared at her with a face void of expression.

For just a moment, Sunny's eyes hardened, and then she broke out her most dazzling smile. "Why . . . you must be Clay! Your father's told me so much about you, I'd know you anywhere." Sunny started toward the girl, but Clay skittered over to her father.

"Clay, honey. Where are your manners?"

Clay extended her hand to Sunny. "How do you do?" she said flatly.

"Your father was just about to take me on the grand tour. Won't you join us? Mac's told me you're an expert equestrienne, and that your favorite horse is named Cartoon. I think that's the cutest name! Can we see him?"

"It's a her. And she's gone to the south pasture for the night."

"Oh, too bad. Well, another time."

Mac opened the champagne and poured. "You want something to drink, baby?"

"No thank you, daddy."

Sunny laughed. "I wish Audrey—that's my daughter— were more like you. She adores champagne, has ever since she was fourteen. I can't wait for you to meet her, Clay. I'm sure you'll be great friends. We only moved here last fall, and she's been off at Hollins, so she hardly knows a soul in town. I hope you'll take her around and introduce her to your friends."

Mac answered for his daughter. "Of course she will. Won't you, Clay? Well, we'd better get outside before it gets dark. Coming with us, baby?"

"No, thanks. I know what the stable looks like."

"Well, we'll see you at dinner. Come with me, Sunny. Did you know that all the bricks for the house and stables were handmade and kilned right here? And that holly over there is three hundred years old . . ."

Dinner had been planned as a very special occasion. Nonah had not seen Mac so anxious that everything be perfect since Eleanor was alive. The oldest Baccarat goblets, Tiffany's Chrysanthemum sterling and their private stock *Jardin de Jade* china, the Irish lace tablecloth that Mac's grandmother had brought with her when the family came from Scotland.

And the food. Nonah had been submitting menus to Mac for days before he finally approved one: her famous chicken and Virginia ham shortcake to start, green turtle soup with sherry, game hens with wild rice and orange sauce, asparagus Hollandaise, a salad of early summer greens, and for dessert, airy apricot mousse and lace cookies. He chose a red bordeaux to accompany the meal, a 1961 Chateaux Latour, and a light Taittinger champagne for dessert.

The room was lit by candles in twelve eighteenth-century silver candelabra around the room and Waterford crystal candle holders on the dining table encircling an Imari porcelain bowl brimming with red Enchantment lilies and milk-white Siberian iris.

During the first two courses, Sunny chatted vivaciously about the splendor of The Willows. She quizzed Mac about its history (the estate, built in 1835, had been purchased by Mac's father in the Twenties) and the ins and outs of the horse-breeding business. Clay answered the questions she was asked but offered no conversation of her own.

"I must say, Mac, you are certainly lucky to have Nonah. She's a fabulous cook. I'm certainly goin' to have to watch my weight."

At dessert, Mac ordered a champagne glass for Clay and insisted she have at least one sip. "I want to make a toast to Sunny," he said. "To my beautiful future bride and hostess of The Willows."

Clay pretended to sip, but let the amber liquid flow out of her mouth and back into the goblet, "Er, daddy, I don't want any dessert. Could I be excused now?"

"No, sweetheart. You don't have to eat, but I'd like you to sit with us until the end of the meal. We have to discuss wedding arrangements, and I wanted to have you in on the conference." He smiled warmly at his daughter.

"Now, Clay," Sunny Yates said, "I'd be very honored if you'd be my bridesmaid, along with Audrey. Audrey's a blonde, like me, and you're dark. I think lavender dresses would suit you both beautifully. And white orchids in your hair—"

"I'm sorry, but I don't want to be a bridesmaid," Clay said quietly.

"Oh, baby, don't be shy," Mac said. "Sunny especially wants you in the wedding."

"I certainly do. A weddin' at The Willows with my daughter and stepdaughter. What could be lovelier?" She looked sweetly at Clay. "I know you have to get used to the whole idea. I mean, it's natural. You've had you daddy to yourself all these years. But Clay, I just want you to know that I hope we'll become warm friends." She laughed, tossing back her head. "I certainly won't be like the classic wicked stepmother you read about in fairy tales."

Clay stared at her, and Sunny could not tell what the

girl was thinking behind her hostile gray eyes and thick lashes, accentuated by her eyeglasses. Sunny continued, to fill the awkward silence. "Now let's get the date set. The last Saturday in June is the twenty-eighth. I checked with Keller and George. They can put a rush on the invitations and have them engraved in three days. That would mean we could have them by next Tuesday. In the meantime, they'll furnish us with the envelopes so Audrey and I can get them addressed and stamped and ready to mail as soon as the invitations are delivered . . ."

Clay stood abruptly. Her napkin fell to the floor. "Daddy, I'm going over to Robin's to spend the night. I'll see you tomorrow." She rushed out of the room.

"Clay!" Mac called out. "Come back here and say good night to Sunny. Clay!" He rose to fetch her, but Sunny put her hand on his arm.

"No, Mac . . . it's all right. Don't worry. Everything will be fine between us. It'll take a little time. Clay has to get used to me. But I think she's a perfectly lovely girl," she added tactfully.

Clay overheard that as she searched the hall for her wallet. *No, Sunny Yates,* she thought, *I'll never get used to you.* And then out loud, as she slammed the heavy screened door, "Bitch!" She ran over to the stable to get the pickup and drove off to her friend's house. Clay knew her father was happy, and she supposed she was happy for him. But she had known the moment she saw Sunny Yates that she could never accept that woman as her mother. There was something she couldn't put her finger on, but she didn't trust Sunny, nor did she think she ever would.

Later, Mac and Sunny sat on the terrace, sipping champagne and enjoying the fragrant orange blossoms. They had finished going over the guest list, and plans for the reception were set. They had had a minor disagreement over the farm hands. Mac had insisted they be included, and Sunny, not wanting to rock the boat, had relented with a gracious shrug.

Mac took her hand. "I want to apologize for Clay's behavior at dinner."

"Oh, Mac, don't be silly. It's hard for her to adjust to the reality of havin' to share her beloved daddy with someone else."

Mac pulled her into his arms and kissed her. "Well, darling, you're very understanding. It's hard for you, too, to take on another daughter."

"I'm lookin' forward to it! I know how difficult teenagers can be. Audrey's always been a delight, but Beau was somethin' else and again when he was Clay's age. Thank God, he seems to have calmed down. I guess it's true. The army really does make a man of you. Beau's grown up a great deal, although I wonder . . ." She trailed off. "Oh, enough of the kids. Let's think about you and me." She draped her hand casually in his lap.

"Oh, Sunny, you've made me so happy." Mac kissed her slowly.

"You know," Sunny whispered, "you haven't given me a tour of the house."

Mac grabbed the champagne. "Well, come on!"

The tour wound up in Mac's bedroom suite.

"Oh, my," Sunny said, giggling from all the champagne. "So this is where you sleep!"

"Yes. I picked up that bed at an auction in Charleston a few years ago. It was made around 1800."

"A few years ago?" She examined the handsome fourposter, which was carved with rice fronds. Her lips curved mischievously. "Now tell me, Mac Fitzgerald, is that a virgin bed?"

He laughed. "It sure is. Here, anyway."

Sunny sat on the white-chenille bedspread and motioned for Mac to sit next to her. She leaned into him and asked, "What say we deflower it . . . tonight?" She probed her tongue slowly into his ear. "Clay's gone to her friend's, remember? What's to stop us?"

"Only the rest of the house and farm staff . . ."

"Oh, pooh." Sunny unzipped the back of her Geoffrey Beene linen dress. "I wanted you to see what a good tan I got today." She slipped the dress down over her slim hips and was naked except for white-lace bikinis.

"Well, Nell Smith is due back. She may even be here."

Sunny unloosened Mac's silk Dior tie. "The night's still young. I'll drive home later." She coaxed her right nipple between his parting lips, and Mac dug his hands into her buttocks and pulled her bikinis off.

Down the hall, Nell Smith sat in her yellow-and-white-chintz bedroom trying to repair a broken doll and listening to the sounds of passion coming from Mac Fitzgerald's room. Nell had been miserable many times in her forty-nine years, but tonight hopelessness engulfed her. She didn't cry; she had run out of tears long ago.

Nell went to the window. The moon was bright, and she watched the silhouettes of the horses in distant pastures. The Willows had been her life for ten years, and she loved it. Now everything was changing. She had known that Mac Fitzgerald would never marry her, but she had dreamed that they would grow old together, be there when Clay came to visit with her children.

Each new trill of Sunny's ecstasy was like a dart being thrown into Nell's heart. She was nearly fifty, and she saw her life for what it was. She had no illusions about her future; Sunny Yates had taken care of that. Nell would be alone, as always. Clay was nearly grown. Mac was getting married.

Nell opened her hands and looked into each palm. A long life line. She clenched her hands into fists and pounded them against the window sash until they hurt. And, as if in response, from down the hall came the rising wail of Sunny Yates's orgasm: "Oh, God! Oh, God! No! Ahhhhh!"

As Nell tiptoed down to the library for a brandy, she kept thinking, *A long life and no one to spend it with.*

Chapter 13

THE three weeks leading up to the dreaded day of her father's remarriage ran together in Clay's mind. The days sped by easily enough, but the evenings were harder. Mac Fitzgerald was often out with Sunny; Clay and Nell usually had a quiet dinner together, but Nell seemed as preoccupied as she. Sometimes Clay went into town to the movies with Robin Randolph and her older brother George.

George Randolph was the only person Clay had ever dated. She liked the handsome prelaw student and believed it when he told her that he was going to be a senator or governor of Virginia someday. George enjoyed being with her, too, Clay could tell, except she was afraid he wouldn't admit it to himself. On the big college weekends, he dated girls from Sweet Briar or Hollins or Mary Baldwin, not her. He took Clay out on off weekends when he wanted to see a movie or talk.

Robin was always telling Clay that she had to learn to flirt, but Clay scoffed at the suggestion. She could never be coy with George; she knew him too well. The other boys she knew were interested in only one thing, and they were not interested in doing it with her. Clay was too intelligent, aloof, caustically witty, gawky. She wished that George would look at her one day and realize he was in love with her. Clay loved to fantasize about that magical day when the rest of her body would fill out to match her height and she would be transformed into a beauty. Clay assured her mirror image that she was a late bloomer, that was all. And she believed it, most of the time. The confidence of that belief kept Clay from fretting over her current lack of dates and the fact that George treated her like a kid sister.

On the day of the wedding, Saturday, June twenty-eighth, Clay was still in bed at eleven o'clock, although she usually rose before six to help Bluejay Cole feed and exercise the horses.

Clay had decided not to get up at all.

"Clay! You should be gettin' dressed now." Nell Smith came in with a tray of toast and grapefruit juice.

Clay groaned. "I can't, Nell. I don't feel well. I think I have flu. Or maybe it's appendicitis."

Nell regarded her sympathetically. "I know how you feel, Clay. I really do. But you have to rise to the occasion. Your father would be heartbroken if you weren't at the ceremony."

"A lot he cares. I don't see why he couldn't just have an affair with Sunny. Why does he have to marry her?"

Secretly, Nell wished the same thing. "Now Clay, you're soundin' like a spoiled brat. This isn't going to be the end of everything. Life at The Willows will go on as usual. Besides, if you give Sunny half a chance, you'll probably discover that she's not so bad."

Clay reached for her glasses on the bedside table. "Oh, come on, Nell. Do *you* like her?"

"She seems like a lovely person."

"Nell! Come off it!"

"Well, she must be. Your father wouldn't have fallen for her if she weren't."

"Answer me, Nell. Do *you* like her?"

Nell shook her head with a rueful laugh. "No, Clay. But neither of us has any say in the matter. We might as well get used to it."

"She's so phony. Dripping with that New Orleans accent. Giving my father those big eyes as if he were playing Tarzan to her Jane."

Nell laughed in spite of herself. "Get up, Clay. I told your father you were gettin' dressed forty-five minutes ago. Think about *him* for a minute. He's happy, but he's bothered that you haven't taken to Sunny. This is his day. Let's not spoil it."

Clay thought about how her father had spoiled her graduation day by springing the news about Sunny. But Nell was right. She owed it to her father to go to his wedding. She had no choice. She loved him and for whatever reasons, Sunny Yates made him happy. Clay got out of bed.

"Okay, Nell, you win. But if I throw up in the punch, don't blame me."

"I'd better go and finish dressin'. See you later." The thin, graying woman went back down the hall to her room.

Clay showered and dressed. She had held firm about not being a bridesmaid but had relented to Mac's request that she wear a long dress. She had chosen an embroidered yellow Mexican peasant dress, and it suited her.

Clay sat at her dressing table and tried to apply eye makeup, her face pushed up to the mirror so she could see without her glasses. Her hand slipped and the mascara wand dipped into the corner of her eye, making her blink in reflex, smudging black blobs under each eye. "Damn it!" she said out loud.

Clay smeared cold cream around her eyes and removed all the makeup, then put her glasses back on. She looked plain, and she was in a rotten mood.

Impulsively, she braided her long chestnut hair into two plaits, and rummaged through a drawer for the scissors.

"Clay? Clay, honey, you ready yet?" Mac Fitzgerald's voice called from somewhere.

Clay stared hard into the mirror.

"Clay! Where are you, anyway?" Mac's voice came nearer.

Clay picked up the scissors and with a savage motion cut off each braid just below her ears. She glared defiantly at her shorn reflection and the plaits dangling limply from her left hand. Then her eyes filled with tears and before she knew it, she was sobbing in loud heaves.

Mac hurried in. "Clay . . . baby." He took her in his arms, held her tight, and comforted her until the tears stopped.

"I know what this is all about," Mac said. "This isn't a day you've been looking forward to."

"It's not too late, daddy, to change your mind."

"I don't want to change my mind, baby." He handed her his handkerchief. "I know it's hard for you. It's always been the two of us, but things will be better than ever now. Nothing will change between you and me. And Sunny really likes you . . . she'll be a fine mother."

"I told you, she'll *never* be my mother!" Clay snapped.

"All right. I understand. But she can be your friend. All I'm asking is that you give her a chance. Will you?"

Clay realized the hopelessness of the situation. "Yes, daddy." She sighed. "I'll try."

"That's my girl!" Mac kissed her on the forehead. "The Fitzgeralds have always been a hearty bunch."

"Do I have to go out of my way to be nice to Beau and Audrey, too?"

Mac smiled. "Get the chip off your shoulder and I'll bet you'll like them."

"Beau gives me the creeps. I mean, anybody who actually *joined* the Special Forces and wasn't drafted is a little weird. I think he actually *liked* being in Vietnam . . ."

"Now honey, there are still some young men who believe in fighting for their country, you know."

"All right, daddy, all right." This was an old and familiar discussion and neither of them wanted it now. "But I don't expect we'll ever hit it off."

"Well, you don't much like boys yet. But Audrey's only a year older than you. You two will find a lot in common, I'm sure."

"Oh, daddy, really! She's conceited because she's so pretty. And she thinks St. Timothy's and Hollins are *the* only places to go. She's just a dumb blonde that boys drool over." Clay pointed to her head. "There's nothing upstairs."

Mac threw up his hands. "Okay, you're determined to be stubborn. But all I'm asking is that you keep an open mind. That's fair, isn't it?"

"Yes."

"So will you?"

"Yes."

"Good. Now come downstairs with me. People will be arriving soon."

"Daddy?"

"Yes, baby?"

"I love you so much!" She threw herself into his arms.

"I love you too, Clay. Nobody is ever going to take your place in my heart." He put his arm around her shoulder and led her to the door. "By the way, I like your hair like that. It looks kind of cute. Nice and cool for the summer."

The wedding ceremony was held in the living room, with guests spilling out into the hall and on to the terrace. Sunny and Mac glowed and held hands as family and close friends stood by. The reception was held in the gardens, and three hundred people milled around, chatting, dancing to Peter Duchin's orchestra, and sipping champagne or Wedding Punch, a lethal Virginian concoction of rum, whiskey, wine, sugar, and lemon and orange juice.

In spite of Clay's prayers to the contrary, the day was rare perfection for Virginia at the end of June: sunny, breezy, not too humid. Pete Hughes and a special crew had worked overtime to groom the gardens. The herbaceous borders were beautifully manicured, the Rose Walk had never looked so delicate, and the flowers in both the cloistered and botanical gardens appeared to have waited until that morning to bloom. Water lilies glazed the reflecting pool, and the old-fashioned secret garden was enclosed by a yew hedge put in especially for the occasion. The fountain, which had not worked in Clay's lifetime, spewed jets of water in lovely cascades. Mac Fitzgerald had spared no expense to make the new mistress of The Willows feel at home.

"If I have another glass of this punch, I won't be held responsible for my actions." Robin Randolph giggled. "Come on, Clay, shall we have George get us some more?"

Clay wanted to get drunk. She held out her punch cup.

"Okay, George, fill 'er up. And bring a plate of sandwiches when you come back. I'm hungry."

"I want some more shrimp," Robin said. "Maybe we'd better go with you, George and help you carry stuff back." They had been picnicking behind the gazebo where they could hear the music but did not have to mingle with the other guests. "Come on, Clay. Move your ass."

"Oh, all right. But if the shrimp's all gone, I'll never forgive you for forcing me to move. I could sit here forever." Clay headed down the Rose Walk with her friends.

"Oh, Clay . . . *there* you are. I was lookin' for you earlier."

Audrey Yates, in the lavender Halston her mother had picked out for her, stumbled over. Her straight white-blonde hair flowed down to her shoulder blades; two barettes of wild orchids kept the silky mane away from her face. Her date, Schuyler Clark, held up a bottle of champagne.

"We have our own private stock," he said. "We're trying to find a nice secluded spot."

"Won'tch'all join us?" Audrey slurred. "And Clay, you haven't introduced me." She gazed at George Randolph with the innocent, baby-blue-eyed look that Clay despised.

"Oh . . . Robin and George Randolph. Audrey Yates."

"Audrey Yates, your *stepsister*." She giggled. "Isn't it all too excitin'? Imagine! True love at *their* age. I think it's just wonderful." Audrey turned to George. "And where have you been keepin' yourself? Why haven't I met you before?"

George colored. "My bad luck, I guess. I'm a Saint A. at the university. I bet you haven't been favoring our house with your company."

Audrey giggled, again. "Well I spent most of my time last winter with the K.A.s. But I certainly don't want to get in a rut . . ."

"Come on, Audrey," Schuyler said. "Let's find a place to settle down before the champagne goes flat." He grabbed her hand and pulled her down the path.

"See you later, y'all," Audrey called back. "Maybe we can go dancin' at the club tonight."

Robin shook her head. "Whew! Everything you told me is true, Clay. She's something."

George watched until Audrey disappeared with Schuyler behind a shrub. "I'll say! God, she's fantastic!"

Robin and Clay looked at each other. Clay thought George had more sense than to be taken in by someone as brainless as Audrey Yates.

"Come on, George," Robin said. "The punch. The shrimp. Remember?"

They armed themselves with food and drink.

"I want to see Beau Yates," Robin said. "If Audrey's so beautiful, he must be a dream."

"Yeah, he's okay looking. But I told you, he's a real loner. He was at the ceremony, but he split right after. I don't know. I've never had a real conversation with him. He's supposed to be moving into one of the great cottages near the stable, but he hasn't yet."

"Jesus, Clay. A handsome stepbrother. Under the same roof sort of. What an arrangement that could turn out to be." Robin giggled. "It's not incest because you aren't really related."

"Not a chance, Robin. Beau is definitely *not* my type! You can have him, but I wouldn't advise it."

The music came to an abrupt halt. There was a crescendo of drum rolls. Rosemary Clark, Schuyler's mother, raised her musical Virginian voice above the crowd.

"Hush now. For just a minute. The bride and groom are goin' to cut the cake!" The crowd clapped and laughed among shouts of "Hurray" and "It's about time!"

Clay watched her father smile with pleasure as Sunny gaily took his hand and led him over to the cake: fourtiered with magenta roses, sculpted from icing, spilling down the sides.

"A glass of champagne, please." A waiter rushed one over to Mac. "A toast. To my beautiful bride. And to all of you for coming and making this such a happy occasion."

Sunny raised her glass. "And to you, Mac Fitzgerald, for makin' me the happiest woman in the world!" She kissed her husband in front of the approving crowd, and they cut the cake.

Clay stood quietly off to the side. Her father looked as handsome as she had ever seen him in his formal cutaway. He was tall and fit. Even with the gray streaks in his hair he looked ten years younger than he was. Sunny was attractive, too, Clay had to admit, in the coral Oscar de la Renta chiffon she had flown to New York to buy. Still, there was a toughness beneath the tan and blonde charm. Clay could not figure out why her father had not picked up on it. She decided that love must be blind, after all, and hoped that when she fell it would be for someone worthwhile.

"How's my little Clay? My favorite girl in the whole world." Bill Sinclair draped a heavy arm over her shoulder. He was a middle-aged bachelor friend of Mac's, and Clay had always been put off by his oily good humor. Now, drunk as usual, he was using her to hold him up.

Out of spite, Clay lurched slightly and spilled her punch down the front of his pale-blue shirt.

"Oh, Mr. Sinclair! I'm *so* sorry." The man blinked, stunned. "I'll run and get you a towel."

As Clay headed for the bar, Mac glided through the crowd and grabbed her. "I've been hunting all over for you. You all right? Having fun with your friends?"

"Yes . . . sure. It's a good party."

Tears came to Mac Fitzgerald's eyes. "Oh, Clay, sweetheart, I love you more now than I ever have in my whole life." He hugged her tenderly. Clay closed her eyes, clinging hard to him.

"Mac! Mac . . . hurry now." Sunny called out the window from the upstairs bedroom where she had gone to change into her traveling outfit.

"Okay, honey. Clay, I'm going to change. We're going to slip away quietly now. I don't want any rice or rose petals or anything."

They walked slowly to the house; Mac still had his arm around her. "You behave yourself while we're gone. Do everything Nell asks you to. We'll be back a week from Tuesday."

"Mac, darlin'." Sunny walked out on the porch wearing a white Corrèges suit with its skirt several inches above her knees and white patent boots. "If you don't hurry, we'll never get away from here."

Mac whispered in Clay's ear, "Give Sunny a good-by kiss. It'd make her so happy."

Clay went over to her stepmother, who smiled at her warmly. "We're going to be great friends, Clay. I know we will." She extended her cheek, and Clay kissed it quickly, averting her eyes.

"Well, have a nice time at Sea Island," Clay said unenthusiastically.

"Thank you, Clay. Now don't dally, Mac. I'm goin' to tell Audrey good-by."

Later, on her way to change back into jeans, Clay stopped off at Nell's room. The spinster's eyes were red, and Clay was embarrassed at having barged in.

"No, no. It's okay, Clay. I'm all right. How are *you* holdin' up? Are your friends still here?"

Clay shook her head. "Robin got plastered, and George drove her home. After that, he's going out dancing with Audrey."

"Audrey?" Nell exclaimed. "George Randolph has hooked up with her?"

"Love at first sight," Clay said with disgust. "His eyes just about popped out of his head when he saw her. You should have seen the way she flirted with him."

"Oh, Clay, I'm sorry. I'm sure he'll come to his senses."

"I suppose. I really don't care." Clay lied.

"Well, I don't feel like sticking around here and entertainin' the stragglers," Nell said.

"I guess they'll go home eventually. The bar closed over an hour ago." Clay sat down on the bed next to Nell. "I love you, Nell. *You're* the closest thing to a real mother I have. Not *her*."

"I know, honey. And I'll always be around for you. Whenever you need me. No matter where you go or I go."

"Well, neither of us is going anywhere soon." Clay picked up the rag doll resting on Nell's pillow. It was the first one Clay had ever made. She had given it to Nell the first Christmas after Nell came to live with them.

"Yes, we are." Nell stood. "Let's get changed and go in town to a movie. *Bedazzled* is back at the University. I think we need some laughs."

"Good idea," Clay said eagerly, then jumped up. "Oh, God, I just remembered! I never did get poor old Bill Sinclair a towel after spilling that drink on him."

"I doubt if he ever noticed. He passed out down in the living room. Let's get movin'! The last show's at nine."

Nell splashed water on her face. She tore the note Sunny had left for her into tiny pieces and watched them disappear down the toilet. There was no point in telling Clay now. She would find out soon enough.

Chapter 14

NELL Smith moved out the day after Sunny and Mac Fitzgerald returned from their honeymoon. Clay helped her pack and load the car.

"Nell, *please* don't go. How am I going to exist without you here?"

"It'll be okay. This is the best thing. Besides, my apartment can be your *pied-à-terre* in town. I'll have a set of keys made for you."

Clay hugged Nell. "Who knows? I may move in for good."

"Give it a chance, Clay. Once school starts, you'll be busy. And there's always the telephone. Call me whenever you feel like talkin'." Nell put the last suitcase in the car. "Well . . . *adios, amigo*," she said brightly. "Now run inside before I start bawling. Go on. Scram!"

Clay kissed Nell on the cheek. "I'll come in with Pete tomorrow when he brings the rest of the stuff. I'll help you fix the place up. Okay . . . see you!" Clay ran up to her room to cry.

Nell drove off, down the drive of The Willows for the last time. Of course, she would see the place again, but she would never live there. It would be hard adjusting to a one-bedroom apartment on Rugby Road after the splendor of the mansion. How would she manage without Nonah's cooking?

Think forward, she told herself, *and you'll get through it*. Mostly she tried not to think at all. At least Sunny had lined up a job for her, managing a new hobby shop in the Barracks Road shopping center. Why, she wondered? Probably to keep her quiet about having fired her. She knew Sunny had told Mac that it was Nell's decision to leave, and Mac had believed it. Just as well. Nell did not want Clay to learn the truth. Clay hated Sunny enough for taking her father away from her.

But Sunny was probably right. If Nell had stayed there, things would have been awkward for all of them, especially her. Nell loved Mac Fitzgerald. Mac had never suspected it, but his new wife probably did.

It's amazing, she thought, *how quickly your entire life can change.*

Nell Smith pulled over to the side of the road. She was crying too hard to drive safely.

Clay spent July working full time at the stable, helping Buck Smith get things set for Fasig-Tipton's fifty-first annual sale at Saratoga, the most prestigious sale of the year for the farm. The Willows Stud had sixteen yearlings to sell. At least two of them, one sired by Nashua, the other by Graustark, were expected to bring top dollar.

For the first time since she was eight, Clay would not be going to Saratoga with her father. Mac had made a point of inviting her, but Clay knew he was still playing the loving bridegroom to Sunny. And Clay did not think she could take it.

"Clay, would you give Dr. Sydnor a call?" Mac Fitzgerald asked, poking his head in the office. He had on a summer tweed suit, was freshly shaven, and smelled of the fancy after-shave lotion Sunny had given him. "Jack says that Kettle Drum's running a fever."

"Sure, daddy. What're you up to? I thought we were going for a ride together at three."

Mac snapped his fingers. "Damn! I knew there was something. I'm sorry, sweetie. We'll do it tomorrow. Sunny's dragging me up to Washington to look at some antiques. She's found some new decorator in Georgetown she wants me to meet."

"Why?"

"She thinks some of the rooms are a little threadbare. I told her to do them over if she wanted."

"That's ridiculous. The house looks fine."

"Don't worry. If Sunny replaces any of the furniture your mother bought, I'll have it put in storage for you. For later, when you have a place of your own."

Clay shrugged. "Okay." She knew she didn't have any say in the matter, anyway.

"I've got to run now. We'll be back tomorrow afternoon. Let's have our ride then. We'll go over to the Randolphs. I have to discuss something with Hunter, and you can visit Robin."

Clay blew her father a kiss. "Okay, you're on. Have fun." It was hard to get used to Mac these days, dressed up most of the time running here and there with Sunny. But he seemed to thrive on it. Clay had begrudgingly admitted to Nell the other day that her father looked better than ever.

As Clay was dialing the vet, Audrey Yates came in, gracing the stable office with one of her rare appearances. Clay motioned that she would be off the phone in a minute. The gorgeous eighteen-year-old blonde, wearing a micro-mini Betsey Johnson dress, wandered aimlessly around the office. She glanced at the bookcase, full of magazines and books on horses and breeding: the Jockey Club's *American Stud Book*, yearly *Breeder's Guides*, *Foals of 1970*, the *Thoroughbred Record* and *Daily Racing Form*, *Index to Stakes' Winners*, and hundreds of other reference indexes and sales catalogues from the various horse sales around the country. She sighed and sat on the window sill, crossing her legs. Her hair was piled up on her head, held in place by one silver clip. Her makeup was perfectly applied. Clay had seen her without any and knew that with her blonde coloring Audrey had to wear a lot to achieve her "natural" look.

Clay put down the phone. "Hi, Audrey. Haven't seen you much lately." Clay was still annoyed with Audrey for flirting with George Randolph. It didn't seem fair. Audrey had plenty of boy friends, and George was the only one Clay had ever had even though he treated her as more of a pal than a real girl friend.

"You won't believe what I've been doing. Don't breathe a word. Mother'd have a fit if she knew."

Buck Smith walked into the outer office to pick up some papers. Audrey glanced at him and pushed the door closed with her foot. To her, everyone who worked at The Willows was "help," faceless peons whom she could completely ignore. "Anyway I've been goin' out with the most divine man. He's twenty-eight! He's a junior partner at one of the big law firms in town. . . ."

"Oh? Who?" Clay knew that Audrey expected her to take an interest in her affairs. It was the relationship they had evolved into as stepsisters. Audrey would confide to Clay about her latest conquest. Clay would ask a few questions. Audrey would make her promise not to tell Sunny and launch into the most intimate secrets of her sex life. When the subject was exhausted, Audrey usually asked to borrow something from Clay; scarf, money, car, toenail clippers. Clay knew that whatever the item, it was what Audrey was after in the first place. She seemed to have no idea that Clay could see through her, and Clay suspected that Audrey actually believed that they had established a sisterly rapport.

Maybe they had. Clay had never had a sister, and although she did not want this one, Audrey made few demands on her. Audrey was totally self-absorbed, but she wasn't around much. Clay had discovered that she did not really have to listen as Audrey bubbled over with the day-to-day scenarios of her sex life. All that was required of Clay was an occasional question or a rote response such as "That's super" or "What a drag."

"Promise you won't tell mother?"

Clay nodded.

"Larry Taliaferro. Do you know him?"

"I know who he is. I went to school with his youngest sister."

Audrey helped herself to a Chicklet from a pack on Clay's desk. "Well, let me tell you. He's really smooth." She giggled and lowered her voice. "*If* you know what I mean."

Clay nodded.

"We went out on this moonlight picnic last night. Back

around the seventh hole at Farmington? We were drinkin'
purple passions. That's vodka and grape juice."

"Yes, Audrey, I know."

Audrey held out her long-fingered hand and inspected
her nail polish. "So we were lyin' on a blanket lookin' at
the stars, and the next thing I knew my blouse was completely unbuttoned! I mean, I hadn't even felt him doin' it
at all."

"Oh?" Clay was sorting through a stack of *Maryland
Horse* magazines, trying to locate an article Buck wanted
her to have copied. "Then what?"

"Well, *you* know. Or actually, maybe you don't."
Audrey lit a cigarette. "But Clay, honey, you just wouldn't
believe how much *better* older men are. They're really experienced. They know how to *do* so much more. Not like
those dumb college boys who throw themselves on top of
you and get all sweaty and—you know. I mean, boys like
your friend George. They're so *fumbling*. They get all flus-
tered and anxious, and they don't think about a girl's
enjoyment at all." She smiled. "Oh, I'm sorry, Clay. You
probably don't really understand what I'm talkin' about at
all. But you will, one of these days."

Clay refrained from responding. Audrey loved to make
references to what a child she considered Clay to be. That
didn't bother Clay: she did not aspire to be like Audrey. It
did bother Clay, however, that Audrey could go out with
George Randolph a couple of times a week and then talk
about how sexually unsophisticated he was. "I guess it's
over between you and George, then?"

"No, not really." Audrey shrugged. "George is taking
me to the Simon and Garfunkel concert in Washington on
Friday."

"That's . . . nice," Clay managed to say. Since Audrey
had appeared on the scene, George still took Clay to an
occasional movie, but during the long drive back from
town, all he ever wanted to talk about was Audrey. He
never seemed to pick up on the fact that Clay was not
particularly interested in talking about her half sister.

"Listen Clay . . . would you be terriby peeved if I
borrowed ten dollars? Mother's gone out of town, and I

forgot to get some money from her before she left. By the time I get to town, the bank'll be closed."

Clay handed her the money from a change purse she kept in the desk. "Here."

"Oh, you're a darlin'! A *real* sister couldn't be sweeter. I'll pay you back tomorrow." She stood and adjusted the skirt, which barely covered her buttocks. "Don't wait up for me tonight." She giggled.

As if Clay ever did.

Clay told Nonah to take the night off since everyone else was out. After work, Clay and Bluejay Cole and two other boys went for a sunset ride, as they had done on similar summer nights since their childhood. Galloping through the distant meadows, Clay felt free as a bird. Riding cleared her mind; it had a way of pushing problems out of her head, or putting them into perspective. It also helped her figure things out. She always did her best thinking on horseback.

Something nagged at her as she galloped ahead of the others. Something Audrey had told her, repeating a conversation between Mac and Sunny that she had overheard. "Better watch yourself!" Audrey had warned Clay. Sunny wanted to put a stop to Clay's palling around with the black stable boys. Mac had objected, Audrey reported, but Sunny had been adamant that Clay was a young woman on the verge of adulthood and it was "out of place." Clay was prepared to fight for her rights, but so far her father had not broached the subject.

It was a beautiful evening, and Clay looked forward to having the house to herself. After she had changed out of the faded jeans and plaid shirt that were her uniform, she showered, put on a pink terry-cloth wrapper, and went barefoot to the kitchen.

She was sitting at the round oak table eating a lettuce and tomato sandwich and reading the latest issue of *The Blood Horse* when Beau Yates burst in. He had become a sort of hippie since his return from Vietnam. His blond hair straggled over his shoulders and there was a thick stubble on his face. Clay was unsure whether he was growing a beard or had neglected to shave. He was tan, but his Paul Newman blue eyes had ashen circles around them. Clay guessed that it was the result of drugs. Audrey had told her that Beau consumed anything he could obtain through a secret network at the university.

"Hey . . . where's everybody?"

"Audrey's on a date. Sunny and my father are in D.C. till tomorrow."

"Shit!" Beau opened the refrigerator and took out a Michelob and a platter of fried chicken. He sat down at the table and ate and drank messily in silence.

Clay went back to reading an article about some friends of her father's.

Beau finished the chicken and belched loudly. He tilted his chair back and put his feet on the table.

"So . . . how're things?"

"Okay." Clay continued reading.

"How'd you like to lend me fifty bucks?"

"You have to be kidding. I gave your sister ten, and that cleaned me out." She would never loan money to Beau. Audrey had warned her that he seldom repaid debts.

"Well, er, does Mac keep any cash around the house? You know, for emergencies or somethin'?"

Clay shrugged. "Not that I know of." She looked down at her article, but Beau grabbed it out of her hands and tossed it in the sink.

"Come on. Talk to me! I know you're pissed off that your old man married Sunny. But I haven't done anything wrong."

"I don't have anything against you, Beau." Clay felt uneasy, realizing the two of them were alone. "Look why don't you go over to Buck's? He might have some petty cash you could borrow." She knew Buck would never give Beau money, but at least it would get Beau out of the house.

"Nah, you know he wouldn't fork over anything without authorization. Say, you got any grass?"

"No. I don't smoke."

He fished in the breast pocket of his embroidered denim shirt. "Aha! Eureka." He produced half a joint, lit it, and inhaled deeply, closing his eyes. "Here," he said, still holding the smoke in his lungs; "have a toke."

"No thanks. I told you."

"Come on, try it . . . you might like it."

"I *have* tried it. Lots of times. It doesn't do anything for me."

"This is good stuff. Hawaiian. I promise you'll get off on this."

Clay shook her head. "You finish it."

"Oh, yeah. I forgot. Miss Priss. Daughter of the local royalty."

"Come off it, Beau." Clay put her plate in the sink, retrieved the magazine, and headed for the door.

"Hey! Where're you goin'?"

"To get some stuff together. I have to be up before six."

"It's still early." Beau followed her into the dining room. "Wanna go over to the Road House and have a beer?"

"No, Beau."

"Why don't you come over and see my place? One of the farm hands told me it used to be your playhouse when you were a kid." He laughed. "We could play there tonight."

"Not interested, Beau. I have to be up early to exercise the horses."

Beau grabbed her arm and pulled her toward him. "Well, little stepsister, horseback ridin' is no substitute for a good fuck." Clay tried to move away, but he held her arm tightly. "Audrey can't imagine that any girl your age is still a virgin. But I told her I'd bet you were. And I don't think you wanna be. I think you lie in bed at night and jack off . . . and dream about doin' it with your father."

"Stop it! Get away from me . . . you're disgusting!" She struggled, but although Beau was her height and thin, he was much stronger than Clay.

Her anger gave way to panic. She decided she had better use tact; no one would hear her scream. "Beau . . ."

His thin lips pressed against hers, and his arms locked around her waist. He pressed his pelvis into her, and she could feel his erection. His tongue probed roughly around her mouth.

The phone rang. Clay tried to pull away, but Beau held firm. "It's not important," he whispered. He grabbed her hand and pulled it down over the hard bulge in his jeans. He forced her hand to rub him.

"No, Beau. Listen . . . I have my period. It's not a good time."

Beau cackled. "Since when did that make a difference? Come on," he said coaxingly, "your place or mine?"

Clay backed up and bumped against the mahogany sideboard. She was trapped. Beau unzipped his fly, and his penis sprang out like a jack in the box.

"Here's as good a place as any . . ." He clumsily tugged at the knotted sash around her robe.

Clay summoned all her strength and pushed as hard as she could against him, accidentally knocking a large silver samovar on to the oak floor. It crashed as if a bomb had exploded into the still night.

Beau jerked away, his erection withering back into his jeans. "Jesus! Why did you have to do that?" He stared right through her with his pale-blue eyes. He looked down in horror. "Oh, my God! Look what you've done!"

Clay followed his eyes to the floor. The antique samovar lay there dented. Its alcohol lamp had broken, and the liquid was seeping toward the Chinese carpet. Clay was too frightened to speak.

Beau grabbed her shoulders and shook her. "You're just like all the others. You think you can get away with it. But I saw you . . . I saw you! This time I'm going to report it . . ." He stopped shaking her, but his eyes were wild and frightened.

Clay found her voice and tried to whisper calmly. His fingers still dug hard into her shoulders. "It's all right, Beau. Everything's all right . . ."

"You say that!" Beau snapped. "You say that now. But *I'm* the one . . . I'm the one who takes the rap. Shit! This time I'm gettin' the fuck out. I'm not goin' to stick around and wait for the fuckin' CO. This time it's on your ass." He jerked his head toward the French doors and lowered his voice to an urgent whisper. "Oh, Jesus, fuck . . . they're still after us. We've gotta get the fuck outa here . . ."

Beau vaulted over the dining room table and took off. Clay heard the screen door in the front hall slam shut and her stepbrother shrieking into the night.

Clay was shaking uncontrollably. She ran to the phone to call Buck Smith, but as she dialed, she heard Beau start up his motorcycle and streak down the drive. She put the receiver back in its cradle.

Clay ran up to her bedroom and locked the door. She stayed awake for the rest of the night, trying to figure out what had happened.

"Clay!" Sunny Fitzgerald's voice called out from the library. "Could you come here a minute? I'd like to talk to you." Sunny had been sorting through fabric swatches for the carved cherry-wood Chippendale side chairs.

"Actually, Sunny, I'm in a hurry. I have to pick up the brochures from the printers. Buck has to have them for Saratoga."

"Well, this will only take a couple of minutes."

Clay sighed and pushed the bangs out of her eyes. Robin had talked her into having a professional cut, and although every time Clay looked in the mirror her short hair reminded her of her father's wedding day, she was beginning to adjust to her new look.

"Have a seat, honey."

Clay hated Sunny to call her "honey." "I'll stand. I've been riding all morning."

Sunny settled herself on the sofa. In a navy and white Adolfo suit, she appeared overdressed for a morning at home. "That's the main thing I want to talk to you about. You spend entirely too much time at the stable."

"Sunny," Clay said impatiently, "my summer job is helping out at the office. Where would you like me to work?"

"Don't use that tone of voice with *me,* young lady." She lit a cigarette. "The problem with you is that you've been accustomed to gettin' your own way for too long. Anything you want, your daddy sees that you get it. You're a very spoiled young lady."

"That's a laugh! As if Audrey has been pitifully denied . . ."

"My daughter has nothing to do with this. I'm talkin' about *you*, Clay Fitzgerald. You think you have your father wrapped around your little finger."

"I think nothing of the kind!" Clay's face burned with fury.

Sunny lowered her voice. "We've gotten off on an unpleasant tangent. My point is . . . you've got to start growin' up. You have to realize who you are, what's expected of you."

"And what do *you* expect from me, Sunny?"

"Stop that sarcasm. Immediately!" Sunny crushed out her cigarette. "If you're goin' to live here, you're goin' to have to conform to a few rules. First of all, no more hangin' around with those black stable boys. You have no idea how bad it looks. It's out of place for a girl your age, and who knows what'll happen if it continues."

"I've grown up with Bluejay Cole and Jack and Ronnie . . ."

"Be that as it may. You're no longer a child. Use your brain, for goodness' sake! I don't have to spell it out for you."

"What does my father say about this?" Clay was beginning to pace around the room like a caged animal.

"He agrees with me one hundred percent. He asked me to speak to you." Sunny relaxed back into the sofa.

Clay was upset that her father had not discussed it with her in person.

"As you know, we're leavin' for Saratoga in the mornin'. And I don't want to hear reports when I get back that you've been out ridin' around the countryside with farm hands. D'you understand?"

Clay stared at her stepmother with loathing.

"I asked you . . . is that *understood*, young lady?"

"No! It isn't. If my father agrees with you, he can damned well tell me himself. I don't have to take *any* orders from you."

Sunny controlled her temper. "We'll see about that, Clay. You will not get away with talkin' to me like this."

"And *you* won't get away with trying to tell me what to do. Stick with your own kids. They could use a little motherly supervision."

"Why you little . . ." Sunny started for her.

Before Sunny could slap her stepdaughter, Nonah Hughes appeared in the doorway. "Er, excuse me, Miz Fitzgerald." She handed a piece of paper to Clay. "This is some more things Mr. Buck wants from town."

"Thanks, Nonah." Clay started out the door.

"Clay," Sunny said evenly, "we haven't finished our chat."

"Oh, yes, we have." Clay called back.

Sunny smiled at the large black woman and shrugged. "My goodness, I'd forgotten what a difficult age seventeen is! You may bring me my lunch on the patio, Nonah. Fruit and cottage cheese will be fine. In half an hour." Sunny closed the library door.

Taking out her party book, Sunny began working on the menu for the celebration she and Mac were planning on their return from Saratoga. She was not a woman who allowed an unpleasant scene to disrupt her routine. Neither was she a woman to forget.

She had known even before she married Mac that his daughter would be a problem. Spoiled all these years by that drab nanny and a doting father, Mac had said that Clay would come to love her, but Sunny knew better. There was bad chemistry between them, made worse by the relationship that was foisted upon them.

And it had nothing to do with Clay's being at a difficult age, although Sunny had been far more mature than Clay at seventeen. At seventeen, Sunny was engaged to be married.

What a year that had been . . .

There was a drought, and her family's farm was in the red. It was nip and tuck as to whether Sunny could return to Madeira for her senior year. At the last minute, she had been granted a scholarship. It meant that she had to work in the bookstore during lunch, and some of the snobbier girls, friends in former years, looked down on her with pity. Sunny hated their condescension.

Then a miracle had happened. Scott Yates, the most divine senior at Woodbury Forest, had invited Sunny to Midwinters. Scott was from one of the wealthiest families in New Orleans, and he was fair and handsome, the best-looking boy Sunny had ever laid eyes on. That weekend had been perfect; by the end of it, they were in love. She spent spring vacation in Louisiana, and in spite of both families' initial objections, she returned to school in April with an antique diamond and topaz engagement ring. They were married in the summer, honeymooned in Europe, and arrived back in Louisiana several days before Scott started at Tulane.

Around the time Scott began rushing for fraternities, Sunny discovered she was pregnant. Things changed. Scott stayed out late and came in drunk. The only time he brought his friends around was to be fed, and as Sunny grew huger, she became more resentful and unhappy. But the birth of Beau brought another change. Scott became tender again, and Sunny began making friends of the other married coeds. Their social life became more couple oriented, although Scott still took off on weekend drunks with his fraternity brothers from time to time.

During one of those weekends, Sunny began her affair with Jack Rutherford, an old friend of Scott's. Over the next few months, the relationship became intense. Once again, she was pregnant. Only that time she did not know who the father was. She sent Jack away. She agonized over the next months, but when baby Audrey arrived, there was no problem; she looked exactly like her mother. Sunny never knew whether Audrey's father was Scott or Jack.

After college, Scott and Sunny moved into a small mansion in the Garden District of New Orleans, and Scott went to work for his grandfather's department store. Life was a graceful social whirl, but gradually Scott began drinking more and working less. Around that time, Scott's father, J. K. Yates, took Sunny to lunch and announced that it was *her* fault that his son was becoming shiftless.

He gave her an ultimatum: pull him together or he would cut them both off without a nickel.

Sunny had tried. She canceled most social commitments and monitored Scott's drinking. But Scott sneaked alcohol late at night and often pulled her out of bed to quarrel. Once he hit her over the head with a vase full of roses. She still had a tiny scar on her forehead from that.

One evening, Scott returned home and announced that he had quit the family business and was taking off for Africa. It was something about a deal involving a tanzanite mine. He was gone five months.

Scott had left ninety dollars in the bank account, and his father had refused to help. Somehow Sunny scraped together money from sympathetic friends and, when that ran out, from pawn shops. They survived. But during that awful time, two things emerged as clear facts: she loved her children. They were keeping her sane. And she did not love Scott. He was ruining her life. When he returned from Tanzania, empty-handed, she asked for a divorce. He refused. If she left, he said, it would be without the kids. His family's influence made it more than an idle threat. Scott began drinking before breakfast, and they went through most of Scott's stock portfolio.

One weekend, on the day before their tenth wedding anniversary, Scott took off on a hunting trip with some buddies. Sunny was forced to call off a party she had planned. On the night of her anniversary, as she sat alone with a glass of Jack Daniel's watching Carol Burnett on television, she received a phone call. Scott was dead. He had shot himself. None of his buddies had seen it, but they assumed it was an accident.

For the sake of their only grandchildren, Scott's parents agreed to a reasonable allowance for Sunny on the condition that she remain in New Orleans. Life was much better than it had been. She had the same house, jewels (what was left of them), a car and spending money, and she was without a sullen alcoholic husband who beat her up. She was a glamorous widow and became a renowned hostess. When celebrities passed through, one could be sure to meet them at Sunny's Sunday afternoon soirées.

Audrey and Beau adjusted to life without their father, and Sunny continued her intense interest in them. Audrey was pretty and popular, never a moment's trouble, but Sunny worried about her son. He was a great deal like his father: restless, handsome, and although he ran around with a set of wealthy kids, he was basically a loner. Beau resented having to suck up to his grandfather for money when he needed things. He was one of the elite, he had told Sunny, but was pushed aside because he had no easy access to money. In school, he was brilliant in subjects he liked, science and math, but failed the others. He was an excellent athlete but shunned team sports. He took up long-distance running and won top medals at school meets. Suddenly, he gave up running and switched to riflery. Sunny told herself that he would settle down eventually.

After a while, Sunny became bored. Her suitors were all like Scott. They had the same background, the same lack of curiosity about the world outside of New Orleans society, the same interests: partying, drinking, gossiping. Sunny was no longer attracted to, or intimidated by, the type. They had money but lacked flair.

Sunny took to escaping every once in a while. The first time it happened, Audrey and Beau were touring Europe with their grandparents. Sunny had been spending the evening with friends listening to jazz in the French Quarter. She had made eye contact with the black saxophone player and later got rid of the friends and ended up with the musician. That night and for many others, he took her to sexual heights she had never before allowed herself to fantasize. After him, there had been others—not all musicians, not all black. Sunny had prided herself during these years on the discretion with which she conducted her double life.

Then, one day, it was all over. Sunny's father-in-law, J. K. Yates, it seemed, had been having her followed ever since Scott's death. He had a dossier on Sunny that left her nothing to bargain with. The old man cut Sunny off without a penny and banished her from New Orleans. He also took custody of Beau and Audrey; they were only allowed to visit their mother during school vacations.

Beau became wilder. His grandfather blamed Sunny, but it was clear to her that his grandparents were too old to raise teenagers. Finally, after he graduated from prep school, Beau disappeared. A few weeks later, it was discovered that he had joined the Special Forces and was on his way to Vietnam. At that point, Audrey ran away to Sunny's and refused to return to New Orleans. The real reason, it turned out, was that she was pregnant and the boy refused to marry her. Sunny arranged for an abortion and sent Audrey to St. Timothy's, a boarding school in Maryland. She also finagled J. K. Yates into paying for it.

Sunny gave Atlanta another year or so, but she did not like it. En route to Audrey's graduation, Sunny dropped in on an old school friend, Rosemary Clark, who lived in Charlottesville, Virginia. Rosemary told her that Albemarle County contained some of the wealthiest men in the country. And there were always a few between wives.

Three months later, Sunny moved to Virginia, and in less than a year she had married Mac Fitzgerald. Her troubles were finally over, and she deserved every minute of her happiness. She was not going to let her snippy stepdaughter ruin it.

"Miz Fitzgerald! You want your lunch in there?" Nonah called through the door.

"No, Nonah. I told you. Set it on the patio. I'll be right out."

Sunny sipped tea and listened to the bobwhites calling to one another. Pete's lawn mower hummed in the distance. Mac Fitzgerald wandered through the French doors from the dining room. He snatched a coral rose growing up a trellis on the side of the house.

"A peace offering." He handed her the rose and kissed her. "I ran into Clay . . . I gather you two had words."

"Nothing serious, darlin'. Clay's just experiencin' growin' pains."

"She said you've forbidden her to go riding with the boys."

"Well, I didn't put it that strongly. I merely suggested that she's gettin' too old for it."

Mac threw up his hands. "Well, I'm staying out of it. I told you, it doesn't seem so terrible to me. But being a woman, I suppose you're a little more in tune with that kind of thing."

Sunny handed Mac a strawberry. "Let's not talk about Clay now. What about Saratoga? I've packed everything you laid out. And five ball gowns for me. Do you think I'll need more?"

"You are going to be the most beautiful woman in Saratoga. I can't wait to show you off."

"Mac, let's go upstairs. I feel like bein' alone with you." Her blue eyes closed in a sultry glance.

Mac hugged her. Sunny was the most exciting woman he had ever known. There seemed to be no limit to her ability to please him. "We have to make it a quickie. I promised Clay I'd go ridin' with her a little later."

Sunny smiled. She was not yet certain, but she suspected that she would soon provide an antidote for Mac's obsessive devotion to his daughter.

Chapter 15

THE Willows Stud did well at the 1971 yearling sales in Saratoga, New York. The Graustark colt brought in $600,-000, and the Nashua offspring closed in at half a million. The fourteen other yearlings averaged fifty thousand each. Mac Fitzgerald told everyone modestly that Sunny was responsible for his good luck.

The Saturday after their return, Mac and Sunny threw a celebration party for five hundred friends and business associates. Mac had taken on two silent partners some years before when he had decided to expand the business he had inherited from his father, and he had recently brought in several additional investors. The horse-breeding business was precarious, with bad years to offset the good and a large travel and entertainment expense. That was apart from the upkeep of The Willows: the cattle and grain farm, horse stables, main house, and outbuildings. Mac Fitzgerald had always been a generous spender.

Sunny shimmered around the newly redecorated living room in a black-sequined Bill Blass. The amethyst choker around her neck was a gift from Mac.

"Oh, Sunny," Rosemary Clark said, "I'm wild about what you've done with this room."

"You like it? I'm so pleased."

Clay, of course, resented what Sunny had done to the first-floor rooms. Not only had walls been repapered and furniture recovered, but her mother's antiques were switched around to make way for new antiques. It annoyed Clay not to have objects where she expected to find them. The rare 1832 Mitchell clock at the head of the stairway, for example, had been moved to the library. The original whale-oil prism lamps in the dining room were now on the Queen Anne table, formerly of the living room, now in the hall. Sunny had even had the audacity to replace the house's original wallpaper in the parlor.

Robin Randolph found Clay in the crowd. "Jeans? I thought you were going to dress up."

"I did. I bought this blouse for the occasion." It was green and blue flowered chiffon.

Robin lowered her voice. "I had my first real conversation with Beau. Just now. God, he's so good-looking, and—aloof. Actually, I guess it wasn't much of a conversation. I talked while he drank. I'm goin' to try again." Robin fluffed up her dark curly hair in the mirror and dashed off.

Clay had not seen Beau alone since that strange night. He had never made any reference to it, and she had avoided the subject as well. She wandered into the dining room. The servants under Nonah's charge were setting up the buffet supper: smoked turkeys and hams cured at The Willows smokehouse, rabbit fricassee, New Orleans crab cakes, spoon bread, corn pudding, creole squash, beaten biscuits, and a dozen other dishes.

"Nonah, have you seen daddy?"

"He was out on the terrace dancin' with Miz Jefferson a while ago."

"Thanks, Nonah. I can't find anybody in the dark." The house lights had been extinguished in favor of twenty dozen candles, a romantic whimsy of Sunny's.

"Oh, *there* you are!" Audrey said, slinking up in a long white jersey, slit to midthigh. The dress exposed her entire back, scarcely concealing the cleft between her buttocks. "I've been lookin' all over for you."

"And now you've found me." Over the summer, Clay had concluded that a little of Audrey went a long way. Audrey was selfish; she used people.

"Hmmm, you look sweet tonight. I like your blouse. But honestly, I don't know what you've got against good clothes. If Mac were my real daddy, I'd make sure I was the best-dressed girl in the state."

"Well, you don't seem to be doing badly for yourself."

"Oh, everybody's seen this at least a dozen times."

"With that figure, who could remember the dress?" George Randolph came up and put his arm around Audrey. She pulled away. Clay had been miffed over George's obvious crush on her stepsister, but now she was beginning to feel a little sorry for him. Audrey had obviously used George to meet more boys, and now Audrey made it evident that she had no more need of him.

"Oh, George, you scat now. I have to talk to Clay in private."

"Okay, but you owe me a dance. You too, Clay," he added politely.

"In a few minutes, sugar. I'll find you." When George was out of earshot, Audrey said, "He won't leave me alone. I don't know what I'm goin' to do. Anyway, come with me." She directed Clay into the crimson-and-black living room.

"Don't you have a date for tonight?" Audrey asked.

"Of course . . . he's up in my bedroom waiting for me."

Audrey laughed. "Oh, Clay, you have the best sense of humor. Oops, just a minute." She grabbed two glasses of Fish House punch from one of the circulating waiters and handed one to Clay. "I know you don't drink much, but you will when you hear this!"

"What?"

Audrey pointed to the center of the room. "Take a look at mother."

Sunny and Mac were standing together, his arm around her, chatting animatedly with friends. Sunny glowed, and Mac kept giving her adoring glances.

"So?" Clay said. "What's new about that?"

"When she turns to the side, check out her belly."

"What?"

"See . . . Mother's gettin' a little thick around the waist? And since she always watches her weight, it could only mean one thing."

Clay was stunned. "But . . . no! Sunny's too *old* to have a baby. It isn't possible."

"Thirty-nine's *not* too old, silly. It's perfectly possible."

"I don't believe it! Did she tell you?"

"Of course not. I'm only guessing. But it sure looks like it to me."

Clay sipped the drink. The rum burned her tongue, but the fruit juices left a pleasant aftertaste. "A baby . . . at their age? Oh, God . . . I refuse to believe it."

Audrey shrugged. "Well, it may not be. Just a hunch. Oh, there's Jeffrey. My date. See you later."

Clay downed her punch and took another while she stood there watching her father and Sunny. It had never occurred to her that there could be a baby. Clay had never bothered to consider Sunny's age; she had assumed she was in her forties like her father. But it was certainly possible to reproduce at thirty-nine; even Robin Randolph's mother had done that.

If there was a baby, Clay realized that she would no longer be her father's only child. The thought sent chills through her. She began to feel dizzy, in part from the strong punch, so she walked shakily to the garden.

"Hey, Clay. Want to dance?" George Randolph came over.

"No, thanks. Now now. I don't feel well. I think I'll take a ride on Cartoon."

"Want me to come with you?"

"No, thanks, George. I want to be alone for a while. I'll see you later."

The moonlight ride through the hot, dewy evening eased the throbbing in Clay's brain. She rode Cartoon all out for four miles or so, then slowed the horse to a canter and later to a walk so that she could begin to think clearly.

It was time to call a truce with the devil on her shoulder. Time to face facts. Mac was in love with Sunny, and now, if there was a baby, Sunny's lifetime reign at The Willows would be assured. As for Audrey and Beau, they would be going their own way soon enough; for that matter, so would she. She was already planning to live with Nell in the fall, to be closer to the university.

Clay knew her father loved her and would go on loving her no matter how many other children he fathered. But it was still difficult to accept that he was not hers alone anymore. And Sunny was right about one thing: she had been acting like a brat. It was time to grow up.

She leaned over and kissed Cartoon's neck. Mac had given her the filly for her twelfth birthday, and Clay had broken and trained the horse herself. "Good girl. It's you and me, baby. I'll fix you a nice treat when we get back to the stable. Would you like that?"

As Clay rode into the stable courtyard, she listened to the din of music and laughter, still going strong. She could make out the silhouettes of couples dancing in the glow of the Japanese lanterns strung around the gardens. It was not a bad party; maybe she would dance with George, after all.

Then she heard other noises coming from the barn. Thuds, and grunts . . . and a scream. She jumped off Cartoon, hastily tied her to the nearest post, and ran the few yards to the ivy-covered barn.

As her eyes became accustomed to the dim light, Clay recognized the familiar figure of Bluejay Cole, the exercise boy. There was a deep cut above his eye, bleeding down his cheek. He was gasping for breath, backed up against a bale of hay. Clay could not see anyone else.

"Bluejay! Are you all right? What happened?"

He did not react to her. He was breathing heavily.

A loud screech pierced from the hayloft above. Clay looked up and made out a figure looming above them in the shadows.

"I've got you now, you geek," the man shouted. "You're not gettin' the fuck away this time." He hurled himself down from the loft, landing on the stunned black boy.

"Beau!" Clay yelled. She tried to pull him off Bluejay, but her stepbrother, reeking of bourbon, knocked her halfway across the room with the butt of his elbow. Clay doubled over from the pain in her side. She tried to stand, but her knees buckled under her. She watched with horror as Beau raised himself off of Bluejay. The young black remained motionless, but she saw his lips move. She moved closer to hear better.

"Please, Mr. Beau," Bluejay whispered. "I'm not—"

Beau grabbed Bluejay as if he were a weightlifter and raised him high above his shoulders. Then, with a terrible grunt, he hurled the slight black boy into the shadows.

Bluejay crashed into the fender of a tractor and let out an excruciating cry. There was a sickening crunch as Bluejay's bloody body crumpled to the floor. A trickle of blood spurted from his mouth.

Clay remained stationary, frozen with terror.

Beau leaned against a bale of hay, breathing heavily. "Think . . . think . . . think . . ." he chanted in gulps. Then, suddenly, he became aware of Clay. He whirled around and stared at her. "Clay . . ." he said slowly. "Why are you lookin' at me like that?"

She ran as fast as she could. A voice that did not seem connected to her let loose a barrage of screams. She felt as detached from the voice as she did from the legs that were carrying her to the main house.

Other faces rushed toward her.

"What happened?"

"Quick! Get Mac . . ."

"I'm here. Clay! Calm down. What's wrong?" Mac Fitzgerald grabbed her and held her tight. "Try to tell me . . ."

"The barn," she said raspily. Her throat hurt from the screaming. "Bluejay . . ."

Mac and a dozen or so others raced for the stable. Clay trailed after them. The other party goers who had heard the ruckus remained at the edge of the garden in silence.

As they reached the barn, Beau Yates met them. "Get a doctor! He's hurt bad."

Dr. Long, one of the guests, rushed into the barn. "Somebody go back to the house and get my bag," he called back.

"Mac . . . I'm sorry . . . I didn't mean to hit him so hard." Beau seemed sober and lucid.

"What happened?" Mac asked.

"Well . . . I don't know exactly. I walked down here to get away from the party for a while. I'd been drinkin' a lot of that punch, and I had a headache."

"Go on," Max coaxed gently.

"I became aware of voices comin' from the barn. I went to check, and there was Clay . . . and Bluejay. Bluejay was tryin' to kiss her . . . and she was strugglin'. When I ordered him to stop, Bluejay came after me. We fought . . . then I knocked him against the tractor. He must've hit his head or somethin' . . . he fell down unconscious . . ."

Clay came up. "No! That's not what happened at all! I went for a ride, and when I came back, Beau was beating Bluejay up. He kept hitting Bluejay even after he was hurt and bleeding!"

"Oh, come on, Clay," Beau said. "You can at least be grateful to me for protectin' your honor."

"What do you mean? I wasn't in the barn with . . ."

Dr. Long came back outside. "We'd better call the county coroner. The boy's dead. Fractured skull . . . subarachnoid hemorrhage."

When Clay woke up twelve hours later, Nell Smith was sitting by her bed. She had closed the curtains to the midmorning sun, and the room was quiet except for the hum of a small table fan.

"Ohhh." Clay tried to sit, but her ribs hurt, and there was a sharp pain in her head.

"Take it easy, honey. You'll be all right."

"What . . ." And then she remembered the events of the night before. "Bluejay . . . Bluejay is dead! It's not true . . . please tell me it's not!" Clay started to cry.

Nell held her. "I know . . . I know. It's awful. Here . . . Dr. Long gave me some tranquillizers for when you came to."

"No. No, I don't want anything. Where's daddy?"

"At his lawyer's. He'll be back soon."

"How long have you been here?"

Nell smiled. "Since about midnight when your father called me. I slept over there on the chaise."

"Oh, Nell . . ." Clay hugged her and started crying again.

"What happened, Clay? Do you feel up to talking about it?"

Clay nodded. "I guess." She described the fight and afterward. "Beau lied. He said he was protecting me . . . that Bluejay and I . . . Oh, Nell, you know Bluejay. We grew up together. He would never . . . and now he's dead."

"I know . . . I know. Maybe you should take a pill and try to get some more sleep . . ."

There was a soft rap on the door, and Mac Fitzgerald entered. He was unshaven, and he looked as if he had not slept. He came over and hugged and kissed Clay. "How do you feel, baby?"

"Terrible."

"Nell, I'd like to talk to Clay alone for a few minutes."

"Of course. I'll go have Nonah fix a tray of something."

Mac looked at his daughter tenderly. "Do you feel up to talking, or should I wait till later?"

Clay shrugged. "I guess I can talk as well now as later. This is all so unreal."

"I've spent the morning with Jack Russell trying to figure out the quietest way to handle this situation."

"Where's Beau? Where is he?"

"State cops have him in Culpeper. He took off last night just after you fainted. When the cops caught him, he was doing a hundred and ten. He told them that he had been forced to kill a black man in self-defense . . ."

"But daddy, that's *not* the way it happened!"

Mac sighed. "I believe you, baby. But George Randolph saw you going down to the stable, and Audrey says she saw Bluejay following you."

"Audrey! She was off somewhere with her date. She's trying to cover for Beau because she's his sister. How could anybody believe her?"

"Now, now. Try to calm down. I'm only giving you a play-by-play description of what's been going on around here since midnight."

"Daddy, you *do* believe me, don't you?"

Mac paused. "Of course, I do. Now I'll be back later. You try to eat something. Then take some of those tranquillizers the doctor left. Tomorrow, when you're feeling a little stronger, Jack would like to come by and talk to you. I've hired him to defend Beau. He's charged with manslaughter."

"Defend Beau? But . . ."

"Now, honey, Beau is family now. He's Sunny's only son, and she's very upset . . ."

Suddenly, Clay saw very clearly what was going to happen. Sunny would obviously believe her son's story instead of Clay's. And Sunny had accused Clay of spending too much time with the stable boys. She would try to convince Mac that Clay was lying.

"Daddy, I'm telling the truth. Beau was beating up Bluejay when I came in from my ride . . ."

"Sure, honey." Then a puzzled look came over Mac Fitzgerald's face. "Why were you out riding in the middle of our party?"

"Because"— She did not want to repeat Audrey's speculation that Sunny was having a baby—"I wasn't in a party mood. Oh, daddy, *please* believe me."

"I do, baby. Now you get some rest. I'll check back in later."

Sunny Fitzgerald wore no makeup, and when she smiled, which she was trying to do, claws of fine lines imprinted themselves on the skin beneath her eyes. She was propped up in bed sipping a cup of herb tea.

"Come sit by the bed, Clay. I have somethin' important to discuss with you. First of all, your father tells me that you're stickin' to your story, that you walked in as Beau was beatin' up that black boy."

"It's *not* a story. It's the truth!"

"Well, your father wants to believe you . . ." Sunny trailed off. They sat in silence for a few moments.

"Beau is my son," she continued. "I love him as much as your father loves you. And I happen to believe what he says. But if you stick to your story, there'll be a full-scale trial. Beau won't be able to get a suspended sentence for self-defense. He'll be tried as a deliberate murderer."

"He can plead temporary insanity. He *is* crazy, you know."

"He is not!" Sunny yelled, then lowered her voice. "The

coroner's inquest and preliminary hearing's on Friday. And I'm willin' to make a deal with you, Clay."

"A deal? What do you mean?"

"I mean I want you to change your story . . . go along with Beau's. That way, the whole sordid mess will be over with. Your father's lawyers can get a speedy hearin', with a . . . discreet judge. It can be kept quiet, without a sensational trial and all that publicity." She stared hard at Clay. "Surely you don't want to have to get on the stand and talk about your friendship with Bluejay and what happened . . ."

"What *about* my friendship with Bluejay?" Clay demanded, outraged. "I have nothing to hide. I won't dishonor his memory and lie to protect Beau."

"If not Beau, think about your father. Think what all this could do to him."

Clay hesitated a moment. "It's still perjury," she said. "Perjury is a crime, you know. If anyone found out, I'd be sent to jail. Or is that what you have in mind. Framing *me* for your son's crime?"

"Perjury is a crime only if someone accuses you of lyin'. If you corroborate Beau's story, it will be an open and shut case."

"Beau killed Bluejay. That's the open and shut case!"

Sunny leaned back and closed her eyes. She sighed. "Clay, there's somethin' I have to tell you . . . and it cannot leave this room. About your father."

Lines of concern creased Clay's brow. "What?"

"He made me promise not to tell anyone, especially you. But in light of all this, I feel I must." She paused.

"What about my father?"

"When we were in Saratoga, he started havin' chest pains. On the way home, we stopped off in Manhattan, and Mac saw a specialist at Columbia Presbyterian. It turns out he has somethin' called idiopathic myocardiopathy—some sort of heart abnormality. He's seein' a doctor here at the University Hospital, and he has some pills to take, but—"

"How serious is it?" Clay asked, frightened. "I mean, could he die?"

Sunny nodded. "Well, it's not a certainty. He could live to a ripe old age if . . . Actually, there're two big ifs. One, he takes it easy and rests a lot. You know how hard it is to get your father to sit down for five minutes. And . . ."

Clay leaned forward. "And what?"

"If nothin' drastic happens to upset him. Of course, with what's happened already he's upset. But if the whole thing drags on—a trial, publicity—the emotional trauma could kill him."

Clay shook her head slowly. "Daddy? I can't believe it. He's always been so healthy." But she thought about how haggard he had looked that morning.

"So you see, Clay, if you insist on stickin' to your story and testifyin' against Beau, it could literally *kill* your father. If you don't believe me, I'll give you the name of the heart specialist in town. You can talk to him."

Clay could not think. Bluejay, her childhood friend, a boy whom everyone had liked, was dead. Now her father had heart disease—he could die. She felt so alone, so scared.

"I know this is a shock. But I thought you should know the truth." Sunny lit a cigarette and then said, almost casually: "There's somethin' else I think you should know. I'm pregnant."

"I thought so."

"You did? That's very perceptive of you. Well, your father's delirious with happiness. For a man his age, with his only child nearly grown, havin' a new baby, a new family, is like gettin' a new lease on life."

"I'm sure my father is very happy," Clay managed to say. "He and my mother wanted another child after me, but she had a miscarriage."

"That's why your father is doubly concerned about this pregnancy," Sunny said softly. "After Audrey, I had two miscarriages. Mac wants me to be very careful this time. I'm thirty-nine. The older you are, the more dangerous it becomes. And now this . . . the ordeal of Beau goin' through a scandalous murder trial. Well, I don't know what might happen."

"What do you mean, Sunny?"

"If you testify against Beau, I could have a miscarriage. In fact, I can almost guarantee it."

"Oh, my God, Sunny, you wouldn't—"

Sunny stubbed her cigarette out in the ashtray by the bed and looked coolly at Clay. "And if I were to lose this baby and *you* were responsible, your father would never forgive you. If he lived through the shock."

Chapter 16

IF you took into account the wind-chill factor from the gusts blowing inland from the Hudson River, it was ten below zero, the kind of bitter, blustery cold day that Clay Fitzgerald had never adjusted to even after two and a half years at Bard College in upstate New York. Despite the weather, she preferred being there to Virginia. In New York, at least occasionally, she could block out the painful memories of the past.

Out of concern for her father's health, Clay had made a deal with Sunny. She agreed to corroborate part of Beau's story. Sunny, in turn, pledged to send Beau to live in California and undergo psychiatric treatment there.

At the hearing, Clay had testified that she had been in the barn, merely discussing horses with Bluejay. Beau Yates had walked in, "misinterpreted" what was going on, and freaked out because he was drunk. Mac's lawyer cited the fact that Beau suffered from an increasingly common aftereffect of Vietnam, a condition termed post-traumatic stress disorder. Beau was "an action junkie" who experienced headaches and mental flashbacks rooted in Vietnam combat. During these episodes, he was unable to control his actions. The judge had given him a two-year suspended sentence, with mandatory psychiatric treatment.

Afterward, the strain of the emotional tension on Clay had sent her into a severe depression and made her physically ill. She and Mac had decided that she needed to get away. So instead of the University of Virginia, she enrolled at Bard, one of the other colleges where she had been accepted.

She returned to Virginia as seldom as possible.

ring to spend vacations in Connecticut with her best friend
and roommate, a black girl named Garnet Turner. When
she did visit The Willows, she was never able to spend
much time alone with her father. Sunny seemed to go out
of her way to keep him occupied. Their young son,
Kenyon McCracken Fitzgerald V was a sweet child. In
spite of her predisposition to resent his existence, Clay was
fond of Kenny and enjoyed playing with him. Mac, to
make up for the little time he spent with Clay at The Willows, came to New York City twice a year, and they spent
a week together at the Pierre, going to Broadway shows
and haunting art galleries that specialized in equestrian
paintings. Sunny never accompanied Mac on these trips,
and Clay cherished them. Her father was due to visit
again next month, and she looked forward to it.

Clay pulled her scarf up over her nose to shield it from
the wind and trudged through the snow to her English
literature class.

"Clay! Clay! I've been looking all over for you!" Garnet
Turner ran up, breathless. "Call home right away. Your
father's had a heart attack!"

Because of the rush, Clay had to take a limousine to La-
Guardia, the shuttle to Washington, and a Piedmont to
Charlottesville. When she finally arrived, in the midst of a
snowstorm, Nell and Buck Smith were waiting at the airport to rush her to the University of Virginia Hospital
where her father lay in intensive care, in critical condition.

Clay hugged both her old friends. "How is he?"

Tears welled up in Nell's eyes, and she shook her head.

Buck spoke up. "Not good, honey. He's hangin' on . . .
but just barely."

"What do the doctors say?"

"Well . . ." Nell blinked away the tears and took a
deep breath. "There's always hope for a miracle."

"You mean . . ."

"The doctor doesn't give him much of a chance," Buck
said solemnly.

When Clay arrived at the hospital, Sunny was there, looking thin and pale. Audrey, Nonah and Pete, and several of the farm managers were there, too. They exchanged somber greetings with Clay and waited in silence for the doctor who was in with Mac.

The door opened, and the strong-jawed, white-haired doctor appeared.

"How is he?" came a chorus of concerned friends and family.

"Very weak . . . but conscious. He's asked to see his daughter . . ."

Clay stood. Her round gray eyes were shrouded with concern.

"Only a minute or two. He hasn't much strength."

Mac Fitzgerald was surrounded by machines and tubes and wires. His eyes were closed, and his face appeared colorless and sunken and old. Clay took his hand. It felt cold.

"Daddy," she whispered hoarsely. "It's me . . . Clay."

Mac Fitzgerald opened his eyes and stared at her, without recognition.

"Daddy! I love you. It's . . . me."

There was a flicker of acknowledgment. The eyes closed, then opened again.

"Clay . . ." Mac's voice was so weak that she had to put her ear to his lips. "You got here . . ."

"Yes, daddy. I love you so much. You're going to be all right," she said, trying to convince herself.

"I'm . . . sorry for what I did to you . . ."

"What, daddy? No, don't try to talk. Just rest now."

"Beau . . . I know you were right. I didn't have . . ." Mac trailed off. He flinched with pain. "I love you . . ." His eyes closed.

"Daddy!" Clay ran to get the doctor.

Clay stayed in town with Nell so they could comfort each other. After the funeral, she drove to The Willows to see Kenny and ride her horse, Cartoon. With her father gone, The Willows was merely a farm, a house, Sunny's house. Clay's stepmother was surrounded by sympathetic friends.

"Poor Sunny," they said, "widowed twice. How terrible." These same friends bestowed condolences on Clay, too, but nothing anybody said or did could dispel the pain of her father's death.

The will was read. Mac had remembered many people, including Nell and Buck Smith, Nonah and Pete, and Bluejay's mother. The bulk of his estate, The Willows, and the bloodstock business and cattle farm was to be divided equally between his two children and Sunny.

The next day, Clay made an appointment to see Jack Russell, her father's lawyer and executor of the estate.

"Jack, I don't want any part of The Willows. I'd just as soon sell off my share of the estate and stud business to Sunny. She can do whatever the hell she wants with it."

"Hold on a minute, Clay. You're still upset. The best advice I can give you is to wait a while before you attempt to make any major life decisions." He riffled through a stack of papers on his Jeffersonian desk. "Actually, you don't have any choice. You'd have to wait a year, until you're twenty-one, before you could legally sell it."

Russell sat back in his swivel chair and puffed on his pipe. He took off his glasses and contemplated Clay with fatherly concern. "There's something else. Your father had been overextending himself over the past few years. Everything is tied up in horses and property. And I happen to know Sunny doesn't have any money of her own. Even owning a third of The Willows, she couldn't generate enough cash to buy you out."

"You mean my share of The Willows is worthless?" Clay said, startled.

"No, I'm not exactly saying that. It's worth a great deal. On paper and probably in tangible assets in a few years' time. Buck will continue managing the business, and in a matter of time it should be solidly in the black again. The last few years, Clay, your father spent a lot of money."

On Sunny, Clay speculated. "So except for the stocks my mother left me, I'm basically land poor."

Jack laughed. "You do have a flair for the dramatic, Clay. In a few years, you'll be sittin' pretty."

"What if The Willows were sold?"

"Well, you own a third, and Sunny controls two-thirds since she's Kenny's guardian until he comes of age. You'd have to get Sunny to agree to sell The Willows. I happen to know that she would never go along with that."

Jack Russell had been right. Sunny laughed down Clay's idea as preposterous. The Willows was her life now, and she would never relinquish it. She would be willing, however, to buy Clay's third of the estate if she could raise the money over the next year.

Clay said she would consider it but would not commit herself. Faced with the actuality of letting Sunny have complete control of The Willows, Clay backed off some. Clay made the decision, however, to sever her tangible ties with The Willows. She packed up her clothes, books, pictures, and other memorabilia and stored them in the attic of the house Nell had recently bought with the profits from her crafts' business.

Clay spent one last night there in her childhood bed, and the next morning played with Kenny, who was not quite two. She saddled up Cartoon and took a final ride around the snow-covered pastures, rolling hills, and woodlands. The familiar Blue Ridge Mountains nestled imposingly in the west. After she had covered every acre of the property, Clay cantered over to the Randolphs' adjoining estate, crying all the way. She gave the horse to Robin, and the two of them reminisced for the rest of the afternoon. After that, Clay was ready to leave Virginia.

By that time, Bard College had let out for midwinter field period. Her friend Garnet had settled herself in Key West, Florida, for six weeks to work as a research assistant for a writer who was an old friend of her mother's.

Clay had planned to spend her field period working on her thesis, a photographic essay on Opus 40, a six-and-a-half-acre environmental sculpture near Woodstock by a former Bard professor. But after the ordeal of her father's death, Clay was not sure she could face the bleakness of winter in New York. She telephoned her friend and told her to put out a sleeping bag; she was on her way to Florida.

Clay said good-by to everyone except her stepmother.

Chapter 17

THE poster on the wall of Garnet Turner's studio room in Old Town bore the words "Key West: the Last Resort." Garnet herself wore, over her well-shaped breasts, a yellow T-shirt with the slogan "Key Wasted." Garnet pushed Clay's two suitcases through the door with her bare foot.

"Well, this is it. Home."

"Very nice. Where's the rest of it?"

"Well, Miz Clay, we done had ta sell da big house and shoot da servants. We is po' now."

Clay headed for the tiny refrigerator. "No beer after that drive? It's only a hundred and fifty miles from Miami. How come it took four and a half hours?"

"Just lucky, I guess. It's usually five or six. All those bridges where you can't pass anybody. Anyway, my friend Tom is bringing some beer and stuff. He's dying to meet you.

"What have you told him?"

"That you're a nymphomaniac."

"Oh, nice."

"No, that you're a really fantastic photographer. He's into underwater photography. The coral reef is full of some dynamite fish. You're going to flip out when you see it."

"I'm wiped out. I want to lie on the beach and do nothing for at least a week."

"Didn't anybody tell you? There are no beaches in the Keys. At least not honest-to-gosh ones. Just man-made stretches of powdered marl and a few handfuls of sand. You also have to be real careful when you swim because

159

of the coral. If you cut yourself on fire coral, you can get a hideous rash."

"Wow, what a swell vacation spot."

"You'll get used to it. This island grows on you. Anyway, you must be dying in those clothes. Time to change seasons." The beautiful leggy black girl pointed to a door. "I cleared a space for you in the closet."

"Is that where I'll be sleeping?" Clay looked around quizzically.

"Sleeping bag and screened sleeping porch are off the kitchen."

"You call that a kitchen?" Clay gave her friend a big hug. "God, it's good to be here. I really appreciate your taking me in. I couldn't face going north."

"I'm glad you're here, too. I was getting lonely. Anyway, you'll like it. A total change of scene is exactly what you need."

There was a knock, and the door opened. A tall young man with shoulder-length black hair pulled back into a pony tail tripped over a suitcase and lurched into the room. "Delivery's here," he said, laughing.

"Clay," Garnet said, "this rather clumsy person is Tom Schultz. He came here from the University of Colorado last year for spring vacation. As you can see, he decided to stay on."

Tom nodded to Clay. "I got hooked up with a group of treasure salvors working out of here. I dive for them and take pictures . . ."

"You mean diving for buried treasure—those old Spanish galleons?" Clay ripped into a bag of potato chips and opened a Budweiser.

Tom nodded. "Yeah, do you know about them?" Clay shrugged, so Tom continued. "A fleet of Spanish ships left Cuba in 1622 loaded with treasure and headed north on the Gulf Stream. They ran into a hurricane off the Keys that totally demolished twenty-eight ships and killed hundreds of people. Most of the gold and stuff is still down there waiting to be scooped up. And lots of other ships have gone down in these waters."

"I've read about that man Mel Fisher. The one who found a lot of Spanish coins . . ."

"Tons of other stuff, too. His group is called Treasure Salvors Incorporated. He's been at it full time since the early Sixties, and finally he found one of the 1622 ships, the *Nuestra Señora de Atocha*." Tom talked with intensity. "They dug up records of the shipwreck of the *Atocha* in some archives in Seville. That's how Fisher finally proved the ship he was salvaging was the *Atocha*. The records contained a detailed list of the ship's contents, including a lot of silver bars, each one numbered and its exact weight recorded."

Garnet sighed.

Tom opened a beer and sat crosslegged on the floor. "Am I boring you?"

"Yes," Garnet said. "I've heard all this before."

"No!" Clay insisted. "I'm fascinated."

"Well, it was really incredible. Fisher *found* some silver bars, and last July, with all these people and press and everything, he had a weighing ceremony. This one silver bar, number four thousand and something according to the records, was supposed to weigh sixty-three pounds and six ounces. Fisher set the scale for that exactly. Then he put the silver bar on it, and the needle bobbed and quivered. Then it leveled off. That was his proof that the silver was actually from the *Atocha!*"

"That's really incredible," Clay said.

Garnet nodded. "From what I hear, it was the big event around here last summer."

"Do you dive for Mel Fisher?" Clay asked Tom.

"Nah, he's all set up. I freelance, but mostly I work for a guy named Will Stone. He's a real character. He owned a dive shop in New Jersey, renting scuba equipment and stuff. He used to come down to the Keys on vacation and dive for old ships. Then he found a Spanish galleon and came up with some muskets and a really rare astrolab and a couple of gold coins. So he sold everything, bought a salvage boat and a houseboat, and moved here to salvage full time."

"What a life," Garnet said. "I can't believe I only have a month left before I head back to school."

"You, too?" Tom asked Clay. "Or are you gonna stick around for a while?"

Clay shrugged. "I have to go back to school, too. Although at this moment I can't think of one good reason why."

Clay's focus had always been horses. She had spent very little time at the seashore; an occasional weekend at Virginia Beach and Nags Head, North Carolina, were the extent of it. Now that she was in Key West, she was determined to enjoy it. The town was pleasant; the weather was clear and hot. She spent her first week checking out the beaches: Smathers, Memorial, and a couple of smaller ones. Each attracted its regulars, and invisible dividing lines marked out sections for hippies, gays, couples, college kids, and families. The spot with the best sand on the island, and her favorite, was the private beach at the Sands Restaurant. Tom had shown her the little lane off Vernon where locals parked their bikes so they could wander on to the beach for free.

There was a sailing center nearby, and Clay often rented snorkeling equipment, a pair of fins, mask, and snorkel. She loved the slow-paced life, looking for shells and swimming under the transparent blue-green water in the psychedelic world of the coral reef. The only drawback was her nearsightedness; everything was a beautiful blur since it was impossible to wear her glasses under her face mask. Even so, the reef was such a riot of color and activity that she began experimenting with underwater photography by covering her Nikon with a waterproof plastic bag.

"I don't see why you don't get contact lenses," Garnet said. They were eating conch fritters and hot bollos, deep-fried fritters of garlic and chick peas, that Garnet had brought home from Daniello's Bollo Stand.

"I had a pair once, but they really bothered my eyes. I stopped using them."

"Hard lenses, right? Just about anybody can wear the soft ones."

"I doubt if I could."

"Clay Fitzgerald, you're a dope! You hide behind those glasses. You check out the world and stay removed from it all. I mean, with contacts, not only would you be able to see, you'd be *seen*. You'd look gorgeous. Or are you afraid boys will start making passes . . ."

"Who's making passes?" Tom Schultz entered without knocking. "Listen, I have Wednesday off, Clay. Wanna go diving with me? A friend of mine has a Hobie Cat we can borrow. We can sail over to Man Key and some other islands. I'll even let you use my camera. You're gonna ruin yours if you don't shell out and get a good waterproof housing."

"Thanks, Tom. I took a course in scuba diving last year, at the 'Y' near school."

"Great. I promise you'll love it better in the ocean than a swimming pool. Wanna come, Garnet?"

The black girl shook her head. "Can't. Wednesday I have to drive up to Marathon Key and get some books for my boss. And pick up his TV from the repair shop. And go grocery shopping, then take his clothes to the Margaret Truman Launderette and . . ."

Clay laughed sympathetically. "All this comes under the jurisdiction of researcher? Why can't the guy run his own errands?"

"Because the *New York Review of Books* says he's a creative genius." Garnet flashed her big mahogany eyes. "And we all know that creative geniuses cannot be bothered by such mundane things as mayonnaise and matched socks."

Garnet Turner had been trying since their freshman year at Bard to make over Clay. Finally, in Key West, because she needed summer clothes and she wanted to be able to see under water, Clay relented. She bought soft contact lenses, several new bikinis, shorts, and T-shirts that showed off her small but perfectly shaped breasts. Garnet made her invest in waterproof eye makeup, too.

Clay had to admit that the image staring back at her in the ophthalmologist's mirror was changed almost beyond recognition. Glasses had flattened out her soft gray eyes and high cheekbones. Without them, her features were as striking as a model's, set off by her healthy five feet nine frame. Garnet was nearly as tall, and when they walked down the street together, even the gays turned around to look at their black and white beauty. Clay loved being able to see without glasses, but she felt awkward and conspicuous when people looked back.

On Wednesday, when he picked her up, Tom smiled approvingly but said nothing. Clay was grateful to him for not making a big deal out of her new appearance.

The tropical sky was cloudless, and the breeze was perfect for sailing. Tom handled the sailfish with expertise, and Clay relaxed as Tom described what they could expect to see that day, the vivid palette in the underground oasis of the coral reef that ran parallel to the Keys, from south of Miami to the Dry Tortugas, seventy miles west of Key West. First there was the coral itself: the hard limestone-like elkhorn, staghorn, fire, and finger coral and the soft coral sea fans and whips and feathers that fluttered lazily in the currents.

"You know," Tom said, "there're about twenty-five hundred species of coral. They can only live in tropical water where the temperature's above seventy-two degrees Fahrenheit."

"Ah, but what degree Celsius? Tell me that." Clay smiled and put on an extra shirt of Tom's to keep her shoulders from burning.

"Fuck Celsius. I'm teaching you marine biology, not conversion math." He grinned.

"I'd never seen coral before I came here," she said, "except on bric-a-brac shelves."

"Yeah, you know, it's against the law here to take coral from the reef. People take home souvenirs, and they damage the coral. Every year, the reef's being pushed closer to extinction. They say only ten percent of the reef's healthy now. And it takes generations for a coral head to grow or a damaged one to heal." Tom steered the boat toward an island in the distance. "Did you know that thousands of tiny animals live in coral? They come out at night to feed. Tiny plants live inside too. They feed on the waste products from the animals."

"Nature does it again!" Clay handed Tom a piece of the mango she was slicing with her Swiss army knife. "I feel as if I'm doing the ocean with Jacques Cousteau."

Tom laughed. "Ah, yez, *ma chère*. Just you and *moi* romping through ze fields of elkhorn coral, ze meadows of sea fans." He pointed toward the horizon. "Okay, land ahoy. Let's head around to the far side of the island."

Clay and Tom pulled the boat up on the empty beach and unloaded their gear. He checked the scuba equipment.

"You're going to flip out when you see what's in store for you. God, the fish—the spectrum of color is unreal. Damsel fish, parrot fish, dragonfish . . ."

"Forget the pretty ones. I want to know about sharks and barracudas."

"Oh, the barracudas are harmless unless you provoke 'em. They're attracted to shiny objects, so you make sure not to wear any bracelets or chains. I've only seen a couple of sharks in the entire time I've been diving in these waters. One of the writers in town told me that your chances of being attacked by a shark around here are roughly the same as being run over by an airplane on the beach."

Clay pointed above Tom's head. "Look out! A 747!"

Tom laughed and showed her the scuba equipment. "Okay, with this diving lung on your back, you could technically go down a hundred and fifty feet, but today we're not going below about thirty."

"What if I get claustrophobia? It's a lot different from the 'Y'."

"You'll be fine. Anyway, I'll stay with you." He helped her strap on her tank. "Did you know this tank was invented by Cousteau and another engineer named Gagnan? In 1943." He smiled. There was a chip missing from one of his front teeth. "I'm a storehouse of trivia. Tell me if you want me to shut up."

"No, Tom. I'm really interested."

"Okay, don't forget, this mouthpiece makes it possible for the air you inhale to be delivered at the correct pressure for the depth you're swimming in." He handed Clay her mask and flippers. "Before we start, I want to show you my camera so you can shoot a roll underwater." He took out a roll of Plus-X film.

"This incredible fantasia of color around the reef and you want me to shoot black and white?" Clay asked.

Tom nodded. "Less expensive for experimenting. Look, if you can take decent pictures topside, you can do just as well underwater. But there're a few things you have to get used to." He handed her his Nikonos amphibious camera. "You can set this underwater, but if you buy a good aluminum case for your Nikon, you'll have to figure out the intensity of the sun and the depth you'll be shooting at . . . then you have to preset your shutter speed and aperture opening before you go down." He handed her a piece of paper. "Memorize this chart. It'll make the whole thing easier."

Clay looked at the sky and then the chart. "Okay . . . it's a bright day, and you said we'd be diving about thirty feet. So I'd set it for 1/250th at f/8 . . ."

"Right on. Now if you were using a camera housing without a focusing control unit, then your next step would be prefocusing. In general, if you set it for ten to fifteen feet, you're gonna be fine for most pictures you'll want to shoot." Tom handed Clay a plastic dictagraph pad and a grease pencil. "Write down the data for each picture you shoot today—exposure, shutter speed, aperture opening, depth of water, time of day, conditions of the water surface. Then, when we develop 'em, you'll know exactly what you did wrong."

"Or right. Shouldn't I think positively?"

Tom put his deep tan arm around her and kissed her quickly on the lips. "I have a feeling you do just about everything right. But I guarantee you . . . the film you shoot today will be a disappointment."

Clay watched Tom as he loaded the camera and put on his scuba gear. He was nice. She knew he liked her, and his kiss indicated that he had more in mind. She enjoyed being with him, but he did not kindle any internal fires.

She was twenty and still a virgin. It was not a condition of which she was especially proud. In 1974, there were few twenty-year-old virgins walking the streets. Clay had told Garnet that she might as well wear a scarlet "V" around her neck or, more appropriately, a white one.

Because it was a fact of her life, Clay had become more, not less, choosy as to who should win the honors, so to speak. She had waited this long; she could wait longer for the right man to come along. But how much longer? She was out of her teens and began to fear she was wearing her virginity as if it were a porcelain shell, protecting her, yet rendering her more vulnerable at the same time. She was afraid she was becoming too precious; she wanted to be free.

On several occasions over the past year, Clay had decided she should sleep with someone, anyone, to get the first-time stigma over with. But when actually confronted by the boy and the bed, she had always panicked. She knew that this was not psychologically healthy. She kept hoping that a man would appear who would make her want to give herself willingly and freely. Tom Schultz was a nice friend, but he was not the one.

"Okay. Are you ready for your adventure in coral land?"

Clay smiled. "All set, Monsieur Cousteau. Take me to your underwater castle."

Chapter 18

THE live music drowned out the whir of the ceiling fans at Sloppy Joe's Bar on Duval Street, a Key West landmark, the guidebooks decreed, straight out of a Bogart movie. Papa Hemingway was known to do some heavy drinking there, probably around the time he was writing *To Have and Have Not*, back in the Thirties when the bar was still on Greene Street. Key West was suffering through the Depression then, stuck at the end of U.S. Route 1, the southernmost city of the United States. It was the end of the line for those who wanted to get away from it all or run away from it all. It still was.

Nearly half a century later, locals and visitors were still eager to spend a regular chunk of time at the long 'U'-shaped bar. Clay, Garnet, and Tom Schultz sat sipping beer while Tom went over Clay's black-and-white contact sheets with a magnifying glass.

"Don't get discouraged," Tom said. "I told you it's all an experiment." He held up the magnifying glass for Clay. "See, what you did here was compensate for magnification instead of focusing at the distance the fish appeared. The refraction of light underwater magnifies things and makes them appear about twenty-five percent larger. So if you judge a fish to be about ten feet away, you have to focus for ten feet. The camera lens will record the same degree of magnification that your eyes see."

"Okay," Clay said glumly, "that explains my focusing problem. But every shot is badly framed, badly exposed . . ."

"Hell, my first shots were much worse than these. I

ended up missing fish entirely. You'll be ninety percent better next time you shoot. I guarantee it."

"Or you can always stay above water," Garnet said. "My boss loves those pictures you took of him sitting on his porch by the wisteria. He's thinking about using one for his next book jacket. That'd be a great credit."

An attractive blond man of medium height came up and tapped Tom on the shoulder. "Hey! I've been looking for you." His skin was incredibly tanned. His face was weathered, with tiny laugh lines etched beneath his eyes and in the corners of his mouth. Clay guessed he was in his mid-thirties.

"I need you for the next few days, Tom. You free?"

"You bet," Tom said. "Anything special?"

"We want to take the magnetometer boat over toward the Marquesas Keys. We had some luck there last year, then got sidetracked. I have a hunch we ought to go back and poke around some more."

"Great! I'm free as long as you need me."

"Good. We'll leave from over by the shrimp docks around five in the morning." The man turned to leave but paused as his blue eyes met Clay's. "Hello there, pretty lady—ladies," he amended as he saw Garnet.

"Hello." Clay could think of nothing else to say. The man's gaze made her forget to breathe.

"Oh . . ." Tom said. "Clay Fitzgerald and Garnet Turner. This is Will Stone. Remember I was telling you about him, Clay?"

She nodded, hoping her voice would come back when she started to speak. "The man who roams the sea looking for pearls. In treasure chests instead of oyster shells."

Stone laughed heartily. "Well said, love. You a diver?"

"In the beginning throes. I'm a photographer. Tom's teaching me to shoot underwater."

"Look me up when you've got it mastered. Tom can tell you I don't pay much, but I'm always looking for divers. Especially ones who can take decent pictures underwater."

"Thanks. I'd love to see what you're doing. Are there really millions of dollars worth of treasure under the seas around here?"

"I hope so. I gave up everything to live here full time. Including a wife who thought I was nuts." He smiled. "See you bright and early, Tom. Nice to meet you, uh . . ."

"Clay . . . Fitzgerald."

"See you around, Clay Fitzgerald." Will Stone looked at Clay for a beat longer than was necessary before making his way through the crowd to the door.

"Nice stuff," Garnet said. "Forget the treasure. I wouldn't mind diving for him."

Tom laughed. "He has dozens of women. I heard he was real upset when his wife divorced him. Now he's making up for it."

They ordered one last round before Tom headed off to get some sleep. Garnet and Tom chatted, but a portion of Clay's lower abdomen kept knotting and unknotting as she replayed Will Stone's riveting glance. She had always sneered at the concept of love at first sight. Now she knew the condition was not mythical. Perhaps it was lust at first sight. No matter, Will Stone was it. She had been holding out for him without ever knowing who he was.

Now she knew.

There was an unusually clear stretch of weather over the next few weeks, and Tom spent most of his time diving with Will and his crew. Every day, Clay rented scuba equipment and went out diving, usually with people she met at the dive shop. She bought a good Ikelite housing for her camera, and a subsea Mark 150 marine strobe attachment. She shot rolls of Plus-X and Tri-X, meticulously developing them herself in the apartment's tiny bathroom. She analyzed her errors and corrected them. Pretty soon, she began to be pleased with her results, and Tom, on one of his rare evenings in town, proclaimed that she was ready to switch to color.

The undersea world had become a subject of intense interest to Clay. She realized that she was devoting herself to it with the fanaticism of a convert to a new religion. But it helped fill her waking hours and kept her from dwelling, as she did during many sleepless nights, on the fact that she would never see her father again or The Willows. She had told Nell that she would return to Virginia for the summer, but she knew that she could not visit Charlottesville without seeing The Willows, and she could not bear seeing The Willows reigned over by her stepmother.

And so she bought books on the Keys, diving, treasure salvaging, and underwater photography and pored over them late every evening, often until dawn. Before long, Clay could identify hundreds of tropical fish, shells, and sea fauna and flora by name. She read about deep-water photography which she had not yet tried, and how to compensate, by using a red filter, for the color cast that exists in the turquoise waters off the Keys. She memorized what filters to use in every color water and remedies for dozens of other conditions that were unique to underwater photography.

During the days, gliding weightlessly among the corridors and in and out the crags and mazes of the reef, Clay felt as if she were somewhere over the rainbow in an aquamarine city of shells, starfish, sea biscuits and urchins, sand dollars, and sea anemones. The gaudy luminescent tropical fish appeared in every color and pattern: stripes, dots, lozenges. Even though she never dove alone, time sped by so rapidly when she was photographing underwater that she bought a Rolex marine watch to help her keep track of it. The reef was the most beautiful place she had ever been with the exception of The Willows. And that seemed so far off.

"Wow . . . these are fantastic! That parrot fish resembles one of my ex-professors," Tom Schultz said. He and Clay were having a drink at the Full Moon Saloon. It was late.

Clay had not seen Tom for over a week and was pleased by his enthusiasm over her color photographs. Clay had hoped Will Stone would show up; she had not laid eyes on him since their first meeting.

And then she saw him. He was at a table with an attractive woman who was dressed far more fashionably than the others in the place.

Clay nudged Tom. "There's your boss. Who's that with him?"

Tom looked over. "Oh, she's a newspaper reporter from Atlanta. She's been hanging out with him all day. She came down to do a story on treasure salvors. Will's been charming the pants off her—or if they haven't come off yet, they probably will later on."

Clay examined the chic brunette and felt a pang of jealousy. The woman was around thirty, and she sat there, legs crossed, with a sophisticated tilt to her head as she dragged on a cigarette and listened attentively. Will Stone was talking animatedly, casually brushing his hand against hers from time to time. A compact Sony cassette recorder perched on the table between their drinks.

As if suddenly picking up on Clay's interest in the scenario, Stone glanced toward the bar and spotted them. He waved to Tom and Clay and signaled for them to join him.

As Clay and Tom set their beers on the table and pulled up chairs from an adjoining one, Will Stone introduced the reporter, Jackie Lowenstein. She nodded perfunctorily, clearly displeased by their intrusion.

"Tom can tell you firsthand about the euphoria we experience when we find treasure," Will said. "See that piece of eight he's wearing around his neck? He found it last summer when he was by himself off the Matecumbe Keys."

"Yeah," Tom said, unfastening the necklace and handing it to Jackie. "See . . . the coin's angular? It's a 1715 Spanish peso cob. They minted money back then by cutting it from a bar of silver and hand stamping it." Tom grinned. "Treasure salvaging has taught me a lot of history."

"Very interesting," Jackie said, fingering the coin. "It must be worth a lot of money. Why do you wear it around your neck?"

Tom shrugged. "For luck. It was the first valuable treasure I ever found. You can bring up a lot of crap—old nails, anchors, winches, fish traps, old rubber boots. I bring it all up. I can't stand litter, especially on the ocean floor."

Jackie handed him back the necklace. "And what about

the state of Florida? Aren't they entitled to twenty-five percent of it?"

"Yeah"—Tom smiled mischievously—"but how are they gonna divide up a coin?"

"It's okay for Tom, finding one coin while diving by himself," Will added. "But the rest of us, the ones who are into treasure salvaging as a business, we have to obtain annual search permits for *each* location we salvage. We have to keep a catalogue of every item we bring up. There's a state agent posted on board to make sure nothing is pocketed on the sly." He chuckled. "A hundred years ago, I'm sure I would've been a pirate. And it would have been a lot more fun than hassling with the authorities nowadays."

Jackie laughed throatily and lit another cigarette. "I can see you now, Will. With a bandanna around your forehead, a patch over one eye, and a skull-and-crossbones flag waving in the breeze from the mast."

"And what about you, sweetheart?" Will stared at Clay. "Hasn't Tom convinced you to become a treasure hunter?"

"I've been reading up on it. It's not exactly the best way to get rich quick," Clay said.

"You said it, kiddo. I'm in hock all the way into the twenty-first century. It's expensive as all hell. And that's merely bankrolling the day-to-day operations: boat maintenance, fuel, salaries." He finished off his bourbon and lime. "And just when you find a new investor and get a little ahead, your main motor quits on you, or some bill collector presses in, and there you are, back at 'Go'."

"You're obviously hooked," Jackie said. "That old American frontier spirit, the Gold Rush, getting something for nothing."

Will looked at her intently. His voice became serious. "For nothing? You put in everything you've got. All of yourself, physically and mentally, all the resources you can get your hands on. You take other people's loyalty and squeeze as hard as you can." He bummed one of Jackie's cigarettes and lit it. "Each year, you tally it up. A year older, still in the red, and a few less friends. The treasure's there, like a dancer in the fog. It keeps floating out of your grasp. Treasure salvors have to be one hundred percent dedicated . . ."

"And one hundred percent crazy." Tom grinned.

"And one hundred percent romantic," Clay said before she even realized she was speaking.

Will looked at Clay, the same riveting gaze that had made her stomach do flip-flops the night they met, and nodded.

Jackie Lowenstein caught the glance and, sensing competition, took the offensive. "Well, what do you say we go back to your houseboat? I want to see those photos you mentioned earlier." She flicked off the cassette player and tossed it in her straw bag. "Nice to meet you, Tom. You, too," she said without looking at Clay.

Will paused and turned back to Clay. "I've been granted a new search permit, and I need more divers. You interested?"

"What are the odds of actually finding treasure?" Clay asked.

"I don't know. A thousand to one—a million to one."

Even if it had been a billion to one, Clay would have said yes to Will Stone.

"Yes," she said.

Chapter 19

"THESE are really decent. Best pictures I've ever seen of me." Will Stone set the photo contact sheet on top of the log book of his eighty-foot salvage boat, *Camelot III*. "Damned flattering, of course . . ."

"Of course," Tom Schultz interrupted. "You don't look half as good as that in real life."

Oh, but you do, Clay thought. "Now you know how gifted I really am. A female photographic Pygmalion!"

Will laughed. They had arrived back in Key West after a frustrating twelve-hour day of diving. Clay had developed the film the night before, but this was the first chance she had had to show it to Will. The roll had been shot several days before, the day that she, Tom, and two other divers had brought up thirty silver pieces of eight. Since then, they had turned up empty. But on that afternoon, Will looked as if he owned the world, and it showed on his face in the photographs.

"I'd like a couple of copies of this one here . . . when you have time." Stone took a slug of J & B and passed the bottle around. "Clay Fitzgerald . . . alias F-Stop Fitzgerald . . ." He chuckled, along with the others. "Hey, F-stop. Good name for you."

"Oh, come on, Will. It's corny."

"Yeah," Tom said, "that's how people get nicknames. They're corny, but they stick. Better get used to it, F-stop." He patted her sympathetically on the back. Tom had not given up, although he knew Clay was intent on their being pals only. Garnet had told him, without furnishing details, that Clay had been going through a rough time. Tom did not want to force her into a relationship; so far, Clay had retreated from his most tentative advances.

"Okay, gang, let's go over to Shorty's diner. I'll buy you some dinner," Will said.

"Wow, what a cheapskate," Carlos Abeyta, one of the divers, said.

"Yeah . . . after the day we put in for you, I think you should spring for the patio at the Pier House," said Sally Kincaid, another diver.

"What do you mean 'after the day you put in'? Sure it was long. But did you find any silver coins? Did you uncover any gold chains? Not even a shell-encrusted musket ball." Will shook his head with mock solemnity. "No, I'm afraid it's Shorty's or nothing if you want me to pick up the tab."

"Any place is fine with me as long as they serve big portions. I'm starved," Tom said.

"Me, too," Clay said, gathering up her camera gear.

"Well, come on then. Or we can stand around all night and listen to the waves slurp against the sides of the boat." Will locked the cabin that housed his office, although nothing of value was kept there. The treasure he had found to date was in bank vaults, waiting to be divvied up by the state of Florida. He desperately needed his seventy-five percent share of the coins and artifacts he had salvaged over the past two years.

Will Stone was deeply in debt. Treasure hunting was exciting but expensive. He needed his cut from the state as collateral for new bank loans. Stone was accustomed to raising money, but he wished he could spend more time searching for treasure and less time searching for capital. What spurred him on was the ever-present possibility that real wealth was hiding behind the next reef. It was a frustrating, dangerous, foolhardy method of getting rich. But for a born adventurer, it was the only way to live, the only way he wanted to live.

For this life, Stone had given up his wife, Maxie, his business in New Jersey, and his friends. Some had cheered him on when he decided to move to Key West. A few had envied him. Most had sided with Maxie, calling him a crazy, irresponsible bastard. Stone, of course, did not see it that way. He was not irresponsible, or crazy, even if he was obsessed with finding Spanish treasure buried beneath the sea. It had been his dream ever since he had read *Treasure Island* as a boy and, later on, Ferris Coffman's *Treasure Atlas* and John S. Potter, Jr.'s *Treasure Diver's Guide*.

Will Stone's fantasy had lured him to the coasts of Florida, the Bahamas, and Mexico on vacations. In those days, the Sixties, Maxie had been with him, sharing his spirit of adventure. But as treasure eluded them, Maxie yearned for a more direct path to security. She wanted a nice house, kids, and all the accoutrements of middle-class suburban life. Will wanted only to dive, to search for a vision as mythical, to Maxie, as Atlantis.

Their final separation had been difficult. Will was beginning to consider that he had been a bastard. It was hard, even now, for him to review the facts objectively. In 1970, he was thirty-three, no longer a kid, although he felt the same as always. He had the usual outdoorsman's lines in his face. Small permanent grids, not merely fleeting laugh lines, were nibbling their way into his face.

The dream kept nagging at him. He wanted to move to Florida and treasure salvage full time before he became too settled, too old. His own father had been a man of unfulfilled visions, and he had instilled in his only son the importance of action, the pointlessness of sitting back and waiting for something to happen. And so Will made his decision.

Maxie had shrieked, pleaded, and cried. She told him that she was pregnant, that it was no time to switch life-styles. Will tried to convince her that she would love Florida; it was a healthy place to raise a kid. Not that a child was on his agenda, nor could he afford one at the time. They fought . . . and fought. Will refused to budge; so did Maxie.

Soon after that, Maxie told him that she was having an abortion. She did not want to carry his child. Will begged her to change her mind about moving to Florida. They had been together for eight years. Maxie told him to get out, if he was going, as soon as possible.

What she did not tell him, what Will did not learn until a year later from a mutual friend, was that she did not have the abortion. She had a baby girl, Angela. When he learned about their daughter, he telephoned Maxie and asked her to reconsider coming to live with him. Maxie declined.

"It's not your child," she had said.

"What do you mean? Who were you screwing around with?" Will asked, outraged.

"You're the biological father. But it ends there. You didn't want a kid. You want everybody else to revolve around you—you're totally self-centered! You didn't care that I had a job up here, that I *wanted* to get pregnant."

"Hell, Maxie, you're so stubborn."

"I'm stubborn? Look—I wanted a kid, I had one. I paid all the expenses myself, and I intend to continue. Unless I get married again. Which I may."

"If you had loved me at all, you'd have seen that *I* had needs, too. I was running out of air up there. I wanted a better life, for *both* of us."

"Listen, Will, it's over. I've got to go. Angie's crying. You'll be getting the divorce papers in a few weeks."

"But the baby? She's mine. What about my rights?"

Maxie's voice turned icy. "You don't have any." And she hung up.

When the divorce came through, Will vowed that he was finished with serious commitment. His life was chock full; treasure salvaging took most of his time and all of his money. There were plenty of women in Key West, both permanent and transient, to satisfy his needs. So even with his money hassles, Will Stone, at thirty-six, considered himself a lucky man. His life revolved around a dream, and he was on his way toward making it come true.

After hamburgers, French fries, and milk shakes at Shorty's, Clay managed to get herself invited back, alone, to Will's houseboat on the pretense of borrowing a book on shipwrecks. Moored off Roosevelt Boulevard, the houseboat was painted barn red and was peeling in places. Dangling from the roof on one side was a large rusty chain that held a two-foot anchor, and a clay pot containing a large, scraggly night-blooming cereus cactus stood by the door.

Clay was enchanted by his living quarters. "This is wonderful, Will."

"Well, I wouldn't exactly call it that. But it's just fine for me." He flipped on the light in the space that served as living-dining room-kitchen.

The cozy room was decorated with straw matting, worn and unraveling, and wicker and rattan furniture in the basic Key West motif. In one corner, a brightly colored Guatemalan hammock hung diagonally from hooks in the ceiling.

"Is that where you sleep?" Clay asked.

Will shook his head. "I'm not *that* gung-ho seafaring. I have a Japanese *futon* mat I pull out at night. I usually tuck in on deck, surrounded by a veil of mosquito netting." He squeezed the back of Clay's neck lightly. "Love to have you share it with me sometime."

Clay darted across the room to examine a model of an old Spanish galleon. "I'll bet a record number of Key West women already have."

Will searched through the overflowing bookcase for the volume he wanted to lend Clay. "Hmmm, possibly. I'm not one to kiss and tell."

"Good for you. A silent man of the sea. Women go for that."

Will surveyed her with his intense blue eyes. "Do you?"

Clay shrugged off his gaze with a bravado she did not feel in her stomach. "Of course," she said casually. "How could I resist? Anyway, this place is terrific. It must be great to live on a boat all the time."

Will shrugged. "Cheaper than owning a regular house, that's for sure. There are drawbacks. This thing nearly sank on me last summer. An electric bilge pump went on the blink during the night, and the water was washing on the deck when I woke up. I was having a dream that I was taking a bath." He laughed. "Turns out I really was.

What a mess! The fire department had to come help me pump the water out. Took days to get it repaired and dried out."

"Ah, the joys of home owning . . ." Clay accepted a snifter of cognac from Will and a book he had pulled from the shelf. It was a novel about life in Cuba and Key West when the wealthy Spanish ruled the Caribbean. She flipped through some illustrations in the middle. "Thank you, Will. I'll get this back to you in a few days."

"No hurry. You know, I don't lend my books to just anybody. Some people can read character by looking at faces or examining palms. I can tell by how a person talks about books. Not what they read but how they care about reading. Remember the other day when you were telling me about that book you'd read on treasure hunting? I knew then that you're a returner."

"Returner?"

Will nodded. "People lend you things. You return them."

Clay grinned. Being alone with Will Stone had been her goal since the night she met him. "But what if you're wrong about me? I just might have a trunkload of other people's volumes decaying in an attic somewhere."

Will brought over the Hennessey V.S.O.P. and refilled their snifters. "I can tell you're not that sort of person. You're honest . . . hard working . . ."

"And loyal? God, you make me sound like a Canadian Mountie!"

Will laughed. "Oh, these sassy college gals."

"*Women.* College women. I've been meaning to tell you. You use 'girl' and 'gal' much too often. It's demeaning. This is 1974, after all."

Will leaned over and kissed the top of her curly head. "A woman after my own heart. I'll try to be more courteous in the future. To you and the rest of your bimbo friends." He ducked, in time to miss the pillow Clay pitched at him.

"You creep!" She looked pointedly at her watch. "Eleven-thirty. I have to go."

"Why? Do you have a curfew?"

"Yes. There's this treasure salvor I know who pays lousy wages and expects his crew to be ready by six A.M."

"You're young, for God's sake. How much bloody sleep do you need? Come over here. I want to show you something."

Will opened his desk drawer and handed her an old book, its pages yellow and crackling. It was handwritten in Spanish. "This is a diary . . . a woman in Cuba whose husband was a sea captain. She talks about her life in Havana with him away for months, sometimes a year, at a time. Finally, his ship was lost at sea, somewhere off the Keys. Her son was part of the expedition that went to salvage the wreck. The Spanish salvaged many of their own wrecks back then. Did you know that?"

Clay shook her head. "Does it ever give you an eerie feeling when you bring up something that used to belong to somebody in another time? Something that's been lying untouched for hundreds of years?"

"Of course," Will said. "I even feel it when I go to antique shops. The sense of handling something that someone else has owned or made . . ."

"The other day," Clay said quietly, "when we found those tarnished silver coins? I was exhilarated at first. But that night, I don't know, I began to feel strange. I wondered who they had belonged to and how horrible it must have been to be drowned at sea. I began to feel as if I had no right to interfere."

"I suppose most archeologists are sensitive to that," Will agreed. "Treasure salvaging is marine archaeology, you know. What we find will help scholars learn more about the past. Maybe some things they never speculated about." He carefully replaced the book in his drawer. "I'm not trying to deny that I'm hunting treasure for the money. But there's a lot more to it than just a job. I really care about what I'm doing."

Clay's soft gray eyes gazed gently into Will's. "But what if you never hit it big? I mean, lots of people have tried to find the mother lode and skulked home with empty hands. Or empty pockets, I should say."

"I won't give up! Not as long as I have a dime left. I

thrive on challenge." Will rested his hands on Clay's shoulders. He was scarcely an inch taller than she. He contemplated her face for a moment and touched his lips to hers. He pulled her close to him.

Clay shivered involuntarily and hoped Will had not noticed. She responded to his kiss, parting her lips to allow the gentle mingling of their tongues. She perceived the aftertaste of cognac for a moment; then her awareness dissolved into experiencing the texture of his tongue. Their mouths parted and came together again urgently. Clay's breathing quickened, and in a panic she pulled away from Will.

"You're a challenge to me, F-stop," Will murmured softly. "Tall, athletic women are very sexy. But you're aloof, which also attracts me. You're seductive without trying to be."

As much as Clay wanted to be with Will, part of her wished she were far away. It was her big chance to give away her virginity to a man whom she admired and who was also devastatingly appealing. Will was older, more experienced than the men she knew. The tropical moon was full, and the quaint houseboat was rocking gently in the calm waters. She had drunk enough cognac to loosen her inhibitions. Will switched on the radio, and the mellow rock and roll beat of a golden oldie, the Flamingos singing "In the Still of the Night," permeated the air with a whiff of nostalgia. Everything was perfect. But Clay was scared stiff.

"I really have to go." She picked up the book Will had lent her.

He took it out of her hand and led her out on deck. "Not yet. It's still early. I like having you here." He draped his arm around her waist, sticking a thumb under the waistband of her cut-off jeans. "An exceptionally fine night," he said matter-of-factly. "Did you know that the most stars the human eye can see is about six thousand? Not millions at all."

Clay was nervous. She wanted to answer with something witty and trivial, but her vocal cords felt locked. She stood, lovely and vulnerable, in the moonlight.

"I want you, F-stop. Stay here tonight."

It was the moment Clay had both craved and fought off for years. She did not want to be a virgin forever.

"All right." She took a quiet deep breath. The ordeal, the "dirty deed," she and her friends had joked about in eighth grade was about to become a *fait accompli*.

Will kissed her hand. He pressed it gently to his cheek, his chest, then to the hardness in the crotch of his jeans. "Why don't I bring out the bed and the cognac?"

Clay took off her sneakers and gazed over the rail into the water shimmering in the moonlight. *Last chance to jump in and swim away,* she thought. She unbuttoned the front of her pink Oxford shirt and buttoned it back up again.

Will reappeared, naked, and handed Clay her snifter of cognac. It was too dark for him to see the flush that Clay felt shoot up her neck into her cheeks. She stared into the copper liquid trembling in her glass and swilled down all of it.

Will busily unfolded the Japanese mat, covered it with a blue sheet, and tossed five or six vivid pillows from Woolworth's on top. He set a bamboo tray next to the mat. It contained the Hennessey, a red-glassed hurricane candle, an ashtray, cigarette papers, a Coleman dry mustard can, and a perfect cluster of green grapes. Finally, he lowered the gauze netting, rigged on a homemade frame around the bed.

"Where's the bathroom," Clay asked.

"Two steps past the fridge on the right. Light switch's on the outside wall. Bring the radio when you come back, will you, love?"

Clay stood in the bathroom for a couple of minutes trying to conjure up everything her friends had told her about sex. Men love you to suck their earlobes, one friend had said. And their toes. And. . . . Clay laughed out loud. This was ridiculous. Since it would be Will's first time with her, he would be as anxious to please her as she was to satisfy him. She was making a big deal out of a biological function as natural as drinking water. So what if she wasn't great? She had read, and heard, that the first time, a couple seldom orgasmed together. She could fake it. Will Stone would never know that she had never been with a man before. And this was not merely sex; she would be making love.

Clay took off her shorts but kept the shirt on, unbuttoned and open. She had sunbathed nude on the roof of the conch house where she shared the tiny apartment with Garnet, and her tan was even all over. Her chestnut hair had been streaked with gold highlights by the sun.

"My God, you're beautiful," Will said when she crawled under the gauze netting to be with him. He propped the pillows against the side of the wall. "Come lie here. Let me look at you."

Clay took off her shirt and leaned back. She began to feel more natural, and to relax.

"Feel like a smoke?" Will sprinkled some of the contents of the mustard can into a cigarette paper. "This is Jamaican—strong. A couple of tokes is all you need."

"Later. I've had a lot of cognac. I don't want to pass out."

"And I don't want you to, either. I want you to have the most enjoyable night of your life." He pulled Clay to him. His skin was glistening with sweat from the humidity.

Clay could feel his hardness poking into her belly, but Will seemed in no hurry to do anything besides lick and nibble her breasts. At first, it tickled, but before long, her nipples hardened under the insistent flicking of his tongue. Clay gasped with joy. "Oh . . . oh, my . . ." she said.

Will laughed and kissed his way over to her shoulder and up her neck to the back of her ear. He moved over to her lips and kept on kissing her until she felt that there were stars inside her and they were about to burst through her pores.

"Oh, Will . . . I can't believe this is happening."

"I can. And it's still early. Just tell me what you like. I'm here to please."

"Anything. Everything. What do you want me to do?"

"Nothing now. I want to get to know your body. You can get to know mine later on." Will kissed her again and stretched out next to her, his knee draped over her belly.

"You're unique, F-stop. Gals—women your age usually bore me." He kissed her black eyebrows. "But I was attracted to your personality before I even noticed what a nonstop body you have."

Clay laughed. "I was attracted to your nonstop body before I even noticed you had a personality."

"Those are fighting words, my dear." He lunged at her, laughing.

Clay ducked, shimmied under the gauze net, and ran into the living room with Will in pursuit.

Will caught her and pulled her on to the rattan sofa. "I'm too old and out of shape for this sort of athletics."

"Funny," Clay whispered. "You don't look old at all." She ran her hand down over his penis and grabbed hold of him for the first time. "And you certainly don't seem out of shape." She paused in her boldness. Once holding on to him, she was not sure what to do next.

But Will solved the problem. "Oh, F-stop. You are an enticing creature." With that, his lips found hers, and he guided his stiff penis into her ready vagina.

Clay gasped, shocked by the twinge of pain at the moment of penetration. But once Will was inside, moving in and out of her with tender force, she opened all of herself to him completely. He was expert, holding back, thrusting forward, manipulating her clitoris with his skillful fingers, bringing her to the edge, then slowing again. Clay, in all of her fantasies, had never imagined that it could feel that good. Then, without willing it, her body began to shudder with climactic delight. She moaned, hearing a voice that sounded like hers, off in the distance.

"Oh . . . baby . . ." Will came seconds after her. "Oh, wow."

For a long time Clay listened to the rhythm of their breathing as it slowed to normal. She absorbed the intense wet heat from where their bodies were welded together. She felt total commitment, and love, for the man who had done all those wonderful things to her.

Afterward, as they were eating grapes and smoking a joint, Clay said, "I wish I had lost my virginity to you when I was fourteen. Think of all the fun we could've been having all these years."

Will kissed her shoulder. "I wish I had been the first one in your life."

Clay remained silent for a moment. "You were," she said softly.

"What? The first one? Not likely, F-stop. You're too good."

"No, I mean it. I was really a virgin until tonight."

Will looked at her. "You're really serious?" He kissed her. "Oh, baby, I never guessed. I feel so . . . flattered. That you would choose me the first time out."

"You're special, Will. I knew it the minute I saw you."

"You're special, too. I . . . my goodness . . . a virgin!" Will whistled under his breath.

Clay and Will did not sleep that night. They talked and made love and talked some more. And made love some more.

By morning, Clay knew that she had been right to wait for Will Stone. He was the most wonderful man she had ever met, with the exception of her father. She loved him. She wanted to spend the rest of her life with him.

Will was very taken with Clay. He was not one to make a commitment from one night to the next. But when he made breakfast the next morning and Clay looked into his eyes across the table, he decided that she was pretty special.

Chapter 20

THE *Camelot III* was docked in Key West for a few weeks while Will Stone used a chartered thirty-five-foot Chris-craft, the *Tra La La*. The Chris-craft was rigged to tow a magnetometer, a device that tracked metal buried on the ocean floor. If the magnetometer head detected any sunken metal—a rusted anchor of a Spanish galleon, for instance—an anomaly would register on the mag dial. Then day-glo orange buoys attached to concrete blocks would be tossed out to mark the location. The crew took turns manning the magnetometer dial and diving to explore the area under the buoy markers. Usually, nothing more exciting turned up than a newish anchor or a bomb shell. The area around the Marquesas Keys had been used since World War II as a navy bombing range.

Early March was not the best time for salvaging because of the shifting winter winds and six- to nine-foot swells. But the Keys were experiencing an unseasonal calm, and Will Stone wanted to take advantage of it. He had narrowed down a target area about ten square miles in a zone between Key West and the Marquesas, past Boca Grande. In this stretch, Will had found most of his treasure to date. He speculated, and had nearly convinced himself, that his cache was all from one ship, one of the many galleons that had sunk in storms three hundred and fifty years before.

Will had a hunch that he was getting close. Unless, of course, the wreck he found had been picked clean by Spanish salvors or pirates or even twentieth-century fortune hunters. The research Stone had conducted, leading him to the archives in St. Augustine and, finally, to those

in Seville, Spain, indicated that the area still hoarded
wealth in abundance, waiting to be uncovered. By him.
After four years of searching as often as he could finance
gasoline for his boat or the rental of the magnetometer
boat, he felt lucky. His palms itched, he felt so close to
genuine booty.

The *Tra La La* was anchored by a day-glo buoy. While
the crew ate Cuban sandwiches for lunch, Will Stone
dived down to check out an anomaly. After an hour,
bubbles appeared on the surface of the water off the stern.
Will bobbed to the top and pulled himself up on the boat.
He spit out his mouthpiece and pushed his face mask on
top of his head. Clay, Tom, and the others waited with an-
ticipation.

"No cigar," he said. "Probably a meteorite or an old
winch, buried deep."

"But it registered so strong on the mag dial," Tom said.

"Yeah . . . I really think it warrants another look. Tomorrow, if this weather holds, we'll set up the blower and
see if we can stir up anything at all." Will took off his wet
suit and twin air tanks. Underneath, he had on frayed
khaki shorts and a T-shirt that read: "Henry Jennings is
alive and well and living in Will Stone." One of Will's
former girl friends had given it to him. Henry Jennings
was a famous freebooter, or pirate, in the Keys.

"Okay, how much more gas do we have, Victor?" Will
asked.

"About seventy-five gallons."

"Let's get to it, then! Clay," Will ordered, "your turn
for the mag. Tom, you and Jack go down next time. I'm
going to study the map and do some more figuring."

The others disappeared to do their various chores, but
Will lingered over the mag dial with Clay. No one except
Garnet Turner knew that Clay and Will were having an
affair, although Tom Schultz had picked up the signals
and suspected it.

"You were down a long time," Clay said, "to come up
empty-handed."

"I know." Will paused and put his arm around her
waist. To anyone who might have noticed, the gesture ap-

peared casual. But even after two weeks, Clay continued to quiver every time Will brushed near her.

"Something happened to me down there," Will said quietly.

"Oh, no! What?" Clay said with alarm.

"Nothing dangerous. No sharks or anything. But I experienced something . . . mystical. A lot of divers talk about it, but I've never felt it before. It was . . . as if I were being touched by someone, a presence. I actually felt a hand on my shoulder. I turned around, and I swear I saw a flicker of yellow light for a split second. Then I blinked, and it vanished."

Will leaned over to shield himself from the breeze and lit a Camel. "But the sensation that I wasn't alone stayed with me," he continued. "I tried to meditate . . . to see if I was being drawn to something. I dug in the sand in a few spots where I felt particular urges . . . but . . ." Will shrugged. ". . . nothing. Then I lost the feeling that a friendly force was hovering around me. I began to feel paranoid, that I was in danger. That's when I came back up. I still feel a little strange."

"Are you sure you should go back there tomorrow? Your ESP may be picking up on something," Clay said, concerned.

Will smiled with his mouth, not his eyes. "Listen. I'm not spooked. I want to check this spot out again, that's all. Forget it, mother hen. I was probably hallucinating because I didn't get enough sleep last night."

"Sorry about that." Clay grinned.

Will patted her on the back. "Anyway, all those superstitions of the sea are just that. Get back to work."

Clay wondered if Will was miffed at her for showing concern. Their relationship was easygoing, punctuated by the high notes when they made love. But Will did not keep it a secret that he had other women around town whom he saw at whim. It bothered Clay, but Will had warned her not to expect anything from him. If she wanted to keep him, she had to play by his rules. She tried hard to appear casual with him, and she succeeded most of the time.

Clay was convinced that if she could hold on long enough, Will Stone would come to need her. She would burrow her way under his skin and into the part of his heart that had been stomped on by his ex-wife. Clay would make Will love again: he would love her.

"Sit down, Clay. We've got to talk." Garnet Turner was painting her toenails a deep apple red.

Clay pulled a clean white-cotton T-shirt over her head, to match her clean white duck pants. She was on her way over to Will's. "Yeah, I know. But I'm late now."

Garnet and Clay were due back at Bard at the end of the week. Clay had told her friend that she was not leaving Key West. Garnet had figured that Clay would come around, but now the deadline was almost upon them.

"Wait a minute. We've got to hash this out. I've hardly seen you the past few weeks except when you pop in to change clothes."

Clay sat by her friend on the lumpy green sofa. "I'm sorry, Garnet. It's just that I'm happier now than I have been in a long time. Will's the most incredible man I ever met, and I love working for him. What's up north for me?"

"Nothing except a degree. Which you'll need to get a decent job. Come on, Clay. Use your brain. Even if this is the real thing, you can come back for the summer and next year for field period. And then we'll graduate, and you can do whatever you want."

"I don't give a damn about graduating. College is a big fat waste of time, and—"

"Shit!" Garnet interrupted. "Will Stone is a lot older than you, and Tom says he's as selfish as they come. You've fallen for him because he's your first. But I know this dude is the kind of guy who'll hurt you. He doesn't want to get involved. He's told you that, but you refuse to believe him."

"He told me that he's not *ready* to get involved again. But he is! I can tell from the way he acts when we're together."

"I know he likes you, Clay. But looking at the facts—

which is easy for me since I hardly know him—Will Stone is a lousy bet to stake your life on."

"I'm *not* staking my life on him!"

Garnet sighed. "Then go back to school. Come back to Key West in the summer and see how you feel about him then. And how he feels about you."

"You think I'm afraid if I leave he'll find somebody else."

"Shit, he *has* somebody else. Five or six somebody elses, from what I hear."

"Oh, Garnet Turner, private eye. Where do you get your information? Are you and Tom busy gossiping behind my back?"

"Will Stone is one of the island characters, Clay. And this is a small town. It's not hard to pick up information about him." Garnet pleaded with her dark eyes.

Clay stood. "Look, I'm really late. I'm sorry if I flew off the handle. You're right. I admit it."

"You mean you'll go back to school?"

Clay nodded. "I suppose I have to. But I'm definitely coming back here in the summer." She grabbed the canvas bag with her camera gear and clothes for the next day.

Garnet hugged her. "Oh, thank God. You haven't gone over the hill, after all."

Biking to Will's, Clay felt terrible. She hated lying to her best friend. She would miss Garnet, but she was determined to stay in Florida. Besides, if things did not work out, she could always return to Bard in the fall and make up her courses in summer school. If things with Will *did* work out, there was nothing to worry about. She would not need a college degree.

Clay snapped photographs of the shrimp fleet, the cucumber boats from British Honduras, a coast guard cutter, and some navy subs as the *Camelot III* left Mallory Dock and headed west. She had decided to do a photo journal about Will Stone's treasure-salvaging operation. She was the newest member on the team, but not many of them were experienced salvors. Will hired divers whom he did not have to pay well; his was a crew of enthusiastic young people, mostly college dropouts looking for adventure before settling down to the realities of making a living.

Doing a photo journal was an excuse for Clay to photograph Will Stone as often as she wanted for her private scrapbook. She still felt overwhelming pangs of loneliness when she thought about her father and The Willows.

But she was proud of herself. She had sketched out a new life, one as different from breeding horses in Virginia as she could imagine. And she liked it. She had learned a lot in a short time: how to scuba dive, how to photograph underwater, how to make love with the best of them. She felt good about herself.

The salvage boat churned through mildly choppy green water, past the small mangrove keys called *chiquimulas,* or brothers, by the Indians because of their similarity to one another. Past the larger keys, out into the channel where the Marquesas Keys, an oval of islets around a three-mile lagoon, speckled the distant horizon.

"There's the buoy!" Tom Schultz pointed to the bright-orange object bobbing in the water several hundred yards off port side. "Hey, Victor, we've got it!" Victor Lopez, a Cuban whose family had been in Key West for over a century, slowed the large salvage boat. As Will's chief mechanic and navigator, Victor was a minor partner in Will's salvage company and would receive a cut of the profits, if there were profits.

"Okay, wet suits on the double. I don't like the look of those clouds ganging up over the Dry Tortugas," Will said. "Clay, I want you to stay close to me and take pictures while I look around. Tom and Carlos, drop the anchors and make sure they're in place. Jack, Sally, you get the blower ready."

"Ay, ay, captain." Tom saluted as Victor maneuvered the boat into position with a final twist of the wheel.

Clay put on her scuba gear, adjusted her mask, picked up her camera, and somersaulted backward from the diving ladder into the water. Will followed. The search area was shallow, only twenty feet to sea bottom. In spite of the clouds on the horizon, the visibility underwater was good. The neon marine life was going about its cyclical business, paying little attention to the divers. Clay clicked a shot of a school of iridescent yellow surgeon fish being pursued by a barracuda. Will signaled her to follow him through a thick patch of sea fans and fauna.

He pointed to a section of the ocean floor, making a wide sweep with his hand to indicate that it was the scene of his mystical experience. Clay looked around. Aside from some litter, debris from conch fishermen of the past, she guessed, she could see no sign of a shipwreck. Nor did she experience any peculiar vibrations. A curious barracuda swam by as Clay leaned over to pick up a large lamb conch. The predator darted back to look at her and disappeared.

Clay felt a gentle tug. She looked around, half expecting an apparition. But it was Will, signaling excitedly. She followed him around the coral reef to a spot several yards away.

He picked up a black shell-encrusted ball. A cannon ball. He dug excitedly with his hands while Clay photographed, stirring up a storm of sand from the ocean bottom. Clay came in close to see better. She could not help him dig because of her camera and flash gear. Then they both spotted something large and rusty through the cloudy water. He looked at her and smiled, and she realized it could be the anchor to a Spanish galleon. Will pointed upward, and Clay headed back to the surface, as straight up as she could manage, to have Tom mark the location with a buoy so Will could position his concrete block correctly on the sea floor.

"What do you think it is?" Tom asked Clay, back on the boat.

"I hope it's an anchor. It's buried pretty deep."

Will surfaced, handed the cannon ball to Carlos, and pulled himself on deck. "It's probably nothing more than Excedrin headache number five-0-two, but let's get the blower down and dredge the spot first."

"We're ready to go," Carlos said. He went below and turned on the air compressor Will had bought secondhand. It roared noisily, drilling into the serenity of the hot day.

Will shouted to Victor over the rumble. "The damned thing's knocking. I thought I told you to fix it."

Victor shrugged. "I did. This is something new. I'll work on it tonight when we go back."

"Will it hold out till then?"

Victor shrugged and grinned. The small good-natured man had repaired, mended, rewelded, glued, and sewn together nearly all the apparatus and equipment Will owned. Most of it was used when Stone acquired it, and the Cuban had squeezed several lifetimes out of it since then. Victor was well aware of Stone's financial straits, so he did not complain. He continued to repair, mend, and reweld. He prayed the equipment would hold out until they struck paydirt or pay sand, as Will liked to say.

Big-time treasure salvaging was a relatively new enterprise. For as long as there had been ships that went to the bottom, there had been men diving down to them to bring up their treasure. But now the ancient practice was being approached on a grander scale. Fortune hunters were going after the sunken hulls with the intention of bringing up everything, not just isolated objects. The men who engaged in this endeavor were resourceful out of necessity. They lacked the capital for the best equipment; often, the right paraphernalia did not exist. So they invented what they needed as the particular circumstances arose. The sea floor varied; it was coral reef in places or sand or bedrock or mud in others. Both marine archeologists and treasure salvors were underwater pioneers and ingenious when it came to improvising what was needed for excavation.

Will and Victor invented their Rube Goldberglike contraption to excavate the ocean floor. It was based on similar devices used by salvor Mel Fisher and by Jacques Cousteau when he was exploring a shipwreck on the Silver Bank reef north of the Dominican Republic. The "blower," dubbed the "giraffe" by Tom Schultz, was a gizmo that reached down to the ocean floor by extension pipe from a powerful motor inside the *Camelot*. A large tongue drilled through bedrock, when necessary. Otherwise, an attachment resembling an enormous mouth ate into the sand, dispersing it in neat piles, once the particles had settled.

After an area was cleared several feet down, the divers took ninety-minute shifts picking through the loosened sand, looking for objects from ancient shipwrecks. If a particularly ripe vein of artifacts was uncovered, the blower tube would be brought in and, in reverse gear, suctioned back on to the ship's deck, spewing it, along with sand and shells, into an area nicknamed the "sandbox." Crew members on deck could search through the sandbox more quickly than the divers could underwater.

"Okay, shut it off. We're hitting against something," Will said. The blower had been at work for nearly forty-five minutes. "Tom, Carlos, you dive with me. Clay, you be ready to come down with your camera when we signal."

Clay, Victor, Jack Devine, and Sally Kincaid waited anxiously on deck for ten minutes before a fast tug on the buoy line signaled Clay to dive down.

"Okay, F-stop. Go to it!" Sally said.

On the ocean floor, Clay saw Will, Tom and Carlos standing around an object she could not make out.

Will made a "V" with his gloved fingers. She set the shutter speed and aperture opening of the camera and focused. Will stepped aside, and her camera lens made out a large greenish object. She moved closer, adjusting the focus. It appeared to be—it was—a bronze cannon, listing on its side.

Tom and Carlos were busy cleaning the exposed side with scrapers they had attached to belts around their waists. The cannon was obviously old, and Spanish. Tom waved excitedly: he had scraped away enough to see part of a Spanish crest with a lion etched onto it. Under that was an inscription, *Ano 1625:* the date the cannon was made.

Clay photographed Will Stone, eyes shining with joy through his face mask, and snapped the scene from every angle until she ran out of film. Will moved the concrete base of the buoy over next to the cannon and twisted part of the cable around the barrel of the gun to make sure the location would be accurately marked from above.

All four divers surfaced to tell the others the good news.

"Why can't we bring it up now?" Sally asked.

"Look at that sky," Tom said. "The wind's starting to shift. We won't have time."

"We can't bring it up, anyway. I've got to put through for a salvor's contract on this location," Will said. He burst into a hearty laugh. "But we're cooking, guys! We're getting close to that pot of gold."

Clay would always remember the way Will looked at that moment. She was so in love with him she forgot to take a picture.

During the next few weeks, the crew's mood changed daily, alternating between elation and frustration. Clay remained in Key West in spite of Garnet's last-minute pleas at the airport. Clay could not leave Will on any count, especially when he was on the brink of success.

With Garnet gone, Clay wanted to move in with Will, but he insisted the houseboat was too small for two, so she kept the studio on Whitehead Street. She missed Garnet. Although Tom Schultz had become a buddy and confidante, there were certain times when Clay longed to talk to a woman. She knew Will continued to see other women, but he insisted that she was his "main lady—the one I really care about."

There were evenings when Clay cried herself to sleep on the porch at the studio. The tears were always triggered by the loneliness of missing her father and imagining that Will was bedding down another woman. On those nights, usually, Will had sent her home, saying he felt like being alone. Clay knew he was the sort who enjoyed solitude for perhaps half an hour before heading to Sloppy Joe's or the Chart Room at the Pier House or one of his other hangouts.

The treasure excavation was on again, off again. Because of high winds, treacherous underwater currents, and recurring mechanical failures, they averaged only two days a week at the target site. The rest of the time, Will spent trying to get bank loans and find new partners to help finance the summer's excavation.

Will had applied to the state of Florida for a salvage contract on the site where he had found the cannon, some twenty miles from the location Mel Fisher and his Treasure Salvors company were digging up the treasure of the 1622 Spanish galleon, the *Atocha*. Until Will's permit was granted, a state agent was posted aboard the *Camelot*, allowing only exploratory digging to establish the legal boundaries of the possible shipwreck.

In late May, Will and Clay flew to Tallahassee to check on his salvage application. He had not yet received a favorable recommendation from the advisory committee to the Division of History, Archives and Records Management, a branch of the Florida Department of State. Will met in person with the head of the commission and afterward felt certain that he would be granted the contract.

"Okay, F-stop," Will said on the plane to Miami after the meeting. "Good vibes. We'll get the contract. How about a celebration dinner before we head back?"

"I'd love it." Usually, they ate on Will's houseboat: grouper or jewfish or hog-snapper that they had caught during the day at sea. If they went out, it was to have a beer at Captain Tony's or to listen to the jukebox with Thirties' tunes at Sloppy Joe's. On the infrequent occasions when they ate out, Will favored good, cheap Cuban restaurants—Eddie's, El Cacique, The Fourth of July—or Howard Johnson's, the only place on the island open all night.

At the Ember's in Miami Beach, they gorged themselves on rare steaks, salad, and baked potatoes. Clay was wearing a sun dress of bright Key West-printed fabric. Will had on a sport jacket and tie because of his meeting in Tallahassee.

"Gee . . . we're both dressed up. It's like a date that real people go on." Clay grinned. "And a bottle of wine. You haven't spent this much money on me the entire time we've known each other."

"Don't let it go to your head."

"The wine?"

"No, the fancy restaurant. We're only pretending to be real people." Will laughed and peered into her eyes, Svengali-like. "At midnight, we'll be on the plane to Key West. When we get there, you will remember nothing of this evening, nothing of this restaurant. You will become my slave again. You will—"

"What do you mean, your slave again? Is that what you think of me? A kid who rushes over when you snap your fingers?"

Will laughed. "No, F-stop. Don't flare up like that. I was only kidding."

"No, you weren't! Not really. I'm not at all important to you, am I? You don't take me to nice places, on real dates, because you don't care about me."

"Of course I care about you, F-stop."

"And *stop* calling me F-stop!" The family at the next table stared at her.

Will sighed. "Clay, you know how I feel about you. I'm not the kind of guy who lives high off the hog. I'd take you to expensive restaurants more often if I went to them. But I don't. I take you to my kind of places. I've always been very up front with you, and I thought you understood the situation."

"Situation?" Clay poured the rest of the wine in to her glass.

"We're together because we like each other. Because we have fun. I've never made any promises to you. I know myself well enough to know that I wouldn't keep any promises I made."

"I don't want promises," Clay said softly. "I just want you to love me."

Will put his hand gently over Clay's. "I do, honey. But let's just take it slow. No looking at your glass ball into the future." He warmed her with his smile. "Okay?"

"Okay." But Clay admitted to herself for the first time that she loved Will more than he loved her. It was a fact she would have to deal with and try to change. Will would come around sooner or later; she was sure of it. He would realize how indispensable she was to him.

It was merely a matter of time. And she had plenty of that.

Chapter 21

BEFORE the salvage contract was awarded to Will Stone, an on-site inspection by a state marine archeologist had to be conducted. The serious middle-aged man, Gene Knickerbocker, and his assistant dived to examine the cannon and take possession of the artifacts found to date that had been replaced underwater, according to protocol: the silver coins, a clay pipe, some broken pottery and an intact Spanish jar, cannonballs, a harquebus matchlock gun, hand-cut nails, two rapiers, and a sword. Will received a receipt for the items. He would not see them again until the state had divided them up and taken its twenty-five percent share for the archeological archives.

While they awaited the go-ahead, Will bought an old tugboat, the *Cornelius,* and anchored it securely near the target site above the cannon. The boat's propeller would enable them to excavate deeper in the coarse sand and bedrock. In addition, Will needed more space for supplies, extra parts and equipment, and the freshwater tanks (large garbage cans) that the treasure was stored in. Will hired a security guard, Mike O'Hara, to live on the tug and make sure it was not vandalized at night when the *Camelot* was in port. A regulation applying to federal salvage areas stipulated that to keep claims alive, a vessel had to be kept on site permanently.

At last, in early June, in time for the year's best diving weather, the salvage contract was granted. A state field agent, Tony Echevarria, was assigned to the *Camelot* to observe the excavation. He was a pudgy, humorless man who added an inhibiting presence. Clay knew he was watching their every move to make sure they did not pocket any of the treasure. She realized the man was necessary, from the point of view of the state of Florida, and even for Will's sake, so he would not be accused of doing anything underhanded. But Clay resented the field agent. The atmosphere and the language on the salvage boat became more formal.

Clay also sensed a pressure building within Will. He did not discuss the nitty-gritty of his finances with her, but she knew that he was having trouble raising the money he needed to carry him through the summer's excavation. He had finally received his share of the artifacts he had found over the previous two years. After he had divided them with his silent partners, he had to sell his share or use it as collateral for a loan.

"Good news, F-stop," he said one morning. "A rich Texan's real interested in buying my coins for his numismatic collection. We're having lunch together. Our money problems are as good as over."

Clay hugged Will. "Hurray! I'll get a bottle of champagne."

After the meeting, Will told her to save the champagne. The Texan was offering peanuts, a fraction of the real value. No deal.

It happened over and over again. The stock market was down, Will told Clay, but added optimistically that the Wall Street forecast was looking up. He was sure he would be able to sell the coins in another month or so. Still, the strain showed in Will's face, and when they made love, Will seemed less anxious to have the mood linger through the night. He often left before midnight after a perfunctory sexual performance. Clay tried to reach out to him, but Will became more withdrawn.

Back on the *Camelot*, Clay became full-time photographer of artifacts, since Tom preferred diving for treasure. When an item was uncovered, she would shoot it underwater and again on deck for the official catalogue of artifacts. In addition, she helped Sally Kincaid tag the objects they found and kept a written log. Will, she knew, was a lousy record keeper.

For weeks, they were blessed with sunny weather. The

calm azure water was perfect for diving and photographing, and nearly every day the divers came up with shell-encrusted muskets, rusted harquebuses, and blackened silver coins. Will still did not know from what ship this treasure came, if indeed it was all from one wreck.

Several days a week, Will chartered the magnetometer boat to crisscross the target area, tracing a grid back and forth like needlepoint. The rest of the week would be spent diving to check the areas that had registered strongly on the mag dial. By the end of June, they had dug out three major finds: a rusty three-foot Spanish anchor, another cannon, and two feet of gold chain. Still, there was nothing that could be positively linked with a specific shipwreck. Meanwhile, in the main target area, the "giraffe" continued to burrow through the sand.

On July first, Will spied a shiny brass something through the dim green underwater light. He signaled for Clay to bring her camera and shoveled quickly. He extracted two bars out of the sand, weighing roughly a pound apiece.

"Eureka!" Will shrieked, back on deck. "Look at this! Silver turns black underwater . . ."

"But gold is forever!" Tom said, squinting from the glare of the bars glittering in the midday sun.

"They're high carat, for sure," Will said.

Sally fetched the magnifying glass so Will could examine them. The markings on one were indistinguishable, but on the other he could make out a carat stamp and the royal seal of King Phillip IV, the Spanish king who ruled from 1621 to 1665.

"Now we're getting somewhere. From the research I did in St. Augustine last year, I have a hunch that this is from the *Santa Teresa*. It was a Spanish trading ship that went down in a hurricane in 1660."

"Wow, that gold's been lying there for three hundred years," Carlos said.

"Clay," Will said, "I want you to do me a favor. Write the archives in Seville and see if you can get a copy of the ship's *manifesto*."

"*Manifesto?*"

"The registry—the Spanish kept meticulous records."

"Unlike some people we know," Clay said.

Will laughed. "*As* I was saying, they listed each item of every ship's cargo. If this is the *Santa Teresa,* then we may finally be able to prove it."

Elation ran high the next two weeks. The divers found more gold chain, a hundred and fifty gold two-*escudo* coins in an engraved silver box, a ruby ring, a gold and garnet rosary, a pearl bracelet preserved in a pottery jar, dozens of cannonballs, and a gold disc weighing over three pounds.

The records from Seville arrived. Will checked what they had found with the manifest of the *Santa Teresa.*

"It matches . . . it matches . . . it matches!" He shouted to the crew. "Our wreck *is* the *Santa Teresa!*"

Tom laughed. "We've got our wreck . . . now all we need is the ship."

But the remains of the ship itself eluded them. It was evidently embedded too deeply for the magnetometer to pick up a reading.

In late July, tropical storms began keeping them away from the site. They stayed in Key West for two solid weeks, and when they returned, another week passed without uncovering so much as a rusty musket. Will managed to borrow enough money to rent an eighty-foot salvage barge with enormous airlifts, powerful enough to dig deep into the ocean floor. The motors dug quickly but overheated easily, and seashells often clogged the pumping system, which would then have to be cleaned before they could work again. After two weeks of start-and-stop frustration and no sign of the actual *Santa Teresa,* Will decided the barge was more expensive than it was worth.

The bad weather returned. The outlook in Key West was not much better. The Internal Revenue Service issued an audit of Will's books for the past three years. They had ruled that federal income taxes on Will's treasure would be deferred until it was sold, but they accused him of tax evasion of some of the money he had raised from his partners. To worsen the situation, Will's records were a shambles. He had also run out of money. The telephone and electricity on his houseboat were shut off. He owed back pay to his crew. On top of that, he had exhausted his bank-loan possibilities.

The crew began to make other plans. Sally Kincaid decided to return to college; so did Jack Devine. Tom Schultz and Carlos Abeyta signed up to spend the winter at the deep-water diving school at Ft. Pierce. Victor Lopez was exhausted and planned to move in with his son, to help him run a marina on Fiesta Key.

Will managed to sell enough coins to a numismatist in Atlanta to pay his crew and get his utilities turned back on. But his spirits were low. He had come so close to finding the riches of the *Santa Teresa*: millions of dollars of booty were down there still. Now he had to retrench and wait until spring before he could continue his search.

There were other potentially hazardous legalities brewing over the status of treasure beyond the three-mile limit. The federal government, for the first time since the passage of the Antiquities Act of 1906, had told the Treasure Salvors group that it covered shipwrecks on the outer continental shelf. Since Will's site covered a wide area on both sides of the three-mile limit, he was holding his breath. He knew it was a matter of time before the state of Florida and the U.S. government got around to picking the meat off his bones. Then he would need more money to cover legal expenses.

On September first, Will's birthday, Clay announced that she wanted to take him to the Buttery for dinner.

"Save your money, F-stop. Thirty-seven's not starting out to be a good year."

"No, silly. It's the *end* of your thirty-seventh year. You're starting out on thirty-eight. I'm sure your luck will change."

Will pinched Clay's buttock, reaching his hand up under her cut-offs. "Somehow that doesn't make me feel a hell of a lot better. You're only twenty, for chrissakes. You have no idea what it's like to see your body getting older when you feel as young under your skin as you ever did."

Clay kissed him. "I can't believe you ever looked better

than you do now. You're not old at all. Come on . . . let's
have a really good dinner."

"No, Clay. I don't feel like going out."

"But we have something to celebrate. I have a surprise
for you."

"I told you, I don't want a present."

"It's not exactly." Clay urged him with her eyes. "Oh,
please."

Will reneged. "All right. If you'll iron me a clean shirt."

At the Buttery's bar, Will ordered three bourbons with a
twist of lime while Clay sipped on a planter's punch. In
the restaurant's tropical garden, they feasted on garlicky
shrimp and spiny lobster, but Will remained quiet while
Clay chatted about some friends of Tom's who were renting a boat to transport all their friends to Bimini for a
week-long wedding celebration.

The waiter appeared to take their dessert order. Will
passed.

"What about Richard's incredible chocolate cake?" Clay
urged. "It's your birthday, after all."

"No cake. I'll have coffee and a celebratory Cour-
voisier."

Clay smiled mysteriously. "Anyway, it's time for your
surprise. I want you to know, first, that this isn't meant in
any way to make you feel obligated to me personally. This
is a business deal."

"A business deal?" Will laughed skeptically. "What do
you know about business?"

"A lot more than you think. I'm not blind. I know everything that's going on with your company. What you'd
spend money on if you had it and what hassles you're facing." Her hair had grown over the summer and framed
her face in a soft frizz. Her big gray eyes glowed with excitement.

Will sighed. "I suppose it's pretty obvious that I'm
broke. That's why I feel strange having you take me to
dinner. If I were flush and you brought me here, I'd be
amused. But I couldn't pick up the tab if I wanted to, and
that makes me uncomfortable."

"Oh, Will. You know it's only temporary. You'll be a millionaire soon. Everything'll work out."

"I suppose." Will lit a cigarette and leaned back.

"Anyway, back to the point," Clay said. "I have money that I inherited from my father. I want to invest it in your company. As a partner."

Will was astonished, though he had guessed that she had some money. Clay lived beyond the salary he paid her in an overpriced studio. And she was generous, always bringing him little presents—books, cognac, T-shirts. "A partner?"

"Yes! You're a better gamble than the stock market. I can't give you the money until my birthday, in January. When I come of age. But I wanted you to know now that it's all yours." She smiled. "So you'd stop worrying so much."

"Oh? You think I worry too much?" Will signaled the waiter for another cognac. "Well, I *know* everything'll turn out okay. I appreciate your offer, but I'm not about to take candy from a baby. You hold on to your inheritance. With the way things are going these days, everybody needs a cushion to fall back on."

Clay's eyes moistened. "But Will, you're missing the point. I'm not giving you money. I'm *investing* in the *Santa Teresa*—in the future."

"And what if we don't find anything more? Or what if we find the ship and discover it's already been picked clean by pirates?"

"Well, *you* don't think the *Santa Teresa*'s a dead end. I've heard you talk to newspaper reporters. You're confident there are millions of dollars . . ."

"I think you have the romantic notion that we'll turn up old wooden chests filled with gold and jewels, just like in the movies," Will snapped.

"Oh, Will, you *know* I don't! I've been working for you for seven months now. I know it's hit or miss."

"And what do you expect in return for your investment?"

"The share of the treasure that my money will finance—if you find the rest of it. You think I'm naive, but I know what I'm doing."

"I don't think you really do." Will looked at the pretty girl across the table from him. He knew Clay Fitzgerald was in love with him. He liked her. But she was still a kid and harbored fantasies about the two of them living together and having babies. If Clay became a financial partner, it would be a bond almost as strong as marriage. And if he lost all her money, Will knew he would feel guilty as hell. He could not accept her offer. She would want too much in return.

The waiter brought their check, and Will allowed Clay to pull out her BankAmericard. He flashed an uncomfortable smile at the waiter. "My birthday," he said. "I'm a king for the evening."

Will was silent as they walked down Duval over to the Chart Room. By the time they had wedged themselves into the crowded bar, he knew what he had to do.

"Why are you mad at me?" Clay asked.

"I'm not mad at you."

"I'm only trying to help you out of your financial troubles. And make some money for myself. What's so wrong about that?"

"Do you love me, Clay?"

"What does that have to do with it?"

"Everything. I *can't* take your money. I don't want to be obligated to you."

"But you wouldn't be."

"Jesus, Clay, wake up! We've had a good time together. You're a terrific lay. But we've had our run. I told you, I don't want to be tied down—*ever*." He looked down at his drink.

Clay looked puzzled. "Have I tried to tie you down?"

"You bet your sweet ass you have! What other reason would you have for investing in my company?"

"To make money," Clay repeated.

"Bullshit!" Will snapped. "You're really full of it, F-stop. You want an emotional guarantee out of your investment in me. And I'm not prepared to give you one."

Clay rested her hand on his arm. "Will, I don't *want* one. I told you—this is strictly a business deal."

"And would you still invest in my company if you knew that I was having an affair with someone else? Someone closer to my own age who doesn't feel sorry for me?"

"Shit, Will! You know I don't feel sorry for you."

"Then why the fuck don't you go back and finish college?"

Clay's eyes flared. "Is that what you *want* me to do?"

"*Yes!* It'll get you out of my hair. I don't want to be obligated to be faithful to you."

Clay was devastated. "Okay . . . okay. If that's what you want, that's what you'll get! Good-by."

Will's voice softened. "Try to understand, F-stop. It's not meant to be."

"I told you, I *hate* being called F-stop!" Clay paused and looked at the man she loved. And hated. "Good-by." She turned and wove her way to the door, ignoring greetings from several acquaintances.

Will ordered another cognac. He felt rotten. He knew he would miss Clay for a while and her money for longer than that. He drank alone for a few minutes before he spotted a breathtaking redhead at the other end of the bar. She smiled at him.

As Will Stone nodded for the gorgeous creature to join him, he knew that he had done the right thing. Clay was sweet, but she had wanted too much of him.

Clay took a plane to New York City. Fall semester at Bard had not yet begun, but Clay did not want to return to school because she felt there was nothing there for her anymore. Tom Schultz, who had driven her to the airport in Miami, had given her the names of some friends in Manhattan and some work contacts. She had put together an impressive portfolio of underwater photographs and had the photo journal of her months with Will Stone to show as well.

Clay rented a room in the Evangeline on West Thirteenth Street, an inexpensive residence for young women run by the Salvation Army. She and Garnet Turner made plans to share an apartment after Garnet graduated in June.

Clay spent weeks writing a story about her treasure-salvaging experience to accompany her photographs and sold it to *Mademoiselle* where a friend of Garnet's mother was editor. Next, she landed a studio job as a gofer for a commercial photographer. During off hours, she continued to hustle for freelance magazine assignments.

In January, when Clay was twenty-one, she sold as many stocks as her lawyer would allow and wired $80,000 to Will Stone, anonymously. She still loved Will and thought about him all the time, but she began to understand why he had sent her away. Nevertheless, she often had fantasies of a future reunion when he would beg her to come back to him. In the meantime, she hoped he would find the *Santa Teresa* and the fortune and fame that went with it.

Sunny Yates Fitzgerald did not come up with the capital to buy out Clay's third interest in The Willows. Although Clay told Nell Smith that she never wanted to see the farm again, she was glad that a part of it would always belong to her. She agreed to be a silent partner in The Willows Stud, waving all rights concerning the day-to-day operations of the bloodstock business. The Willows seemed far away from the new life she was building for herself.

Clay worked hard, made friends, and fell in love with New York. One night at a party, she met David and Annie Doubilet, underwater photographers for *National Geographic*. She showed them her portfolio and wound up with a job as their apprentice, a job that she kept for several years before striking out on her own, confident that she possessed a real talent for underwater photography. Her career took off, and she was the youngest professional in that specialized field of photography.

Clay Fitzgerald was not the sort of person to waste time feeling sorry for herself.

PART THREE
The Present

Chapter 22

THE Oriental Hotel was a short waterfront block from the public river-taxi landing stage. A walk down the path through a well-tended garden adorned with neoclassic statues brought one to the elegant white-porticoed entrance of the hotel's old wing. It was used only occasionally, because the back door was convenient to traffic and deliveries. But Clay Fitzgerald preferred using the front entrance. It made her feel as if she were entering a bygone era—1876, the year the Oriental was built on the banks of the legendary Chao Phya, River of Kings. Clay liked to pretend that she had just disembarked from her own private yacht into the languid splendor of pastel-organdied women and white-suited men sipping limeades with mint or being served high tea to the accompaniment of a string quartet.

Adjusting a loose strap on her espadrille, Clay paused at the memorial marker for Anna Leonowens, the Anna of *Anna and the King of Siam* and, subsequently, *The King and I*, who had arrived in Siam in 1862 as governess to the children of King Mongkut. Next to the brass plaque, the Louis T. Leonowens Company, Ltd. had embedded a time capsule containing "a wide range of items in use in 1980," to be opened in the year 2055. With a smile, Clay speculated on what sorts of *items* might have been chosen, as she headed on into the hotel, past the Regency Room filled with Oriental paintings, into the Author's Lounge to check the Associated Press news ticker.

The lounge was white, with touches of light green and yellow, full of wicker tables and armchairs and beach umbrellas. In each corner, a bamboo tree climbed forty feet to a translucent domed canopy that allowed light to filter down a suspended double staircase that led to the hotel's poshest rooms, the Somerset Maugham and Joseph Conrad suites. Clay loved the lounge, a quiet retreat for reading or drinks or afternoon tea that had been enjoyed over the years by such famous literati as Conrad, Maugham, Noël Coward, John Steinbeck, Tennessese Williams, James Michener, John Le Carré, Philip Roth, and Gore Vidal. Leather-bound volumes of their books were displayed in locked mahogany-and-glass cases.

Clay noticed Linda Zaidenberg sitting in a wicker princess chair in a corner writing postcards. Clay walked over and sat down next to her.

"Clay! Where've you been? I was looking for you."

"Over at the Thai Bureau of Public Information, running an errand for Fred Justin. May I have a sip of your iced tea? I'm dying of thirst."

"Sure, finish it. I have to meet Peter in a couple of minutes. Josh asked me to give you a message. He wonders if you're free for dinner this evening. Just the two of you, as far as I could gather."

"Hmmm, should I play hard to get?" Clay asked with a playful toss of her head. Her chestnut hair was pulled back into a short pony tail, which made her look like a schoolgirl. "I'd planned to go to Soi Cowboy tonight with Bill Lacy for an injection of racy Thai night life."

"Oh, you didn't hear?"

"What?"

"Bill's been rushed to the hospital. He has a really high fever. It came on right after lunch."

"Oh, no. Is anybody with him?"

"Fred, and Lars just headed over there. He's going to be all right. Don't worry. Anyway," Linda counseled, "*don't* play hard to get. You and Josh need to be alone, to talk." Under the strong Bangkok sun, Linda's fair complexion had broken out with dozens of new freckles.

"You're right. What else did Josh say?"

"Nothing. Believe me, I pumped for info. He just said he needed to discuss something and that if I saw you before he did, to pass along the invitation."

"My watch band broke. What time is it?"

Linda peeked under the sleeve of her gauze peasant blouse. "Five-thirty. Doesn't it drive you crazy that there are no public clocks around here? The Thais must not believe in keeping time."

"Well, you know, if you get used to not wearing a watch for a while, you usually know what time it is instinctively."

"I'm not that psychically tuned in—I can barely get by with a watch." She giggled and gathered up her postcards. "Have fun tonight with Josh. Oh, by the way, what's happening with your sexy-looking blond friend? The man from your past?"

"Will Stone? I wish I knew. I haven't seen him since that first night. I've left dozens of messages at his hotel. He must be away."

"Are you interested in him? Rekindling old flames and all that?" Linda's red hair glowed as the sun streamed in through the skylight.

"No, nothing left to rekindle. But I'd like to see him again, just to talk." Clay wanted to learn more about his connection with Beau Yates.

"Here, would you mail these for me? I'm late." Linda handed Clay her postcards. "See you at breakfast," she said. "Hope things go well tonight."

"You're not the only one."

Clay wandered into one of the lobby shops and bought a pair of tiny gold earrings, in the shape of Buddha, for luck. On her way up to her room, she stopped by the inquiry desk to leave Linda's postcards and to pick up any messages: one from Josh about dinner; one from Lars Knudsen wanting her to fill in for Bill Lacy while he was sick; a call from Owen Thomas in New York; still nothing from Will Stone.

Clay retraced her steps through the huge windowed lobby, which was modern with ancient Siamese touches—chandeliers that were giant replicas of Buddhist brass chimes, ebony elephant sculptures, ancient Thai scrollwork detail on the tables and lamps. In a corner, a Thai quartet played Beethoven for guests lounging on the lime-green lobby sofas, sipping exotic, overpriced fruit punches.

Clustered next to the stairway to the mezzanine ballroom were a group of ladies, all dressed in light green. "Thailand Tupperware Convention," the white letters on the black convention board proclaimed. Clay paused a moment to marvel at the Thai women, dressed in different Western styles of the same fabric and color—Tupperware green, she decided. The green ladies were joined by a group of matrons dressed in holly red and another decked out in turquoise. The latter groups appeared older, suggesting a Tupperware hierarchy.

"It's not polite to stare."

The voice jolted Clay, and she snapped to attention, locking eyes with Josh Lewis, who was wearing white jogging shorts and a sweat-soaked dark-blue polo shirt. His tan face was flushed with the rosy pink of *après*-jogging exertion. He wiped a bead of perspiration off his forehead with the back of his hand.

"You've really been out *there* running?" Clay pointed in the direction of New Road.

Josh nodded. "There's not a hell of a lot of choice. No parks, nothing. Just the wretched uneven sidewalks. Some of them have holes so deep you can look down five feet to the water." Most of Bangkok's roadways had been built over canals.

"Just walking the streets is treacherous enough. I could never *run* them."

Josh steered Clay through the arcade to the old wing. "Yeah. Except I have to run. I'm one of those people who go crazy if they can't sweat out their anxieties."

"I can understand that. But in this polluted city, don't you think you'd better find a gym and play handball or something. It can't be healthy for your lungs."

Josh shrugged. "My lungs have been conditioned by L.A."

"Just be careful. Keep your eyes on the sidewalk at all times."

"Yes, ma'am." Josh saluted. They got on the elevator. Clay pushed three, Josh, four. "Did you get my message? About dinner?"

"Yes. I'd love it. What time?"

"I have to shower and make a few calls. I'll ring your room when—"

"Better yet, stop by. I've stocked my mini-bar with Singha beer, at nonhotel prices."

Josh broke into a smile. "Always resourceful. See you soon."

Clay stepped out of the elevator, then looked back. Their eyes kept in touch until the door slid shut.

Clay changed into a pink Thai silk ruffled skirt that showed off her knees and an over-one-shoulder fuchsia T-shirt. She dabbed between her breasts with Mystère de Rochas and attached a magenta orchid behind one ear. She was determined to get Josh back, but she knew she would have to take it easy. They would be together on this job for the next six to eight weeks, and there would be a lot of work to do. There was plenty of time. At this point, Clay was not anxious to rush or push the relationship.

Josh knocked on the door, and when Clay opened it, he handed her a small, foil-wrapped package. Josh looked tired. There were dark shadows around his eyes, but he had gone to the trouble of dressing up in a beige-gabardine suit with a narrow-lapeled, loose-fitting jacket. His shirt was unbuttoned to midchest. He wore no tie or jewelry.

"What's this?" Clay asked. The package was warm.

"An experiment. I bought it at that open market down the street." Josh helped himself to a large-sized Singha from the mini-bar and divided its contents into hotel glasses.

Clay unwrapped the foil to find a small corn on the cob, with kernels the color of ballpark mustard. "This is the most unusual present I've ever received."

Josh laughed. "Well, I was amazed to see corn being sold on the sidewalks of Asia. I mean, I always considered it strictly Coney Island. But the color—have you ever seen corn that color?"

"Never." Clay held it up, amused. "I'm willing to try it if you will. I've had all my shots and this week's malaria pill." She nibbled a few kernels tentatively. The taste was bland, the texture, mealy. "Well . . ." She handed it to Josh.

He took a large bite, chewed for a moment, then made a face and tossed the cob into the wastebasket. "Not worth risking dysentery," he said. "You heard the news about Bill Lacy?"

"Yes. How is he?"

"Some form of malaria, but there's no danger. Poor guy never got around to getting Fansidar. The pills his doctor in L.A. gave him weren't potent enough for the mosquitoes they have here. Anyway, they're shipping him home as soon as he's well enough to travel."

"Poor Bill. He's the only one of us who really loves it here. He told me he thought he had been Siamese in a former life." Clay opened the door to the balcony. There was a sticker sign on the glass warning patrons to keep windows closed to avoid insects.

Josh followed Clay on to the small balcony that looked over the hotel's swimming pool and outdoor restaurant to the Chao Phya River. Josh placed his hands on the railing and leaned over the side, stretching. He pulled back and looked at Clay. "Clay, I know I've been preoccupied since we've been here . . ." He trailed off, and turned his gaze to a river taxi pulled up alongside the Oriental's pier. Six or seven saffron-robed Buddhist monks were disembarking along with a tourist couple wearing straw peasant hats that they had probably purchased at the Floating Market.

Clay waited for Josh to continue. When he didn't, she said, "You've been busy. And everybody talks about what a maniac you are when you work."

Josh nodded, his dark eyes serious. "I'm borderline ulcers when I'm filming. The pressure's stimulating, but it's still pressure. I get kind of crazy. That's why I become so obsessive about running. I'd go nuts if I couldn't get in a few miles a day." He chipped away a speck of peeling paint from the balcony rail. "I can't let go of any detail. Oh, I'm able to delegate authority, but I still watch over everything like a harpy." He lit a Gitanes, and the breeze blew the smoke toward the river.

Clay took a sip of her beer. She was curious as to where Josh was leading, so she kept silent during his pause.

"Look across the river," Josh said, changing the subject suddenly. The sun was gleaming off the domes and minarets of the hundreds of temples in Thonburi.

"Fabulous. That tall one is *Wat Arun*, the Temple of Dawn. It's one of the nicest. Quiet. Not the carnival atmosphere of some of the others." Sitting on one of the porch chairs, Clay motioned for him to join her.

Josh brought another beer from the bar, poured some into Clay's glass, and sat next to her. "What I'm trying to get to is—we have to take it easy. When I'm working like this, I can't take time out for my personal life. When I have a free moment, I often need to spend it alone. Sorting out crises, trying to relax." He looked at her with intensity. "Besides, I'm not sure where we stand."

"Don't look at me. I'm sure *I* haven't figured it out." Clay brushed a mosquito from her tanned knee.

"Things started out great with us. I think they'll go well again when I can relax. I just want you to understand that you can't expect much from me, at least not now."

"I understand. That's fine with me," Clay said. She could tell that he was surprised by her reaction, that he had expected a lengthy discussion.

Josh grinned back at her slowly. "I'm glad. There's something else on the horizon that's going to drive me up the wall. Harvey Schaffner's coming over to check things out in person."

"Lars told me about your relationship with Harvey. If you'd like me to take him scuba diving with faulty equipment, I'd be happy to." Clay laughed. Josh did, too. The remaining tension between them evaporated.

When the laughter subsided, their eyes stayed on each other, and their lips met. The kiss was tender, not urgent. It was a kiss of truce, hinting of possibilities for later, sealing the friendship for the present. Josh plucked the orchid from behind Clay's ear, kissed it, and tucked it into her shirt between her breasts.

"Somebody told me about a French restaurant, complete with maps of the Paris metro and posters of Toulouse-Lautrec. Are you hungry?"

"*Mais oui, monsieur.* Just let me grab a shawl."

Clay went into the bathroom and touched up her lipstick. Fluffing out her shiny brown hair, she put the orchid back behind her ear. By the time they left Thailand, she hoped, Josh would be hers.

As Josh and Clay were stepping into the taxi to go to the Metro restaurant, Fred Justin called out to them. He sprinted out the lobby door and was followed by Nick Reynolds.

"Josh! We've got a problem." There was a deep crease of worry between Justin's thick brown eyebrows.

"We're on our way to dinner," Josh said. "Have you eaten?"

Justin shook his head and squeezed in back, next to Clay. The actor dashed around the cab and got in the front seat, beside the driver.

"Sorry to interrupt," Fred apologized to Clay. "But this is a major crisis."

"I figured as much," Clay said, resigning herself to her fate: apparently, she was never to see Josh alone again, at least not for more than a few minutes at a time.

Over the house red wine, *pâté de compagne,* and racks of lamb in the wood-paneled upstairs at the Metro restaurant, the problem became clear. Nick Reynolds, who had a reputation for being the most agreeable of stars, absolutely refused to shoot the next day's love scene with Natalia Ferrari, his famous Italian costar. The problem was a delicate one and hard to overcome: Nick found Natalia repulsive in every way.

"She smells of garlic." Nick Reynolds's entire body shivered with disgust. His blond good looks were enhanced by his present mood. Calm, he was too pretty. Angry, he was incredibly sexy, Clay thought, though she knew he was gay. "She smells—period. You don't have to work close to her, Josh. The woman has the personality of an undertalented primadonna and the personal hygiene of Petunia Pig."

Clay laughed, along with the others.

"Laugh if you want," Nick said, also chuckling. "But it's not funny, and it won't be tomorrow. No amount of pleading and cajoling will change my mind. I *won't* do the scene. Maybe you can shoot the whole fucking thing with Don." Don Potter was one of the stuntmen, and also Nick's stand-in.

Josh sighed. "Believe me, I wish we could, but not the way I've set it up. It's an important scene for the development of the characters." Josh signaled for the maitre d' to bring them another carafe of wine. "Have another drink, Nick, and let's mull it over some more."

"Look, Josh . . ." Nick lowered his voice so the people at the next table, a European man with a Eurasian woman, would not eavesdrop. The Hollywood star assumed that everyone understood English. "This isn't prewedding night hysterics because I like boys better than girls. You know I throw myself into my love scenes. On and off camera, I try to please." He paused. "But this time it's totally out of the question. The woman's an insult to her sex." He swallowed the rest of his wine in one gulp. "I'm leaving. I'll do anything in the world for you, Josh, except shoot that fucking scene." He stormed out of the restaurant.

"What about using Natalia's stand-in?" Fred Justin suggested after Reynolds had gone.

"No, for the same reason we can't use Nick's. The shot has to be real to give plausibility to the two characters." Josh idly began pouring salt on the tablecloth, piling it into walls with his knife. "Besides, you can imagine how Natalia would take it. I don't even want to think about that."

"She'd probably walk off the picture," Clay said, "judging from the intensity of her tantrums."

"Maybe you could write around it," Fred suggested.

Josh glared at him. "Cut the major sex scene? Harvey would certainly go for that." He threw several hundred *baht* on the table. "Hell, let's head back. I'll just have to talk Nick into it."

Clay snapped her fingers. "I have an idea. What leads up to the scene in the story?"

"Nothing pertinent—action stuff with Nick. Then he stops by her house to question her. She fixes him a drink, and they end up making love."

"Is she expecting him? No, never mind, it doesn't matter," Clay said excitedly. "She can be in the tub when he arrives. Open the door in a towel, body wet and glistening. . . ."

"And *clean!*" Josh broke into a smile. "Brilliant!"

Fred agreed. "Solves all but one problem."

"What?"

"Her garlic breath."

Josh shrugged. "We all have to make a few sacrifices for art."

Later that night, after Nick Reynolds had agreed to do the scene if a bathtub sequence were written into the script and Natalia Ferrari agreed because it gave her an additional opportunity to bare her body without having to share the shot with Nick, Clay and Josh made their way back to her room.

Josh waited at the door as Clay went around turning on lamps. "I really can't stay," he said. "I have to go write that scene."

Clay tossed her shawl on the sofa. "What's to write? Natalia takes a bath. They go to bed."

Josh grinned. "Yes, but it's a heavy mood scene. I have to do some thinking on that."

"Mood," Clay said. "If it's mood you're after, I'm your girl." She took Josh by the belt and pulled him slowly inside the room, closing the door behind him. "Mood," she said again. "I think I overdid it with the lights. We need candlelight for this. Help yourself to brandy while I change into something more seductive. And you'll find candles on the shelf by the mini-bar."

Josh placed a fresh candle in the candleholder on the coffee table and lit it. He poured two brandies, then turned to see Clay coming down the stairs from the bedroom level in a transparent peach nightgown.

"Hotel room. Interior. Night," Clay said throatily. "The world's sexiest woman descends a staircase clad in nothing but the most diaphanous of gowns."

"The mood is soft, erotic," Josh said, taking a step toward her.

"Heavily erotic," Clay corrected him. "Supercharged with sexual tension."

"Yes. Oriental mood light bathes the lovers in its special glow."

"The hero offers the world's most beautiful woman a brandy," Clay suggested.

"Right." Josh handed her a glass. "Mindful as he does so that a few sips of this intoxicating beverage can turn her into a raging nymphomaniac."

"She drains her glass," Clay said, "and beckons him back up the stairs to her bed."

Josh brought the candle upstairs and sat it on the night table. Clay arranged herself on top of the bedspread.

"I think I'm in the mood," Josh said, unbuttoning his shirt and tossing it on the chair.

As he took off his pants, Clay's eyes sparkled. "I think you are."

"I have an idea." Josh held out his hand and pulled Clay from the bed. "Come with me."

In the bathroom, Josh turned the shower on full force and adjusted the temperature. "Get in."

Clay started to pull the gown up over her head.

"No," Josh said. "Keep it on."

Clay stepped in and felt the warm water splash over her gown. The wet nylon clung to her body, and her erect nipples jutted through the thin fabric. Josh put his lips to them as he stepped in and closed the shower door. His hands cupped her buttocks through the wet gown. Kneeling, he nuzzled his way down the front of her gown. Water cascaded over his dark-brown hair and down his face. He pulled up Clay's gown, seeking refuge underneath. His tongue seemed warmer than the water as it plunged through her soft pubic lips. Clay leaned back, moaning, and accidentally knocked against the faucet. The water changed to icy cold.

"Oh!" Clay yelped, laughing.

"You bitch," Josh joked. "*That* was not conducive to the mood." They were out of the shower now. Clay had peeled off her gown and ran into the bedroom to snuggle under the bed covers and get warm. Josh was right after her. They hugged together, and within a few moments Clay could feel a hardness pressing against her belly. Her lips found Josh's in the candlelight, and he entered her slowly.

An hour later, when the candle had burned out and they were lying in the darkness, their bodies still entwined, Clay felt gloriously happy and refused to worry about tomorrow—or Josh's unpredictable moods.

Chapter 23

BY seven A.M., Clay Fitzgerald, had breakfasted with Lars Knudsen on the hotel's terrace, read the *Bangkok Post* from cover to cover, and now, dressed in white duck pants and a tangerine gauze shirt, she headed toward Oriental Avenue to catch a *thuk-thuk* to take her to the Weekend Market across from the old Royal Palace.

A young Thai boy wearing a cowboy hat came toward her, and Clay recognized the T-shirt, navy blue with white letters, saying "Never Give a Sucker an Even Break." The handsome, happy face broke into a smile at the sight of her.

"Miss! Khun Clay! Hello . . . you remember me? Pat . . . from Pattaya?"

"Hi." Clay smiled. "Of course I remember you."

"I come here to be your guide. I have been waiting a few days, but I never see you."

"I've been pretty busy. I use the other entrance a lot." She pointed toward the front of the hotel. "But, actually, Pat, I don't need a guide here in Bangkok. Maybe in Pattaya because you know the diving there."

Pat nodded, smiling, and offered no argument. "Where you going now?" he asked sweetly; disappointment spread across his face.

"The Weekend Market."

"Have a good time," Pat said, restraining himself admirably.

"Oh, come on if you want."

For the next couple of hours, Clay and Pat wandered around among the more than ten thousand stalls of the

222

Pramane market. It was a giant open-air department store with an incredible mixture of offerings—pet baby boa constrictors, deshelled live snails, roasted sparrows on skewers, microwave ovens. Marveling at the array of foods, flowers, and multifarious merchandise, Clay looked, handled, picked and poked. The vendors ranged from children to ancient ladies with no teeth. Haggling over prices was *de rigueur*. Because of an early-morning rain, the middle section of the market, near the pet birds and the mounds of dried fish and vegetable pastes, looked like manure; the ground was so muddy that the bamboo and cardboard in the aisles had been trampled into the sludge.

Though her sandals were caked with mud, Clay pushed on. She bought remnants of Thai silk and cotton to send to Nell Smith to make doll clothes for her shop, and chose a snowball paperweight with a beach scene that lit up for Kenny and a small *kan*, a gourd flute made by the northern Hill Tribes, for Lars Knudsen's birthday. Pat bought sticky rice confections wrapped in banana leaves.

Clay and Pat returned to the Oriental in the river taxi, and by ten-thirty she was back in the lobby checking her messages. There had been a call from Will Stone, at last, and Clay phoned him as soon as she returned to her room.

"Sorry I haven't been able to connect with you," Will explained. "It's been hectic. Been in and out of town. Can I take you to lunch?"

"I'd love it. How about fresh seafood—in Phuket?"

"Phuket? It's two hours by plane."

"But Will, you promised to show me your pearl farm. I have the day off, and we've been having so much trouble getting together." Clay paused. She knew she would have to flirt with Will to get what she wanted. "I really want to see you, Will. I can get the tickets here at the hotel and pick you up on the way to the airport."

"Oh, God, you are as persistent as ever." Will sounded exasperated, but there was a good-natured lilt to his voice.

"My magazine'll cover expenses. So let's say *I'm* inviting you to lunch—in Phuket. Dinner, actually. I want to photograph the pearl farm first."

Will chuckled. "Okay, you win. Call before you leave
and I'll be in front of my hotel."

On impulse, Clay brought Pat along. He claimed to speak
the dialect of the far south: Phuket Island was just off the
mainland of the Thailand chunk of the Malay Peninsula.

On the plane, Clay and Will sat together, while young
Pat, two rows in front, was ensconced in an aisle seat next
to a Chinese businessman. The Thai boy was clearly enjoying his first air trip. Wide-eyed and curious, he rang for
the stewardess every few minutes, read all the literature in
the seat pocket in front of him and tried to look out the
window across the businessman. When the meal came—a
snack of hot rolls and sticky rice cakes—he devoured every morsel and asked for seconds.

From time to time, Will took a swig of whiskey from an
ivory-carved flask he kept in his jacket pocket.

"This isn't exactly how I'd planned to spend my day,"
Will said. "But I'm glad you talked me into it. Remember
that trip we took to Tallahassee?"

"Of course. And that romantic dinner in Miami after.
Although I seem to recall we ended up having a fight."

Will chortled. "You always were feisty, F-stop. That's
what I liked about you."

Clay looked out at the clouds. It seemed so long ago,
her affair with Will, and so strange now to be halfway
across the world with him talking about old times. Once,
Clay had prayed for a reunion such as this, sure that they
would fall in love all over again. But time had changed
her, she sensed, more than Will, although he appeared less
invincible than he had in the past.

"Tell me, Will. What happened finally? In Key West,
with the *Santa Teresa*?"

Will waved his hand as if to dismiss the subject. "I don't
think back on it anymore. It was a gamble, and even
though I won, I lost. The mythical trunks of gold and jewels never materialized, just scattered bits and pieces of
treasure. In the end, I owed my investors and partners and
the government more money than I made. I wound up de-
claring bankruptcy."

"I'm sorry it didn't turn out, Will." Clay looked at him sympathetically.

"Well, it's not too late. . . ." He trailed off. "I mean, I've shifted careers, but I plan to make a million bucks yet."

"What's your connection with Beau Yates?" Clay asked.

A look of surprise flickered across Will's face.

"I saw you get into a car with him," Clay explained. "That first night."

"Oh, I see." Will drifted into thought for a moment but snapped back with a quick smile. "Beau Yates and I are business associates. Matter-of-fact, he's head of the Siam Gulf Export Company, which owns the pearl farm I manage." He pushed a lock of blond-gray hair away from his cheek. "How do you know Beau Yates?"

"He's my stepbrother," Clay said flatly.

"Oh, God, I remember now. You never wanted to talk about yourself or your family. Beau Yates—I had no idea."

"No reason you should." Clay smiled. "We haven't been in touch for years. I ran into him in Bombay a few months ago. But tell me, how did the two of you get hooked up? I mean, I just can't get over running into you in Southeast Asia."

Will picked up her hand and touched each long, slender finger gently. "An amazing fluke of small worldism, or whatever." He smiled and looked into her gray eyes. "You know, I was a fool to let you go."

Clay shifted her body around so she could face him directly. "Well, that's in the past."

"Yes. Maybe now is the right time for us. To start over."

"Will, I'm really happy to see you again, but—"

Will Stone nodded with sudden comprehension. "There's someone else. Sorry. It was silly of me not to assume there would be."

"We're friends again, Will. That's the important thing."

"You're right, F-stop. I'm glad. I've felt awful all these years about taking your money and—"

Clay put her fingers to his lips. "The past, remember?

Has nothing to do with now." She paused. "But you didn't answer my question. How did you and Beau happen to become business buddies?"

"Associates—hardly buddies."

"I'm glad to hear it."

Will looked at her quizzically but let the comment pass. "Beau saw an article about me and my hassles over the *Santa Teresa*. At the time, he was looking for someone qualified to manage a business, someone who—liked being around the water and who was available to start work at once. It was coincidence, actually. Beau happened to see the article and decided that I was the man he needed. He figured I would be looking around for something to do and that I'd probably welcome a change from Key West. He flew down to see me, offered me the job with a good salary and a chance to forget my troubles. So there you are, and here I am."

"Khun Clay, please. May I sit with you?" Pat's face was pale, and droplets of perspiration trickled down his forehead. The plane had been jouncing through an air pocket for the past few minutes.

"What's the matter, Pat?"

"I don't feel good. I feel better if I sit next to person I know."

Will laughed and stood. "Here, Pat. I can't blame you. Anyway, we'll be there in another ten minutes." Will took the aisle seat Pat had been occupying and looked back at Clay with a wink.

Clay held Pat's hand and spoke soothingly, telling him there was nothing to be afraid of. Her thoughts, however, were on Will Stone. Why, Clay asked herself, would Beau hire someone whose business had declared bankruptcy to run another business? And although Will liked water and diving, what did that really have to do with pearl farming?

The Citröen taxi, a relic from the late Fifties, drove slowly out of the airport and headed down the west coast of the large island of Phuket on the Andaman Sea.

"Some people call this place 'fuck it' island because of

all the secluded beaches." Will laughed. "It's really pronounced like poo-*kette*."

"It's breathtaking. How are you doing, Pat?" Clay asked. The boy still looked a little shaky from the landing. The runway, it turned out, was carved through limestone cliffs, ending at the clear aqua sea. The pilot had landed easily enough, but the runway seemed to Clay a bit shorter than regulation.

"I feel better when we get down to the water," Pat said, slouched down in the seat, head in hands.

"Look out the window, then."

The road paralleled a scenic stretch of beach divided by short rocky promontories jutting into the sea.

"I feel better," Pat said.

Will laughed. "There's beautiful coral—powder-blue surgeon fish, clown trigger fish, royal empress fish. But I suppose those sights don't thrill you the way they once did, F-stop. You used to get so excited when you went underwater with that damned camera of yours."

"I never get tired of it. Will. I still feel the same excitement, especially in places where I've never dived. And one thing always lures me—there's no one to yell at you when you're underwater. Sometimes I don't think I could cope with everyday life if I couldn't get away from it by diving."

"I know what you mean." Will stretched his arm across the back of the seat, casually brushing against Clay's shoulders. "Have you ever been diving, Pat?"

"Oh, sure. I work sometimes for dive shop in Pattaya. I been diving since I was a kid."

"But you're still a kid!" Will laughed. He leaned forward and instructed the driver to turn left at the next fork in the road. "We have to head over to the east coast, which isn't quite as beautiful. All the pearl farms are on islands off the coast. Most of them grow *mabe* pearls, half pearls. Only the Koh Naka Noi farm and ours grow the South Sea pearls that can be worth thousands of dollars apiece."

"You know, I dive for treasure in the Siamese Gulf," Pat said. "Lots of shipwrecks there. They say one of

Marco Polo's ships went down there with millions of *baht* in treasure—gold and real pearls. The legends say this ship was carrying wedding gifts from Kublai Khan to his brother's grandson in Persia."

"But that was the end of the thirteenth century, when Marco Polo was navigating through here," Will said.

"Will knows a lot about sunken treasure, Pat. He used to dive for it in the States."

Pat looked at Will, his eyes full of respect for the handsome older man. "I did not know. You rich, then?"

Will laughed. "No, I'm not rich."

"You ever dive in Siamese Gulf?" Pat asked Will.

"No," Will said. "Well, once, for fun. Not to look for treasure."

"But you know how to bring up treasure? How to take care of it—and sell it?"

"I suppose so."

"Maybe I make you my partner, then. Also, you, Khun Clay."

"What are you talking about, Pat?" Clay wanted to know.

"The ship I find—off of an island near Pattaya. I think it may have treasure. Maybe the Marco Polo ship, but maybe not old enough."

Will, who had been instructing the taxi driver, turned to Pat with interest. "So you found a ship, did you? Is it *very* old?"

Pat shrugged. "Hard to tell. It is foreign, not Thai."

"Hmmm. And where did you say you found it?"

"I take you there sometime. If you like."

"Yes," Will said. "Perhaps," he amended. "If I have time someday."

Fifteen kilometers later, the dusty Citröen pulled up to a small marina where a canopy-covered wooden boat awaited them. The muscular, bare-chested Thai pilot, Clay noticed, had a rifle on the floor next to the helm. He greeted Will stiffly with a nod and glanced at Clay and Pat with suspicion. He steered the boat through the quiet, sheltered waters toward a small island that had jungle growth on one side and craggy limestone cliffs on the other.

"You know, not far from here are the caves where they collect swallows' nests, for bird's nest soup," Will said as the boat headed into a cove. "Here we are. Home on the farm."

On the cliffs, Clay spotted a tall Malaysian with a rifle, and in the brush near the landing dock she saw several other men with guns.

"Security," Will said, following her gaze. "You might think we were in the middle of nowhere. But pearl culturing's a big business, and there are a lot of bandits in these parts."

The Andaman Pearl Farm was a smaller operation than the others Clay had photographed for her article on cultured pearls, but it appeared to be a professional, well-run establishment. While Clay photographed two biologists inserting tiny slivers of mother-of-pearl into the oyster, Will spoke knowledgeably, but with textbook insights, about the pearl business. Much of what he said she had heard before from other pearl farmers she had interviewed. Still, Clay was fascinated by this new side of Will and slightly amazed by the way he threw himself into the standard patter on pearl farming.

"When the sliver or any foreign body is inserted into the oyster, it has to be done with great care," Will remarked. "If the shell is opened too much, the oyster'll die. Come on, I'll show you the pearl beds. They're in a sheltered cove on the west side of the island."

They walked through a tangled garden of hibiscus, frangipani, and large-leafed greens. Pat followed quietly.

"According to the methods developed by the Japanese, Mikimoto, these oysters are allowed to grow naturally for two years. Then they're collected, cleaned, divided into groups, and placed in cages back in the sea. When they're three or four years old, each oyster is brought up, inserted with a nucleus which has been wrapped in living tissue— this reinforces the graft and helps the oyster produce a round pearl. After that, they're put back in the water, hung in cages from rafts." Will pulled the ivory flask from his jacket and took a large swallow. "The cages holding the oysters are periodically dipped in coal tar to prevent corrosion. And the oysters themselves are cleaned monthly—barnacles scraped off, and such. That goes on for three to six years before the oysters are harvested."

Will gave Clay the scuba equipment he kept at the farm, and she went down to shoot the divers, most of them women, who spent the bulk of their working day underwater checking on the oysters and harvesting them. Thousands of white-lipped oysters rested comfortably, in cages, opening and closing to absorb light and the microscopic marine life that nourished them.

"Pearl farmers are lucky. We don't have to feed the livestock," Will joked when Clay had changed back into her khalei jumpsuit. He led her back to the plain whitewashed wood laboratory and into the room where whitecoated Thai technicians placed the flesh of the pearl oysters into a revolving drum that shook out the pearls. After that, the pearls were raked out, washed, and taken to the sorting room. There, the misshapen and seed pearls were culled, and the others were sorted according to size.

"We don't match them for necklaces here. Some farms drill the holes and string the necklaces, but we subcontract a firm in Bangkok to do it for us." Will explained, and then looked at Clay. "So now you've had the tour. Are you impressed with our little operation?"

"Indeed I am." Clay had been pleased to discover that the farm was such a thriving enterprise. She began to feel that Will really had made a new start for himself.

As they wandered back into the main entrance hall, Clay noticed two doors off in an alcove. "What's in there?"

"My office in one of them. Nothing at all worth photographing in there. Just an immense mess."

"And the other?"

"Ah, my dear Clay, a reporter to the end. It's only storage, extra cages, nets, tools, that sort of thing."

"Oh, that might make a good shot. Everything else around here is so neat and methodical. Maybe the storage room would provide a contrast—sort of the guts of the pearl-farming business." Clay headed toward the brown door, and tried the knob, but it was locked.

"No! Really, it's too much of a mess. Take my word for it. Besides I'm starving. There's a wonderful seafood restaurant in the town of Phuket that I think you'll like. The waiters fish for your dinner right before your eyes." He turned to Pat, who had been following them around, fascinated by the pearl business. "What about you, my young friend? Are you hungry?"

Pat smiled. "Oh, yes, Khun Will. You know, I think I want to be a pearl farmer when I get older. You give me a job?"

Will scratched the top of the boy's head good-naturedly. "Sure, look me up in a couple of years."

"But Will." Clay had picked up on Will's anxiety about the locked room. "I really want to photograph the storage."

"My God, F-stop, you're relentless." Will laughed, but there was enough of a look of panic in his eyes to make Clay wonder what really was in the room. But she joined him when he said, "Shall we head back to the boat. It's getting late."

Outside, Clay walked around the building and down the path with Will and Pat, noticing that the storage-room windows were closed and shuttered with padlocks. She was dying to slip away and poke around on her own, but the pearl farm was heavily guarded, and Will would be suspicious if she made up an excuse to go back. Besides, she told herself, she was probably overreacting to the mere hint of something mysterious.

During the twenty-minute journey back to Phuket, Clay busied herself making notes for her article. Then she made her way to the front of the boat where Will and Pat were immersed in talk about the Siamese Gulf and treasure salvaging.

Clay smiled as she joined them. *Old treasure salvors never die*, she thought. And then it occurred to her: they never give up, either. It was strictly intuition, but Clay felt that Will seemed a little *too* interested in Pat's story about the Marco Polo ship.

After a splendid fish dinner in Phuket and a spot of sunset

watching in the nearby town of Surin, the three of them took the last flight back to Bangkok.

"Thanks, Will. I really enjoyed the day," Clay said as their cab inched its way through the traffic from the airport to Bangkok.

"I'm glad you liked my little home away from home," Will said, squeezing her arm. "It's still early. Have you experienced Patpong Road yet? Or maybe you'd enjoy just a quiet drink somewhere?"

"I'll take a rain check." Clay smiled. "I have to be at work bright and early tomorrow. Our cinematographer's assistant was sent home with malaria, so I've taken over his job. Things are really hectic."

Will put his arm around Clay and squeezed her shoulders. "I'm proud of you, Clay. You've really made something of yourself. Jesus, you're still so fucking young."

"Twenty-eight," Clay reminded him.

"Oh, to be under thirty again. I just collided with forty-five. What a shock that was."

"You don't look it, so what does it matter?"

Will kissed her nose. "Thank you." His lips slid down, warm and moist and anxious, and embraced hers. Clay returned the kiss, letting her tongue meet his for a moment, closing her eyes, giving it a chance. Finally, she pulled away and kissed his cheek lightly. She started to speak, but Will interrupted.

"Sorry, F-stop, I couldn't resist. Who is it you're involved with?"

Clay shrugged. "Just someone."

"Oh, that serious." Will looked out the window at a water buffalo grazing by the side of the road. "Well, how do you like me as a gentleman pearl farmer?"

"You're suited for the role perfectly, Will. Except I think I'll have to get you a white Panama and a box of cigars to complete the image." Clay grinned. "I'm very impressed by your knowledge of pearls."

"You know me. I throw myself into whatever I'm doing. Let's see—you know, of course, that pearls are aphrodisiac?"

"Oh, yes. I read that Cleopatra's reputed to have dissolved them in wine to enhance her sexuality." Clay laughed. "I've always meant to try it."

"It works. I mean, pearls dissolve in acid. I tried it. It takes two weeks to dissolve a pearl in a glass of Chianti. I couldn't bring myself to drink it, however."

The taxi pulled up the ramp to the Oriental Hotel.

"You're sure I can't lure you into spending the evening with me?"

"Another time, Will. Thanks."

"What about you, Pat? Want to have a beer?"

Pat was still feeling shaky from his second plane ride of the day. "Yes, Khun Will. I think I need a beer."

"Okay, Clay," Will kissed her cheek. "See you soon."

"Thanks, Will. That was a good tour today. I learned a lot. Let's have dinner next week."

Clay waved good-by as the taxi pulled off with Will and Pat. She still had a feeling that there was something else going on between Will and Beau, but it was only a hunch, and maybe she was wrong. Maybe Beau Yates was really on the straight and narrow these days.

She doubted it, though.

Chapter 24

THE American ex-hippie chauffeur pulled the black Datsun into a tiny parking space outside Bangkok's Don Muang airport.

"Go check on the plane, Jerry. See if it's in yet." The chauffeur nodded and headed over to the terminal. Beau Yates reached into the breast pocket of his navy Armani suit and pulled out a Shark's Eye seashell with a hinged silver top. Flipping it open, he dug the small fingernail of his left hand, kept long for convenience, into the white powder, raised it to his nostrils, and sniffed deeply.

"You want?" Beau asked his companion.

"Might as well." Vincent Lascaux, Beau's partner, took a tiny spoon out of his wallet and reached for the cocaine container. Beau's method did not work for Vincent; the small fingers on both of Vincent's hands were missing. Vincent had never told Beau why, but Beau assumed that they had been extracted for nonpayment of a debt. Vincent had a past full of dealings with shady, sadistic people.

"Okay, as soon as the package comes through, you take a cab back to town. You know where to deliver it?"

Vincent nodded. "*Oui, oui, mon cher.*" He ruffled up Beau's neatly cropped, sandy-blond hair.

"Cut it out!" Beau snapped. "I told you not to touch me—in public."

Jerry, the chauffeur, came back and peered in the window. "Plane's about twenty minutes late," he reported.

"Oh, fuck," Beau said. "That's all we need. Goddamnit! Why can't anything go right in this fuckin' country?"

234

"They said it was due to a storm over the China Sea," Jerry explained.

"That's right, take up for them. Believe their lies." Beau's face had turned crimson with anger.

"Calm down, *mon ami*. You will get a headache. Here." Vincent handed Beau a Quaalude. "Get him something to wash it down with," he instructed Jerry, who took off in a run across the driveway. Vincent massaged the back of Beau's neck with his four fingers. "You've got to learn to take things easy."

Jerry raced back with an iced soft drink in a plastic bag. "It's all they had," he said. "And they announced the plane. It's landing now."

Beau Yates and Vincent Lascaux were a striking pair as they crossed the parking lot to the terminal building. Beau was five-ten, muscular, fair. Vincent Lascaux was five inches shorter, slight, with black hair and eyes, sunken cheeks, and a wide jaw. He, like Beau, was hauntingly handsome, although they were total opposites in looks.

Beau and Vincent had met in Vietnam. Vincent's father, who was French, had moved to Saigon in the early Fifties to open a restaurant. His mother, a Vietnamese, later abandoned the family to run off with an American GI. Vincent's father had died shortly after, and Vincent spent the rest of the war years playing both sides, buying drugs from a North Vietnamese connection, selling them to the Americans. That was how he met Beau Yates, in the late Sixties when Beau was in the Green Berets. At the time of Beau's discharge, Beau had promised Vincent he would return: there were many business opportunities in Southeast Asia.

It had taken Beau several years. He had been under psychiatric treatment in California, but as soon as he could put together enough money, from his mother, his grandfather in New Orleans, and various dope deals, he flew to Bangkok where Vincent Lascaux had settled.

They had been lovers for a while, but Vincent, who was bisexual, as was Beau, took up with a Thai beauty and married her when she got pregnant. Beau and he settled into being business partners and only occasional lovers.

Vincent enjoyed his bisexuality, flaunted it. Beau was more cautious. He was the front man in their business, and a clean image was important. Thus, in public, Beau was seen with beautiful women, usually Eurasian. He confined the darker side of his sex life to clandestine evenings with Vincent when they took opium and arranged not to have any business to conduct before noon the following day.

Beau and Vincent entered the airport as the passengers from Pan Am flight 2 were being cleared through passport control.

"Hi, darlin'." Sunny Yates Fitzgerald, trim, tight-skinned, and blonde, dressed in a crisp white jacket, cerise silk blouse, and lean-cut black pants, waved at them from customs.

Audrey Yates followed her mother. She had recently divorced her husband the lawyer, Babcock, and dropped his name. Her silvery blonde hair was pulled back in a braided chignon, and she looked stunningly beautiful. Both she and her mother wore pearl necklaces.

"Hi, mother." Beau pronounced it "muh-thuh" even though his Southern drawl had evolved into a relaxed American accent with only some words distinctly southern.

"Beau, darlin', I love your suit." Sunny kissed him. "Hello, Vincent," she said coolly, not bothering to extend either cheek or hand.

"What a flight we had!" Audrey kissed both Beau and Vincent cordially. "Headwinds. So we were late gettin' to Tokyo and didn't have time for *sushi* in the airport. Then they wouldn't let us out of the plane in Hong Kong to make up for the lost time. Why do you live in such a difficult place to get to? I'd just recovered from our last trip when it was time to turn 'round and come back again."

"Hmmm," Beau said routinely. "Too bad. Do you have the package, mother?"

"Yes, darlin', of course," she said with the weary tone that a mother might take with a six-year-old. Sunny unzipped her flight bag and handed her son a gift-wrapped package, the size of a box of frozen vegetables. Beau gave it to Vincent, who nodded farewell and drifted out to the taxi stand.

"I don't know why you do business with him," Sunny said. "There's somethin' a little shady about him."

"Well, he likes you, mother." Beau hailed a porter for the baggage.

In the car, Beau sat in the back between his mother and sister.

"How *are* you, sweetheart? What's new?" Sunny patted Beau's knee.

"Business is goin' great. Just got a coupla new accounts." He offered cigarettes to Sunny and Audrey and took one himself. "Somethin' interestin'—you'll never guess who's in town."

"I know already," Audrey said. "Josh Lewis. He's shootin' a movie here, and he's the only reason in the world I'd come back to this Asian hellhole."

"What? Why, sweet sister, I thought you came to see me." Beau mocked his sister's thick southern accent.

"Fat chance, Beau. You don't hang around with an interestin' enough crowd."

"Tough shit, sis. Anyway, Josh Lewis is not who I'm referrin' to. Someone else we know is here workin' for him."

Sunny finished applying fresh lipstick and snapped shut the jade and Burmese ruby compact Beau had given her for Christmas. "I would assume it's Clay. We saw her with him in England."

"I'm surprised they're back together again." Audrey giggled. "After I managed to throw my particular brand of pixie dust on them."

Beau shrugged. "I haven't seen her. Just heard from Will Stone that she's here. Anyway, I got you your favorite suite at the Erawan."

"Drop *me* off at the Oriental," Audrey said. "That's where Josh is stayin', and I booked a suite there. By the way, do you have my private stock for me?"

Beau reached into his pocket and handed Audrey a small rectangular envelope.

"Oh, you all." Sunny sighed. "You're both too old to be foolin' around with drugs."

"As if you don't indulge from time to time, mother," Audrey said sweetly.

After they had dropped Audrey and her five suitcases off at the Oriental, Sunny took Beau's hand and kissed it. "I want to see your new office."

Beau leaned forward. "The office, Jerry. And don't take off. I want you to drop mother at her hotel after she's had a quick look around."

"You're not comin' back to the hotel with me?" Sunny's mouth froze into a pout.

"I'm expectin' a few calls. Later this evenin', we'll have supper. Then, if you want, we'll have a drink on Patpong Road and you can check out all the rich American studs."

Sunny giggled. "Beau! You know I don't like you to talk like that to me. Where is your respect for your poor old mother?"

"Who's that? I thought *you* were my mother. Sexy, terrific you." Beau kissed her cheek. "Here we are."

Beau's office was on the fourth floor of the ultramodern Siam Center, an indoor mall-office building full of touristy shops and Le Drugstore-type restaurants.

The door to the office was lettered "Siam Gulf Export Company" in gold. The reception room and adjoining offices were carpeted in gray, with blue and green floral slipcovers and draperies.

"Honestly, Beau. Why didn't you wait and let me decorate this for you? This is so drably masculine."

"Goddamnit!" Beau flared up. "I had this done in colors I especially thought you'd like!" He went into his office and called back. "You don't mind if I don't escort you back to the car. I have some business to attend to."

Sunny followed Beau into his office, smiling contritely. "Sweetie, I'm sorry. I didn't mean to hurt your feelin's. It's really quite perfect for an office. I tend to forget that business interiors have to be starker. Forgive me?"

Beau shuffled through some papers on his desk, ignoring her.

"Beau—come on, sweetie. I'm sorry."

He looked up, and Sunny could see the hurt in his pale-blue eyes. It was a look she had seen many times when he was a boy. She went over and kissed the top of his head. "I love you so much. I guess I'm just tired from that tryin' flight."

"Okay, mother. I forgive you." He paused. "By the way, you won't mind wearin' another pearl necklace back to New York for me? To give to Mr. Matasiow, like last time."

Sunny sighed. "No, I guess not. But I wish you'd tell me why you want me to smuggle them through customs."

"Hell, mother, you're not smugglin'. It's just it's too risky to mail 'em. The Thai postal service is the pits."

Sunny smiled. "Then there's nothin'—underhanded about this? I get so worried about you. I've never been quite sure what you do. I know there's that pearl farm, but you seem to be involved in so many other things."

"I'm an entrepreneur, mother." Beau stood and led Sunny toward the reception room. "If you knew the export business, you'd understand that it's a close-to-the-vest business. You have a lot of deals goin' on all the time. You can't put all your eggs in one basket." He kissed her mouth quickly. "Don't ask questions and you won't be bored. I'll be over later with champagne. If you don't want to go out, order us a midnight supper from room service."

Sunny left, and Vincent Lascaux arrived moments later.

"How did it go?" Beau asked.

"Perfect. Your friend Matasiow appears to be a man of unerring quality." Vincent spoke with the peculiar accent of a French-Vietnamese who had lived in Thailand for ten years. "I deposited the money already. Except this." He opened a wall safe behind a file cabinet. "Fifty grand, for petty cash."

Beau smiled. "Good boy. I want you to fly to Chiang Mai tomorrow to talk to Chanya."

Vincent shook his head. "He's off in the jungle taking inventory. One of the Hill Tribes has been bought off by the government, not to grow poppies. Chanya's gone to persuade them to change their mind." He opened the top drawer of the file cabinet and brought out a bottle of Thai White Cock whiskey. He poured two neat glasses and handed one to Beau.

"To us," Beau said. "We've come a long way in five years."

Vincent kissed Beau's neck, unbuttoned his shirt, and began to nibble his way down Beau's front. Beau leaned back in his swivel chair and unzipped his bulging pants.

The outer door to the reception room opened. "Oh, shit," Beau whispered. "Didn't you lock it when you came in?"

"Yes, I—" Vincent pulled away from Beau and stood.

Will Stone entered the office, keys in hand. "I was hoping you'd be here." He went directly to the bottle of White Cock and poured himself a drink.

"What's up?" Beau asked.

"I've had an interesting day. With Clay."

Beau leaned forward, discreetly rezipping his pants. "What do you mean 'interesting'?"

Will recounted his afternoon with Clay and Pat and Pat's story about the treasure ship he found in the Siam Gulf. "You know, I've been poring over maps and doing some recalculating. I'm convinced we've been looking in the wrong place—too far west. Where this boy Pat says he found the Marco Polo wreck is exactly where I figure the Kampuchean opium ship went down."

Vincent, who had stretched out on the sofa, opened his eyes. "Yes? But if the Thai is just a kid, how can you believe him?"

"He's *completely* unguarded. After we dropped Clay off, I took him for a beer. Clay's film unit's moving to Pattaya in a few days, and Pat's going with them. He's going to take me out to the spot where he found the ship." Will drained his glass and poured another whiskey. "I have that old lucky feeling. I think this Pat is on to something."

"Good work," Beau said. "But check it out as soon as you can. We have no time to lose. A lotta other people want that ship. 'Course they're still huntin' off the coast of Hua Hin. Too far west, if you're right."

Will chuckled. "I'm ninety-nine percent positive. You

see, the ship was supposed to have sunk near Hua Hin. But my revised calculations indicate the ship could have been washed much farther east."

Beau toasted Will. "I knew you were the right man for the job when I hired you."

"And I've turned into a damned good pearl farmer, too."

Beau snickered. "Yeah. Listen, why'd you take Clay to Phuket?"

"To photograph the place for *International Geography*."

"I wish you hadn't taken her there without informin' me first. There is a lot that an outsider, especially a journalist, should not see."

"I'm well aware of that," Will snapped. "She saw pearls being cultured and nothing else! To hell with it. I'm going home to bed. I've had a long day."

Will sulked out. Beau leaned back, propping his feet on the ebony desk. "Keep close to this one," he instructed Vincent. "Especially when he gets together with the Thai kid. Keep an eye on him in general."

"Okay, Beau. That won't be hard to do. I will enjoy it even. He is very attractive."

"You come over here and unzip my fly. Then you tell me all about what you see in Will Stone."

When she returned to the hotel after her trip to Phuket, Clay ran into Peter and Linda Zaidenberg on their way to the Bamboo Bar for a nightcap.

"Come on," Linda urged.

"I'd love to," Clay said, "but I'm really wiped out."

"You'd better come," Peter whispered. "Rona Barrett Zaidenberg here is going to tell all about Nick and Natalia's love scene behind a closed set."

"You've persuaded me." Clay laughed.

They passed the convention board "Welcome EEC Trade in Tapioca," and Linda led the way to the bar, scanning the crowd as they walked toward the back. "Coast is clear. This is top secret, you understand."

"Hmmm," Clay said to Peter. "That sounds promising."

Linda withheld the story until the waiter had brought

their drinks, then leaned forward. "Okay," she said in a loud whisper. "You've got the basic picture. Bathtub scene. Five takes. By that time, Natalia's cleaner than she's been in years. Her olive skin's a rosy glow—olive *minus* the oil."

Peter groaned. "Now, now, love. Hiss, hiss."

"All right. Back to straight reporting." Linda's red hair was piled on top of her head, Katharine Hepburn style. Although her body was petite, her face was rounded and childlike. She was quintessentially cute, to her everlasting dissatisfaction. "So, according to the rewrite, Nick lets himself in with a key. Natalia calls out from the bathroom, and he saunters in. 'You look like a boy with your hair all slicked back,' he says. And she says, 'Oh, does that turn you on?' "

"Something about this dialogue sounds very familiar," Clay said, remembering the time in London with Josh. "Sorry—continue."

"Well, you can see from an instant flicker on Nick's face that Natalia *does* turn him on. And she realizes it, too, which turns her on."

"Oh, I love it already." Peter laughed.

"Anyway, it's all eye contact between them for the next minute or so until they get into the bedroom. The thing was set up as a continuous shot, to keep the rapport going between them."

"That's amazing. If you could have heard the things Nick was saying about Natalia last night," Clay remarked, *sotto voce*, looking around to make sure neither of the stars had come in. After a quick glance around the room, she did a double take. Josh Lewis was sitting at a side table in front, laughing. His blonde companion was blocked from view, but Clay was sure she knew who it was: Audrey! Obviously she had come to Bangkok to see Josh. Clay turned back to Linda. "Go on! Don't keep us in suspense." She tried hard not to look back at her stepsister and Josh.

"Anyway, they come into the bedroom, fall on the bed, and Natalia, playful, kittenish, starts pulling off Nick's clothes. Slow though, stripteaselike. I mean, it had been written that way, but she was obviously putting something extra into it."

Linda took a swallow of her daiquiri and went on. "You could've plugged a toaster into the scene it was so electric. So when Nick's all undressed, he's got this enormous erection, hidden from camera view, of course. But you can tell *that* really perked up Natalia even more. They continue on with their lines and then fall under the covers together and kiss and writhe around. Cut! Right? Right. The film stops rolling. A wrap in one take, and everyone starts bustling around and—lo and behold—our two stars are *still* getting it on like gangbusters, totally oblivious to the world. And they go on—and *on*."

"Did *you* keep watching after the cameras stopped rolling?" Peter inquired.

Linda looked sheepish. "Yes, sort of. I mean, I didn't stare. But from time to time, I just had to sneak a quick peek. Most everybody else just went about their business, ignoring them."

"Amazing," Clay said.

"Hmmm, I'm truly impressed." Peter raised his glass. "To good old Nick. I never thought he had it in him."

"Not only that. Afterward, they took off together and haven't been seen since."

"Ah, so." Clay smiled. "And they think it can only happen in the movies." She stifled a yawn. "Sorry, Linda, that wasn't a comment on your ability as a master storyteller. But I've had a long day."

"Get some sleep," Linda said, catching sight of Josh and the blonde. "You'll need it."

"Oh, her?" Clay tilted her head in that direction. "No threat." She tried to sound calm, but she was mad as hell that Audrey had come around the world to see Josh. Audrey had to have what Clay wanted; it was compulsive with her.

Peter turned around to see who they were talking about. "Right, Clay. Anyone can see she's just another beautiful, scintillating, stylish, sexy, vacuous blonde. No challenge."

"Peter!" Linda chided. "You're a creep."

"No, it's just a friendly warning, Clay," Peter said.

"That looks like a woman who would devour small children to get what she wants."

Clay kissed Linda and Peter good night and gathered up her camera bag. On the way out, she stopped by Josh's table.

"Hi, Clay," Josh said, startled. "I didn't know you were here. Ah, you know Aud—"

"Hello, Audrey. Surprised to see you in this part of the world. Are you here for the waters?" Clay asked, deadpan.

Josh Lewis grinned.

"I don't know what you mean," Audrey replied.

"No, I didn't think you would." Clay said. "It's a line from *Casablanca.*"

"Won't you join us, Clay?" Josh asked, a little sheepishly, Clay thought.

"No, thanks. I just got back from Phuket with my friend Will. It was beautiful. You'll flip over the pictures I took. Anyway, see you in the morning, Josh. Lovely to see you, Audrey."

Clay told herself that there was no reason to be jealous of Audrey. No man ever satisfied her for long. And Audrey herself was such a mental lightweight, surely Josh woud tire of her soon enough.

Clay took stock of herself in the elevator mirror as the lift whirred slowly to her floor. "Not bad, kid," she said out loud to reassure herself. When Clay was around Audrey Yates, she had to keep reminding herself that she was no longer seventeen and Audrey no longer had the upper hand on beauty and sophistication.

Now, for the first time since Clay was a teenager, she and Audrey were both after the same man. This time, though, Clay was going to fight for what she wanted.

Chapter 25

"BANGKOK is so noisy one can't even hear the thunder," Lars Knudsen observed the day the film unit moved to Pattaya, on the eastern coast of the Gulf of Siam. It was a welcome relief for the crew to move to the seashore.

That day and the next were spent setting up the light and sound equipment for shooting in a teak Thai-style house on a hill south of town. The day after that, the crew was given an unscheduled break: Nick Reynolds and Natalia Ferrari, still an item, had come down with food poisoning from sharing a skewer of barbecued baby squid, bought from a street vendor.

Peter Zaidenberg rented a blue-canopied fishing boat, the *Nahora Samui*, to take Linda and Clay to the off-shore islands for a day of diving exploration. At eight, Clay met Peter on the beach and stashed her cameras on board.

"Where's Linda?" Clay asked after the boatman had arrived back with beer and soda for the trip.

"She had a breakfast meeting with Josh. I wish she'd hurry up."

"Hello!" Linda called out from across the street, in front of the Regent Pattaya Hotel where they were staying. She raced over to them, taking off her shoes when she hit the sandy beach. "I can't come with you," she reported glumly. "Harvey Schaffner and Marcy Sims rolled into town last night. Josh was up most of the night with Harvey, and now he's in a foul mood. I have to spend the day with the two of them and Fred Justin, going over production costs and schedules. Harvey's fit to be tied that we're a couple of days behind."

Peter kissed his wife's forehead. "I'm sorry, honey."

Linda shrugged. "Yeah, the trouble with being Josh's assistant is you have to work as hard as he does."

"What's Harvey Schaffner like?" Clay asked.

"Kind of small and wiry," Linda said, "with dark hair combed judiciously to hide the receding hairline. He's moving all the time, jumping up, on the phone, taking aspirin, ordering coffee. It exhausts me to be around him." Linda sighed. "I've got to get back. Have a good day." She put on her shoes and ran back across the street and over the lawn to the hotel.

"Where's your little Thai sidekick?" Peter asked Clay. "I thought he was coming with us."

"He was supposed to. I got a note in my box this morning saying he was taking Will Stone out to a reef off Koh Lin to show him a wreck he thinks dates back to Marco Polo."

"Highly unlikely that a ship could have survived seven hundred years."

"I know. It's possible, I guess, but I'm amazed that Will would take the time to go out there. Anyway," Clay said, "let's get going."

"Damn! Look at those clouds coming up over there. Just our luck to get more rain on our day off," Peter said as they climbed on board.

That evening, back in her room, Clay was stretched out on her bed, phone in hand. "Okay, Owen. I miss you, too. I'll wire you and let you know when I'm coming back. Call Garnet for me and say hi. Okay, 'by." Owen Thomas had called Clay to say he loved both her and her latest photos for her cultured-pearl article.

A knock on the door was followed by "Clay? It's me. Josh."

Clay unlocked the door, still wrapped in a towel from her shower, and greeted a smiling man. He was holding a bottle of Taittinger in an ice bucket and two crystal, tulip-shaped champagne glasses. "I don't remember ordering anything from room service," she said, smiling back.

Josh walked straight to her bureau and set the champagne down. With a flick, the already-loosened cork exploded to the ceiling, and he poured quickly, handing her a glass. "To our friend, Oriental Pearl."

Clay sipped. "What's the occasion?"

"She won her first start, by *three* lengths, at Santa Anita."

"Oh, Josh!" Clay threw her arms around him; her towel fell to the floor.

Josh checked out her naked, tan body. "Hmmm, I like the way you express enthusiasm."

Clay leaned down for the towel.

"Don't you dare," he warned, steering her gently over to the double bed. They stretched out crosswise, on their sides, facing each other.

"Eddie Landry's doing a great job. He's nominated her for the Oakleaf Stakes there for two-year-old fillies. If she wins that, Landry thinks she's a good candidate for the Kentucky Oaks."

"Or the Derby," Clay said. "Fillies can win that, too."

Josh laughed. "You never give up, do you? She's *my* horse, you know."

"I know," Clay said, laughing, too. "I'm merely an interested bystander."

Josh rubbed a cold hand over her belly. "I don't know if I can believe that, but it doesn't matter. I'm happy you convinced me to buy Oriental Pearl." He kissed her lips, then pulled back. As an afterthought, he said, "I want you to know that Audrey didn't jet to Thailand at my request. So don't be jealous."

"Who's jealous? I'm not especially fond of Audrey, but I certainly can't blame you for falling all over her."

"What? You think I'm falling all over her?" There was a sharp rise to his voice.

"I was *joking*, Josh. I don't care about you and Audrey." She nestled closer to him and began unbuttoning his shirt. "I care about you and me."

Josh held his champagne glass to her lips. "To us."

"We're not an us, Josh. We're taking it easy, remember?"

Josh looked perplexed for an instant, then pulled her close to him. There was the faint aroma of Coppertone suntan oil on his chest. "That's what I need—to take it easy." He recounted his various hassles with Harvey Schaffner. It was obvious to Clay that most of the problems rose out of their mutual dislike; they looked for reasons to disagree with one another.

'You seem tired, Josh. What can I do?"

Josh shifted around and lay back, his shoulders and head resting on the pillows. "I want you," he said. "I want you to take me. Do with me what you will—I'm yours." He closed his eyes. legs and arms stretched out.

Clay undressed him slowly, starting with his shirt and working down. Then she massaged and kissed Josh's toes and worked her way back up his calves and thighs. She licked and kissed his balls and took all of him into her mouth until he grew so large that not all of him would fit.

Josh moaned with pleasure as Clay, slowly and deliberately, aroused him almost to the point of orgasm. She withdrew her lips and moved around to ease herself down on to him. Grabbing his shoulders with her hands, she began to rock back and forth. Shifting her legs to a kneeling position, she began to ride her passive mount like a horse that was hers to control at will—trotting, cantering, faster, with urgency. A few minutes later, at a full gallop, Clay and Josh both came, Josh's fingers digging into Clay's buttocks, their faces contorted in ecstasy.

Afterward, Josh fell asleep. Clay gently dislodged her arms and legs, which were wound around him, and took another shower.

While she was combing out her hair, Clay remembered Pat. He was supposed to call or come by at five. It was after seven. Clay brought the phone into the bathroom so she would not disturb Josh.

The information desk had no message from Pat. She called several of the crew members who knew him, but no one had seen him that day. She hung up the phone, and it rang almost immediately. It was Fred Justin. Natalia Ferrari had had a fight with Nick Reynolds and was in the lobby, checking out. Josh was needed on the scene to intercede and soothe the star's volatile feelings.

Clay awakened Josh and explained the situation.

Josh dressed quickly. "I apologize—twice. For falling asleep and for the hasty exit."

"See you around." Clay grinned good-naturedly but wondered if she would ever have Josh to herself for an entire evening.

The wooden ceiling fan whirred squeakily in Will Stone's dimly lit room in the Hotel Ran Khai in Bangkok.

Will poured another shot of Mekong whiskey into Beau Yates's glass and took his own drink straight from the bottle. They were celebrating. The ship off Koh Lin island that Pat had found was the Kampuchean opium ship, sunk in a storm in 1971.

Beau laughed. "Imagine that dumb kid thinkin' it's some seven-hundred-year-old Marco Polo ship."

Will did not laugh. "He was smart enough to find a ship that a lot of other people have been searching long and hard for."

"That didn't take brains. Just luck. Hit me with some more whiskey." Beau held out his glass, and Will refilled it to the top. "Okay, here's how we'll work it. I've lined up a house for you and Vincent near Pattaya, off a cove past the Royal Cliff Beach. A good secluded place to take off from."

Will scowled. "Look, Vincent isn't a diver. If I have a couple of good men working underwater with me, I can bring that stuff up in a week, maybe less. But alone, at night, with Vincent on watch—"

"Shit," Beau said, "you don't need to tell me we have to work fast. But we can't risk *anybody* knowing about this. The American narcs, the Thai and Kampuchean governments, the Mafia, every fucker in the drug business wants that ship. And *we've* fuckin' got it! I'm not taking any chances." Beau reached into his breast pocket, pulled out a .38 revolver, and tossed it on the table. "Take it."

"No," Will said. "I've never carried a gun. I don't intend to now."

"Listen, stoneface," Beau slurred drunkenly, "you've never been close to this much money, not even if you'd found all the gold in all those Spanish fuckin' ships you were lookin' for. Carry this with you at *all* times."

The phone rang. Will startled, picked it up. "Yes, Will Stone here."

"Hi, Will Stone," said the voice at the other end. "What a surprise to reach you on the first try."

"Hello, Clay. How are you?" Will glanced over at Beau, who seemed to bristle at the sound of his stepsister's name.

"Fine. Listen, I'm calling about my friend Pat. Do you know where he is?"

"No."

"Oh, I thought since you were out with him today—"

"Well, yes—but how did you know that?"

"Pat left a note that he was dragging you out to Koh Lin reef to check out that treasure ship. Anyway, he was supposed to come by here at five, but he never did show up."

"Oops, just a minute, F-stop. There's someone at the door." Will put the phone down and beckoned Beau into the bedroom. "What'll I tell her?"

"What does she know?" Beau queried.

Will repeated Clay's end of the conversation.

"Okay. Tell her Pat's gone to visit relatives, anything to get her off the scent."

Will went back to the phone. "Sorry, love, the lady with fresh towels. Where were we?"

"Pat, do you know—"

"Oh, yes, what a day. He couldn't find the ship after all that. We wound up looking at tropical fish. After that, I bought him a couple of beers, and he said something about heading inland, some relative's birthday, but I don't really remember."

"That's odd," Clay said. "Did he say when he'd be back?"

"No. But you know the Thais. They run on a completely different time schedule than the *farongs*." *Farongs* were what the Thais called Westerners. "It's *now* that's important to them. Now can drag on for days or weeks. Don't worry. I'm sure he'll turn up soon."

"Hmmm, yeah. I just think it's so strange that he didn't stop by here and tell me."

"How long will you be in Pattaya, Clay?" Will asked.

"Couple of weeks. But I'll be back and forth to Bangkok."

"Good. Call me, we'll have dinner. Listen, love, I was just dressing to go out."

"Okay, Will, thanks. Talk to you soon."

After Will put down the phone, he stared at Beau uneasily. "Do *you* know where Pat is?"

"Couldn't begin to tell you." Beau chuckled. "Well, let's say he's achieved *nirvana*."

"What do you mean?"

"Shit, you act like a squeamish old maid, Stone. Go out tonight. Get yourself a massage and a girl. I think you spend too much time in this dingy room, drinkin' and porin' over your fuckin' maps."

"I don't want a woman! That Thai boy didn't harm anyone!"

"Fuck! He had a mouth, didn't he? He told everyone who'd listen about that ship, didn't he? No one else but you bothered to take him seriously. But he'd be in the way from now on—dangerous. Look, he told Clay that he was goin' out with you. What else do you s'pose he told her?"

"Nothing," Will said, suddenly scared. "She didn't know anything at all."

"Hmmm. Well, we'll have to keep an eye on her." Beau pulled out the Shark's Eye shell and sniffed several heaping fingernails worth of cocaine. "Tell me somethin'. Exactly what was it between my stepsister and you?"

Will took another drink. "Just a fling years ago. She had a crush on me. I was the sophisticated older man, you know. But the novelty wore off."

Beau burst out into a loud guffaw. "Yeah, shit, I know what you mean. You're not hung up on her now, are you?" he asked casually.

Will Stone shook his head. "No, it's over between us."

"That's not exactly what I asked you, Will."

"Goddamnit, no! We're business partners, Beau. My private life is of no concern to you. You understand?"

Beau drained the whiskey from his glass and got up to leave.

"Yeah, Will. I understand."

Chapter 26

ROSES, double-headed bougainvillea, hibiscus, and orchids, deep-purple Madame Pompadours, and cerulean blue Rothschildiana spilled out of the hanging baskets on the porch of the fifty-year-old Thai house. Large multicolored butterflies fluttered around a lavish display of fruits—mandarin oranges, bananas, custard apples, wine-colored mangosteens, and furry rambutans—piled neatly on a flat straw mat on the floor.

Natalia Ferrari read the note slowly, and tears welled up in her large soulful eyes as she absorbed the terrible news. She shook her head, the tears spilling down over her high cheekbones, and leaned back into the white-lace hammock. The note fell from her lap. A breeze picked it up and carried it away, over the teak railing toward a tamarind tree where wild parakeets sang.

"Cut! Print it," Josh Lewis said. He hurried over to Natalia and kissed her full lips. *"Bella, carissima,"* he whispered. "You were sensational."

"Grazie, Josh. I love you. You are a wonderful director," the star said in her lilting accent. Josh had succeeded in convincing her to stay without having to point out the legalities and contractual obligations. He had also renegotiated peace between Natalia and Nick Reynolds, although their brief affair had ended.

"That's it for the day," Josh called to the crew. "Linda, go find Don and Zack." They were the chief stuntmen. "Wait a sec, Lars. We have to talk about the boat chase. Fred? What's the story on that warehouse? Do we have the permit to shoot there tomorrow afternoon?"

Fred Justin scowled. "I'm working on it. Damned bu-

253

reaucratic red tape. No one seems authorized to make any decisions in this country. We may have to go up to Bangkok tonight, to be sitting on the bureau's doorstep in the morning when they open."

"Josh . . . Josh," Marcy Sims, ex-lover of Josh, star of his film *Victorian Pastoral*, and current wife of Harvey Schaffner, came over to him. The titian-haired English beauty was wearing white pants and a scooped-neck white T-shirt pulled tight against her ample breasts.

"Where's Harvey?" Josh inquired.

"Oh, he went back to the hotel to make calls. Listen, Josh—"

"Sorry to interrupt," Lars Knudsen said. "Clay and I have to go check the progress on the underwater set. Can we talk later about the chase scene?"

"Sure, Lars." Josh turned back to Marcy. "Listen, Marce, I'm really—"

Marcy Sims brushed her fingers against Josh's hand, then took hold. "I have to talk to you. It can't wait." Her green eyes pleaded.

Josh nodded and walked back out on the porch with her.

"I'm going crazy, Josh. I made such a huge mistake, leaving you and marrying Harvey. He's a demon workaholic, the most jealous man I've ever met. I can't breathe anymore." Marcy put her hands around his waist and dug in her fingers. "I want you, Josh," she said softly. "I want you back." She lifted her face, intending to kiss him, but one of the lighting technicians wandered out.

Josh pulled out his pack of cigarettes. "Want one?"

"Hmmm." Marcy accepted, and Josh lit hers, then his.

Josh dragged slowly, considering the right words. "Marcy, you're a beautiful, talented woman. I'd love to work with you again. But we could never *live* together again. I sympathize, but you went into that one with your eyes open."

"Oh, Josh, I don't want a lecture. Everyone makes mistakes." Marcy looked over the porch to the sea.

"Look, I was hung up on you for a long time. I was pissed as hell when you left me. But a lot has gone down since then." Although Marcy's back was to him, Josh could tell from the way she trembled that she was crying. "I'm sorry you're unhappy, Marcy. Maybe you can talk to Harvey, work it out."

Marcy wiped her eyes with the back of her index fingers. "Oh, fuck you, Josh!"

Half an hour later, Josh Lewis arrived back at the hotel. He hadn't eaten lunch and was trying to decide whether to nip down to the terrace café for some Thai noodles.

"Josh! Darlin'. I was just gettin' ready to track you down." Audrey Yates breezed across the open-air lobby. She had on a black skirt, a Chinese red blouse, and an antique belt fashioned of linked pieces of carved jade. Her blonde hair was plaited in one long braid down her back.

"Well, this is a surprise, Audrey. You hungry?"

"Goodness, it's too early for dinner."

"Call it late lunch or high tea. I'm starving."

Audrey smiled. "I'll come watch you eat. You know, I was so bored in Hong Kong without you. I should never have accepted that invitation, except they're old friends of mother's. Anyway, when I got to the Oriental, they told me you were down here in Pattaya. I decided that a little relaxation by the seashore was just what I needed." Audrey paused for breath. "I have an idea. Why don't you come up to my room and order a snack from room service? You look tired, an' I'm just worn out from my trip."

Josh glanced at his watch. He could spare about forty-five minutes. And none of the film crew would track him down in Audrey's room. Audrey knew just the right distractions, and that's what he needed right now, more than food. "All right, Audrey. Lead the way."

Out of the corner of his eye, at that moment, he saw Clay walking in with Lars. She smiled at him nonchalantly and went down the stairs with Lars to the Viennese coffee shop.

Feast or famine, Josh thought to himself as he pressed the button for the elevator.

The next morning, Fred Justin phoned Linda Zaidenberg

from Bangkok to report that Josh had been out jogging, fallen into a pothole, and broken his ankle. He was in a cast to his knee, and the doctor had ordered him to stay off it for the rest of the day.

On impulse, Clay hired a car to take her to Bangkok, and by noon she was at Josh's hotel door, a stack of the latest American magazines in one hand and a pint of Häagen Dazs ice cream in the other.

Ensconced on the rattan sofa, Josh had his left leg propped up straight, his good foot resting on the floor. He held the phone in his lap, and a paper-strewn coffee table had been pulled up next to him to be used as a desk.

"I come bearing gifts of sympathy."

Josh broke into a smile. "What are you doing here? And *where* did you get Häagen Dazs in Southeast Asia?"

"Oh, I have connections." Clay handed him a spoon from the bar. "I hope you like rum raisin. We've never discussed ice cream preferences."

"One of my all-time favorites." Josh tore off the top and dipped his spoon in. "Ah, already tempered to a soft consistency. Fabulous—have some." He fed her a spoonful.

A bellboy knocked and came in carrying two vases. One held a mixed bouquet, the other, two dozen coral roses.

"Good God, Clay. This, too?"

"I'd love to take credit, but I'm not that extravagant." Clay handed Josh the cards from the flowers.

"From my mother," Josh said, reading the first.

"Your mother? My, news travels fast."

Josh grinned. "I had to call her this morning. It's her birthday."

Clay found it touching that in the midst of all this, a broken ankle, a behind-schedule film, and a dozen daily crises, Josh had remembered his mother's birthday. "What an excellent son you are."

Josh looked down. "Well, after my brother died, there was just me. My mother was in bad shape for a while."

"You never told me. When—"

"Four years ago. He was younger than me. He OD'd on heroin." Josh shrugged. "Sounds like a tawdry movie script. I don't like to talk about it." He glanced at the other card and tossed it on the table.

Clay could not read the message, but it was signed "All my love, Audrey."

"Good thing you're not jealous."

"Yes." Clay kept her tone light, although she experienced a tinge of emotion. Audrey was relentless. "It's a good thing you have her to send you roses. I'm not that romantic."

"I'll take ice cream any day. Why don't you come over here and sit down?" He cleared his lap by putting the phone on the floor. The phone rang immediately.

After a couple of seconds of conversation, Clay gathered from the constraint in Josh's voice that it was none other than her stepsister. Audrey, it seemed, wanted to bring over a picnic. Josh told her he was busy, but after a while, he gave in, emphasizing that he couldn't see her before six.

It annoyed Clay that Josh was putty in Audrey's fingers and that he seemed to think it would be fine to spend the afternoon with Clay, then shoo her out before Audrey got there. By the time Josh cut short his conversation, Clay was livid, though determined not to show it.

"Sorry," Josh said. "Let's see, where were we?"

"I was about to tell you how much I really admire what you're doing with *Golden Triangle*. The rushes look really terrific."

Josh beamed. "God, you think so? I'm so crazy by this point I don't know anything anymore. Thank you."

"Take my word for it. You don't have to worry about Harvey or anyone. You've got a winner." Clay glanced at her watch. "And I have a lunch date, so I'd better be going."

"Oh? Is that what brought you to town?"

"No, of course not. I came to cheer you up." Clay said it convincingly enough to sound unconvincing.

"Can't you stay a while longer?"

"I'd like to, but I really have to go. When are you coming back to Pattaya?"

"Tomorrow. I'm taking a helicopter. I'll be there by seven."

Clay kissed him on the mouth. "Then I'll see you tomorrow. Hope you feel better."

Down in the lobby, Clay felt pleased by her performance but would gladly murder Audrey. She called Will Stone, hoping he would be free for lunch, but the operator said he was out.

"When do you expect him?" Clay asked.

"I not sure. He go south for a while," the Thai operator responded.

Late that afternoon, back in Pattaya, Clay stopped by Dave's Diver's Den to see if anyone there had seen or heard from Pat, but the response was negative. Clay felt more and more disturbed by the boy's disappearance. Every day she expected him to show up back at her hotel. She knew that there had been no formal agreement between them other than the forty *baht* she gave him when she needed him to go around town with her. But Pat had not only liked Clay; he had loved doing odd jobs on the "big American film." It did not seem to Clay that a relative's birthday was reason enough for him to leave town for so many days.

After she left the dive shop, Clay went to meet the Zaidenbergs and Lars for dinner at Wee Andy's Trade Winds, a small restaurant that advertised "Genuine English Food, Prepared Scottish Style With A Gentle Thai Touch." They gorged themselves on fish and chips and barbecued spareribs and talked about the underwater film sequences, including the climactic one that would be coming up soon.

"Feel like a movie tonight?" Linda asked, out on the street. "The English-language cinema's showing *Raiders of the Lost Ark* and *Wolfen*."

"I'll pass," Clay said.

"Then what about going to the Las Vegas disco? That place is extremely colorful," Linda said.

Lars made a face. "How can you have so much energy in this climate?"

"I'm living it up while Josh's away. Tomorrow at seven, I turn back into the pumpkin-haired director's assistant."

Peter and Linda Zaidenberg trundled off to the cinema, and Clay and Lars walked up the beach toward the hotel. Lars was depressed: Harvey Schaffner was getting him down, too. Besides, he missed his wife and two young daughters and was longing to see them. Clay urged Lars to talk, then spent the next hour trying to cheer him up. They were so engrossed in conversation that they passed the hotel and walked two miles farther down the beach, away from town. It was dark by then, although the moon and the neon lights in the distance threw an orange glow over the beach. They continued on farther, enjoying the sound of the waves slapping up over their bare feet. Rounding a cove, they walked past the Royal Cliff Beach Hotel.

"I suppose we should turn around," Lars said, suddenly becoming aware of how far they had come.

"Yes. Look, tied to that pier over there. That's a great-looking boat, larger than most of the ones you see in town." A white fifty-five-foot yacht rocked gently at the end of a wooden pier. There appeared to be some heavy equipment on the pier, and there were dim lights on inside. "Shall we take a look?" Clay and Lars started down the rickety wooden structure.

A blond man emerged from the far side of the boat. "Yes?" he called out. "Can I help you?"

"We were just admiring your yacht." Clay called back. "Sorry, didn't mean to intrude." She and Lars turned back toward the beach.

"Clay? For God's sake, is it you?"

The blond man was Will Stone.

"Will! What a coincidence. I phoned you to have lunch with me today in Bangkok." She introduced Lars to Will.

"I just came down here to check out this baby for a friend who's interested in buying it. Wanted me to give it a test run."

"It's a beauty," Lars said.

"By the way, Will," Clay said, "have you heard anything from Pat?"

"Pat? No, nothing. Haven't you?"

It seemed to Clay that the question had made Will a bit nervous, that he might be covering up something. "No, not a word. Can we have a look around before we hike back to town?"

"Well, it's a mess inside. I've been diddling around with the motor." He paused. "Actually, to tell the truth, this is a little embarrassing. I have a friend inside who's not all dressed," Will grinned sheepishly.

Clay had started toward the boat. Her eyes locked on the equipment—a scuba tank, some underwater strobes, and several commercial lift bags—on the pier. Just the sort of apparatus Will used for treasure salvaging. "Oh, *sorry!*" Clay laughed. "By all means, we won't disturb you."

"I'll call you for dinner," Will said, waving good-by to them. "Soon."

Will Stone watched Clay Fitzgerald and her friend disappear around the cove toward town.

"Who was that?" Vincent Lascaux came on deck.

"Oh, just some people wanting to look at the boat."

"No, I don't think so. I heard the name 'Clay.' That is your friend, no? Beau's stepsister?"

Will nodded. "Look, let's get this stuff loaded on. It'll take us at least an hour to reach the reef."

Vincent did not move. "I watched through the porthole. I saw your friend looking at the salvage equipment. She looked as if she knew what it was."

"Impossible. Come on. Let's get going."

"You finish loading. I have to go back to the house to get something."

Will Stone stood on the pier and stared at the equipment in the moonlight. Of course, Clay would recognize the gear. It made him uneasy that Vincent Lascaux had figured that out, too.

Will saw the light go on back at the house. He didn't like Vincent Lascaux, hated having to work with him. The man was a cold fish, and Will could never tell what he was thinking.

Will looked up at the stars—so clear and close. At that moment, he would have given anything to be back in Key West, Florida, looking at the same stars from the deck of his little red houseboat.

Chapter 27

"WHEW, what a glare." Sunny Fitzgerald put on her dark glasses as she and Beau Yates boarded the *hang yao* at the landing dock in front of the Oriental Hotel. A somber Thai boatman backed the wooden, long-tailed craft into the Chao Phya River and headed north, weaving in and out of the other river traffic—crowded water taxis and ferries, a sleek ship from the Royal Thai Navy, cumbersome sand and rice barges so heavily loaded that their prows were nearly at water level. In the western sky, the sun was an orange ball of fire, almost ready to drop behind the temples of Thonburi, Bangkok's sister city.

Resting her feet on the empty seat in front of her, Sunny said, "I can't wait to see your new house, honey."

Beau lit a Turkish cigarette. "Well, it's kind of my country house. I still use the place in Bangkok when I'm workin' late."

"Imagine, you with a country home—even if the country is Thailand." Sunny smiled. "I'm so pleased your business is goin' so well."

"I'm glad you're proud of me, mother. Finally."

Sunny looked around at the glass-and-ceramic spire of the Buddhist temple, Wat Arun, glistening a fiery gold, and over on the right bank, at the Royal Palace and the minarets of the Temple of the Emerald Buddha. Her eyes caught sight of an old man brushing his teeth in the brown river. Shuddering, she turned her gaze back on her handsome son. "Oh, darlin', I admit there was a time when I was afraid you wouldn't get your life together. But that's in the past."

Passing the Bangkoknoi Railway Station, the boatman

steered left, by the boathouse of the magnificent Royal Barges, and into the large waterway, *Klong Bangkok Noi.* As they traversed deeper into Thonburi, the noise and pollution of Bangkok gave way to the tranquillity of an exotic suburb: graceful Thai houses built over the water on stilts—dilapidated shacks, side by side with elegant teak domiciles; fruit-laden banana trees, orchid and jasmine orchards; Thai and Chinese temples along the riverbanks; floating restaurants serving up hot, spicy dishes. The boat traveled through a maze of watery streets, the nameless, narrow *klongs.*

"I don't see how they can live that way," Sunny said as they passed a family bathing in the murky water in front of their house, modestly wrapped in flower-patterned *sarongs.* "Did you see? One of 'em was washing her hair in that water." They had seen a dead dog float by a few minutes before. "They do their clothes, their dishes—it's *too* unsanitary!"

"They don't drink it, though. They use bottled water. Look, over there." A small boat with a tentlike curtain around the middle paddled by, and a heavily made up Thai woman with a flower in her hair stared over at them. "You don't see many like her anymore on the *klongs.* Floating prostitutes. They're nicknamed 'water babies.' "

"This is quite picturesque, honey," Sunny said. "But we've been skimmin' down these canals for half an hour. When are we gettin' there?" Sunny looked glamorously out of place, for the *klongs,* in a coral Halston and a diamond-and-gold necklace Mac Fitzgerald had given her for her fortieth birthday. "I don't understand why you didn't buy a place in a more fashionable area, like one of those *sois* near the embassies."

"I wanted a place I could get away to. You know how goddamned loud it gets in town."

"Do you still have a problem with those headaches, sweetie?" There was a look of concern in Sunny's eyes.

Beau nodded. "I've tried medicine, even Chinese herbal remedies, acupuncture—nothin' works. They come on when there's a lotta noise or I'm upset. Ah, here we are!"

The boatman turned off the motor of the *hang yao* and guided it over to Beau's porch with a long bamboo pole.

"Suthep!" Beau clapped his hands to summon his young Thai houseboy. The handsome twenty-year-old, wearing a white jacket and black pants, rushed out to the screened veranda and helped Sunny out of the boat, and, smiling, greeted her in the Thai, *sawadee krap.*

"Beau! This is just charmin'," Sunny exclaimed enthusiastically.

"Come on, mother. I'll show you around."

The walls of the Thai-style house were paneled with teak, and the floors were dark wood, except the hallway, bathrooms, and kitchen, which were laid with Chinese black and white tiles. The small rooms were too sparsely furnished for Sunny's taste, but the clutter of mementos from Beau's travels were a tribute to the good taste he had absorbed from his New Orleans grandparents. In the living room, Sunny noted, Beau had placed Burmese lacquer tables at either end of the red-and-black-chintz sofa to display his collection of five-color Bencharong porcelain—made in China for export only to Thailand. The walls held late-eighteenth-century Siamese prints from the Ratanakosin period. Sunny was surprised to see the hodge-podge of sculpture around the house—a Balinese flower god, Cambodian stone figures, wooden Burmese statues, and Thai stone Buddha images. It was hard for her to imagine Beau as a serious art collector. Still, there was a great deal she didn't know about her son and his life in the Orient.

"Did someone help you do this? Come on, tell the truth," Sunny cajoled.

" 'Course not, mother. Only a few people even know about this place. Come upstairs."

The stairs entered directly into Beau's suite of rooms: study, bedroom, dressing room, bath, and a screened-in reading porch. There was a red-and-black Persian rug in the bedroom and, lacquered in the same colors, an ornately carved four-poster opium bed. That was it except for two small palms in matching baskets.

"This is quite spectacular, honey. You must really wow your girl friends with this bed."

"It's what I do *in* it that wows 'em," Beau replied.

"Oh, Beau, really. Is that any way to talk to your mother?"

"You look more like a sister, and you know it." Beau took a red Chinese robe out of the closet. "I'll be down in a minute. I wanna take a quick shower. Suthep'll fix you a drink."

Sunny sat in a rattan chair by the screened picture window. Outside, the back of the house looked out on a tangle of jungle growth—flame of the forest, tamarind, bamboo. Sipping her vodka and tonic, she felt content that Beau, at last, was making a grand success of himself. She wished Audrey would marry again and settle down. Even with her alimony, Audrey spent too much of Sunny's money. The Willows Stud was doing all right, but there never seemed to be enough *extra* money. Since Mac's death, though, Sunny had been happy. She had to be discreet in Virginia about whom she dated and with whom she went to bed, but when she traveled, she was free, still uninhibited enough to indulge in her appetite for younger men.

Beau came downstairs, his hair still wet from his shower. "Suthep! *Rew . . . hiw how!*"

The young Thai hurried in, carrying a bottle of Amarit lager for Beau and a selection of Thai appetizers, garnished with mint and flowers, which he spread out on the Chinese cloisonné coffee table.

"Oh, this looks lovely," Sunny said. "We won't need any dinner after this. What is it all?"

Beau leaned forward. "Suthep's specialties. Let's see, this here's called 'fat horses.' It's spicy meat steamed in banana leaves. And spring rolls . . . *gung tawt kriep*, deep-fried shrimp . . . *kai kwam*, eggs stuffed with pork and crab . . . *kaab muu*, crispy fried pork skin . . . and *nam prik*, red spicy sauce. It's real spicy, though. Be careful."

"My, I can't get over what a host you've become."

Beau went into the dining room and came back with a

suede pouch tied together with brown ribbon. "I have somethin' for you."

Sunny opened the case and took out two double-strand pearl necklaces and a third single-strand. "Oh, Beau, these are divine. But I have the feelin' you're gettin' ready to ask me to do you a favor."

Beau broke into a smile and watched his mother try on the pearls. "The same as last time, mother. You and Audrey wear them when you leave. In New York, Mr. Matasiow will pick you up at J.F.K. and take you to the Pierre. You can give him the two double strands when you get to your room."

"What about the third necklace?"

"I'll have it gift-wrapped in a box of candy. You'll give that to him as a present."

Sunny sighed and looked out the window. "Beau, I know you don't want me to know the ins and outs of your business. But these pearls must be very valuable. Are they real Orientals mixed with cultured? Is that why you don't want to risk payin' duty on them? Is that why you want us to smuggle them in?"

"Now, now, mother. You're not smugglin'. You're only wearin' 'em for a while. And they're all cultured, from my pearl farm."

"But—"

"Ask me no questions and I'll tell you no lies." Beau looked at Sunny with affection.

Sunny sighed. "All right, all right. Subject closed."

Suthep appeared with new drinks. Sunny complimented him on the hors d'oeuvres, and the houseboy broke into a grin and backed out of the room, bowing.

"I think I'll import a bunch of Thais to The Willows. Suthep's a dream."

Beau nodded vaguely, his eyes glazed over. Sunny was not sure whether Beau was lost in thought or one of his sulks was coming on.

"What's the matter, honey? Anythin' troublin' you?"

Beau did not respond.

Sunny went over and sat next to him. She took his hand

and kissed it. "Come on, tell me. I'm sorry I was givin' you the third degree. Come on, tell mama."

"It's business. I don't want to bother you. I wanted our evenin' to be perfect."

"Beau, you won't be botherin' me! You know you can talk to me. You always have."

"I've come upon a kind of dangerous realization. Will Stone is hung up on Clay. And that upsets me."

"Why should you care? Clay's only here long enough to shoot that movie. Audrey told me they'll be finished in Thailand in another week or so."

"Yeah, but if Clay finds out business secrets from Will, she might use the information to try and ruin me."

Sunny was concerned. "Is there really something Clay could find out that *could* affect you?"

"Well, without goin' into details—" The phone rang, and Beau picked it up quickly. "Hello . . . yeah, Vincent. What? When, tonight? Yeah . . . yeah, I see. Okay. Bring up as much as you can tonight. Yeah, I'll think about it." Beau put down the phone and rubbed his head. "Shit!"

"Honey, what's *wrong*?"

"It's that damned Clay. I think she's spyin' on Stone. Vincent just called from Pattaya and says he's pretty sure she knows what's goin' on."

"Beau, what *is* goin' on? Come, sit back here, and tell me, once and for all. How can I help if I don't know the facts?"

"Okay. I guess you'd better know. I have a few deals goin' at once. The cultured pearl farm's my front."

"Your front? But—"

"Don't say anything until you hear me out. I've got everything under control." One of his businesses, Beau explained, was "exporting" genuine Oriental pearls, procured by Vincent Lascaux from the black market, camouflaged among cultured ones. His and Vincent's other activity was smuggling heroin in false-bottom cases that held the pearls to select "jewelers" for fabulous prices. Will Stone, Beau told Sunny, had been brought in for his knowledge of treasure salvaging, to find the famous lost Kampuchean ship and bring up its drug contents. Will was also overseeing the mixing of the real and fake pearls in Phuket.

When Beau finished, he and Sunny sat in silence for a while. All the contentment that Sunny had felt a half hour earlier had vanished. Beau was in a dangerous business, taking major risks. And now Clay Fitzgerald could blow the whistle on him once again.

Loathing for her stepdaughter welled up in her. Beau had to be kept out of danger at all costs.

"What'll I do, mother?" Beau whispered.

"I don't think you have a hell of a lot of choice, honey. You're goin' to have to get Clay out of the picture. Make sure she is unable to continue poking around. But don't you dare do anything yourself. Get Vincent or someone else."

"How? I mean, she's all involved with that movie. Always surrounded by movie people."

Sunny laughed. "Do I have to do *all* your thinkin' for you? Have you forgotten that Clay's an underwater diver? They have accidents all the time—the bends—poisonous fish and sharks—they run out of air. I don't know what. Somethin' that'll get her out of here. That much you can figure out."

Beau hugged Sunny. "Oh, God, I love you. You're the only person in my whole life who *always* comes through for me." He had already decided; he would get Clay out of the way. Permanently.

The voice on the phone sounded clipped and professional.

"This is Linda Zaidenberg reporting from the Gulf of Siam with news of fresh disasters."

"What now?" Clay was still in bed, drinking coffee from room service.

"Peter just got back from the doctor. He went out body surfing with the stunt guys."

"And?"

"He sprained his neck. The doc says it'll be maybe a week before he can go diving."

"Oh, no." Clay knew how terrible a sprained neck could be underwater. Peter would not be able to move or see or look into a view finder or even get into a wet suit without excruciating pain. "But the big underwater scene . . ."

"Is scheduled for two days from now. Everything else *you* can handle. That scene is the big problem."

"Does Josh know?"

"God, yes. He helicoptered in with his cast and crutches a few minutes ago. I won't bother to repeat what he said."

"Listen, is Peter there? Can I speak to him?" Clay asked, and Peter came on the phone. "Peter, the diver's p-o-v shot? Through the porthole? I can do it. We don't have to wait."

"I wish you could, Clay. But it's tricky. You've got to dive down and with all the gear swim smoothly through that hole, around, upside down, and up again. One shot. To do it, you'd need about forty more pounds of muscle on you. I'm not trying to be chauvinistic, but you're not strong enough."

"I can *try* it, can't I?"

"Talk to Lars about it," Peter snapped, sounding miffed. "Oh, hell, Clay, I'm sorry. I'm just so fucking mad at myself. A sprained neck, for chrissakes. Yeah, talk to Lars. It's much more important to get the shot on schedule than to wait for me to do it. It's worth a try."

"Thanks, Peter."

Clay met with Lars in Josh's suite. Josh was not there when she arrived, but he came in just as Clay had managed to convince Lars to let her try the shot.

"What's worth a try?" Josh asked. He propped his crutches against the wall and hobbled over to the sofa.

"Peter's p-o-v shot through the sunken porthole. I'm going to do it."

Josh glared at her. "The hell you are. That's the fanciest shot in this whole picture except for the special effects."

"Why? You don't think I'm good enough to get it? Lars does. Tell him, Lars."

"I didn't say that!" Josh retorted. "You're not strong enough. It's that simple."

"Well, damnit, you can at least let me *try*. If I get the shot, we've got it. If not, then we're just out some film."

"*And* half a day of setting up the lights underwater *and* all the crew's time. A few feet of film and a lot more than a few grand."

"Bull!" Clay snapped.

Lars Knudsen stood. "I have a meeting. You two fight it out. See you at eleven, Clay."

Josh watched Lars leave, then turned back to Clay. "The shot is *dangerous*, Clay. Too many things could go wrong."

"It is *not* dangerous! You're only saying that because you don't think I'm *capable* of getting the shot."

"No, I don't," Josh said. "Peter Zaidenberg's a helluva lot more experienced than you are as a cameraman. I mean, that documentary you did was good, but it was pretty straight stuff."

"I did what the director *wanted* me to do! I know it wasn't splashy."

Josh grinned. "Splashy—very nice."

"Stop making fun of me!" Clay snapped. "I'm trying to suggest a way that your damned picture won't go even more over budget and schedule."

"Oh? You think all the disasters we've encountered are my fault? That I somehow don't run a tight enough ship?" Josh yelled, furious.

"No, I didn't say that," Clay yelled back. "I'm saying that you're a narrow-minded male chauvinist. You don't think I can get the shot because I'm a *woman*, not just *physically* weaker. That's the bottom line, isn't it? *Isn't it?*" Clay glared at Josh.

"No." Josh lowered his voice. "I said before, it's dangerous."

"How dangerous can it be?" Clay softened her voice as well. "I'll be surrounded by people. The lighting gaffers will be under there with me. Peter will be on board the boat. *Please*, Josh. Give me a chance. That's all I'm asking. I'll practice the shot without film in the camera until I get it down."

The phone rang. "Yeah, what is it? Just a second, Harvey. Hold on." Josh put his hand over the mouthpiece. "Okay, Clay, you win. If it doesn't turn out, we'll have Peter reshoot it. In the meantime, we'll get the other underwater stuff out of the way tomorrow and Wednesday. Then Thursday we'll do it."

Clay nodded curtly, and left. She realized Josh was under a lot of pressure, but she was still mad at him.

Sunny Fitzgerald was in her room at the Erawan Hotel, in Bangkok, blow drying her hair when Audrey called from Pattaya.

"Hello, mother? I can't talk long. I'm still in my bikini, and I'm supposed to be meetin' Josh in ten minutes for a drink. But remember? You asked me to report on what's happenin' with Clay?"

"Yes, honey. Anythin' interestin'?"

Audrey laughed throatily. "Well, it seems that Clay's goin' to make some kind of dangerous dive on Thursday. I had lunch with one of the stunt men, and he gave me all the gossip. Josh and Clay had a big fight over it. Josh didn't want her to do it, but Clay insisted."

"Well, we all know how headstrong Clay can be," Sunny pointed out. "If you can, find out the specifics from Josh an' call me back. But—Audrey?"

"Yes, mother?"

"Be discreet."

"That goes without sayin', mother."

"All right, darlin'. Talk to you later."

Sunny, protecting her newly painted fingernails, knocked on the bathroom door with her elbow. "Beau, honey? You still soakin' in that cool water? I have some good news for you."

Chapter 28

BY twelve noon, they were on a boat anchored a mile and a half off the island of Koh Larn. Clay, in her Blue Water wet suit, ran a final check on her scuba and camera equipment as Josh gave her last-minute instructions for the shot.

"Remember, Clay, it's got to be a slow, languorous shot that's going to play against the tension that's building on the sound track. I want an unbroken, inevitable feel to it."

Lars Knudsen came over and tightened the straps of the camera mounting around Clay's chest. "The set's ready, Josh. The dummy's in place. The lighting's set." Lars patted Clay's shoulder. "Good luck," he said.

Josh nodded at Lars and turned his attention back to Clay. "It's got to be continuous, Clay, but getting slower, slower all the time as it gets closer to the hatch. Always moving . . . but slow . . . slower, with a sense of premonition, until Don slides the hatch away and you tilt down into the hold where you see the body. And then I don't want that camera to move for thirty seconds . . . rock steady . . . frozen."

"Okay, Josh," Clay said.

Josh's eyes were burning into hers, and his hand was tight around her elbow. "Go do it," he said to Clay.

Peter Zaidenberg, still in a neck brace, helped Clay on to the diving platform and fitted on the twenty-four-pound weight belt around her waist. He attached her strap to the cable line that would slow her speed in descending to the ocean floor. Don Potter, the stunt man, was already in the water.

Clay put in her mouthpiece, and gave Josh the thumbs-up sign. She pressed the trigger of the camera and lowered

herself gently into the water with the help of two other
stunt men.

Clay felt the slight drag of her control strap as she slid
down the twenty feet of cable to the ocean floor. Her flip-
pered feet touched the sandy bottom, and she flexed her
knees, absorbing the slight impact so that no jarring would
show on the film. Feeling the cable strap fall away as Don
Potter released it from the back, she continued her motion
smoothly toward the sunken hull of the set, fifteen yards
away. A curious surgeon fish darted across her field of
vision as she propelled herself slowly toward the ship.
Reaching the slanted deck, Clay circled the mast, then
glided up over the side and down toward the shadowy
opening of the porthole.

A wave of nausea swept over her. *Oh, no*, she told herself, *this is no time for nerves*. With an effort, she pushed
it back, concentrating on the shot, and slipped smoothly
through the open porthole. Lars Knudsen's subtle side
lighting had turned the hold of the sunken ship into an
eerie grotto.

Clay rolled on to her back for an up-angle shot, and the
nausea came back again, stronger and accompanied by
dizziness. She fought against it, gritting her teeth. *Christ!*
she thought, *I can't fuck up now*. She had fought hard
against Josh's prejudices to be allowed to do this shot. She
was not going to confirm them now.

That time, the nausea did not pass, but Clay kept her
hands steady on the camera as she panned slowly across
the murky interior and began the painfully slow approach
to the partly open hatch cover. She was aware of Don
Potter swimming silently beside her and just behind. As
she reached the hatch, Don slid it back, and she tilted the
camera down through the opening, holding it steady on a
grizzly sight: a dead body, its foot pinned beneath a heavy
chest, one arm raised in a frantic effort to escape. The
eyes were wide open, staring up, and the upraised hand
waved back and forth with the current in a ghastly greeting.

Clay held the shot steady, Josh's voice echoing in her
ears: "I don't want that camera to move for thirty seconds

... rock steady ... frozen." She counted slowly toward thirty. The nausea and dizziness were overpowering, and her body felt cold. Clay opened her other eye and looked down at her hand, which was gripping the handle of the camera. Her fingernails were a livid red.

Twenty-two ... twenty-three ... twenty-four, she counted. Her head was pounding. The scene drifted out of focus and back in again. She kept her finger clamped on the trigger of the camera.

Twenty-nine ... thirty ...

The camera slipped from her grip and Clay lost consciousness.

When she came to, she was lying on the deck of the ship with an ice pack on her head and an oxygen mask over her mouth. Josh, Lars, Peter, and Don Potter were kneeling around her.

Clay pushed the oxygen aside and tried to sit up. "I got the shot," she croaked.

"Lie down," said Josh. "Don't try to talk."

Clay looked at Peter. "It was carbon monoxide," she said, "in my tank."

Peter Zaidenberg nodded grimly in confirmation. "Thank God, Don was right there to bring you up."

Clay smiled wanly at the stunt man. "Thanks, Don."

"You must've known what was going on, Clay," Peter said. "Why the hell did you stay down so long?"

"I had to get the shot, and I did," Clay said again, looking a little defiantly at Josh.

Josh took Clay by speedboat to a waiting helicopter on shore. She was flown to the Mission Hospital in Bangkok for tests and checked out satisfactorily. By six o'clock, she was back in her room at the Oriental Hotel with no worse aftereffects than a splitting headache.

"God, I feel as if the right side of my brain is shooting cannon balls into the left," Clay groaned. "I've never had a headache like this."

Josh wrapped a washcloth around some ice cubes from the mini-bar and laid it gently over Clay's forehead.

"Ohhh," she moaned again, closing her eyes. "I thought that painkiller would have taken effect by now."

Josh pulled a chair up next to the sofa where Clay lay, propped up. "As bad as you feel, consider the alternative and remind yourself how lucky you are."

"I know," Clay said, "I know. Another minute or two and it would have been all over. Oh, Josh." Clay threw her arms around Josh and let him pull her close to him. He held her quietly for a long while. He massaged the crown of her head with his left hand.

After a while, he spoke. "Clay, I have something to say. It's not just the accident and the fact that you nearly died today, although that's probably speeded up my awareness of the situation." He kissed her gently. "I love you, Clay. I've been resisting getting involved. But when Don brought you up unconscious, I realized how involved I really am."

Clay smiled at Josh, although the cannon balls were still exploding in her brain. His dark eyes were full of love and concern. "I love you, too, Josh." She tried to lean forward to kiss him but drew back in pain. "Ohhh, why can't I do this like Camille? Looking beautiful, feeling ill, but not too ill." She managed another half smile.

He lifted his leg on to the coffee table. Naturally, the cast had been signed by everyone in the cast and crew. "What a pair we make. But at least we're both suffering from temporary conditions. The doctor said you'd probably feel okay by tomorrow. Are you hungry? Do you want something from room service?"

"No, thanks. I still feel a little queasy."

"How about some ginger ale?" Josh hobbled over to the bar refrigerator.

"Really, I don't."

"Look, would you let me wait on you? I have to do something to make up for the shitty way I've been acting the past few weeks." Josh set her drink on the table and opened a Singha for himself. "You know, I can't figure out how this happened. I talked to Peter on the phone from the hospital. He said all the air tanks were filled at the same time, last night."

"I know. I stayed on the boat late and checked out all my equipment. The guys filled the aqualung bottles while I was there."

"Which air compressor did they use?"

"The main one—electrical."

"You're sure? Peter said that maybe if they used the gas compressor the intake hose could have bent backwards and sucked in the fumes from the exhaust. That way, carbon monoxide could have inadvertently flowed back into the tank."

Clay shook her head. "Not a chance. I was there. I saw *all* the tanks being filled. Besides, if that had happened, all of us underwater would have blacked out, not just me." She sipped her ginger ale. "No, Josh. I've been trying to figure it out. It couldn't have been an accident. My tank was sabotaged."

"Sabotaged? My God! Who'd want to kill you?"

"Well, it's the perfect way to do in a diver. Syphoning in carbon monoxide doesn't affect the weight of the tank. It's pretty tasteless, odorless. You need only about two parts carbon monoxide to a million to do damage. And it *looks* like an accident."

"Okay, I'll buy the premise. It's a clever way to do somebody in. But who'd want to do *you* in? And how on earth would they know which tank was yours?"

"That's easy. I had all my gear together in a huge duffel bag with my name on it. I *had* to be the target."

"*Who*, then?"

"The most dangerous man I've ever known is here in Bangkok. My stepbrother, Beau Yates. I know he doesn't like me, but I'm not sure why he'd want to kill me."

"Think hard about this, Clay. If we go to the police, we have to have proof of some kind," Josh said.

Clay nodded. "It's hard to think right now. But you know, Audrey wouldn't mind having me out of the way, either."

"Because of me? Come on, Audrey's not that evil or that calculating."

"Hmmm, I agree with the first point, but I'm not sure about the latter. There's my stepmother, too." Clay drained her glass, and Josh got her another ginger ale. "Sunny might want my third of The Willows. It'd go to Kenny, according to my father's will, and she's his guardian. She could control the whole thing."

"Then why didn't she make her move years ago? Why wait till now?" Josh pointed out.

"I'm only listing the possible suspects."

"What about your other boy friend? The good-looking blond guy?"

"Will Stone? No, Will would never—" Clay paused. "He is a diver, though. He'd know about carbon monoxide poisoning, but—No, not Will." Clay trailed off, and leaned back. There was something strange about Will's business association with Beau. But what?

"Are you okay?" Josh asked, worried.

"Yes, the headache's better. The green fuzzy ball's not taking up quite as much of my brain as before. The pill must be working." Clay picked up an ice cube from her glass and sucked on it. "No, I was thinking. Will acted a little strange the other night, kind of nervous." Clay told Josh about her beach walk with Lars and their chance meeting with Will Stone.

"Will had a big boat," Clay continued. "And I'm *sure* the equipment on the dock was for salvaging. Not only that, he wouldn't let us go on board to have a look around." She shook her head in sudden realization. "Of course! How could I not have figured it out before? Beau hired Will *because* he was a treasure salvager! So there must be some ship that Beau's after. Lots of ships go down in the Siamese Gulf. Pat was telling me about—" She stopped talking abruptly.

"What is it, honey? Are you feeling worse?"

Clay shook her head again slowly. "I can't believe it. How could I have been so thick? Pat had found a sunken ship. He took Will out to see it, and then Pat disappeared that same day. He's never shown up again."

"Did you ask Will about it?" Josh leaned forward.

"Of course. He said Pat had taken off to visit relatives. But what if the boat Pat found was, by some fluke, the one Will and Beau were looking for? They wouldn't want

Pat talking about it, especially since he was friendly with me."

"So you think Will Stone killed Pat? And tried to kill you because he was afraid you'd figure it out?"

Clay closed her eyes. "No. I can't believe that Will could harm anybody. But Beau Yates could. I *saw* him kill somebody." Clay began to cry. The pain in her head and the memory of Bluejay and her father and The Willows flooded and choked her brain.

Josh held her and patted her head until she stopped crying. Finally, Clay wiped her eyes and applied more ice to her head. Then she sat back and spent the next hour telling Josh everything about her past.

Josh was stunned. "God, why the hell didn't you tell me any of this before? No wonder you hate your stepfamily. Now I *finally* understand what happened in England and why you stalked off so fast." He removed the washcloth and kissed her head gently. "I'm sorry. All this time I've been using Audrey to keep from getting too involved with you. Christ! Of all the other women in the world for me to fool around with." Josh limped over to the window and looked out at the river traffic. He stood for a long time, then slowly turned back to Clay. "I hope I can make it up to you." There were tears in his eyes.

"Oh, Josh," Clay said. "You've been under such enormous pressure. This is *all* you need. To be caught up in some bizarre family plot."

"Look, if Beau did sabotage your equipment, and he seems the most likely suspect, or if he ordered it done, he would have to *think* you know something. And when he finds out you've pulled through, he isn't going to be pleased. I've got to get you out of here on the next plane. I'll hire a bodyguard for you, and you can stay at my place in California until we're finished shooting here; then I'll join you."

"Wait. First let me call Will. He's out of his league. As soon as Beau gets what he wants, he'll never cut Will in. I know it."

"No, Clay. To hell with Stone. He can take care of himself."

Clay sat up. Her head felt better. "All right. I guess Will knows what Beau's up to. But if it's something illegal, then we'd really have something to tell the police."

"No, Clay! Stone's not going to confess everything to you so you can go to the police. Forget it."

"I *know* Will Stone. I've at least got to warn him."

"Send him a telegram from California," Josh said.

There was a half-empty bottle of Mekong whiskey on the table, and Will Stone lay on his bed, his clothes and shoes on. Beau Yates was in the other room, where he had been talking on the phone. Will hadn't overheard the conversation, but whatever it was, Beau was in a rotten mood when he hung up. He had been sniffing coke every few minutes since he had arrived. When the phone rang, Will made no effort to get it because he assumed it was someone calling Beau. But after Beau had ignored five rings, Will picked it up.

"Will! Thank goodness you're there." It was Clay. She told him how she had nearly died of carbon monoxide poisoning. She suspected sabotage; she suspected Beau. She implored Will to be careful, warning him that Beau was dangerous.

"Okay, sure, thanks for calling." Will Stone felt sick. "I'm glad you're okay."

"Who was that?" Beau questioned.

"Clay had a diving accident today. Only it wasn't an accident."

"Oh?" Beau took a swig of Mekong. "Too bad."

"You had Vincent do it, didn't you? I know he was hanging around the film set yesterday."

"So what?"

"You wanted Clay out of the way because you were afraid she'd find out what we were up to," Will accused.

"Okay—so? I'm not lettin' anybody . . . *anybody* jeopardize this deal! Understand? Two nights from now, we're gonna be multimillionaires. So forget Clay Fitzgerald. Women like her grow on trees." He swallowed more whiskey. "I'm mad as hell at Vincent for botchin' it up.

Just goes to show you gotta do it yourself if you want things to get done right."

"Don't try it again, Beau. Clay doesn't know anything. You're just being paranoid."

"Paranoid? When you're in this business, you'd better be. You're not in the Caribbean lookin' for pirates' treasure anymore. This is the real world. Wake up, you fucker!"

"I've had it, Beau! I'm getting out. Just give me my cut, and—"

Beau Yates burst out laughing. "Jesus, Stone, you really are fuckin' naive. You smell blood, and you wanna hide under the bed." He came over to Will and stood so close their bodies were almost touching. "You ain't dealin' from a position of strength, Stone. Face the facts. That Thai kid's dead, and you were the last known person with him. Clay's scuba tank got sabotaged, and you're a diver who knows all about that kind of thing. And people have *seen* you with her." Beau washed down a pill with a gulp of whiskey. "Look at it from *my* point of view. You know too much to be dealt out now. You try anythin' and I go straight to the cops and pin the kid's murder on you."

Will's head ached. He took another drink.

"Well, actually, you *do* have a choice," Beau sneered. "You can be rich, or you can be dead." He pulled a .38 out of his side pocket.

Will Stone was suddenly terrified. He figured he had better start using his brain. If he could get out of here, he was going to tell Clay everything. Perhaps they could go away together; he could protect her . . . "Okay, Beau. You win."

"I thought you'd see it my way. Except I have a favor to ask. I think it's time for you to *prove* your loyalty to me."

Will poured the rest of the Mekong in his glass. "What do you want?"

Beau opened his wallet and pulled out a packet of aluminum foil. It contained four tiny white pills. He divided the foil in half and wrapped two pills in each packet. He put one back into his wallet; the other he handed to Will. "Okay, take a shower and pull yourself together. Shave, too. I want you to call Clay and take her out for a drink. Later, before you're ready to end the evenin', slip the pills in her drink. And try not to let anyone notice you."

"No! You're crazy. I'm not—"

Beau stuck the gun in his head. "If I pull the trigger, it ain't Russian roulette. You don't stand a chance. What'll it be, buddy? You with me?"

Will Stone nodded slowly and telephoned Clay. Beau held the gun to his ear for the duration of the call.

"Okay," Will said. "She wants me to come to her room for a drink. She doesn't feel well enough to go out."

"Perfect!" Beau chortled. "She's gonna feel worse than that before the evenin's over." He put the gun back in his pocket. "Now you know what to do? And you won't let anybody see you goin' to her room?"

Will nodded. "Okay, Beau. I guess I don't have any choice."

"Right, Will. See you tomorrow." Beau slapped Will Stone on the back jovially. "I knew I could count on you once you understood the situation."

Chapter 29

CLAY Fitzgerald's head felt clearer. She had bathed and changed into fresh clothes that Linda and Peter Zaidenberg had brought her from Pattaya. Once they were assured that she was resting comfortably, the Zaidenbergs and Josh had gone to Lord Jim's, on the hotel's mezzanine, for dinner. Josh had booked Clay on the midnight flight to Los Angeles. He would take her to the airport, and he had arranged for someone to meet her when she arrived in California.

Clay had waited until Josh left before she called Will Stone. She was glad that Will had called back and was coming over. She was anxious to see him before she left to find out what Beau Yates was up to. Perhaps she and Will could go straight to the police and have Beau arrested. Then she wouldn't have to leave Thailand that night.

Fluffing up the pillows on the sofa, Clay relaxed back into them, feeling drowsy. It was good that Josh had gone out, she decided. Will would not talk as freely with Josh there.

She sat up as a loud pounding on the door startled her. "It's me," Will called.

"Come in. It's unlocked," Clay said, realizing that she should have locked it.

Will Stone looked terrible, although he was dressed in a suit and tie. "Clay, you're in danger," he blurted out immediately. "You've got to get out of town. Beau's after you." He threw a foil packet on the table. "He made me call you and threatened me, so I'd slip those pills into your drink." Will went over and knelt beside her on the sofa. Clay could smell whiskey on his breath. "But Clay, dar-

282

ling, you know I could never hurt you. I love you. I have it all figured out. We'll leave together, tonight. I have a friend in Australia. We'll go there. I'll get a job." Will threw his arms around Clay and buried his face in her chest.

"Oh, Will, it's all right," Clay said. "Calm down. Tell me everything. We'll go to the police."

Will pulled back. "No! No, we can't. I'll get blamed for everything. Beau set it up that way. He's too clever. He—"

There was a loud thud, and the door swung open. "You're damned straight I'm too clever." Beau Yates's gun was pointed at them. He pushed the door closed behind him with his foot. "I knew you'd chicken out on me, Stone. And then I came up with a jim dandy plan. One that's foolproof, 'cause I'm not trustin' anybody to botch things up again." He shifted his glance to Clay. "Hi, Clay. Sorry you have a headache. I've got a cure, right here." He pulled back the hammer of his gun. "But first things first. What d'ya have to drink?"

Clay pointed to the bar. "See for yourself."

"Nah. Get me a whiskey, Stone. Neat."

The phone rang. Clay reached for it quickly, but Beau sprang across the room and laid a karate chop down on her knuckles. She pulled her hand away in pain.

"Just let it ring, honey. You don't have time for a chat."

Will handed Beau a White Horse Scotch. While Beau tilted his head back to drink, Will swayed closer, with the intention of grabbing the gun. Beau pivoted around, thrusting a jab to Will's gut. Will fell backward, gasping for air.

"That won't work, Stone. I'm a fifth-degree black belt. Sorry, Will, you blew it. Now I'm gonna have to find another diver to finish bringin' up the opium. It's a drag. I thought I could get the job finished before I sent you on your way."

"What?" Will blinked. His focus was off, from the blow and the whiskey.

"Sure. You don't really think Vincent and I would've split the profits with you? Nah, I was plannin' to send you

off before the end of the week. All I'm doin' is speedin' up
my schedule and clearin' myself at the same time."

Will poured himself some of the scotch. His hand was
shaking, and he was trying to think what to do.

"Move over there! I wanna get this over with. A neat
bullet through Miss Clay's heart and another through your
head with the gun in your hand. The cops'll figure a lovers' quarrel."

Beau backed toward the door, and aimed the gun at
Clay.

"Beau! Wait!," Clay yelled as loud as she could, rolling
on to the floor between the sofa and the coffee table. Will
lunged at Beau. At the same instant, the door burst open,
and Josh jumped toward Beau from the back.

The gun went off. There was a chaotic scuffle, and Peter Zaidenberg hurled himself into the room. Clay lay on
the floor, frozen in fear. She could hear Linda screaming
in the hallway. Peter, in his neck brace, and Josh, with his
foot in the cast, were no match for Beau Yates. Even
drunk, Beau was swift and powerful. With rapid karate
movement—a quick right cross to Peter's jaw and a kick
to Josh's broken ankle—Beau downed both men. He had
lost the gun in the scuffle and looked around for it hastily.
He spotted it, partially under Will Stone, who was lying on
the floor, bleeding.

"Fuck!" Beau shouted, taking off down the hall with the
speed of a sprinter.

Linda Zaidenberg rushed in, and Clay crawled over to
Josh. The floor concierge and several cleaning women arrived on the scene.

"Call a doctor!" Clay ordered, pointing to Will. "A doctor!" she repeated. "Josh, are you—"

"I'm okay. My ankle hurts like hell," Josh said. "Peter?"

"God, I think so." Peter Zaidenberg felt his jaw to see if
it was broken.

Clay knelt over Will. His shirt was soaked in blood. His
eyes were closed. "Will? *Will!*" She grabbed his wrist to
take his pulse, but she could not find a pulse.

Linda put down the phone. "The doctor's on the way.
He's calling the police."

"Are you okay, Clay?" Josh asked.

"Yes." Clay stared at Will Stone's lifeless body.

"I'm sorry, Clay," Josh said. "I don't think there's anything a doctor can do for your friend."

Clay, Josh, and the Zaidenbergs were taken to the Bangrak Police Station, about ten blocks from the hotel.

Inspector Napombesthra, a well-dressed older man, listened to their story while a police translator took down their statements.

"When Clay didn't answer her phone," Josh explained, "we guessed something was wrong. And just as I got to the door, I heard Clay scream, so I burst in. There was a scuffle, the gun went off, Yates shot Will Stone and took off."

Inspector Napombesthra looked at them with tired eyes. "My men are searching for him now." He turned to Clay. "We have had suspicions about Mister Yates for some time. Nothing substantial, no evidence with which to arrest him. Please, miss, can you tell me again everything you know about the opium ship and the pearl farm in Phuket."

A young, uniformed Thai policeman rushed in, spoke quickly to the inspector, and rushed out.

"Mister Yates has disappeared," Inspector Napombesthra announced. "My men have searched his apartment and his office. Yates had been there. Many of the drawers were hastily emptied." He leaned back in his chair and considered the situation for a few moments. "When you are finished here, Miss Fitzgerald, I will have my car and assistant take you to the airport to see that you are safely on the plane to California. Mister Lewis, we will assign a special detail to your film unit in Pattaya to watch out for you and your crew until you are finished. Unless, of course, we find Mister Yates tonight."

"I have an idea," Linda Zaidenberg said as they were heading for the airport in the police car with Clay. "Let's scrap *Golden Triangle* and film this. It's a much better story."

Clay laughed and tried to put out of her mind that Will Stone was dead and Beau Yates was still at large.

After the debacle at the Oriental, Beau Yates had Jerry, his young American driver, take him to the office. He collected all incriminating business documents and fifty thousand dollars from the wall safe, He also tried to track down Vincent Lascaux, but his business partner was nowhere to be reached.

When Jerry dropped him at the Hotel Erawan, Beau handed the boy a five-hundred-dollar bill and told him to get lost.

"Shee-it," Jerry exclaimed. "What about the car?"

"Drive it to Singapore, and sell it. See my friend Raymond at the Kraloana Hotel. Leave now, right away. Drive all night."

"Thanks, Beau. See you again sometime." The happy American took off down Ratchadamri Road.

"Good-by, you jerk," Beau said under his breath. He wanted Jerry out of town so the police could not find him to question him.

From the lobby of the Erawan, Beau called his associate, Raymond, in Singapore. "Hey, Ray. Beau. Listen, I'm goin' on a trip so things'll be quiet for a while. No, don't worry. Vincent or I will be in touch. Listen—favor? Yeah, this American kid, Jerry. He has my car and is headin' down there. I told him to look you up. Yeah, that's right. Take care of him. Fuck! I don't care how. And keep the car for your trouble. Okay, so long."

Beau combed his hair and went up to his mother's room, letting himself in with the extra key Sunny had given him.

"Oh, my God! Beau." Sunny said icily. "I told you *never* to barge in." She was naked. A young Oriental man was lying, erection fading, on the king-sized bed. He appeared to be assessing the situation, trying to decide whether to bolt or protect his territory.

Beau's face twisted with fury. His head began to pound. He pushed Sunny aside and, with a loud moan, jumped on the Chinese in bed.

"Stop it!" Sunny ordered. "This instant!"

Beau and the young man wrestled on the bed, Beau cursing and grunting until he had the Oriental face down and pinned in a full nelson. Beau's arms locked under the younger man's arms; his hands and wrists crushed down on the back of the younger man's neck. Sunny's lover's face was red, and huge veins had popped out on his forehead. Weakened and defenseless, Beau flung him over and ground his knee into the Oriental's groin.

"No! I said *stop* it! Don't hurt him anymore," Sunny demanded. She flung herself on Beau and tried to pull him off her Chinese lover.

"Damnit, mother—damnit." Beau pushed her away, this time more gently, and stood, staring with disgust at the nearly unconscious naked Chinese man. Beau picked him up and walked over to the open window.

"For heaven's sake, Beau. What do you think you're doin'?" Sunny ran to close the window before Beau got there, but he whirled around and ran across the room, out into the hall.

Beau came back several minutes later alone. "Give me his clothes."

"What did you do with him?"

"Never mind. His clothes, where the fuck *are* they?"

Sunny busied herself picking up clothes all around the room. She handed them to Beau, and he went out again.

When Beau returned, he was chuckling to himself.

"Where did you put him?" Sunny asked.

"Down the laundry shoot. Probably landed on a pile of dirty sheets. He'll be okay."

"Beau Yates!" Sunny shrieked. "You're a goddamned fool. Totally out of control. What right have you got bustin' in here without knockin'? Huh? Answer me that!"

Beau appeared stunned by the reprimand. "I—I'm sorry, mama. It's just that—I'm in big trouble. I *need* you!" He rubbed his throbbing temples with his fingers and threw himself face down on the bed.

Sunny sat by him. She put her hand on his back and gently began kneading her fingers down his spine. "What trouble, honey? Tell me."

Beau began to sob. "*Everything's* fucked up. I've got to get away and hide. The police'll be combing the airports. They'll probably be here any minute."

"Wait." Sunny picked up the phone and called the desk. "This is Mrs. Fitzgerald in seven fifteen. I'm ill and do not wish to be disturbed for *any* reason. Do you understand? No phone calls, no visitors. Is that clear? Thank you."

"Shit, mother. That's not gonna keep the cops out."

"It might for a few minutes." Sunny began dialing an outside number.

"Mama, it's no use. I'm fucked."

"Shhh! I'm makin' a call. Khun Kraisri, please. Hello? Ed, darlin', listen I can't chat. I need that favor. Remember?" Sunny giggled sexily into the phone. "Well, my son's in a little trouble. He's been framed, actually. I've got to get him out. Yes, right away. The Erawan. Okay, Ed— Yes. Oh, darlin', *thank* you."

Sunny hung up and dialed another number. "Audrey? Don't ask questions and don't talk to anyone. If anyone wants to know where I am, say I've gone up to Chiang Mai to see the Hill Tribes. Stay out of sight 'til I get in touch with you. Got it? All right, darlin'."

Sunny threw some clothes and makeup into a large shoulder bag and dressed quickly.

Beau lay immobile on the bed, whimpering.

"Now, honey," Sunny said, "it's all goin' to be all right. You can tell me everythin' later." She sat next to him.

Beau turned over on his back and put his head in Sunny's lap. His arms clutched her waist, and he hugged her tight. "Oh, mama, make it all go away. Make me feel okay. Please, mama? Please!"

Sunny kissed Beau's hair. "It's goin' to be all right. I've got a private helicopter to take us to Kuala Lumpur and a jet there to take us to Athens. After that, I'll have to do some more figurin'."

Beau still clung to her. "Bring the pearls," he whispered.

"Don't worry. I have them. Everythin's goin' to be fine."

"Oh, mother, I love you so much. There's no one but you. There's never been anyone else."

"I know, darlin', I know," Sunny crooned. She massaged his stomach and then let her hand slip beneath his belt. "I know what to do, honey. I'll make you happy again."

PART FOUR

Seven Months Later—Kentucky

Chapter 30

"WHAT thoughts are going through your head right now?" asked the attractive brunette reporter for the *Louisville Courier Journal.*

"Positive ones. That—" Josh Lewis answered as he looked at his watch—"seven hours and forty-five minutes from now, we'll be standing in the winner's circle with my filly draped in red roses."

"You're certainly confident, Mr. Lewis." Amy Spalding flipped over the tape in her tiny Sony recorder.

"There sure ain't no point in thinking negative, is there?" Eddie Landry, Oriental Pearl's trainer, opened another Lite beer, though it was not yet ten on the Saturday of the Kentucky Derby. "The Pearl's got a good chance. We wouldn't have nominated her for the Derby or flown her in from California if she didn't. She won the Santa Anita Derby, and the only reason she didn't win the Hollywood Derby was because some loud noise scared her on the way from the stable to the paddock. And she's been restin' plenty since then."

"But she's up against a good field—many people feel a much stronger crop of three-year-olds this year than in 1980 when Genuine Risk won," Amy Spalding said. Genuine Risk had been the first filly since Regret, in 1915, to win the prestigious Run for the Roses; she had also been the first filly to enter the race in twenty-one years.

Eddie Landry unzipped his creased blue windbreaker and leaned back in a leather armchair. "There's no denying we're up against it. Cayenne Pepper's a speed horse, Candle Salad's a strong competitor, so's Coffee Jon. But the Pearl's in great shape. She has speed and stamina, and that's what it takes—plus a lot of luck."

"Have you been doing any special training since you got to Louisville?" Reporter Spalding asked.

"We've been working her this week the same as we would for any big race," Landry said. Landry was a man in his late sixties, with weather-worn face and mostly gray hair, sparse on top. "Oriental Pearl's taken to Kentucky like a pea to a pod. Both her grandparents were bred here, you know. She's got as much natural ability as any horse I've ever trained. I've got a special relationship with the Pearl. She's a real lady. I've got a lot of respect for her."

"What about her—randy urges?" Amy Spalding asked delicately. "A filly in springtime can have a lot of things on her mind besides racing. Is this going to be a problem?"

Josh Lewis grinned. "She's been horsing around a bit since she came here. But, don't forget, she's very competitive. When she gets on a track, the *only* thing her mind seems to fix on is winning."

"And Manuel Maldonado's ridden her in five out of seven starts," Landry interrupted. "He has incredible instincts. He and the Pearl have a real rapport."

Amy Spalding sat forward and directed her dark eyes at Josh Lewis. "The rumors are flying around Louisville"— she said "Loo-a-vul" like a native—"that your constant companion, Clay Fitzgerald, is the daughter of Mac Fitzgerald, who owned The Willows Stud. And since Cayenne Pepper, The Willows' colt, is running against your horse, I wondered if there was any friction, or mixed loyalty."

"Unfortunately," Josh said, "the lady's unavailable for comment."

"Well, *you* can tell me. Is she rooting for *your* horse or *hers*? I mean, she has a financial interest in The Willows, doesn't she?"

"Yes, but Oriental Pearl's almost as much her horse as mine. Does that answer your question?"

"Well, not really." Amy Spalding laughed and turned back to Eddie Landry. "What special advice are you giving your jockey this afternoon?"

"The same advice I always give him. To take his time, relax, and stay out of trouble. Some people predict that Oriental Pearl's got to be in the lead right away in order to win. But that's not true. Manuel's prepared to rate her. It just depends on the conditions. Who the hell knows what will happen?" Eddie Landry crushed the aluminum beer can in his hand. "I've been a trainer thirty-nine years, and this is my fourth Derby. My other horses were good ones, and none of 'em ended up in the money. So who can say? One thing I'll tell you. In all my career, the Pearl's only the third horse I ever fell in love with."

"But why did you enter Oriental Pearl in the Derby, Mr. Lewis, and not the Oaks with the other fillies whom she was sure to beat?"

Josh poured himself another cup of coffee. "I'm a director. I like to feel I can spot star material." He shrugged, and continued, "Look at Gallorette, one of the ten all-time great horses, a filly. She raced forty-nine times and faced males in over two-thirds of her races. Look at Dahlia and Allez France, the two all-time female money winners. Both raced against males most of their careers."

"Yeah," Eddie Landry agreed. "Our Pearl's going to be a star."

Amy Spalding shut off her recorder and, closing her notebook, thanked them for the interview. Josh and Landry walked her to her car and watched as she tore back down the dogwood-lined gravel drive of the Louisville mansion owned by Robin Randolph Lawrence. Josh and Clay were staying in the mansion's guest wing for Derby week. Clay's childhood friend was now married to the Louisville banker, Bruce Tinsdale Lawrence.

"Just between us," Josh inquired, "what *are* our chances today?"

Eddie Landry, looking down at his fancy new cowboy boots, sent a stone skittering down the drive with his foot. "I'm nearly seventy, and I've been around horses all my life. I can tell you one thing for certain."

"What's that?" Josh smiled, knowing the answer.

"*Nothing's* for certain in thoroughbred racing."

Clay Fitzgerald had been avoiding the press and keeping a low profile during Derby week. It was awkward being a silent partner with a third interest in The Willows, yet living with Josh Lewis and loving Oriental Pearl as much as any horse she had ever known. But because Cayenne Pepper, The Willows entry in the Derby, had been raised by her old friend, Buck Smith, Clay felt a peculiar mix of emotions about the situation.

Matters were complicated, of course, by the fact that Sunny Fitzgerald was in town for the festivities; Clay had gone out of her way to avoid her stepmother. Audrey was in Louisville, too, with her new husband, a prominent New York investment banker, Laddie Scott.

Beau Yates was still at large.

While Josh and Eddie Landry were being interviewed by the *Louisville Courier Journal*, Clay sat in the solarium off the kitchen, drinking coffee with Robin.

"You should've stayed longer at the Gentrys'," Robin said. "At midnight, there was the most divine display of fireworks I've ever seen."

Clay buttered an English muffin. "We were tired. Besides Sunny arrived, and that speeded up my departure."

"Did you get close enough to see the diamond ring she was sportin'? Someone said it was twelve carats."

"Of course not." Clay's shiny chestnut hair had grown longer, tumbling now to her shoulder blades. "I'm not interested in anything of Sunny's."

"Well, the big news is that she's gettin' married again."

"You're kidding! To whom?"

"Only one of the wealthiest men in Kentucky—or anywhere, I guess. Porter Mason." Robin wore her hair the same way she always had, short and fluffy, but she had not yet lost the extra twenty pounds she had gained with the birth of her second child.

"The bourbon king? Really?" Clay's eyes widened with amazement.

"It's true. Janie Bell told me last night. It's been a whirlwind romance, and big fat Porter Mason is smitten. You know, he weighs over three hundred pounds."

"He does *not*—there you go exaggeratin' again, honey."
Bruce Tinsdale Lawrence, Robin's husband, walked in.
He was nice-looking, on the stocky side but tall enough to
carry it off. His black hair was trimmed short, and with
his pink cheeks he was an extremely youthful looking
thirty-one. For Derby Day, he had put on forest-green
trousers and a Madras-plaid sportcoat. "Anyway," Bruce
continued, "Josh says the coast is clear. No more reporters
lurkin' around. Unless they're hidin' in the boxwood."

Clay laughed. "You two have been terrific this week.
Not only putting us up, but putting up with us. Josh has
been soaring with all the attention from the press."

"Well, it's excitin' for us. Perks up our humdrum life."
Robin giggled. "Anyway, we'd better be gettin' over to the
track."

In the backstretch at Churchill Downs that first Saturday
in May, Oriental Pearl's groom, Al Butler, rose before
dawn and fed the gray filly a breakfast of oats and only a
handful of the bale of hay she usually munched. He
cleaned out her stall, gave her a bath, picked her hoofs
clean, trimmed her mane, and brushed her coat and tail to
a high silvery sheen. Later, after Eddie Landry arrived,
Oriental Pearl's shoes were checked, the farrier was called
in to make a tiny adjustment, and the filly's hoofs were
filed to parallel exactly the slope of her pasterns, that part
of the feet lying between the fetlock and the coffin joint.
Next, the horse was rubbed with linament to loosen her
muscles and hold her body heat, her lip tattoos were
checked, and the track veterinarian took a blood sample.
Al Butler posed with the filly for all onlookers with
cameras and would not leave the horse for a second.

Oriental Pearl's jockey, Manuel Maldonado, stopped by
her stall to visit with her and pick up Josh Lewis's Victori-
ana Stables racing silks, which he would be wearing for
the Derby. The silks, actually made of parachute nylon,
were dusty rose, ivory, and black, with a fern-green cap
and Josh's initials formed into a repeating "J L" pattern
on the shirt-sleeves. The stall itself was decked out in those

colors, as was almost everything in sight—the medicine kit, blanket, even the water bucket.

When Clay and Josh arrived, Oriental Pearl stuck her head out of the stall and whinnied and whickered.

"Hello, my baby." Clay kissed the horses's muzzle. "Feel like running today?"

"Yes, ma'am. She's sure feelin' good today. Frisky and sassy, you better believe it," Al Butler said.

"She's in great form," Landry added. "Look at her. So calm you could invite her into your living room."

"Well, I'm not too pleased about drawing post position number one," Josh said.

"A lot of horses have won the Derby from the first hole," Landry reassured. "Everybody says that fence seems to protrude out in front of you. But I never seen a horse hit it yet. It's a good hole for us."

Clay was dressed for luck in Josh's racing colors: black suede boots, white knickers with a dusty-rose silk blouse, and a fern-green jacket made of parachute nylon. Around her neck, on a gold chain, she wore the ruby and emerald flower ring her father had given her when she graduated from prep school.

Heywood Hale Broun and the CBS camera crew made their way over to Josh and Eddie Landry. Clay, as she had all week, faded into the background to whisper words of encouragement to the exquisite filly.

"Do you consider Cayenne Pepper—winner of the Blue Grass Stakes and runner-up in the Wood Memorial—your most venerable opponent?" Broun asked Josh.

Josh laughed. "I see all ten of them as our major rivals."

Churchill Downs was packed with an all-time record crowd of 164,971. Walking through the grandstand took a long time. The infield, too, littered with people, looked like a summer park concert. A record amount of money was being bet on the ten-race Derby Day card, close to five million by 5:38, a few minutes before post time. The Derby contenders had been saddled and mounted in the paddock. "My Old Kentucky Home" had been sung, and the post parade to the starting gate was underway.

Up in their grandstand box, Clay took Josh's hand and squeezed hard. "I'm not sure I can survive the next few minutes. Maybe I should have a mint julep, after all."

Josh squeezed back. "Just keep repeating, It's only a race. It's only a race."

"That's right." Robin Randolph Lawrence giggled. "The winner only gets four hundred thousand and incredible prices when the offspring are born. No big deal at all."

"They're getting ready to go in the gates. Oh, Josh. She *does* look good," Clay said.

"The closing odds are thirteen to one. A lot of last-minute action in favor of the boys," Bruce Lawrence said, arriving back at the box with a handful of betting tickets. "If your filly wins, I'm goin' to clean up."

"I put down a hundred on her," Robin said. "If she loses, its nothing but rice and beans for a week."

"How much did you bet, Josh?" Clay asked quietly.

"I'm not saying." Josh smiled and kissed the worried crease between Clay's forehead.

"I'm the only conservative one in the crowd," Clay said. "I put down a two-dollar bet on Oriental Pearl to win and two dollars on Cayenne Pepper to place."

Josh looked at her in astonishment.

"Well, *Buck* raised the horse. Sunny had nothing to do with it. But Oriental Pearl can beat him. I know it!"

"Makes me a little nervous that Cayenne Pepper's big and red like Secretariat," Robin injected. "My palms are soakin'."

The race caller's voice came over the loudspeaker as the horses went into the gates in order: "Number seven, Oriental Pearl, racing out of the first hole, with Manuel Maldonado up and a hundred and twenty-one pounds." Fillies in the Derby were given a 121-pound allowance; the colts carried 126 pounds. "Number ten, Coffee Jon, racing out of the second hole, Angel Cordero up. Number four, Cayenne Pepper, in the third hole with Jaime Velasquez up. Number two, Lord Ming out of the sixth hole . . ."

"The horses are loadin' well," Bruce Lawrence said, handing Clay his binoculars. "And standin' well."

"There they go!" Clay screamed, and gave Josh a quick kiss. "Good luck, darling."

"And they're off!" The race caller's voice echoed into a shuffling hush. "Cayenne Pepper on the outside, Coffee Jon close to the base. Then on the inside is Oriental Pearl and Pueblo Pride. Cayenne Pepper takes the lead by about two lengths. Coffee Jon is second, and Remote Rebel on the outside is third. Candle Salad is fourth, and Lightfoot Dasher, Oriental Pearl, Knickersmith, Moon Dragon, Kalamala, Pueblo Pride, and Lord Ming is eleventh.

"The first quarter—twenty-one and four-fifths, and Cayenne Pepper has the lead by a length. Candle Salad is second by a half, then Remote Rebel, Lightfoot Dasher. On the outside is Moon Dragon, with Pueblo Pride on the rail, followed by Oriental Pearl, Kalamala, Lord Ming, and Knickersmith."

Clay dug her teeth into the knuckle of her index finger. "Oh, Josh," she moaned, "Pearl's too far back. She's never been this far back in a race."

Josh put his arm around Clay's waist but did not speak.

Eddie Landry, who had joined them, chewed on an unlit cigar.

"Come on, Oriental Pearl! You can do it!" Robin shrieked.

"They're approaching the back stretch," the announcer called. The crowd was beginning to explode with excitement. "Cayenne Pepper has the lead by two lengths, Candle Salad is second by a length and a half, Remote Rebel—third and dropping back. Then it's Coffee Jon on the outside. Alongside is Moon Dragon. Then Lightfoot Dasher, Oriental Pearl, Kalamala, Pueblo Pride, all together. And three back to Lord Ming and Knickersmith. The half is forty-five and one-fifth."

Hope began to drain from Clay's face. A negative premonition knotted her stomach. She was suddenly afraid she would burst into tears if Oriental Pearl lost. It would not be a very sporting reaction. If only the filly could break from the pack.

"Oh, God! Come on, Oriental Pearl," Robin yelled as loud as she could.

Eddie Landry kept chewing on the cigar, eyes fixed on the world's fastest three-year-old thoroughbreds as they galloped toward the stretch and the climax of the mile-and-a-quarter horse race. "Come on, Manuel. What are you waiting for? Go to the outside," he muttered under his breath.

"Cayenne Pepper, on the rail, still leads by a half. Coffee Jon on the outside, second by two." The race caller's voice remained calm. "Then Remote Rebel, Candle Salad—with Oriental Pearl. Three back to Moon Dragon and Pueblo Pride with Lightfoot Dasher. Then—Kalamala, Lord Ming, and Knickersmith is eleventh. Around the far turn. The mile—one and thirty-six . . ."

"She's beginning to move!" Clay exclaimed. "Look, Josh!"

"I see . . . I see." He dug his fingers into Clay's waist.

"Cayenne Pepper, on the rail, still leads by a length. Coffee Jon on the outside. Farther out, Oriental Pearl. On the rail, here comes Candle Salad. Remote Rebel is right there. They're approaching the top of the stretch. Coffee Jon is right behind Cayenne Pepper as they enter the stretch. On the outside is Oriental Pearl. Farther out is Remote Rebel and Candle Salad. Then about five back is Moon Dragon . . ."

"Come on, baby. Come on!" Josh whispered.

"Down the stretch, Cayenne Pepper still has the lead by a length. Then Coffee Jon on the rail is second by a neck. Oriental Pearl, on the outside, is third by two. Then Remote Rebel and Candle Salad. Oriental Pearl coming up. And Oriental Pearl takes the lead! Cayenne Pepper is back by a half. Oriental Pearl is in front by a length and a half. Manuel Maldonado on Oriental Pearl, the winner . . . Oriental Pearl going away as they cross the finish! Cayenne Pepper is second; Coffee Jon, third. Time—two minutes and two." The time was two and three-fifths seconds off the track record set by Secretariat.

Clay burst into tears. Josh squeezed her tight.

"We did it! We did it!" Robin yelled.

"Damned if we didn't." Eddie Landry threw his still-unlit cigar on the ground and stamped on it, out of habit. "Four tries on the Derby and I finally get to the winner's circle after I thought I'd retired from this business."

Buck Smith came up and offered his hand to Josh. "Good race." He handed Clay a handkerchief and kissed her cheek. "Better stop cryin' before you get your trophy. People'll think you're crazy."

The governor and his wife presented the award in the closing ceremony. Clay photographed Josh standing next to Oriental Pearl, decked out in roses, with Manuel Maldonado beaming from the saddle. After that, Clay kissed the filly, Eddie Landry, Manuel Maldonado, and Josh, in that order.

At thirteen to one, Oriental Pearl paid $28.60 on each two-dollar bet.

Chapter 31

"OH, darlings, I'm so happy for you." Noni Pinckney kissed Clay and Josh on both cheeks. "I even had money on Oriental Pearl, so it'll help defray the costs of the party."

Nelson Pinckney, who had bred horses in Kentucky for the past twenty-five years, pumped Clay's and Josh's hands jovially as they walked into the grand hall of the Pinckney estate, Sapphire Farm. An impressive walnut horseshoe staircase rose above them on both sides as they entered the grand hall. "Yes, sir. A good mare's like a blue-chip stock. A depreciating asset that is actually multiplying in value."

The Pinckneys were hosting their annual post-Derby Pimm's party. "You know, we stole the idea from the one given every year during Goodwood week in England by Lord and Lady Gordon-Lennox," Noni Pinckney confided. "At this point in Derby week, everybody's sick and tired of mint juleps. Come with me, I have oodles of people who're dying to meet you."

Her hair twisted into an elaborate chignon, Clay looked tall and sleek in a gold-piped Saint Laurent evening suit, satin-and-sequin Andrea Pfister pumps, and the gold-and-diamond chain choker by Paloma Picasso that Josh had given her for her birthday. "Josh, my love," Clay announced, "you're on your own. This is your big night to bask in the glory. I'm going to mingle."

Josh Lewis raised a wary eyebrow as Noni Pinckney started to escort him off to meet a group of worshipers. He glanced back at Clay and mouthed "Help!"

"You'll be able to flirt better without me," Clay whispered. "I'll come rescue you in a little while."

Clay helped herself to a Pimm's cup number one, an English punch made with gin and garnished with lemon and cucumber slices, from the silver tray of a circulating waiter and a cheese puff from another tray. Wandering into the immense living room, Clay chatted with old friends and acquaintances and eavesdropped on other amusing conversations.

The party glittered with the elite of the racing and breeding world—old money mixed with new: Whitneys, Mellons, Guests, DuPonts, Phippses, and Wildensteins; Bunker Hunt; Canadian E. P. "Eddie" Taylor; Robert Sangster from the Isle of Man; Texan Will Farish; Greek Stavros Niarchos; Saudi Arabian construction magnates Mahmoud and Moustapha Fustok, now horse breeders; the incomparable Liz Whitney Tippett; the Van Cliefs from Virginia; Venezuelan dynamo, Dr. José "Pépé" Sahagún; Italian Carlo d'Alessio; Mme. Ettie Plesch and her daughter, Countess Esterhazy; the famous Kentucky Hancocks; assorted blood-stock agents and European trainers; and Dolly Green, from Hollywood, who entered the thoroughbred racing world in 1980 with the dramatic purchase of a Northern Dancer colt for $1.4 million. They were all decked out in their finery and jewels and black ties—a rich group, if not an altogether comely one.

A portly, craggy-faced *grande dame* said to her portly, craggy-faced escort, "Goin' to France is what I love about racin'. June and August for Deauville. And there's the *Arc* in October. It's great fun, and of course the expenses are less."

"The purses are larger, too." The old man chuckled. "The horses aren't nearly so apt to break down gallopin' strictly on turf."

"Oriental Pearl only cost Lewis fifty-five thousand, but then Seattle Slew was knocked down for a mere sixteen. Genuine Risk, as I recall, went for thirty-two thousand." A small, dapper man with his arm in a cast was standing so close to his companion that she was tilting backward, about to lose her balance.

"We got twenty-five hundred this week for rentin' our house. Moved into the Brown Hotel and still made a profit," said a horsy-looking matron with streaked hair and an alto voice.

Robin Randolph Lawrence joined Clay, laughing. "Amazin', isn't it? The racin' world's about the *only* place where it's socially acceptable to talk about money. You havin' fun?"

Clay smiled. "Yes. I haven't been to a party like this since daddy was alive."

All through the post-Civil War mansion, candelabra and chandeliers glowed a flattering pink-gold. In the dining room and on the terraces, tables were covered with white eyelet tablecloths and baskets of spring flowers. The buffet included seafood jambalaya, ham and beaten biscuits, cold salmon, duck and oyster gumbo, and *crudités* in ceramic swans. The centerpiece on the mahogany hors d'oeuvres table was a doll house-sized replica of Sapphire Farm—the brick Georgian house with its identical front and back white-pillared pedimented porticoes—as well as miniatures of the stable and barn, gardens, gazebo, and Japanese garden house.

Clay started for the pool area to listen to the reggae band, but a hand brushed her shoulder lightly.

Clay pivoted around. "Sunny!" she said, taken aback.

"Clay, I have to have a word with you." Sunny Fitzgerald looked elegant in a gold and paisley Bill Blass and younger than ever from a face lift and a week at the Golden Door. Her gold Angela Cummings spiderweb necklace was woven with 291 diamonds. Obviously, landing Porter Mason had been a stroke of luck for her.

"I don't know what we could possibly have to say to each other," Clay responded icily. "Unless you'd like to fill me in on what Beau's up to these days."

Sunny's eyes grew larger. "I don't know where he is. No one's heard from him."

Clay turned to go, but Sunny touched her arm again. "I think you'll be interested in what I have to say. It's about The Willows."

"Do you want to sell it?"

"It's too noisy to discuss here. Let's meet tomorrow."

Clay shook her head. "Josh and I are leaving early."

Josh's film, *Golden Triangle*, was having a sneak preview in New York the next night.

"Then let's go outside, away from the noise. This is important, Clay."

"All right, Sunny. I'll meet you at the garden house. In ten minutes." Clay wanted to find Josh and bring him along to hear what her stepmother had to say.

Clay caught sight of Josh in the living room, surrounded by assorted matrons, starry-eyed belles, and two beautiful reporters from *Town and Country* who had been covering him all week. Josh was lapping up the attention, so Clay decided not to interrupt. Instead, she winked and blew him a kiss and thought about what fun she would have teasing him when they finally got to bed that night.

Clay went alone down the brick steps to the west garden, away from the cacophony of Jamaican music and gin-induced laughter. The walkway to the garden house was flanked by lilacs in full bloom. In the main garden, masses of tulips and daffodils were enclosed by a dwarf boxwood border to form a horseshoe. The air was warm; it had been an early spring. The aroma of the flowers was heady.

As the Japanese-inspired garden house came into view, Clay heard voices. She slowed her pace, instinctively remaining in the shadow of a thick forsythia hedge.

"*Why* did you have to do this to me?" a woman's voice said.

A man responded in a harsh whisper. "Because I *needed* you!"

"You *know* you shouldn't have come here!"

"I couldn't stand it any longer without you."

"You fool! Do you want to *ruin* everything?" Clay identified the voice as Sunny's and stepped back farther out of sight. "Someone'll surely see you. The place is crawlin' with security guards and police."

At first, Clay thought Sunny was quarreling with a discarded lover. But then, shuddering involuntarily, she allowed herself to realize that the man's voice belonged to Beau Yates.

"Mama, listen, *please*," Beau implored. "I've been stuck in that fuckin' mountain shack for months now."

"It's *hardly* a shack. And you certainly haven't wanted for anythin'. Darlin', we've been over and over this. You have to stay put 'til I get everythin' worked out."

"Hell, I'm going stir crazy. I *had* to get out. I knew you'd be here."

Very slowly, Clay pushed through the forsythia, to see and hear better. Sunny's blonde hair picked up the moonlight. She and her son were standing just outside the greenery-filled garden house. Beau's hair had grown well below his ears, and he had a thick, untrimmed beard. He appeared to have lost weight, but his body seemed in excellent condition, taut and muscular.

"Darlin', I told you I'd work it out, and I have," Sunny said softly. "I'm goin' to marry Porter Mason."

"*What?*" Beau shrieked.

"Hush, lower your voice! I'm doin' it for you, darlin'. He has all the money in the world to hire the best lawyers, if we need to. And he has financial posts in South America. I'll be able to get you set up down there, runnin' one of his businesses. You'll be safe, and you'll make a fortune." Sunny smiled. "You see, I—"

There was a sharp thud, and Sunny reeled back against an immense elm. She gasped and held her jaw. Beau's body blocked Clay's sight line, but he seemed to have slapped his mother very hard.

"You bitch!" Beau exclaimed. "Sure, you're lookin' out for me. Get me out of the way in Brazil or Peru so you an' your lover can get it on without havin' to worry about me showin' up."

"Beau—" Sunny recovered and walked slowly toward her son. "Honey," she spoke quietly, "you're not actin' rational. I don't love Porter Mason. I can barely stand to be in the same room with him."

"Yeah? What about the same bed?"

Sunny's eyes flared with anger. She grabbed Beau's shoulders and shook them hard, although she was a good eight inches shorter than her son. "Stop talkin' like that!

I've done *everythin'* for you. How can you think I want Porter? His body disgusts me. *He* disgusts me."

Beau ignored her. "When he does it to you, do you let him touch you all over?"

"Beau, stop it! You're drunk."

"*Do you*?" he yelled. "Can he keep it up long enough for you to come? Huh? Does he?"

The anger in Sunny's turquoise eyes turned to fright. "Please, Beau! Someone'll hear you. Clay's on her way here to talk to me . . ." She trailed off, obviously realizing the mention of Clay's name might make her son fly further out of control.

"Oh, so you're makin' up with her, too? You don't seem to give a damn about me anymore," Beau hissed. "You hate me! You want me hidin' out in some fuckin' shack forever. Oh, my God," he moaned, "for the *rest* of my *life*!" He reached for his mother's neck. "You bitch! All these years I thought you loved me. But you *lied*." There were tears in Beau's pale eyes.

Sunny struggled to wrench her body away from Beau's grasp. Unsuccessful, she dug her long fingernails into his hands and tried to pull them away from her neck. There was more of a scuffle. A harsh guttural sound burst from deep within her. "Ohhhh . . ." Sunny's eyeballs rolled up in her head.

"You women are all alike," Beau continued. "You're filthy, nasty . . ." He squeezed harder, tears rolling down his cheeks. "You only *pretended* to love me . . ." He shook harder and Sunny's petite body jiggled with each motion, her arms limp at her sides.

For a moment, Clay was frozen with horror; finally, she understood what was happening, and she screamed as loud as she could. "Help! The garden house!"

Beau wheeled around to look at her, and Clay panicked, remembering Beau's strength. She was alone. The music and the conversation were louder than a scream.

Beau loosened his grasp on Sunny, and her limp body crumpled to the grass. Beau stared at the forsythia thicket that Clay was standing behind. His eyes darted wildly, and he seemed unaware of Sunny's body lying in the dew.

Clay tore off down the path, running in terror for her life, screaming as loud as she could. Beau sprinted after her. The heel of Clay's black satin pump caught on a tree root, causing her to trip. As she regained her balance, Beau caught up with her.

"It's all *your* fault! Everything—you're the one who ruined my life." His hands reached for her throat. "I've been waitin' for this opportunity for a long time."

Clay saw the hands coming at her. The pounding in her head quickened. She took a fast breath and let out a blood-curdling *keyiii*, the karate yell of spirit she had learned in a self-defense course. Beau's eyes clouded with momentary confusion. Adrenalin surged through Clay's body while she tried to think what to do. *Run,* the voice in her head called out, *keep screaming and run.*

With one shoe off, Clay headed down the moonlit path toward the party lights and music. The pebbles in the path cut through her stocking and dug sharply into her bare foot. The high-heeled pump on the other foot made it difficult to run fast. Clay paused, breathing hard, and kicked off the remaining shoe. She could hear Beau's footsteps on the path, closing in behind her, but she did not dare look back.

"Help!" Clay screamed. She began to realize that her chances of being heard over the roar of the party were practically nonexistent. "The path to the garden house! Help!" she called again.

Clay sprinted ahead. The lights became closer, the music and the guests' voices louder. She heard Beau's steps gaining on her. They were very close now. "Help!" she yelled into the deserted boxwood garden.

The next instant, Clay felt the back of her jacket rip as Beau yanked her backward into the gravel and shoved her to the ground. Sinking to his knees, he pinned her down, thighs straddling her hips. Clay tried to call out, but this time her vocal cords locked in terror. Beau's eyes blazed with rage and loathing as he leaned over her. Clay watched the flattened palm of his hand whisk toward the side of her face. She heard the impact of the blow but was so numbed with fear that she could not feel it.

Beau's hands reached for Clay's throat. All at once, the action seemed to slow down. She saw clearly how white Beau's fingers appeared in the moonlight, how long his fingernails were, how his hands trembled. Beau's irregular breathing sounded unbearably loud.

Clay tried again to scream. This time, she heard something that sounded like a croak escape from her lips as Beau's fingers made contact with her throat. A thought skittered through her brain: she wished she could tell Josh one last time how much she loved him. Beau's fingers locked around her neck and began squeezing. Clay tried to push Beau away, but her arms behaved as if they were rubber. *Why is this happening to me?* Gasping for breath and blinking involuntarily, Clay knew that there was nothing more she could do.

"Look! There!" shouted a Southern voice. A split second later, Clay forced her eyes open to see three uniformed security guards jump through the bushes and grab hold of Beau, pulling him off of her.

Beau punched and kicked wildly, knocking one guard to the ground and another against the hedge before more police arrived on the scene. It finally took four men to subdue him and two more to force Beau's arms behind his back and encase his wrists with handcuffs.

"Are you all right, miss?" One of the guards helped Clay up from the ground.

She nodded, unable to find her voice.

A number of curious guests arrived, hearing the commotion. A doctor and ambulance were summoned, and Clay sent someone to find Josh. As Beau Yates was being dragged over to the sheriff's car, he saw Sunny's body lying lifeless on the ground in the distance, and with incredible force he wrenched away from his captors and threw himself down on his mother, nuzzling his nose into her hair.

"Please," Beau began to whimper in a small voice. *"Please* let me hold her. Oh, God." He uttered a guttural moan, sobbing, begging Sunny to come back to life.

Josh rushed up and took Clay into his arms. "Are you okay?"

"Yes, yes," Clay mumbled into his chest.

"What happened?"

Clay clung to Josh, trembling and weak kneed as the reality of the past few minutes finally got to her. With a hoarse, shaky voice, she told Josh what had happened.

"It's okay," Josh comforted. "It's all over now. It really *is* over. You're safe."

Audrey Yates Scott, hysterical, arrived on the scene. Clay looked at her, all done up in Italian black lace, and felt a momentary flicker of pity for the beautiful blonde who probably did not understand any of it.

A stocky deputy sheriff escorted Josh and Clay to a police car. "I'm sorry, Miss Fitzgerald. We need a statement down at the station." He shook his head. "What a thing to happen. Especially on Derby Day."

As they speeded toward town, Josh put his arm around Clay and brushed a curly wisp of hair away from her eye. "God"—he smiled—"I can't leave you alone for a minute."

Clay, still shaken, broke out into a grin. "You know, before I met you, I led a very calm life."

"And you will again," Josh said. "Let's get married."

"What? I thought you didn't want to be tied down. You said there was no point in making it legal."

Josh's thick-lashed brown eyes beamed down at her. "Well, I've changed my mind. A man has a right to change his mind, hasn't he?" Josh quipped. "With you around, my life will never be boring."

"Oh, Josh, don't joke about it."

"I'm not joking, Clay. I love you. There's no one else I want to be with. So—shall we do it?"

Clay nodded slowly and looked out the car window at the rolling blue-grass pastures of the Pinckney estate. "A good man is hard to find. So I'd better take you." Clay started to grin, but Josh's lips pressed down on hers and the grin gave way to a long, relaxed kiss.

Clay had a hunch that the deputy sheriff was watching them through his rear-view mirror, but she did not care.

Chapter 32

JOSH Lewis leaned back and swung his feet up on the desk in the library at The Willows. "Okay, Harvey. Shooting will start March first. I'll be out on the coast the day after New Year's so we can finish ironing it out. Sure, you, too. Merry Christmas. Yeah? Well, if you think back, I wished you a happy Hanukkah, too. Okay, see you soon." Josh hung up the phone. *Golden Triangle* had garnered rave reviews and broken summer box-office records around the country. Josh and Harvey Schaffner had patched up their differences and were preparing to team up on the filming of a hit Broadway drama. "Harvey and Marcy send love."

"Oh?" Clay said. "Are they back together?"

Josh shrugged. "This week."

"I'm glad you and Harvey are friends again. Makes living with you a lot more peaceful."

Josh poured a cup of espresso from the pot that Nonah Hughes had set on the desk before she went home. "Want some?"

"Not yet. I just have one more to go." Clay was kneeling on the wool Heriz carpet in front of the fireplace. "We need another log." Dressed in old jeans and a plaid shirt, Clay was surrounded by end bits of ribbon, rainbow colors of tissue paper, and a leaning tower of Christmas presents. "And after that, could you start putting these under the tree?"

"I remember the days," Josh said, "when I dreamed of being a country gentleman."

"You *are* a country gentleman. That's what they do. Put logs on the fire and tend to mundane household matters."

"Oh, I thought they smoked their pipes and sipped brandy."

"Only on Sundays." Clay smiled. "Oh, listen, I talked to Garnet while you were out. She and Melvin are coming for New Year's weekend, after all." Clay's old roommate, Garnet Turner, had recently married a well-known writer.

"Clay!" Kenny Fitzgerald, Clay's eleven-year-old half brother called out from the hall closet. "We can't find the stockings."

"I saw them when we were getting out the tree ornaments," Clay called back. "Nell? Did you check that Bonwit's hat box?"

Nell Smith, her hair completely gray now, came in the room, just ahead of Kenny. Nell wore brown corduroy pants and a Tyrolean sweater. "We've looked everywhere."

"Hmmm, I can't think, then. Why don't you use one of your regular socks, Ken?" Clay suggested.

"Aw, they're all full of holes." The lean-jawed young boy looked more like Mac Fitzgerald every day. It had been a difficult year for him. He had loved his mother even though she had spent a minimal amount of time with him. Sunny Fitzgerald's death had upset him deeply, as the death of her own mother had affected Clay. And since she had been through the experience firsthand, Clay was a great comfort to Kenny. She, Nell, and Josh all made an effort never to say anything derogatory about Sunny. The boy had lost his father at the age of two; Sunny was the only parent he had known. But having Nell and Clay helped.

Nell put on her coat. "I've got to get to that party if I'm goin'."

Clay blew her a kiss. "Drive carefully. The weatherman said it might snow."

"Oh, it hasn't snowed for Christmas since . . ."

"Since I was born," Kenny said. "I wish it *would* snow. But not 'til you get home."

Nell kissed Kenny. "Good night, all. Don't wait up for me." Nell Smith had moved back to The Willows to care for Kenny. It was a job she had taken for love, not money. The boy was sweet and bright, and her crafts business practically ran itself. It was doing so well, Nell had hired a general manager and opened branch shops in Richmond, Norfolk, and Arlington.

"I just remembered where the stockings are," Clay said to Kenny. "Look in the top drawer of the hall table. But I don't know why you want a stocking. You don't believe in Santa Claus anymore."

Kenny's blue eyes sparkled. "Well, I believe in the personification of Santa Claus by beloved family members."

Clay and Josh laughed. "Okay, wise guy," she said. "It's time for bed."

"Aw, I want to watch the late show. *Rio Bravo*."

"*Rio Bravo* on Christmas Eve?" Clay asked, astonished that the station wasn't showing *A Christmas Carol* or *Miracle on Thirty-fourth Street*.

"Sure. On the videotape." Kenny giggled, running to the living room.

Clay and Josh had put on old parkas to take a walk through the crystal-clear, freezing air to the stable. On the way, they dropped off gifts to the various farm hands and to Buck and Sally Smith and their kids. Josh put his arm around Clay as she gave carrots to the horses and kissed them all. When they reached Oriental Pearl's stall, the gray filly whinnied with joy to see them. She had been beaten out by a longshot in the Preakness but had gone on to win the Belmont, capturing two out of three races of the Triple Crown.

Josh had sold his California ranch and shipped his horses east. Although Josh and Clay were based at The Willows now, Josh still commuted to the Coast and had maintained his Bel-Air house as his Los Angeles base. Clay still took on assignments for Owen Thomas at *International Geography*. She had recently returned from working in the cold waters of the Strait of Georgia, the inland sea that separated mainland Canada from Vancouver Island.

"Josh, you know if it weren't for Philippine Airlines we

wouldn't have met. We wouldn't be here at The Willows, and Oriental Pearl wouldn't have won the Derby."

"Oriental Pearl didn't win the Derby because of Philippine Airlines," Josh retorted.

Clay laughed. "Well, you know what I mean."

Josh looked at his watch. "Ah ha! Just past midnight." He reached into his parka and pulled out a split of Dom Perignon. After he popped the cork, he handed her the bottle. "I forgot to bring glasses."

"Doesn't matter. Merry Christmas, Josh. I love you." Clay sipped the champagne and handed the bottle back to Josh.

"I love you, too. And now, it's present time."

"Oh, no. You have to wait 'til I get yours from under the tree."

"Mine first." Josh reached into his parka again and produced a fat envelope full of typed sheets of paper.

"What's all this?" Clay asked. "I thought you were getting me a new bike."

"It's The Willows."

"The Willows!" Clay exclaimed. "But—"

"Audrey sold me the share that Sunny left her." Sunny's estate was to be divided between Audrey and Beau. Beau never knew about it, though. He had hung himself in a Kentucky jail, awaiting trial.

Clay threw her arms around Josh's neck and kissed him. "Oh, Josh, you're wonderful! The Willows—mine! I can't believe it."

"Only two-thirds yours," Josh reminded her. "Let's not forget Kenny."

"Oh, no," Clay said. "I don't want to forget him. The Willows should be as much his as mine. I know that's what daddy would have wanted." She turned back to Josh. "Can we give Kenny part of this? So the place will be split fifty-fifty?"

"Of course," Josh said. "It's yours. You can do what you want."

"Are you sure? I don't want to hurt your feelings, darling."

Josh put his hands on Clay's shoulders. "Don't be silly," he said. "I think it's a wonderful thing to do."

Outside, the snow had begun to fall.

"Let's go for a ride," Clay said.

"Now?"

"Now—I want to see The Willows."

They saddled up a pair of horses and led them out into the courtyard. It was snowing hard, and the snow was beginning to cover the ground.

"Where should we ride?" Josh asked.

"Let's go see my half," Clay said. She started off at a canter across the whitening fields.

Josh laughed and took off after her.

A selection of bestsellers from SPHERE

FICTION

DECEPTIONS	Judith Michael	£2.50	☐
BROTHER ESAU	D. Orgill & J. Gribbin	£1.75	☐
ONCE IN A LIFETIME	Danielle Steel	£1.95	☐
WHALE	Jeremy Lucas	£1.75	☐
PACIFIC VORTEX!	Clive Cussler	£1.95	☐

FILM & TV TIE-INS

WIDOWS	Lynda La Plante	£1.50	☐
E.T. THE EXTRA-TERRESTRIAL	William Kotzwinkle	£1.50	☐
THE IRISH RM	E. E. Somerville & M. Ross	£1.95	☐
THE YEAR OF LIVING DANGEROUSLY	C. J. Koch	£1.50	☐
HONKYTONK MAN	Clancy Carlile	£1.95(P)	☐

NON-FICTION

SIOP	P. Pringle & W. Arkin	£2.95	☐
THE SINGLE FILE	Deanna Maclaren	£1.95	☐
NELLA LAST'S WAR	Nella Last	£1.95	☐
JAIL JOURNAL	John Mitchel	£3.50	☐
THE SAS	Philip Warner	£1.95	☐

All Sphere books are available at your local bookshop or newsagent, or can be ordered direct from the publisher. Just tick the titles you want and fill in the form below.

Name _____

Address _____

_____

Write to Sphere Books, Cash Sales Department, P.O. Box 11, Falmouth, Cornwall TR10 9EN

Please enclose cheque or postal order to the value of the cover price plus:

UK: 45p for the first book, 20p for the second and 14p per copy for each additional book ordered to a maximum charge of £1.63.

OVERSEAS: 75p for the first book and 21p for each additional book.

BFPO & EIRE: 45p for the first book, 20p for the second book plus 14p per copy for the next 7 books, thereafter 8p per book.

Sphere Books reserve the right to show new retail prices on covers which may differ from those previously advertised in the text or elsewhere, and to increase postal rates in accordance with the PO.